149–150
W9-BRQ-944
Flem Snopes
221- Spotted Horses
to 317

THE HAMLET

The HAMLET

William Faulkner

Vintage Books
A Division of Random House
New York

 Published in the United States by Random House, Inc., New York, and simultaneously in Canada by Random House of Canada Limited, Toronto.
Originally published by Random House, Inc., in 1940.
Portions of *The Hamlet* appeared as short stories as follows: "Spotted Horses" and "Fool About a Horse" in *Scribner's Magazine;* "The Hound" in *Harper's Magazine;* "Lizards in Jamshy's Courtyard" in *The Saturday Evening Post.*

Library of Congress Cataloging in Publication Data
Faulkner, William, 1897-1962.
The hamlet.
Reprint of the 1940 ed.
The 1st vol. of the author's trilogy, Snopes; the 2d of which is The town, and the 3d, The mansion.
I. Title.
[PZ3.F272Ham16] [PS3511.A86] 813'.5'2 72-8035
ISBN 0-394-70139-9

Manufactured in the United States of America

Vintage Books Edition, March 1956

PUBLISHER'S NOTE

This third edition of *The Hamlet,* corrected and entirely reset, has been prepared for the occasion of publishing *Snopes* as a three-volume set. A collation of the author's typescript and the first (1940) and second (1956) editions has made it possible to correct a number of errors that occurred in either or both of the earlier editions. Several time references in the last chapter were changed by the author to avoid a discrepancy of chronology within the trilogy. For any other discrepancies the reader might find between *The Hamlet* and the other two volumes of the trilogy—*The Town* (1957) and *The Mansion* (1959)—he is referred to the author's note at the beginning of *The Mansion.*

VOLUME ONE

Snopes

TO PHIL STONE

CONTENTS

BOOK ONE

Flem

CHAPTER ONE

Frenchman's Bend was a section of rich river-bottom country lying twenty miles southeast of Jefferson. Hill-cradled and remote, definite yet without boundaries, straddling into two counties and owning allegiance to neither, it had been the original grant and site of a tremendous pre-Civil War plantation, the ruins of which—the gutted shell of an enormous house with its fallen stables and slave quarters and overgrown gardens and brick terraces and promenades—were still known as the Old Frenchman's place, although the original boundaries now existed only on old faded records in the Chancery Clerk's office in the county courthouse in Jefferson, and even some of the once-fertile fields had long since reverted to the cane-and-cypress jungle from which their first master had hewed them.

He had quite possibly been a foreigner, though not necessarily French, since to the people who had come after him and had almost obliterated all trace of his sojourn, anyone speaking the tongue with a foreign flavor or whose appearance of even occupation was strange, would have been a Frenchman regardless of what nationality he might affirm, just as to their more urban coevals (if he had elected to settle in Jefferson itself, say) he would have been called a Dutchman. But now nobody knew what he had actually been, not even Will Varner, who was sixty years old and now owned a good deal of his original grant, including the site of his ruined mansion. Because he was gone now, the foreigner, the Frenchman, with his family and his slaves and his magnificence. His dream, his broad acres were parcelled out now into small shiftless mortgaged farms for the directors of Jefferson banks to squabble over before selling finally to Will Varner, and all that remained of him was the river bed which his slaves had straightened for almost ten miles to keep his land from flooding and the skeleton of the tremendous house which his heirs-at-large had been pulling down and chopping up—walnut newel posts and stair spindles, oak floors which fifty years later would have been almost priceless, the very clapboards themselves—for thirty years now for firewood. Even his name was forgotten, his pride but a legend about the land he had wrested from the jungle and tamed as a monument to that appellation which those who came after him in battered wagons and on muleback and even on foot, with flintlock rifles and dogs and children and home-made whiskey stills and Protestant psalm-books, could not even read, let alone pronounce, and which now had nothing to do with any once-living man at all—his dream and his pride now dust with the lost dust of his anonymous bones, his legend but the stubborn tale of the money he buried somewhere about the place when Grant overran the country on his way to Vicksburg.

The people who inherited from him came from the northeast, through the Tennessee mountains by stages marked by the bearing and raising of a generation of children. They came from the Atlantic seaboard and before that, from England and the Scottish and Welsh Marches, as some of the names would indicate—Turpin and Haley and Whittington, McCallum and Murray and Leonard and Littlejohn, and other names like Riddup and Armstid and Doshey which could have come from nowhere since certainly no man would deliberately select one of them for his own. They brought no slaves and no Phyfe and Chippendale highboys; indeed, what they did bring most of them could (and did) carry in their hands. They took up land and built one- and two-room cabins and never painted them, and married one another and produced children and added other rooms one by one to the original cabins and did not paint them either, but that was all. Their descendants still planted cotton in the bottom land and corn along the edge of the hills and in the secret coves in the hills made whiskey of the corn and sold what they did not drink. Federal officers went into the country and vanished. Some grament which the missing man had worn might be seen—a felt hat, a broadcloth coat, a pair of city shoes or even his pistol—on a child or an old man or woman. County officers did not bother them at all save in the heel of election years. They supported their own churches and schools, they married and committed infrequent adulteries and more frequent homicides among themselves and were their own courts judges and executioners. They were Protestants and

Democrats and prolific; there was not one Ne
in the entire section. Strange Negroes would absolutely refuse to pass through it after dark.

Will Varner, the present owner of the Old Frenchman place, was the chief man of the country. He was the largest landholder and beat supervisor in one county and Justice of the Peace in the next and election commissioner in both, and hence the fountainhead if not of law at least of advice and suggestion to a countryside which would have repudiated the term constituency if they had ever heard it, which came to him, not in the attitude of *What must I do* but *What do you think you think you would like for me to do if you was able to make me do it.* He was a farmer, a usurer, a veterinarian; Judge Benbow of Jefferson once said of him that a milder-mannered man never bled a mule or stuffed a ballot box. He owned most of the good land in the country and held mortgages on most of the rest. He owned the store and the cotton gin and the combined grist mill and blacksmith shop in the village proper and it was considered, to put it mildly, bad luck for a man of the neighborhood to do his trading or gin his cotton or grind his meal or shoe his stock anywhere else. He was thin as a fence rail and almost as long, with reddish-gray hair and moustaches and little hard bright innocently blue eyes; he looked like a Methodist Sunday School superintendent who on week days conducted a railroad passenger train or vice versa and who owned the church or perhaps the railroad or perhaps both. He was shrewd secret and merry, of a Rabelaisian turn of mind and very probably still sexually lusty (he had fathered sixteen children to his wife, though only two of them remained at home, the others scattered, married and buried, from El Paso to the Alabama line) as the spring of his hair which even at sixty was still more red than gray, would indicate. He was at once active and lazy; he did nothing at all (his son managed all the family business) and spent all his time at it, out of the house and gone before the son had come down to breakfast even, nobody knew where save that he and the old fat white horse which he rode might be seen anywhere within the surrounding ten miles at any time, and at least once every month during the spring and summer and early fall, the old white horse tethered to an adjacent fence post, he would be seen by someone sitting in a home-made chair on the jungle-choked lawn of the Old Frenchman's homesite. His blacksmith had made the chair for him by sawing an empty flour barrel half through the middle and trimming out the sides and nailing a seat into it, and Varner would sit there chewing his tobacco or smoking his cob pipe, with a brusque word for passers cheerful enough but inviting no company, against his background of fallen baronial splendor. The people (those who saw him sitting there and those who were told about it) all believed that he sat there planning his next mortgage foreclosure in private, since it was only to an itinerant sewing-machine agent named Ratliff—a man less than half his age—that he ever gave a reason: "I like to sit here. I'm trying to find out what it must have felt like to be the fool that would need all this"—he did not move, he did not so much as indicate with his head the rise of old brick and tangled walks topped by the columned ruin behind him—"just to eat and sleep in." Then he said—and he gave Ratliff no further clue to which might have been the truth—"For a while it looked like I was going to get shut of it, get it cleared up. But by God folks have got so lazy they wont even climb a ladder to pull off the rest of the boards. It looks like they will go into the woods and even chop up a tree before they will reach above eyelevel for a scantling of pine kindling. But after all, I reckon I'll just keep what there is left of it, just to remind me of my one mistake. This is the only thing I ever bought in my life I couldn't sell to nobody."

The son, Jody, was about thirty, a prime bulging man, slightly thyroidic, who was not only unmarried but who emanated a quality of invincible and inviolable bachelordom as some people are said to breathe out the odor of sanctity or spirituality. He was a big man, already promising a considerable belly in ten or twelve years, though as yet he still managed to postulate something of the trig and unattached cavalier. He wore, winter and summer (save that in the warm season he dispensed with the coat) and Sundays and week days, a glazed collarless white shirt fastened at the neck with a heavy gold collar-button beneath a suit of good black broadcloth. He put on the suit the day it arrived from the Jefferson tailor and wore it every day and in all weathers thereafter until he sold it to one of the family's Negro retainers, so that on almost any Sunday night one whole one or some part of one of his old suits could be met—and promptly recognised—walking the summer roads, and replaced it with the new succeeding one. In contrast to the unvarying overalls of the men he lived among he had an air not funereal exactly but ceremonial—this because of that quality of invincible bachelorhood which he possessed: so that, looking at him you saw, beyond the flabbiness and the obscuring bulk, the perennial and immortal Best Man, the apotheosis of the masculine Singular, just as you discern beneath the dropsical tissue of the '09 halfback the lean hard ghost which once carried a ball. He was the ninth of his parents' sixteen children. He managed the store of which his father was still titular owner and in which they dealt mostly in foreclosed mortgages, and the gin, and oversaw the scattered farm holdings which his father at first and later the two of them together had been acquiring during the last forty years.

One afternoon he was in the store, cutting lengths of plowline from a spool of new cotton rope and looping them in neat seamanlike bights onto a row of nails in the wall, when at a sound behind him he turned and saw, silhouetted by the open door, a man smaller than common, in a wide hat and a frock coat too large for him, standing with a curious planted stiffness. "You Varner?" the man said, in a voice not harsh exactly, or not deliberately harsh so much as rusty from infrequent use.

"I'm one Varner," Jody said, in his bland hard quite pleasant voice. "What can I do for you?"

"My names is Snopes. I heard you got a farm to rent."

"That so?" Varner said, already moving so as to bring the other's face into the light. "Just where did you hear that?" Because the farm was a new one, which he and his father had acquired through a foreclosure sale not a week ago, and the man was a complete stranger. He had never even heard the name before.

The other did not answer. Now Varner could see his face

—a pair of eyes of a cold opaque gray between shaggy graying irascible brows and a short scrabble of iron-gray beard as tight and knotted as a sheep's coat. "Where you been farming?" Varner said.

"West." He did not speak shortly. He merely pronounced the one word with a complete inflectionless finality, as if he had closed a door behind himself.

"You mean Texas?"

"No."

"I see. Just west of here. How much family you got?"

"Six." Now there was no perceptible pause, nor was there any hurrying on into the next word. But there was something. Varner sensed it even before the lifeless voice seemed deliberately to compound the inconsistency: "Boy and two girls. Wife and her sister."

"That's just five."

"Myself," the dead voice said.

"A man dont usually count himself among his own field hands," Varner said. "Is it five or is it seven?"

"I can put six hands into the field."

Now Varner's voice did not change either, still pleasant, still hard: "I dont know as I will take on a tenant this year. It's already almost first of May. I figure I might work it myself, with day labor. If I work it at all this year."

"I'll work that way," the other said. Varner looked at him.

"Little anxious to get settled, aint you?" The other said nothing. Varner could not tell whether the man was looking at him or not. "What rent were you aiming to pay?"

"What do you rent for?"

"Third and fourth," Varner said. "Furnish out of the store here. No cash."

"I see. Furnish in six-bit dollars."

"That's right," Varner said pleasantly. Now he could not tell if the man were looking at anything at all or not.

"I'll take it," he said.

Standing on the gallery of the store, above the half dozen overalled men sitting or squatting about it with pocket knives and slivers of wood, Varner watched his caller limp stiffly across the porch, looking neither right nor left, and descend and from among the tethered teams and saddled animals below the gallery choose a gaunt saddleless mule in a worn plow bridle with rope reins and lead it to the steps and mount awkwardly and stiffly and ride away, still without once looking to either side. "To hear that ere foot, you'd think he weighed two hundred pounds," one of them said. "Who's he, Jody?"

Varner sucked his teeth and spat into the road. "Name's Snopes," he said.

"Snopes?" a second man said. "Sho now. So that's him." Now not only Varner but all the others looked at the speaker—a gaunt man in absolutely clean though faded and patched overalls and even freshly shaven, with a gentle, almost sad face until you unravelled what were actually two separate expressions—a temporary one of static peace and quiet overlaying a constant one of definite even though faint harriedness, and a sensitive mouth which had a quality of adolescent freshness and bloom until you realised that this could just as well be the result of a lifelong abstinence from tobacco—the face of the breathing archetype and protagonist of all men who marry young and father only daughters and are themselves but the eldest daughter of their own wives. His name was Tull. "He's the fellow that wintered his family in a old cottonhouse on Ike McCaslin's place. The one that was mixed up in that burnt barn of a fellow named Harris over in Grenier County two years ago."

"Huh?" Varner said. "What's that? Burnt barn?"

"I never said he done it," Tull said. "I just said he was kind of involved in it after a fashion you might say."

"How much involved in it?"

"Harris had him arrested into court."

"I see," Varner said. "Just a pure case of mistaken identity. He just hired it done."

"It wasn't proved," Tull said. "Leastways, if Harris ever found any proof afterward, it was too late then. Because he had done left the country. Then he turned up at McCaslin's last September. Him and his family worked by the day, gathering for McCaslin, and McCaslin let them winter in a old cottonhouse he wasn't using. That's all I know. I aint repeating nothing."

"I wouldn't," Varner said. "A man dont want to get the name of a idle gossip." He stood above them with his broad bland face, in his dingy formal black-and-white—the glazed soiled white shirt and the bagging and uncared-for trousers—a costume at once ceremonial and negligee. He sucked his teeth briefly and noisily. "Well well well," he said. "A barn burner. Well well well."

That night he told his father about it at the supper table. With the exception of the rambling half-log half-sawn plank edifice known as Littlejohn's hotel, Will Varner's was the only house in the country with more than one storey. They had a cook too, not only the only Negro servant but the only servant of any sort in the whole district. They had had her for years yet Mrs Varner still said and apparently believed that she could not be trusted even to boil water unsupervised. He told it that evening while his mother, a plump cheery bustling woman who had borne sixteen children and already outlived five of them and who still won prizes for preserved fruits and vegetables at the annual County Fair, bustled back and forth between dining room and kitchen, and his sister, a soft ample girl with definite breasts even at thirteen and eyes like cloudy hothouse grapes and a full damp mouth always slightly open, sat at her place in a kind of sullen bemusement of rife young female flesh, apparently not even having to make any effort not to listen.

"You already contracted with him?" Will Varner said.

"I hadn't aimed to at all till Vernon Tull told me what he did. Now I figure I'll take the paper up there tomorrow and let him sign."

"Then you can point out to him which house to burn too. Or are you going to leave that to him?"

"Sho," Jody said. "We'll discuss that too." Then he said—and now all levity was gone from his voice, all poste and riposte of humor's light whimsy, tierce quarto and prime: "All I got to do is find out for sho about that barn. But then it will be the same thing, whether he actually did it or not. All he'll need will be to find out all of a sudden at gathering time that I think he did it. Listen. Take a case like this." He leaned forward now, over the table, bulging, protuberant, intense. The mother had bustled out, to the kitchen, where her brisk voice could be heard scolding cheerfully at the Negro cook. The daughter was not listening at all. "Here's a piece of land that the folks that own it hadn't actually figured on getting nothing out of this late in the season. And here comes a man and rents it on shares that the last place he rented on a barn got burnt up. It dont matter whether he actually burnt that barn or not, though it will simplify matters if I can find out for sho he did. The main thing is, it burnt while he was there and the evidence was such that he felt called on to leave the country. So here he comes and rents this land we hadn't figured on nothing out of this year nohow and we furnish him outen the store all regular and proper. And he makes his crop and the landlord sells it all regular and has the cash waiting and the fellow comes in to get his share and the landlord says, 'What's this I heard about you and that barn?' That's all. 'What's this I just heard about you and that barn?' " They stared at one another—the slightly protuberant opaque eyes and the little hard blue ones. "What will he say? What can he say except 'All right. What do you aim to do?' "

"You'll lose his furnish bill at the store."

"Sho. There aint no way of getting around that. But after all, a man that's making you a crop free gratis for nothing, at least you can afford to feed him while he's doing it.—Wait," he said. "Hell fire, we wont even need to do that; I'll just let him find a couple of rotten shingles with a match laid across them on his doorstep the morning after he finishes laying-by and he'll know it's all up then and aint nothing left for him but to move on. That'll cut two months off the furnish bill and all we'll be out is hiring his crop gathered." They stared at one another. To one of them it was already done, accomplished: he could actually see it; when he spoke it was out of a time still six months in the future yet: "Hell fire, he'll have to! He cant fight it! He dont dare!"

"Humph," Will said. From the pocket of his unbuttoned vest he took a stained cob pipe and began to fill it. "You better stay clear of them folks."

"Sho now," Jody said. He took a toothpick from the china receptacle on the table and sat back. "Burning barns aint right. And a man that's got habits that way will just have to suffer the disadvantages of them."

He did not go the next day nor the one after that either. But early in the afternoon of the third day, his roan saddle horse hitched and waiting at one of the gallery posts, he sat at the roll-top desk in the rear of the store, hunched, the black hat on the back of his head and one broad black-haired hand motionless and heavy as a ham of meat on the paper and the pen in the other tracing the words of the contract in his heavy deliberate sprawling script. An hour after that and five miles from the village, the contract blotted and folded neatly into his hip pocket, he was sitting the horse beside a halted buckboard in the road. It was battered with rough usage and caked with last winter's dried mud, it was drawn by a pair of shaggy ponies as wild and active-looking as mountain goats and almost as small. To the rear of it was attached a sheet-iron box the size and shape of a dog kennel and painted to resemble a house, in each painted window of which a painted woman's face simpered abouve a painted sewing machine, and Varner sat his horse and glared in shocked and outraged consternation at its occupant, who had just said pleasantly, "Well, Jody, I hear you got a new tenant."

"Hell fire!" Varner cried. "Do you mean he set fire to another one? even after they caught him, he set fire to *another* one?"

"Well," the man in the buckboard said, "I dont know as I would go on record as saying he set ere a one of them afire. I would put it that they both taken fire while he was more or less associated with them. You might say that fire seems to follow him around, like dogs follows some folks." He spoke in a pleasant, lazy, equable voice which you did not discern at once to be even more shrewd than humorous. This was Ratliff, the sewing-machine agent. He lived in Jefferson and he travelled the better part of four counties with his sturdy team and the painted dog kennel into which an actual machine neatly fitted. On successive days and two counties apart the splashed and battered buckboard and the strong mismatched team might be seen tethered in the nearest shade and Ratliff's bland affable ready face and his neat tieless blue shirt one of the squatting group at a crossroads store, or—and still squatting and still doing the talking apparently though actually doing a good deal more listening than anybody believed until afterward—among the women surrounded by laden clotheslines and tubs and blackened wash pots beside springs and wells, or decorous in a splint chair on cabin galleries, pleasant, affable, courteous, anecdotal and impenetrable. He sold perhaps three machines a year, the rest of the time trading in land and livestock and second-hand farming tools and musical instruments or anything else which the owner did not want badly enough, retailing from house to house the news of his four counties with the ubiquity of a newspaper and carrying personal messages from mouth to mouth about weddings and funerals and the preserving of vegetables and fruit with the reliability of a postal service. He never forgot a name and he knew everyone, man mule and dog, within fifty miles. "Just say it was following along behind the wagon when Snopes druv up to the house De Spain had give him, with the furniture piled into the wagon bed like he had druv up to the house they had been living in at Harris's or wherever it was and said 'Get in here' and the cookstove and beds and chairs come out and got in by their selves. Careless and yet good too, tight, like they was used to moving and not having no big help at it. And Ab and that big one, Flem they call him—there was another one too, a little one; I remember seeing him once somewhere. He wasn't with them. Leastways he aint now. Maybe they forgot to tell him when to get outen the barn.—setting on the seat and them two hulking gals in the two chairs in the wagon bed and Miz Snopes and her sister, the widow, setting on the stuff in back like nobody cared much whether they come along or not either, including the furniture. And the wagon stops in front of the house and Ab looks at it and says, 'Likely it aint fitten for hawgs.' "

Sitting the horse, Varner glared down at Ratliff in protuberant and speechless horror. "All right," Ratliff said. "Soon as the wagon stopped Miz Snopes and the widow got out and commenced to unload. Them two gals aint moved yet, just setting there in them two chairs, in their Sunday clothes, chewing sweet gum, til Ab turned round and cussed them outen the wagon to where Miz Snopes and the widow was wrastling with the stove. He druv them out like a pair of heifers just a little too valuable to hit hard with a stick, and then him and Flem set there and watched them two strapping gals take a wore-out broom and a lantern outen the wagon and stand there again till Ab leant out and snicked the nigh one across the stern with the end of the reins. 'And then you come back and help your maw with that stove,' he hollers after them. Then him and Flem got outen the wagon and went up to call on De Spain."

"To the barn?" Varner cried. "You mean they went right straight and——"

"No no. That was later. The barn come later. Likely they never knowed just where it was yet. The barn burnt all regular and in due course; you'll have to say that for him. This here was just a call, just pure friendship, because Snopes knowed where his fields was and all he had to do was to start scratching them, and it already the middle of May. Just like now," he added in a tone of absolutely creamlike innocence. "But then I hear tell he always makes his rent contracts later than most." But he was not laughing. The shrewd brown face was as bland and smooth as ever beneath the shrewd impenetrable eyes.

"Well?" Varner said violently. "If he sets his fires like you tell about it, I reckon I dont need to worry until Christmas. Get on with it. What does he hâve to do before he starts lighting matches? Maybe I can recognise at least some of the symptoms in time."

"All right," Ratliff said. "So they went up the road, leaving Miz Snopes and the widow wrastling at the cookstove and them two gals standing there now holding a wire rat-trap and a chamber pot, and went up to Major de Spain's and walked up the private road where that pile of fresh horse manure was and the nigger said Ab stepped in it on deliberate purpose. Maybe the nigger was watching them through the front window. Anyway Ab tracked it right across the front porch and knocked and when the nigger told him to wipe it offen his feet, Ab shoved right past the nigger and the nigger said he wiped the rest of it off right on that ere hundred-dollar rug and stood there hollering 'Hello. Hello, De Spain' until Miz de Spain come and looked at the rug and at Ab and told him to please go away. And then De Spain come home at dinner time and I reckon maybe Miz de Spain got in behind him because about the middle of the afternoon he rides up to Ab's house with a nigger holding the rolled-up rug on a mule behind him and Ab setting in a chair against the door jamb and De Spain hollers 'Why in hell aint you in the field?' and Ab says, he dont get up or nothing, 'I figger I'll start tomorrow. I dont never move and start to work the same day,' only that aint neither here nor there; I reckon Miz de Spain had done got in behind him good because he just set on the horse a while saying 'Confound you Snopes, confound you Snopes' and Ab setting there saying 'If I had thought that much of a rug I dont know as I would keep it where folks coming in would have to tromp on it.' " Still he was not laughing. He just sat there in the buckboard, easy and relaxed, with his shrewd intelligent eyes in his smooth brown face, well-shaved and clean in his perfectly clean faded shirt, his voice pleasant and drawling and anecdotal, while Varner's suffused swollen face glared down at him.

"So after a while Ab hollers back into the house and one of them strapping gals comes out and Ab says, 'Take that ere rug and wash it.' And so next morning the nigger found the rolled-up rug throwed onto the front porch against the door and there was some more tracks across the porch too only it was just mud this time and it was said how when Miz de Spain unrolled the rug this time it must have been hotter for De Spain than before even—the nigger said it looked like they had used brickbats instead of soap on it—because he was at Ab's house before breakfast even, in the lot where Ab and Flem was hitching up to go to the field sho enough, setting on the mare mad as a hornet and cussing a blue streak, not at

Ab exactly but just sort of at all rugs and all horse manure in general and Ab not saying nothing, just buckling hames and choke strops until at last De Spain says how the rug cost him a hundred dollars in France and he is going to charge Ab twenty bushels of corn for it against his crop that Ab aint even planted yet. And so De Spain went back home. And maybe he felt it was all neither here nor there now. Maybe he felt that long as he had done something about it Miz de Spain would ease up on him and maybe come gathering time he would a even forgot about that twenty bushesl of corn. Only that never suited Ab. So here, it's the next evening I reckon, and Major laying with his shoes off in the barrel-stave hammock in his yard and here comes the bailiff hemming and hawing and finally gets it out how Ab has done sued him——"

"Hell fire," Varner murmured. "Hell fire."

"Sho," Ratliff said. "That's just about what De Spain hisself said when he finally got it into his mind that it was so. So it come Sat-dy and the wagon druv up to the store and Ab got out in that preacher's hat and coat and tromps up to the table on that clubfoot where Uncle Buck McCaslin said Colonel John Sartoris his-self shot Ab for trying to steal his clay-bank riding stallion during the war, and the Judge said, 'I done reviewed your suit, Mr Snopes, but I aint been able to find nothing nowhere in the law bearing on rugs, let alone horse manure. But I'm going to accept it because twenty bushels is too much for you to have to pay because a man as busy as you seem to stay aint going to have time to make twenty bushels of corn. So I am going to charge you ten bushels of corn for ruining that rug.' "

"And so he burnt it," Varner said. "Well well well."

"I dont know as I would put it just that way," Ratliff said, repeated. "I would just put it that that same night Major de Spain's barn taken fire and was a total loss. Only somehow or other De Spain got there on his mare about the same time, because somebody heard him passing in the road. I dont mean he got there in time to put it out but he got there in time to find something else already there that he felt entitled to consider enough of a foreign element to justify shooting at it, setting there on the mare and blasting away at it or them three or four times until it run into a ditch on him where he couldn't follow on the mare. And he couldn't say neither who it was because any animal can limp if it wants to and any man is liable to have a white shirt, with the exception that when he got to Ab's house (and that couldn't a been long, according to the gait the fellow heard him passing in the road) Ab and Flem wasn't there, wasn't nobody there but the four women and De Spain never had time to look under no beds and such because there was a cypress-roofed corn crib right next to that barn. So he rid back to where his niggers had done fetched up the water barrels and was soaking tow-sacks to lay on the crib, and the first person he see was Flem standing there in a white-colored shirt, watching it with his hands in his pockets, chewing tobacco. "Evening,' Flem says. 'That ere hay goes fast' and De Spain setting on the horse hollering 'Where's your paw? Where's that—' and Flem says, 'If he aint here somewhere he's done went back home. Me and him left at the same time when we see the blaze.' And De Spain knowed where they had left from too and he knowed why too. Only that wasn't neither here nor there neither because, as it was just maintained, any two fellows anywhere might have a limp and a white shirt between them and it was likely the coal oil can he seen one of them fling into the fire when he shot the first time. And so here the next morning he's setting at breakfast with a right smart of his eyebrows and hair both swinged off when the nigger comes in and says it's a fellow to see him and he goes to the office and it's Ab, already in the preacher hat and coat and the wagon done already loaded again too, only Ab aint brought that into the house where it could be seen. 'It looks like me and you aint going to get along together,' Ab says, 'so I reckon we better quit trying before we have a misunderstanding over something. I'm moving this morning.' And De Spain says, 'What about your contract?' And Ab says, 'I done calcelled it.' and De Spain setting there saying 'Cancelled. Cancelled' and then he says, 'I would cancel it and a hundred more like it and throw in that barn too just to know for sho if it was you I was shooting at last night.' And Ab says, 'You might sue me and find out. Justices of the Peace in this country seems to be in the habit of finding for plaintiffs.' "

"Hell fire," Varner said quietly again. "Hell fire."

"So Ab turned and went stomping out on that stiff foot and went back——"

"And burnt the tenant house," Varner said.

"No no. I aint saying he might not a looked back at it with a certain regret, as the fellow says, when he druv off. But never nothing else taken all of a sudden on fire. Not right then, that is. I dont—"

"That's so," Varner said. "I recollect you did say he had to throw the balance of the coal oil into the fire when De Spain started shooting at him. Well well well," he said, bulging, slightly apoplectic. "And now, out of all the men in this country, I got to pick him to make a rent contract with." He began to laugh. That is, he began to say "Ha. Ha. Ha." rapidly, but just from the teeth, the lungs: no higher, nothing of it in the eyes. Then he stopped. "Well, I can't be setting here, no matter how pleasant it is. Maybe I can get there in time to get him to cancel with me for just a old cottonhouse."

"Or at least maybe for a empty barn," Ratliff called after him.

An hour later Varner was sitting the halted horse again, this time before a gate, or a gap that is, in a fence of sagging and rusted wire. The gate itself or what remained of it lay unhinged to one side, the interstices of the rotted palings choked with grass and weeds like the ribs of a forgotten skeleton. He was breathing hard but not because he had been galloping. On the contrary, since he had approached near enough to his destination to believe he could have seen smoke if there had been smoke, he had ridden slower and slower. Nevertheless he now sat the horse before the gap in the fence, breathing hard through his nose and even sweating a little, looking at the sagging broken-backed cabin set in its inevitable treeless and grassless plot and weathered to the color of an old beehive, with that expression of tense and rapid speculation of a man approaching a dud howitzer shell. "Hell fire," he said again quietly. "Hell fire. He's been here three days now and he aint even set the gate up. And I dont even dare to mention it to him. I dont even dare to act like I knowed there was even a fence to hang it to." He twitched the reins savagely. "Come up!" he said to the horse. "You hang around here very long standing still and you'll be a-fire too."

The path (it was neither road nor lane: just two parallel barely discernible tracks where wagon wheels had run, almost obliterated by this year's grass and weeds) went up to the sagging and stepless porch of the perfectly blank house which he now watched with wire-taut wariness, as if he were approaching an ambush. He was watching it with such intensity as to be oblivious to detail. He saw suddenly in one of the sashless windows and without knowing when it had come there, a face beneath a gray cloth cap, the lower jaw moving steadily and rhythmically with a curious sidewise thrust, which even as he shouted "Hello!" vanished again. He was about to shout again when he saw beyond the house the stiff figure which he recognised even though the frock coat was missing now, doing something at the gate to the lot. He had already begun to hear the mournful measured plaint of a rusted well-pulley, and now he began to hear two flat meaningless loud female voices. When he passed beyond the house he saw it—the narrow high frame like an epicene gallows, two big absolutely static young women beside it, who even in that first glance postulated that immobile dreamy solidarity of statuary (this only emphasised by the fact that they both seemed to be talking at once and to some listener—or perhaps just circumambience—at a considerable distance and neither listening to the other at all) even though one of them had hold of the well-rope, her arms extended at full reach, her body bent for the down pull like a figure in a charade, a carved piece symbolising some terrific physical effort which had died with its inception, though a moment later the pulley began again its rusty plaint but stopped again almost immediately, as did the voices also when the second one saw him, the first one paused now in the obverse of the first attitude, her arms stretched downward on the rope and the two broad expressionless faces turning slowly in unison as he rode past.

He crossed the barren yard littered with the rubbish—the ashes, the shards of pottery and tin cans—of its last tenants.

There were two women working beside the fence too and they were all three aware of his presence now because he had seen one of the women look around. But the man himself (Durn little clubfooted murderer, Varner thought with that furious helpless outrage) had not looked up nor even paused in whatever it was he was doing until Varner rode directly up behind him. The two women were watching him now. One wore a faded sunbonnet, the other a shapeless hat which at one time must have belonged to the man and holding in her hand a rusted can half full of bent and rusted nails. "Evening," Varner said, realising too late that he was almost shouting. "Evening, ladies." The man turned, deliberately, holding a hammer—a rusted head from which both claws had been broken, fitting onto an untrimmed stick of stove wood—and once more Varner looked down into the cold impenetrable agate eyes beneath the writhen overhang of brows.

"Howdy," Snopes said.

"Just thought I'd ride up and see what your plans were," Varner said, too loud still; he could not seem to help it. I got too much to think about to have time to watch it, he thought, beginning at once to think, Hell fire. Hell fire, again, as though proving to himself what even a second's laxity of attention might bring him to.

"I figure I'll stay," the other said. "The house aint fitten for hogs. But I reckon I can make out with it."

"But look here!" Varner said. Now he was shouting; he didn't care. Then he stopped shouting. He stopped shouting because he stopped speaking because there was nothing else to say, though it was going through his mind fast enough: Hell fire. Hell fire. Hell fire. I dont dare say Leave here, and I aint got anywhere to say Go there. I dont even dare to have him arrested for barn-burning for fear he'll set my barn a-fire. The other had begun to turn back to the fence when Varner spoke. Now he stood half-turned, looking up at Varner not courteously and not exactly patiently, but just waiting. "All right," Varner said. "We can discuss the house. Because we'll get along all right. We'll get along. Anything that comes up, all you got to do is come down to the store. No, you dont even need to do that: just send me word and I'll ride right up here as quick as I can get here. You understand? Anything, just anything you dont like——"

"I can get along with anybody," the other said. "I been getting along with fifteen or twenty different landlords since I started farming. When I cant get along with them, I leave. That all you wanted?"

All, Varner thought. All. He rode back across the yard, the littered grassless desolation scarred with the ashes and charred stick-ends and blackened bricks where pots for washing clothes and scalding hogs had sat. I just wish I never had to have but just the little I do want now, he thought. He had been hearing the well-pulley again. This time it did not cease when he passed, the two broad faces, the one motionless, the other pumping up and down with metronome-like regularity to the wheel's not-quite-musical complaint, turning slowly again as though riveted and synchronised to one another by a mechanical arm as he went on beyond the house and into the imperceptible lane which led to the broken gate which he knew would still be lying there in the weeds when he saw it next. He still had the contract in his pocket, which he had written out with that steady and deliberate satisfaction which, it now seemed to him, must have occurred in another time, or more likely, to another person altogether. It was still unsigned. I could put a fire-clause in it, he thought. But he did not even check the horse. Sho, he thought. And then I could use it to start shingling the new barn. So he went on. It was late, and he eased the horse into a rack which it would be able to hold nearly all the way home, with a little breathing on the hills, and he was travelling at a fair gait when he saw suddenly, leaning against a tree beside the road, the man whose face he had seen in the window of the house. One moment the road had been empty, the next moment the man stood there beside it, at the edge of a small copse—the same cloth cap, the same rhythmically chewing jaw materialised apparently out of nothing and almost abreast of the horse, with an air of complete and purely accidental which Varner was to remember and speculate about only later. He had almost passed the other before he pulled the horse up. He did not shout now and now his big face was merely bland and extremely alert. "Howdy," he said. "You're Flem, aint you? I'm Varner."

"That so?" the other said. He spat. He had a broad flat face. His eyes were the color of stagnant water. He was soft in appearance like Varner himself, though a head shorter, in a soiled white shirt and cheap gray trousers.

"I was hoping to see you," Varner said. "I hear your father has had a little trouble once or twice with landlords. Trouble that might have been serious." The other chewed. "Maybe they never treated him right; I dont know about that and I dont care. What I'm talking about is a mistake, any mistake, can be straightened out so that a man can still stay friends with the fellow he aint satisfied with. Dont you agree to that?" The other chewed steadily. His face was as blank as a pan of uncooked dough. "So he wont have to feel that the only thing that can prove his rights is something that will make him have to pick up and leave the country next day," Varner said. "So that there wont come a time some day when he will look around and find out he has run out of new country to move to." Varner ceased. He waited so long this time that the other finally spoke, though Varner was never certain whether this was the reason or not:

"There's a right smart of country."

"Sho," Varner said pleasantly, bulging, bland. "But a man dont want to wear it out just moving through it. Especially because of a matter that if it had just been took in hand and straightened out to begin with, wouldn't have amounted to nothing. That could have been straightened out in five minutes if there had just been some other fellow handy to take a hold of a fellow that was maybe a little high-tempered to begin with say, and say to him, 'Hold up here, now; that fellow dont aim to put nothing on you. All you got to do is consult with him peaceable and it will be fixed up. I know that to be a fact because *I got his promise to that effect.*'" He paused again. "Especially if this here fellow we are speaking of, that could take a hold of him and tell him that, was going to get a benefit out of keeping him quiet and peaceable." Varner stopped again. After a while the other spoke again:

"What benefit?"

"Why, a good farm to work. Store credit. More land if he felt he could handle it."

"Aint no benefit in farming. I figure on getting out of it soon as I can."

"All right," Varner said. "Say he wanted to take up some other line, this fellow we're speaking of. He will need the good will of the folks he aims to make his money off of to do it. And what better way——"

"You run a store, dont you?" the other said.

"—better way—" Varner said. Then he stopped. "What?" he said.

"I hear you run a store."

Varner stared at him. Now Varner's face was not bland. It was just completely still and completely intent. He reached to his shirt pocket and produced a cigar. He neither smoked nor drank himself, being by nature so happily metabolised that, as he might have put it himself, he could not possibly have felt better than he naturally did. But he always carried two or three. "Have a cigar," he said.

"I dont use them," the other said.

"Just chew, hah?" Varner said.

"I chew up a nickel now and then until the suption is out of it. But I aint never lit a match to one yet."

"Sho now," Varner said. He looked at the cigar; he said quietly: "And I just hope to God you and nobody you know ever will." He put the cigar back into his pocket. He expelled a loud hiss of breath. "All right," he said. "Next fall. When he has made his crop." He had never been certain just when the other had been looking at him and when not, but now he watched the other raise his arm and with his other hand pick something infinitesimal from the sleeve with infinitesimal care. Once more Varner expelled his breath through his nose. This time it was a sigh. "All right," he said. "Next week then. You'll give me that long, wont you? But you got to guarantee it." The other spat.

"Guarantee what?" he said.

Two miles further on dusk overtook him, the shortening twilight of late April, in which the blanched dogwoods stood among the darker trees with spread raised palms like praying nuns; there was the evening star and already the whippoorwills. The horse, travelling supperward, was going well in the evening's cool, when Varner pulled it to a stop and held it for a full moment. "Hell fire," he said. "He was standing just exactly where couldn't nobody see him from the house."

CHAPTER TWO

1

Ratliff, the sewing-machine agent, again approaching the village, with a used music box and a set of brand-new harrow teeth still fastened together by the factory shipping wire in the dog-kennel box in place of the sewing machine, saw the old white horse dozing on three legs at a fence post and, an instant later, Will Varner himself sitting in the home-made chair against the rise of shaggy lawns and overgrown gardens of the Old Frenchman place.

"Evening, Uncle Will," he said in his pleasant, courteous, even deferent voice. "I hear you and Jody got a new clerk in the store." Varner looked at him sharply, the reddish eyebrows beetling a little above the hard little eyes.

"So that's done spread," he said. "How far you been since yesterday?"

"Seven-eight miles," Ratliff said.

"Hah," Varner said. "We been needing a clerk." That was true. All they needed was someone to come and unlock the store in the morning and lock it again at night—this just to keep stray dogs out, since even tramps, like stray Negroes, did not stay in Frenchman's Bend after nightfall. In fact, at times Jody Varner himself (Will was never there anyhow) would be absent from the store all day. Customers would enter and serve themselves and each other, putting the price of the articles, which they knew to a penny as well as Jody himself did, into a cigar box inside the circular wire cage which protected the cheese, as though it—the cigar box, the worn bills and thumb-polished coins—were actually baited.

"At least you can get the store swept out every day," Ratliff said. "Aint everybody can get that included into a fire insurance policy."

"Hah," Varner said again. He rose from the chair. He was chewing tobacco. He removed from his mouth the chewed-out wad which resembled a clot of damp hay, and threw it away and wiped his palm on his flank. He approached the fence, where at his direction the blacksmith had contrived a clever passage which (neither the blacksmith nor Varner had ever seen one before or even imagined one) operated exactly like a modern turnstile, by the raising of a chained pin instead of inserting a coin. "Ride my horse on back to the store," Varner said. "I'll drive your rig. I want to sit down and ride."

"We can tie the horse behind the buckboard and both ride in it," Ratliff said.

"You ride the horse," Varner said. "That's close as I want you right now. Sometimes you are a little too smart to suit me."

"Why, sho, Uncle Will," Ratliff said. So he cramped the buckboard's wheel for Varner to get in, and himself mounted the horse. Then went on, Ratliff a little behind the buckboard, so that Varner talked to him over his shoulder, not looking back:

"This here fire-fighter——"

"It wasn't proved," Ratliff said mildly. "Of course, that's the trouble. If a fellow's got to choose between a man that is a murderer and one he just thinks maybe is, he'll choose the murderer. At least then he will know exactly where he's at. His attention aint going to wander then."

"All right, all right," Varner said. "This here victim of libel and mis-statement then. What do you know about him?"

"Nothing to mention," Ratliff said. "Just what I hear about him. I aint seen him in eight years. There was another boy then, besides Flem. A little one. He would be about ten or twelve now if he was there. He must a been mislaid in one of them movings."

"Has what you have heard about him since them eight years ago caused you to think he might have changed his habits any?"

"Sho now," Ratliff said. What dust the three horses raised blew lightly aside on the faint breeze, among the dogfennel and bitterweed just beginning to bloom in the roadside ditches. "Eight years. And before that it was fifteen more pretty near I never saw him. I growed up next to where he was living. I mean, he lived for about two years on the same place where I growed up. Him and my pap was both renting from Old Man Anse Holland. Ab was a horse-trader then. In fact, I was there the same time the horse-trading give out on him and left him just a farmer. He aint naturally mean. He's just soured."

"Soured," Varner said. He spat. His voice was now sardonic, almost contemptuous: "Jody came in last night, late. I knowed it soon as I saw him. It was exactly like when he was a boy and had done something he knowed I was going to find out about tomorrow and so he would figure he better tell me first himself. 'I done hired a clerk,' he says. 'What for?' I says. 'Dont Sam shine your shoes on Sunday no more to suit you?' and he hollers, 'I had to! I had to hire him! I had to, I tell you!' And he went to bed without eating no supper. I dont know how he slept; I never listened to see. But this morning he seemed to feel a little better about it. He seemed to feel considerable better about it. 'He might even be useful,' he says. 'I dont doubt it,' I says. 'But there's a law against it. Besides, why not just tear them down instead? You could even sell the lumber then.' And he looked at me a while longer. Only he was just waiting for me to stop; he had done figured it all out last night. 'Take a man like that,' he says. 'A man that's independent about protecting his-self, his own rights and interests. Say the advantages of his own rights and interests is another fellow's advantage and interest too. Say his benefits is the same benefits as the fellow that's paying some of his kinfolks a salary to protect his business; say it's a business where now and then (and you know it as well as I do,' Jody says) '—say benefits is always coming up that the fellow that's going to get the benefits just as lief not be actively mixed up in himself, why, a fellow that independent——' "

"He could have said 'dangerous' with the same amount of breath," Ratliff said.

"Yes," Varner said. "Well?"

Ratliff didn't answer. Instead, he said: "That store aint in Jody's name, is it?" Only he answered this himself, before the other could have spoken: "Sho now. Why did I need to ask that? Besides, it's just Flem that Jody's mixed up with. Long as Jody keeps him, maybe old Ab will——"

"Out with it," Varner said. "What do you think about it?"

"You mean what I really think?"

"What in damnation do you think I am talking about?"

"I think the same as you do," Ratliff said quietly. "That there aint but two men I know can risk fooling with them folks. And just one of them is named Varner and his front name aint Jody."

"And who's the other one?" Varner said.

"That aint been proved yet neither," Ratliff said pleasantly.

2

Besides Varner's store and cotton gin and the combined grist mill and blacksmith shop which they rented to the actual smith, and the schoolhouse and the church and the perhaps three dozen dwellings within sound of both bells, the village consisted of a livery barn and lot and a contiguous shady though grassless yard in which sat a sprawling rambling edifice partly of sawn boards and partly of logs, unpainted and of two storeys in places and known as Littlejohn's hotel, where behind a weathered plank nailed to one of the trees and lettered ROOMƧ AND BORD drummers and livestock-traders were fed and lodged. It had a long veranda lined with chairs. That night after supper, the buckboard and team in the stable, Ratliff was sitting here with five or six other men who had drifted in from the adjacent homes within walking distance. They would have been there on any other night, but this evening they were gathered even before the sun was completely gone, looking now and then toward the dark front of Varner's store as people will gather to look quietly at the cold embers of a lynching or at the propped ladder and open window of an elopement, since the presence of a hired white clerk in the store of a man still able to walk and with intellect still sound enough to make money mistakes at least in his own favor, was as unheard of as the presence of a hired white woman in one of their own kitchens. "Well," one said, "I don't know nothing about that one Varner hired. But blood's thick. And a man that's got kinfolks that stays mad enough all the time to set fire to a man's barn——"

"Sho now," Ratliff said. "Old man Ab aint naturally mean. He's just soured."

For a moment nobody spoke. They sat or squatted along the veranda, invisible to one another. It was almost full dark, the departed sun a pale greenish stain in the northwestern sky. The whippoorwills had begun and fireflies winked and drifted among the trees beyond the road.

"How soured?" one said after a while.

"Why, just soured," Ratliff said pleasantly, easily, readily. "There was that business during the War. When he wasn't bothering nobody, not harming or helping either side, just tending to his own business, which was profit and horses—things which never even heard of such a thing as a political conviction—when here comes somebody that never even owned the horses even and shot him in the heel. And that soured him. And then that business of Colonel Sartoris's ma-in-law, Miss Rosa Millard, that Ab had done went and formed a horse- and mule-partnership with in good faith and honor, not aiming to harm nobody blue or gray but just keeping his mind fixed on profit and horses, until Miz Millard had to go and get herself shot by that fellow that called his-self Major Grumby, and then Colonel's boy Bayard and Uncle Buck McCaslin and a nigger caught Ab in the woods and something else happened, tied up to a tree or something and maybe even a double bridle rein or maybe even a heated ramrod in it too though that's just hearsay. Anyhow, Ab had to withdraw his allegiance to the Sartorises, and I hear tell he skulked for a considerable back in the hills until Colonel Sartoris got busy enough building his railroad for it to be safe to come out. And that soured him some more. But at least he still had horse-trading left to fall back on. Then he run into Pat Stamper. And Pat eliminated him from horse-trading. And so he just went plumb curdled."

"You mean he locked horns with Pat Stamper and even had the bridle left to take back home?" one said. Because they all knew Stamper. He was a legend, even though still alive, not only in that country but in all North Mississippi and West Tennessee—a heavy man with a stomach and a broad pale expensive Stetson hat and eyes the color of a new axe blade, who travelled about the country with a wagon carrying camping equipment and played horses against horses as a gambler plays cards against cards, for the pleasure of beating a worthy opponent as much as for gain, assisted by a Negro hostler who was an artist as a sculptor is an artist, who could take any piece of horseflesh which still had life in it and retire to whatever closed building or shed was empty and handy and then, with a quality of actual legerdemain, reappear with something which the beast's own dam would not recognise, let alone its recent owner; the two of them, Stamper and the Negro, working in a kind of outrageous rapport like a single intelligence possessing the terrific advantage over common mortals of being able to be in two places at once and directing two separate sets of hands and fingers at the same time.

"He done better than that," Ratliff said. "He come out exactly even. Because if it was anybody that Stamper beat, it was Miz Snopes. And even she never considered it so. All she was out was just having to make the trip to Jefferson herself to finally get the separator and maybe she knowed all the time that sooner or later she would have to do that. It wasn't Ab that bought one horse and sold two to Pat Stamper. It was Miz Snopes. Her and Pat just used Ab to trade through."

Once more for a moment no one spoke. Then the first speaker said: "How did you find all this out? I reckon you was there too."

"I was," Ratliff said. "I went with him that day to get the separator. We lived about a mile from them. My pap and Ab were both renting from Old Man Anse Holland then, and I used to hang around Ab's barn with him. Because I was a fool about a horse too, same as he was. And he wasn't curdled then. He was married to his first wife then, the one he got from Jefferson, that one day her pa druv up in a wagon and loaded her and the furniture into it and told Ab that if he ever crossed Whiteleaf Bridge again he would shoot him. They never had no children and I was just turning eight and I would go down to his house almost every morning and stay all day with him, setting on the lot fence with him while the neighbors would come up and look through the fence at whatever it was he had done swapped some more of Old Man Anse's bob-wire or busted farm tools for this time, and Ab lying to just exactly the right amount about how old it was and how much he give for it. He was a fool about a horse; he admitted it, but he wasn't the kind of a fool about a horse Miz Snopes claimed he was that day when we brought Beasley Kemp's horse home and turned it into the lot and come up to the house and Ab taken his shoes off on the gallery to cool his feet for dinner and Miz Snopes standing in the door shaking the skillet at him and Ab saying, 'Now Vynie, now Vynie. I always was a fool about a good horse and you know it and aint a bit of use in you jawing about it. You better thank the Lord that when He give me a eye for horseflesh He give me a little judgment and gumption with it.'

"Because it wasn't the horse. It wasn't the trade. It was a good trade because Ab had just give Beasley a straight stock and a old wore-out sorghum mill of Old Man Anse's for the horse, and even Miz Snopes had to admit that that was a good swap for anything that could get up and walk from Beasley's lot to theirn by itself, because like she said while she was shaking the skillet at him, he couldn't get stung very bad in a horse-trade because he never had nothing of his own that anybody would want to swap even a sorry horse for. And it wasn't because Ab had left the plow down in the far field where she couldn't see it from the house and had snuck the wagon out the back way with the plow stock and the sorghum mill in it while she still thought he was in the field. It was like she knowed already what me and Ab didn't: that Pat Stamper had owned that horse before Beasely got it and that now Ab had done caught the Pat Stamper sickness just from touching it. And maybe she was right. Maybe to himself Ab did call his-self the Pat Stamper of the Holland farm or maybe even of all Beat Four, even if maybe he was fairly sho that Pat Stamper wasn't going to walk up to that lot fence and challenge him for it. Sho, I reckon while he was setting there on the gallery with his feet cooling and the side-meat plopping and spitting in the kitchen and us waiting to eat it so we could go back down to the lot and set on the fence while the folks would come up and look at what he had brung home this time, I reckon maybe Ab not only knowed as much about horse-trading as Pat Stamper, but he owned head for head of them with Old Man Anse himself. And I reckon while we would be setting there, just moving enough to keep outen the sun, with that empty plow standing in the furrow down in the far field and Miz Snopes watching him outen the back window and saying to herself, 'Horse-trader! Setting there bragging and lying to a passel of shiftless men with the weeds and morning glories climbing so thick in the cotton and corn I am afraid to tote his dinner down to him for fear of snakes'; I reckon Ab would look at whatever it was he had just traded the mailbox or some more of Old Man Anse's bob-wire or some of the winter corn for this time, and he would say to his-self, 'It's not only mine, but before God it's the prettiest drove of a horse I ever see.'

"It was fate. It was like the Lord Himself had decided to buy a horse with Miz Snopes's separator money. Though I will admit that when He chose Ab He picked out a good quick willing hand to do His trading for Him. The morning we started, Ab hadn't planned to use Beasley's horse a-tall because he knowed it probably couldn't make that twenty-eight-mile trip to Jefferson and back in one day. He aimed to go up to Old Man Anse's lot and borrow a mule to work with hisn and he would a done it except for Miz Snopes. She kept on taunting him about swapping for a yard ornament, about how if he could just git it to town somehow maybe he could swap it to the livery stable to prop up in front for a sign. So in a way it was Miz Snopes herself that put the idea in Ab's head of taking Beasley's horse to town. So when I got there that morning we hitched Beasley's horse into the wagon with the mule. We had done been feeding it for two-three days now by forced draft, getting it ready to make the trip, and it looked some better now than when we had brung it home. But even yet it didn't look so good. So Ab decided it was the mule that showed it up, that when it was the only horse or mule in sight it looked pretty good and that it was standing by something else on four legs that done the damage. 'If it was just some way to hitch the mule under the wagon, so it wouldn't show but could still pull, and just leave the horse in sight,' Ab says. Because he wasn't soured then. But we had done the best we could with it. Ab thought about mixing a right smart of salt in some corn so it would drink a lot of water so some of the ribs wouldn't show so bad at least, only we knowed it wouldn't never get to Jefferson then, let alone back home, besides having to stop at every creek and branch to blow it up again. So we done the best we could. That is, we hoped for the best. Ab went to the house and come back in his preacher's coat (it's the same one he's still got; it was Colonel Sartoris's that Miss Rosa Millard give him, it would be thirty years ago) and that twenty-four dollars and sixty-eight cents Miz Snopes had been saving on for four years now, tied up in a rag, and we started out.

"We wasn't even thinking about horse-trading. We was thinking about horse all right, because we was wondering if maybe we wasn't fixing to come back home that night with Beasley's horse in the wagon and Ab in the traces with the mule. Yes sir, Ab eased that team outen the lot and on down the road easy and careful as ere a horse and mule ever moved in this world, with me and Ab walking up every hill that tilted enough to run water offen it, and we was aiming to do that right in to Jefferson. It was the weather, the hot day; it was the middle of July. Because here we was about a mile from Whiteleaf store, with Beasley's horse kind of half walking and half riding on the double tree and Ab's face looking worrieder and worrieder every time it failed to lift its feet high enough to step, when all of a sudden that horse popped into a sweat. If flung its head up like it had been touched with a hot poker and stepped up into the collar, touching the collar for the first time since the mule had taken the weight of it when Ab shaken out the whip in the lot, and so we come down the hill and up to Whiteleaf store with that horse of Beasley's eyes rolling white as darning eggs and its mane and tail swirling like a grass fire. And I be dog if it hadn't not only sweated itself into as pretty a dark blood bay as you ever saw, but even its ribs didn't seem to show so much. And Ab that had been talking about taking the back road so we wouldn't have to pass the store at all, setting there on the wagon seat like he would set on the lot fence back home where he knowed he was safe from Pat Stamper, telling Hugh Mitchell and the other fellows on the gallery that that horse come from Kentucky. Hugh Mitchell never even laughed. 'Sho now,' he says. 'I wondered what had become of it. I reckon that's what taken it so long; Kentucky's a long walk. Herman Short swapped Pat Stamper a mule and buggy for that horse five years ago and Beasley Kemp give Herman eight dollars for it last summer. What did you give Beasley? Fifty cents?'

"That's what did it. It wasn't what the horse had cost Ab because you might say all it had cost Ab was the straight stock, since in the first place the sorghum mill was wore out and in the second place it wasn't Ab's sorghum mill nohow. And it wasn't the mule and buggy of Herman's. It was them eight cash dollars of Beasley's, and not that Ab held them eight dollars against Herman, because Herman had done already invested a mule and buggy in it. And besides, the eight dollars was still in the country and so it didn't actually matter whether it was Herman or Beasley that had them. It was the fact that Pat Stamper, a stranger, had come in and got actual Yoknapatawpha County cash dollars to rattling around loose that way. When a man swaps horse for horse, that's one thing and let the devil protect him if the devil can. But when cash money starts changing hands, that's something else. And for a stranger to come in and start that cash money to changing and jumping from one fellow to another, it's like when a burglar breaks into your house and flings your things ever which way even if he dont take nothing. It makes you twice as mad. So it was not just to unload Beasley Kemp's horse back onto Pat Stamper. It was to get Beasley Kemp's eight dollars back outen Pat someway. And that's what I meant about it was pure fate that had Pat Stamper camped outside Jefferson right by the road we would have to pass on that day we went to get Miz Snopes's milk separator; camped right there by the road with that nigger magician on the very day when Ab was coming to town with twenty-four dollars and sixty-eight cents in his pocket and the entire honor and pride of the science and pastime of horse-trading in Yoknapatawpha County depending on him to vindicate it.

"I dont recollect just when and where we found out Pat was in Jefferson that day. It might have been at Whiteleaf store. Or it might have just been that in Ab's state it was not only right and natural that Ab would have to pass Stamper to get to Jefferson, but it was foreordained and fated that he would have to. So here we come, easing them eight dollars of Beasley Kemp's up them long hills with Ab and me walking and Beasley's horse laying into the collar the best it could but with the mule doing most of the pulling and Ab walking on his side of the wagon and cussing Pat Stamper and Herman Short and Beasley Kemp and Hugh Mitchell; and we went down the hills with Ab holding the wagon braked with a sapling pole so it wouldn't shove Beasley's horse through the collar and turn it wrong-side-out like a sock, and Ab still cussing Pat Stamper and Herman and Beasley and Mitchell, until we come to the Three Mile Bridge and Ab turned the team outen the road and druv into the bushes and taken the mule out and knotted up one rein so I could ride and give me the quarter and told me to ride for town and get a dime's worth of saltpeter and a nickel's worth of tar and a number ten fish hook and hurry back.

"So we didn't get into town until after dinner time. We went straight to Pat's camp and druv in with that horse of Beasley's laying into the collar now sho enough, with its eyes looking nigh as wild as Ab's and foaming a little at the mouth where Ab had rubbed the saltpeter into its gums and a couple of as pretty tarred bob-wire cuts on its chest as you could want, and another one where Ab had worked that fish hook under its hide where he could touch it by drooping one rein a little, and Pat's nigger running up to catch the headstall before the horse run right into the tent where Pat slept and Pat his-self coming out with that ere cream-colored Stetson cocked over one eye and them eyes the color of a new plow point and just about as warm and his thumbs hooked into his waist band. 'That's a pretty lively horse you got there,' he says.

" 'You damn right,' Ab says. 'That's why I got to get shut of it. Just consider you done already trimmed me and give me somthing in place of it I can get back home without killing me and this boy both.' Because that was the right system: to rush right up and say he had to trade instead of hanging back for Pat to persuade him. It had been five years since Pat had seen the horse, so Ab figured that the chance of his recognising it would be about the same as a burglar recognising a dollar watch that happened to get caught for a minute on his vest button five years ago. And Ab wasn't trying to beat Pat bad. He just wanted to recover that eight dollars' worth of the honor and pride of Yoknapatawpha County horse-trading, doing it not for profit but for honor. And I believe it worked. I still believe that Ab fooled Pat, and that it was because of what Pat aimed to trade Ab and not because Pat recognised Beasley's horse, that Pat refused to trade any way except team for team. Or I dont know: maybe Ab was so busy fooling Pat that Pat never had to fool Ab at all. So the nigger led the span of mules out and Pat standing there with his thumbs in his pants-top, watching Ab and chewing tobacco slow and gentle, and Ab standing there with that look on his face that was desperate but not scared yet, because he was realising now he had got in deeper than he aimed to and that he would either have to shut his eyes and bust on through, or back out and quit, get back in the wagon and go on before Beasley's horse even give up to the fish hook. And then Pat Stamper showed how come he was Pat Stamper. If he had just started in to show Ab what a bargain he was getting, I reckon Ab would have backed out. But Pat didn't. He fooled Ab just exactly as one first-class burglar would fool another first-class burglar by purely and simply refusing to tell him where the safe was at.

" 'I already got a good mule,' Ab says. 'It's just the horse I dont want. Trade me a mule for the horse.'

" 'I dont want no wild horse neither,' Pat says. 'Not that I wont trade for anything that walks, provided I can trade my way. But I aint going to trade for that horse alone because I dont want it no more than you do. What I am trading for is that mule. And this here team of mine is matched. I aim to get about three times as much for them as a span as I would selling them single.'

" 'But you would still have a team to trade with,' Ab says.

" 'No,' Pat says. 'I aim to get more for them from you than I would if the pair was broken. If it's a single mule you want, you better try somewhere else.'

"So Ab looked at the mules again. They looked just exactly right. They didn't look extra good and they didn't look extra bad. Neither one of them looked quite as good as Ab's mule, but the two of them together looked just a little mite better than just one mule of anybody's. And so he was doomed. He was doomed from the very minute Hugh Mitchell told him about that eight dollars. I reckon Pat Stamper knowed he was doomed the very moment he looked up and seen that nigger holding Beasley's horse back from running into the tent. I reckon he knowed right then he wouldn't even have to try to trade Ab: all he would have to do would be just to say No long enough. Because that's what he done, leaning there against our wagon bed with his thumbs hooked into his pants, chewing his tobacco and watching Ab go through the motions of examining them mules again. And even I knowed that Ab had done traded, that he had done walked out into what he thought was a spring branch and then found out it was quicksand, and that now he knowed he couldn't even stop long enough to turn back. 'All right,' he says. 'I'll take them.'

"So the nigger put the new team into the harness and we went on to town. And them mules still looked all right. I be dog if I didn't begin to think that Ab had walked into that Stamper quicksand and then got out again, and when we had got back into the road and beyond sight of Stamper's tent, Ab's face begun to look like it would while he would set on the lot fence at home and tell folks how he was a fool about a horse but not a durn fool. It wasn't easy yet, it was just watchful, setting there and feeling out the new team. We was right at town now and he wouldn't have much time to feel them out in, but we would have a good chance on the road back home. 'By God,' Ab says. 'If they can walk home at all, I have got that eight dollars back, damn him.'

"But that nigger was a artist. Because I swear to God them mules looked all right. They looked exactly like two ordinary, not extra good mules you might see in a hundred wagons on the road. I had done realised how they had a kind of jerky way of starting off, first one jerking into the collar and then jerking back and then the other jerking into the collar and then jerking back, and even after we was in the road and the wagon rolling good one of them taken a spell of some sort and snatched his-self crossways in the traces like he aimed to turn around and go back, maybe crawling right across the wagon to do it, but then Stamper had just told us they was a matched team; he never said they had ever worked together as a matched team, and they was a matched team in the sense that neither one of them seemed to have any idea as to just when the other one aimed to start moving. But Ab got them straightened out and we went on, and we was just starting up that big hill onto the Square when they popped into a sweat too, just like Beasley's horse had done just beyond Whiteleaf. But that was all right, it was hot enough; that was when I first noticed that that rain was coming up; I mind how I was watching a big hot-looking bright cloud over to the southwest and thinking how it was going to rain on us before we got home or to Whiteleaf either, when all of a sudden I realised that the wagon had done stopped going up the hill and was starting down it backwards and I looked around just in time to see both of them mules this time crossways in the traces and kind of glaring at one another across the tongue and Ab trying to straighten them out and glaring too, and then all a sudden they straightened out and I mind how I was thinking what a good thing it was they was pointed away from the wagon when they straightened out. Because they moved at the same time for the first time in their lives, or for the first time since Ab owned them anyway, and here we come swurging up that hill and into the Square like a roach up a drainpipe, with the wagon on two wheels and Ab sawing at the reins and saying 'Hell fire, hell fire' and folks, ladies and children mostly, scattering and screeching and Ab just managed to swing them into the alley behind Cain's store and stopped them by locking our nigh wheel with another wagon's and the other team (they was hitched) holp to put the brakes on. So it was a good crowd by then, helping us to get untangled, and Ab led our team over to Cain's back door and tied them snubbed up close to a post, with folks still coming up and saying, 'It's that team of Stamper's,' and Ab breathing hard now and looking a right smart less easy in the face and most all-fired watchful. 'Come on,' he says. 'Let's get that damn separator and get out of here.'

"So we went in and give Cain Miz Snopes's rag and he counted the twenty-four sixty-eight and we got the separator and started back to the wagon, to where we had left it. Because it was still there; the wagon wasn't the trouble. In fact, it was too much wagon. I mind how I could see the bed and the tops of the wheels where Ab had brought it up close against the loading platform and I could see the folks from the waist up standing in the alley, twice or three times as many of them now, and I was thinking how it was too much wagon and too much folks; it was like one of these here pictures that have printed under them, *What's wrong with this picture?* and then Ab began to say 'Hell fire, hell fire' and begun to run, still toting his end of the separator, up to the edge of the platform where we could see under it. The mules was all right too. They was laying down. Ab had snubbed them up pretty close to the same post, with the same line through both bits, and now they looked exactly like two fellows that had done hung themselves in one of these here suicide packs, with their heads snubbed up together and pointing straight up and their tongues hanging out and their eyes popping and their necks stretched about four foot and their legs doubled back under them like shot rabbits until Ab jumped down and cut them down with his pocket knife. A artist. He had give them just exactly to the inch of whatever it was to get them to town and off the square before it played out.

"So Ab was desperate. I can see him now, backed off in a corner behind Cain's plows and cultivators, with his face white and his voice shaking and his hand shaking so he couldn't hardly hand me the six bits outen his pocket. 'Go to Doc Peabody's,' he says, 'and get me a bottle of whiskey. Hurry.' He was desperate. It wasn't even quicksand now. It was a whirlpool and him with just one jump left. He drunk that pint of whiskey in two drinks and set the empty bottle down in the corner careful as a egg and we went back to the wagon. The mules was still standing up this time and we loaded the separator in and he eased them away careful, with folks still telling each other it was that team of Stamper's. Ab's face was red instead of white now and the sun was gone but I dont think he even noticed it. And we hadn't et too, and I dont believe he knowed that either. And I be dog if it didn't seem like Pat Stamper hadn't moved either, standing there at the gate to his rope stock pen, with that Stetson cocked and his thumbs still hooked in the top of his pants and Ab sitting in the wagon trying to keep his hands from shaking and the team Stamper had swapped him stopped now with their heads down and their legs spraddled and breathing like a sawmill. "I come for my team,' Ab says.

" 'What's the matter?' Stamper says. 'Don't tell me these are too lively for you too. They dont look it!'

" 'All right,' Ab says. 'All right. I got to have my team. I got four dollars. Make your four-dollar profit and give me my team.'

" 'I aint got your team,' Stamper says. 'I didn't want that horse neither. I told you that. So I got shut of it.'

"Ab set there for a while. It was cooler now. A breeze had got up and you could smell the rain in it. 'But you still got my mule,' Ab says. 'All right. I'll take it.'

" 'For what?' Stamper says. 'You want to swap that team for your mule?' Because Ab wasn't trading now. He was desperate, sitting there like he couldn't even see, with Stamper leaning easy against the gate post and looking at him for a minute. 'No,' Stamper says. 'I dont want them mules. Yours is the best one. I wouldn't trade that way, even swap.' He spit, easy and careful. 'Besides, I done included your mule into another team. With another horse. You want to look at it?'

" 'All right,' Ab says. 'How much?'

" 'Dont you even want to see it first?' Stamper says.

" 'All right,' Ab says. So the nigger led out Ab's mule and a horse, a little dark brown horse; I remember how even with it clouded up and no sun, how that horse shined—a horse a little bigger than the one we had traded Stamper, and hog fat. That's just exactly how it was fat: not like a horse is fat but like a hog: fat right up to its ears and looking tight as a drum; it was so fat it couldn't hardly walk, putting its feet down like they didn't have no weight nor feeling in them at all. 'It's too fat to last,' Ab says. 'It wont even get me home.'

" 'That's what I think myself,' Stamper says. 'That's why I want to get shut of it.'

" 'All right,' Ab says. 'I'll have to try it.' He begun to get outen the wagon.

" 'Try it?' Stamper says. Ab didn't answer. He got outen the wagon careful and went to the horse, putting his feet down careful and stiff too, like he never had no weight in his feet too, like the horse. It had a hackamore on and Ab taken the rope from the nigger and started to get on the horse. 'Wait,' Stamper said. 'What are you fixing to do?'

" 'Going to try it,' Ab says. 'I done swapped a horse with you once today.' Stamper looked at Ab a minute. Then he spit again and kind of stepped back.

" 'All right, Jim,' he says to the nigger. 'Help him up.' So the nigger holp Ab onto the horse, only the nigger never had time to jump back like Stamper because soon as Ab's weight come onto the horse it was like Ab had a live wire in his britches. The horse made one swirl, it looked round as a ball, without no more front or back end than a Irish potato. It throwed Ab hard and Ab got up and went back to the horse and Stamper says, 'Help him up, Jim,' and the nigger holp Ab up again and the horse slammed him off again and Ab got up with his face just the same and went back and taken the rope again when Stamper stopped him. It was just exactly like Ab wanted that horse to throw him, hard, like the ability of his bones and meat to stand that ere hard ground was all he had left to pay for something with life enough left to get us home. 'Are you trying to kill yoursel'?' Stamper says.

" 'All right,' Ab says. 'How much?'

" 'Come into the tent,' Stamper says.

"So I waited in the wagon. It was beginning to blow a little now, and we hadn't brought no coats with us. But we had some croker sacks in the wagon Miz Snopes had made us bring along to wrap the separator in and I was wrapping it in the sacks when the nigger come outen the tent and when he lifted up the flap I seen Ab drinking outen the bottle. Then the nigger led up a horse and buggy and Ab and Stamper come outen the tent and Ab come to the wagon, he didn't look at me, he just lifted the separator outen the sacks and went and put it into the buggy and him and Stamper went and got into it and drove away, back toward town. The nigger was watching me. 'You fixing to get wet fo you get home,' he said.

" 'I reckon so,' I said.

" 'You want to eat a snack of dinner until they get back?' he said. 'I got it on the stove.'

" 'I reckon not,' I said. So he went back into the tent and I waited in the wagon. It was most sholy going to rain, and that soon. I mind how I thought that anyway we would have the croker sacks now to try to keep dry under. Then Ab and Stamper come back and Ab never looked at me that time either. He went back into the tent and I could see him drinking outen the bottle again and this time he put it into his shirt. And then the nigger led our mule and the new horse up and put them in the wagon and Ab come out and got in. Stamper and the nigger both holp him now.

" 'Dont you reckon you better let that boy drive?' Stamper says.

" 'I'll drive,' Ab says. 'Maybe I cant swap a horse with you, but by God I can still drive it.'

" 'Sho now,' Stamper says. 'That horse will surprise you.'

"And it did," Ratliff said. He laughed, for the first time, quietly, invisible to his hearers though they knew exactly how he would look at the moment as well as if they could see him, easy and relaxed in his chair, with his lean brown pleasant shrewd face, in his faded clean blue shirt, with that same air of perpetual bachelorhood which Jody Varner had, although there was no other resemblance between them and not much here, since in Varner it was a quality of shabby and fustian gallantry where in Ratliff it was that hearty celibacy as of a lay brother in a twelfth-century monastery—a gardener, a pruner of vines, say. "That horse surprised us. The rain, the storm, come up before we had gone a mile and we rode in it for two hours, hunched under the croker sacks and watching that new shiny horse that was so fat it even put its feet down like it couldn't even feel them, that every now and then, even during the rain, would give a kind of flinching jerk like when Ab's weight had come down onto its back at Stamper's camp, until we found a old barn to shelter under. I did, that is, because Ab was laying out in the wagon bed by then, flat on his back with the rain popping him in the face and me on the seat driving now and watching that shiny black horse turning into a bay horse. Because I was just eight then, and me and Ab had done all our horse-trading up and down that lane that run past his lot. So I just drove under the first roof I come to and shaken Ab awake. The rain had cooled him off by then and he waked up sober. And he got a heap soberer fast. 'What?' he says. 'What is it?'

" 'The horse!' I hollered. 'He's changing color!'

"He was sober then. We was both outen the wagon then and Ab's eyes popping and a bay horse standing in the traces where he had went to sleep looking at a black one. He put his hand out like he couldn't believe it was even a horse and touched it at a spot where the reins must every now and then just barely touched it and just about where his weight had come down on it when he was trying to ride it at Stamper's, and next I knowed that horse was plunging and swurging. I dodged just as it slammed into the wall behind me; I could even feel the wind in my hair. Then there was a sound like a nail jabbed into a big bicycle tire. It went *whishhhhhhhhhh* and then the rest of that shiny fat black horse we had got from Pat Stamper vanished. I dont mean me and Ab was standing there with just the mule left. We had a horse too. Only it was the same horse we had left home with that morning and that we had swapped Beasley Kemp the sorghum mill and the straight stock for two weeks ago. We even got our fish hook back, with the barb still bent where Ab had bent it and the nigger had just moved it a little. But it wasn't till next morning that Ab found the bicycle pump valve under its hide just inside the nigh foreshoulder—the one place in the world where a man might own a horse for twenty years and never think to look at it.

"Because we never got home till well after sunup the next

day, and my pap was waiting at Ab's house, considerable mad. So I didn't stay long, I just had time to see Miz Snopes standing in the door where I reckon she had been setting all night too, saying, 'Where's my separator?' and Ab saying how he had always been a fool about a horse and he couldn't help it and then Miz Snopes begun to cry. I had been hanging around them a heap by now, but I never had seen her cry before. She looked like the kind of somebody that never had done much crying to speak of nohow, because she cried hard, like she didn't know just how to do it, like even the tears never knowed just exactly what they was expected to do, standing there in a old wrapper, not even hiding her face, saying, 'Fool about a horse, yes! But why the horse? why the horse?'

"So me and Pap went on. He had my arm a right smart twisted up in his hand, but when I begun to tell him about what happened yesterday, he changed his mind about licking me. But it was almost noon before I got back down to Ab's. He was setting on the lot fence and I clumb up and set by him. Only the lot was empty. I couldn't see his mule nor Beasley's horse neither. But he never said nothing and I never said nothing, only after a while he said, 'You done had breakfast?' and I said I had and he said, 'I aint et yet.' So we went to the house then, and sho enough, she was gone. And I could imagine it—Ab setting there on that fence and her coming down the hill in her sunbonnet and shawl and gloves too and going into the stable and saddling the mule and putting the halter on Beasley's horse and Ab setting there trying to decide whether to go and offer to help her or not.

"So I started the fire in the stove. Ab wasn't much of a hand at cooking, so by the time he got his breakfast started it was so late we just decided to cook enough for breakfast and dinner too and we et it and I washed the dishes and we went back to the lot. The middle buster was still setting down yonder in the far field, but there wasn't nothing to pull it with nohow now lessen he walked up to Old Man Anse's and borrowed a span of mules, which would be just like going up to a rattlesnake and borrowing a rattle: but then, I reckon he felt he had stood all the excitement he could for the rest of that day at least. So we just set on the fence and looked at that empty lot. It never had been a big lot and it would look kind of crowded even with just one horse in it. But now it looked like all Texas; and sho enough, I hadn't hardly begun to think about how empty it was when he clumb down offen the fence and went across and looked at a shed that was built against the side of the barn and that would be all right if it was just propped up and had a new roof on it. 'I think next time I will trade for a mare and build me up a brood herd and raise mules,' he says. 'This here will do all right for colts with a little fixing up.' Then he come back and we set on the fence again, and about middle of the afternoon a wagon druv up. It was Cliff Odum, it had the side-boards on it and Miz Snopes was on the seat with Cliff, coming on past the house, toward the lot. 'She aint got it,' Ab says. 'He wouldn't dicker with her.' We was behind the barn now and we watched Cliff back his wagon up against a cut bank by the gate and we watched Miz Snopes get out and take off her shawl and gloves and come across the lot and into the cow shed and lead the cow back and up onto the cut bank behind the wagon and Cliff said, 'You come hold the team. I'll get her in the wagon.' But she never even stopped. She faced the cow into the tail gate and got behind it and laid her shoulder against its hams and hove that cow into the wagon before Cliff could have got out. And Cliff put up the tail gate and Miz Snopes put her shawl and gloves back on and they got into the wagon and they went on.

"So I built him another fire to cook his supper and then I had to go home; it was almost sundown then. When I come back the next morning I brung a pail of milk. Ab was in the kitchen, still cooking breakfast. 'I am glad you thought about that,' he says when he seen the milk. 'I was aiming to tell you yesterday to see if you could borrow some.' He kept on cooking breakfast because he hadn't expected her that soon, because that would make two twenty-eight-mile trips in not much more than twenty-four hours. But we heard the wagon again and this time when she got out she had the separator.

When we got to the barn we could see her toting it into the house. 'You left that milk where she will see it, didn't you?' Ab says.

" 'Yes sir,' I says.

" 'Likely she will wait to put on her old wrapper first,' Ab says. 'I wish I had started breakfast sooner.' Only I dont think she even waited that long, because it seemed like we begun to hear it right away. It made a fine high sound, good and strong, like it would separate a gallon of milk in no time. Then it stopped. 'It's too bad she aint got but the one gallon,' Ab says.

" 'I can bring her another one in the morning,' I said. But he wasn't listening, watching the house.

" 'I reckon you can go now and look in the door,' he says. So I went and did. She was taking Ab's breakfast offen the stove, onto two plates. I didn't know she had even seen me till she turned and handed the two plates to me. Her face was all right now, quiet. It was just busy.

" 'I reckon you can eat something more too,' she said, 'But eat it out yonder. I am going to be busy in here and I dont want you and him in my way.' So I taken the plates back and we set against the fence and et. And then we heard the separator again. I didn't know it would go through but one time. I reckon he didn't neither.

" 'I reckon Cain showed her,' he says, eating. 'I reckon if she wants it to run through more than once, it will run through more than once.' Then it stopped and she come to the door and hollered to us to bring the dishes up so she could wash them and I taken the plates back and set them on the step and me and Ab went back and set on the fence. It looked like it would have held all Texas and Kansas too. 'I reckon she just rode up to that damn tent and said, 'Here's your team. You get my separator and get it quick because I got to catch a ride back home.', he said. And then we heard it again, and that evening we walked up to Old Man Anse's to borrow a mule to finish the far piece with, but he never had none to spare now. So as soon as Old Man Anse had finished cussing, we come on back and set on the fence. And sho enough, we could hear the separator start up again. It sounded strong as ever, like it could make the milk fly, like it didn't give a whoop whether that milk had been separated once or a hundred times. 'There it goes again,' Ab says. 'Dont forget that other gallon tomorrow.'

" 'No sir,' I says. We listened to it. Because he wasn't curdled then.

" 'It looks like she is fixing to get a heap of pleasure and satisfaction outen it,' he says."

3

He halted the buckboard and sat for a moment looking down at the same broken gate which Jody Varner had sat the roan horse and looked at nine days ago—the weed-choked and grass-grown yard, the weathered and sagging house—a cluttered desolation filled already, even before he reached the gate and stopped, with the loud flat sound of two female voices. They were young voices, talking not in shouts or screams but with an unhurried profundity of volume the very apparent absence from which of any discernible human speech or language seemed but natural, as if the sound had been emitted by two enormous birds; as if the aghast and amazed solitude of some inaccessible and empty marsh or desert were being invaded and steadily violated by the constant bickering of the two last survivors of a lost species which had established residence in it—a sound which stopped short off when Ratliff shouted. A moment later the two girls came to the door and stood, big, identical, like two young tremendous cows, looking at him.

"Morning, ladies," he said. "Where's your paw?"

The continued to contemplate him. They did not seem to breathe even, though he knew they did, must; bodies of that displacement and that apparently monstrous, that almost oppressive, wellness, would need air and lots of it. He had a fleeting vision of them as the two cows, heifers, standing knee-deep in air as in a stream, a pond, nuzzling into it, the level of the pond fleeing violently and silently to one inhalation, exposing in astounded momentary amaze the teeming lesser subaerial life about the planted feet. Then they spoke exactly together, like a trained chorus: "Down to the field."

Sho now, he thought, moving on: Doing what? Because he did not believe that the Ab Snopes he had known would have more than two mules. And one of these he had already seen standing idle in the lot beyond the house; and the other he knew to be tied at this moment to a tree behind Varner's store eight miles away, because only three hours ago he had left it there, tied where for six days now he had watched Varner's new clerk ride up each morning and tie it. For an instant he actually halted the buckboard again. By God, he thought quietly, This would be exactly the chance he must have been waiting on for twenty-three years now to get his-self that new un-Stampered start. So when he came in sight of the field and recognised the stiff, harsh, undersized figure behind a plow drawn by two mules, he was not even surprised. He did not wait until he had actually recognised the mules to be a pair which until a week ago at least had belonged to Will Varner: he merely changed the tense of the possessing verb: Not *had* belonged, he thought. They still do. By God, he has done even better than that. He aint even trading horses now. He has done swapped a man for a span of them.

He halted the buckboard at the fence. The plow had reached the far end of the field. The man turned the team, their heads tossing and yawning, their stride breaking as he sawed them about with absolutely needless violence. Ratliff watched soberly. Just like always, he thought. He still handles a horse or a mule like it had done already threatened him with its fist before he even spoke to it. He knew that Snopes had seen and even recognised him too, though there was no sign of it, the team straightened out now and returning, the delicate mule-legs and narrow deer-like feet picking up swiftly and nervously, the earth shearing dark and rich from the polished blade of the plow. Now Ratliff could even see Snopes looking directly at him—the cold glints beneath the shaggy ill-tempered brows as he remembered them even after eight years, the brows only a little grayer now—though once more the other merely swung the team about with that senseless savageness, canting the plow onto its side as he stopped it. "What you doing here?" he said.

"Just heard you werehere and stopped by," Ratliff said. "It's been a while, aint it? Eight years."

The other grunted. "It dont show on you, though. You still look like butter wouldn't melt in your mouth."

"Sho now," Ratliff said. "Speaking of mouths." He reached beneath the seat cushion and produced a pint bottle filled apparently with water. "Some of McCallum's best," he said. "Just run off last week. Here." He extended the bottle. The other came to the fence. Although they were now not five feet apart, still all that Ratliff could see were the two glints beneath the fierce overhang of brow.

"You brought it to me?"

"Sholy," Ratliff said. "Take it."

The other did not move. "What for?"

"Nothing," Ratliff said. "I just brought it. Try a sup of it. It's good."

The other took the bottle. Then Ratliff knew that something had gone out of the eyes. Or maybe they were just not looking at him now. "I'll wait till tonight," Snopes said. "I dont drink in the sun any more."

"How about in the rain?" Ratliff said. And then he knew that Snopes was not looking at him, although the other had not moved, no change in the harsh knotted violent face as he stood holding the bottle. "You ought to settle down pretty good here," Ratliff said. "You got a good farm now, and Flem seems to taken hold in the store like he was raised storekeeping." Now the other did not seem to be listening either. He shook the bottle and rasied it to the light as though testing the bead. "I hope you will," Ratliff said.

Then he saw the eyes again, fierce and intractable and cold. "What's it to you if I do or dont?"

"Nothing," Ratliff said, pleasantly, quietly. Snopes stooped and hid the bottle in the weeds beside the fence and returned to the plow and raised it.

"Go on to the house and tell them to give you some dinner," he said.

"I reckon not," Ratliff said. "I got to get on to town."

"Suit yourself," the other said. He looped the single rein

about his neck and gave another savage yank on the inside line; again the team swung with yawing heads, already breaking stride even before they had come into motion. "Much obliged for the bottle," he said.

"Sho now," Ratliff said. The plow went on. Ratliff watched it. He never said, Come back again, he thought. He lifted his own reins. "Come up, rabbits," he said. "Let's hit for town."

CHAPTER THREE

1

On the Monday morning when Flem Snopes came to clerk in Varner's store, he wore a brand-new white shirt. It had not even been laundered yet; the creases where the cloth had lain bolted on a shelf, and the sun-browned streaks repeated zebra-like on each successive fold, were still apparent. And not only the women who came to look at him, but Ratliff himself (he did not sell sewing machines for nothing. He had even learned to operate one quite well from demonstrating them, and it was even told of him that he made himself the blue shirts which he wore) knew that the shirt had been cut and stitched by hand and by a stiff and unaccustomed hand too. He wore it all that week. By Saturday night it was soiled, but on the following Monday he appeared in a second one exactly like it, even to the zebra-stripes. By the second Saturday night that one was soiled too, in exactly the same places as the other. It was as though its wearer, entering though he had into a new life and milieu already channelled to compulsions and customs fixed long before his advent, had nevertheless established in it even on that first day his own particular soiling groove.

He rode up on a gaunt mule, on a saddle which was recognised at once as belonging to the Varners, with a tin pail tied to it. He hitched the mule to a tree behind the store and untied the pail and came and mounted to the gallery, where already a dozen men, Ratliff among them, lounged. He did not speak. If he ever looked at them individually, that one did not discern it—a thick squat soft man of no establishable age between twenty and thirty, with a broad still face containing a tight seam of mouth stained slightly at the corners with tobacco, and eyes the color of stagnant water, and projecting from among the other features in startling and sudden paradox, a tiny predatory nose like the beak of a small hawk. It was as though the original nose had been left off by the original designer or craftsman and the unfinished job taken over by someone of a radically different school or perhaps by some viciously maniacal humorist or perhaps by one who had

had only time to clap into the center of the face a frantic and desperate warning.

He entered the store, carrying the pail, and Ratliff and his companions sat and squatted about the gallery all that day and watched not only the village proper but all the countryside within walking distance come up singly and in pairs and in groups, men women and children, to make trivial purchases and look at the new clerk and go away. They came not belligerently but completely wary, almost decorous, like half-wild cattle following word of the advent of a strange beast upon their range, to buy flour and patent medicine and plow lines and tobacco and look at the man whose name a week ago they had never heard, yet with whom in the future they would have to deal for the necessities of living, and then depart as quietly as they had come. About nine oclock Jody Varner rode up on his roan saddle horse and entered the store. They could hear the bass murmur of his voice inside, though for all the answer he got he might have been talking to himself. He came out at noon and mounted and rode away, though the clerk did not follow him. But they had known anyway what the tin pail would contain, and they began to disperse noonward too, looking into the store as they passed the door, seeing nothing. If the clerk was eating his lunch, he had hidden to do it. Ratliff was back on the gallery before one oclock, since he had had to walk only a hundred yards for his dinner. But the others were not long after him, and for the rest of that day they sat and squatted, talking quietly now and then about nothing at all, while the rest of the people within walking distance came and bought in nickels and dimes and went away.

By the end of that first week they had all come in and seen him, not only all those who in future would have to deal through him for food and supplies but some who had never traded with the Varners and never would—the men, the women, the children—the infants who had never before crossed the doorsteps beyond which they had been born, the sick and the aged who otherwise might never have crossed them but once more—coming on horses and mules and by wagonsful. Ratliff was still there, the buckboard still containing the music box and the set of virgin harrow teeth standing, a plank propping its tongue and the sturdy mismatched team growing vicious with idleness, in Mrs Littlejohn's lot, watching each morning as the clerk would ride up on the mule, on the borrowed saddle, in the new white shirt growing gradually and steadily a little more and more soiled with each sunset, with the tin pail of lunch which no man had ever yet seen him eating, and hitch the mule and unlock the store with the key which they had not quite expected him to have in his possession for a few days yet at least. After the first day or so he would even have the store open when Ratliff and the others arrived. Jody Varner would appear on the horse about nine oclock and mount the steps and jerk his head bluffly at them and enter the store, though after the first morning he remained only about fifteen minutes. If Ratliff and his companions had hoped to divine any hidden undercurrent or secret spark between the younger Varner and the clerk, they were disappointed. There would be the heavy bass matter-of-fact murmur, still talking apparently to itself for all the audible answer it ever got, then he and the clerk would come to the door and stand in it while Varner finished his instructions and sucked his teeth and departed; when they looked toward the door, it would be empty.

Then at last, on Friday afternoon, Will Varner himself appeared. Perhaps it was for this Ratliff and his companions had been waiting. But if it was, it was doubtless not Ratliff but the others who even hoped that anything would divulge here. So it was very likely Ratliff alone who was not surprised, since what did divulge was the observe of what they might have hoped for; it was not the clerk who now discovered at last whom he was working for, but Will Varner who discovered who was working for him. He came up on the old fat white horse. A young man squatting on the top step rose and descended and took the reins and tied the horse and Varner got down and mounted the steps, speaking cheerily to their deferential murmur, to Ratliff by name: "Hell fire, aint you gone back to work yet?" Two more of them vacated the knife-gnawed wooden bench, but Varner did not approach it at once. Instead, he paused in front of the open door in almost exactly the same attitude of the people themselves, lean, his neck craned a little like a turkey as he looked into the store, though only for an instant because almost at once he shouted, "You there. What's your name? Flem. Bring me a plug of my tobacco. Jody showed you where he keeps it." He came and approached the group, two of whom vacated the knife-gnawed wooden bench for him, and he sat down and took out his knife and had already begun his smoking-car story in his cheerful drawling bishop's voice when the clerk (Ratliff had not heard his feet at all) appeared at his elbow with the tobacco. Still talking, Varner took the plug and cut off a chew and shut the knife with his thumb and straightened his leg to put the knife back into his pocket, when he stopped talking and looked sharply upward. The clerk was still standing at his elbow. "Hey?" Varner said. "What?"

"You aint paid for it," the clerk said. For an instant Varner did not move at all, his leg still extended, the plug and the severed chew in one hand and the knife in the other just about to enter his pocket. None of them moved in fact, looking quietly and attentively at their hands or at wherever their eyes had been when Varner interrupted himself. "The tobacco," the clerk said.

"Oh," Varner said. He put the knife into his pocket and drew from his hip a leather purse about the size and shape and color of an eggplant and took a nickel from it and gave it to the clerk. Ratliff had not heard the clerk come out and he did not hear him return. Now he saw why. The clerk wore also a new pair of rubber-soled tennis shoes. "Where was I?" Varner said.

"The fellow had just begun to unbutton his over-halls," Ratliff said mildly.

The next day Ratliff departed. He was put into motion not by the compulsion of food, earning it. He could have passed from table to table in that country for six months without once putting his hand into his pocket. He was moved by his itinerary, his established and nurtured round of newsmongering, the pleasure of retailing it, not the least nor stalest of which present stock he had spent the last two weeks actually watching. It was five months before he saw the village again.

His route embraced four counties. It was absolutely rigid, flexibie only within itself. In ten years he had not once crossed the boundaries of these four, yet one day in this summer he found himself in Tennessee. He found himself not only on foreign soil but shut away from his native state by a golden barrier, a wall of neatly accumulating minted coins.

During the spring and summer he had done a little too well. He had oversold himself, selling and delivering the machines on notes against the coming harvest, employing what money he collected or sold the exchanged articles for which he accepted as down-payments, to make his own down-payments to the Memphis wholesaler on still other machines, which he delivered in turn on new notes, countersigning them, until one day he discovered that he had almost sold himself insolvent on his own bull market. The wholesaler made demand upon him for his (the wholesaler's) half of the outstanding twenty-dollar notes. Ratliff in his turn made a swift canvass of his own debtors. He was affable, bland, anecdotal and apparently unhurried as ever but he combed them thoroughly, not to be denied, although the cotton had just begun to bloom and it would be months yet before there would be any money in the land. He collected a few dollars, a set of used wagon harness, eight White Leghorn hens. He owed the wholesaler $120.00. He called on the twelfth customer, a distant kinsman, and found that he had departed a week ago with a string of mules to sell at the mule curb-market at Columbia, Tennessee.

He followed at once in the buckboard, with the wagon harness and the hens. He not only saw a chance to collect his note, provided he got there before someone sold the kinsman some mules in his own turn, but he might even borrow enough to appease the wholesaler. He reached Columbia four days later, where, after the first amazed moment or so, he looked about him with something of the happy surmise of the first white hunter blundering into the idyllic solitude of a virgin African vale teeming with ivory, his for the mere shooting and fetching out. He sold a machine to the man whom he asked the whereabouts of his cousin, he went with the kinsman to pass the night at the home of the kinsman's wife's cousin ten miles from Columbia and sold a machine there. He sold three in the first four days; he remained a month and sold eight in all, collecting $80.00 in down-payments, with the $80.00 and the wagon harness and the eight hens he bought a mule, took the mule to Memphis and sold it at curb auction for $135.00, gave the wholesaler $120.00 and the new notes for a quit-claim on the old ones in Mississippi, and reached home at gathering-time with $2.53 in cash and full title to the twelve twenty-dollar notes which would be paid as the cotton was ginned and sold.

When he reached Frenchman's Bend in November, it had returned to normal. It had acquiesced to the clerk's presence even if it had not accepted him, though the Varners seemed to have done both. Jody had used to be in the store at some time during the day and not far from it at any time. Ratliff now discovered that for months he had been in the habit of sometimes not appearing at all, customers who had traded there for years, mostly serving themselves and putting the correct change into the cigar box inside the cheese cage, now having to deal for each trivial item with a man whose name they had not even heard two months ago, who answered Yes and No to direct questions and who apparently never looked directly or long enough at any face to remember the name which went with it, yet who never made mistakes in any matter pertaining to money. Jody Varner had made them constantly. They were usually in his own favor to be sure, letting a customer get away with a spool of thread or a tin of snuff now and then, but getting it back sooner or later. They had come to expect mistakes of him, just as they knew he would correct them when caught with a bluff, hearty amiability, making a joke of it, which sometimes left the customer wondering just a little about the rest of the bill. But they expected this too, because he would give them credit for food and plow-gear when they needed it, long credit, though they knew they would pay interest for that which on its face looked like generosity and openhandedness, whether that interest showed in the final discharge or not. But the clerk never made mistakes.

"Nonsense," Ratliff said. "Somebody's bound to catch him

sooner or later. There aint a man woman or child in twenty-five miles that dont know what's in that store and what it cost as well as Will or Jody Varner either."

"Hah," the other said—a sturdy short-legged black-browed ready-faced man named Odum Bookwright. "That's it."

"You mean aint nobody ever caught him *once* even?"

"No," Bookwright said. "And folks dont like it. Otherwise, how can you tell?"

"Sho," Ratliff said. "How can you?"

"There was that credit business too," another said—a lank man with a bulging dreamy scant-haired head and pale myopic eyes named Quick, who operated a sawmill. He told about it: how they had discovered almost at once that the clerk did not want to credit anyone with anything. He finally flatly refused further credit to a man who had been into and out of the store's debt at least once a year for the last fifteen, and how that afternoon Will Varner himself came galloping up on the old fat grumble-gutted white horse and stormed into the store, shouting loud enough to be heard in the blacksmith shop across the road: "Who in hell's store do you think this is anyway?"

"Well, we know whose store it is yet, anyway," Ratliff said.

"Or whose store some folks still thinks it is yet," Bookwright said. "Anyhow, he aint moved into Varner's house yet."

Because the clerk now lived in the village. One Saturday morning someone noticed that the saddled mule was not hitched behind the store. The store remained open until ten and later on Saturdays and there was always a crowd about it and several men saw him put out the lamps and lock the door and depart, on foot. And the next morning he who had never been seen in the village between Saturday night and Monday morning appeared at the church, and those who saw him looked at him for an instant in incredulous astonishment. In addition to the gray cloth cap and the gray trousers, he wore not only a clean white shirt but a necktie—a tiny machine-made black bow which snapped together at the back with a metal fastener. It was not two inches long and with the exception of the one which Will Varner himself wore to church it was the only tie in the whole Frenchman's Bend country, and from that Sunday morning until the day he died he wore it or one just like (it was told of him later, after he had become president of his Jefferson bank, that he had them made for him by the gross)—a tiny viciously depthless cryptically balanced splash like an enigmatic punctuation symbol against the expanse of white shirt which gave him Jody Varner's look of ceremonial heterodoxy raised to its tenth power and which postulated to those who had been present on that day that quality of outrageous overstatement of physical displacement which the sound of his father's stiff foot made on the gallery of the store that afternoon in the spring. He departed on foot; he came to the store the next morning still walking and still wearing the tie. By nightfall the countryside knew that since the previous Saturday he had boarded and lodged in the home of a family living about a mile from the store.

Will Varner had long since returned to his old idle busy cheerful existence—if he had ever left it. The store had not seen him since the Fourth of July. And now that Jody no longer came in, during the dead slack days of August while the cotton ripened and there was nothing for anyone to do, it had actually seemed as if not only the guiding power but the proprietorial and revenue-deriving as well was concentrated in that squat reticent figure in the steadily-soiling white shirts and the minute invulnerable bow, which in those abeyant days lurked among the ultimate shadows of the deserted and rich-odored interior with a good deal of the quality of a spider of that bulbous blond omnivorous though non-poisonous species.

Then in September something happened. It began rather, though at first they did not recognise it for what it was. The cotton had opened and was being picked. One morning the first of the men to arrive found Jody Varner already there. The gin was unlocked and Trumbull, Varner's blacksmith, and his apprentice and the Negro fireman were overhauling the machinery, getting it ready for the season's run, and presently Snopes came out of the store and went across to the gin and entered it and passed from sight and so, for the moment, from remembering too. It was not until the store closed that afternoon that they realised that Jody Varner had been inside it all day. But even then they attached little importance to this. They thought that without doubt Jody himself had sent the clerk to superintend the opening of the gin, which Jody himself had used to do, out of laziness, assuming himself the temporary onus of tending store so he could sit down. It took the actual firing-up of the gin and the arrival of the first loaded wagons to disabuse them. Then they saw that it was Jody who was now tending store again, fetching and carrying for the nickels and dimes, while the clerk sat all day long on the stool behind the scale-beam as the wagons moved in turn onto it and so beneath the suction pipe. Jody had used to do both. That is, he was mostly behind the scales, letting the store take care of itself, as it always had, though now and then, just to rest himself, he would keep a wagon standing upon the scales, blocking them for fifteen minutes or even forty-five minutes, while he was in the store; maybe there would not even be any customers during that time, just loungers, listeners for him to talk to. But that was all right. Things got along just as well. And now that there were two of them, there was no reason why one should not remain in the store while the other did the weighing, and there was no reason why Jody should not have designated the weighing to the clerk. The cold surmise which now began to dawn upon them was that——

"Sho," Ratliff said. "I know. That Jody should have stayed there a-tall. Just who it was that told him to stay there." He and Bookwright looked at each other. "It wasn't Uncle Will. That store and that gin had been running themselves at the same time for nigh forty years all right, with just one fellow between them. And a fellow Uncle Will's age aint likely to change his notions. Sho now. All right. Then what?"

They could watch them both from the gallery. They would come in on their laden wagons and draw into line, mule-nose to tail gate, beside the road, waiting for their turn to move onto the scales and then under the suction pipe, and dismount and wrap the reins about a stanchion and cross to the gallery, from which they could watch the still, impenetrable, steadily-chewing face throned behind the scale-beam, the cloth cap, the minute tie, while from within the store they could hear now and then the short surly grunts with which Varner answered when his customers forced him to speak at all. Now and then they would even go in themselves and buy sacks or plugs of tobacco or tins of snuff which they did not actually need yet, or maybe just to drink from the cedar water bucket. Because there was something in Jody's eyes that had not been there before either—a shadow, something between annoyance and speculation and purest foreknowledge, which was not quite bafflement yet but was certainly sober. This was the time they referred to later, two and three years later, when they told one another: "That was when he passed Jody," though it was Ratliff who amended it: "You mean, that was when Jody begun to find it out."

But that was to be sometime in the future yet. Now they just watched, missing nothing. During that month the air was filled from daylight until dark with the whine of the gin; the wagons stood in line for the scales and moved up one by one beneath the suction pipe. Now and then the clerk would cross the road to the store, the cap, the trousers, even the tie wisped with cotton; the men lounging upon the gallery while they waited their turns at the suction pipe or the scales would watch him enter the store now and a moment later hear his voice this time, murmuring, matter-of-fact, succinct. But Jody Varner would not come to the door with him to stand for a moment as before, and they would watch the clerk return to the gin—the thick squat back, shapeless, portentous, without age. After the crops were in and ginned and sold, the time came when Will Varner made his yearly settlement with his tenants and debtors. He had used to do this alone, not even allowing Jody to help him. This year he sat at the desk with the iron cash box while Snopes sat on a nail keg at his knee with the open ledgers. In the tunnel-like room lined with canned food and cluttered with farming implements and now crowded with patient earth-reeking men waiting to accept almost without question whatever Varner should compute he owed them for their year's work, Varner and Snopes resembled the white trader and his native parrot-taught headman in an African outpost.

That headman was acquiring the virtues of civilization fast. It was not known what the Varners paid him, except that Will Varner had never been known to pay very much for anything. Yet this man who five months ago was riding eight miles back and forth to work on a plow mule and a cast-off saddle with a tin pail of cold turnip greens or field pease tied to it, was now not only sleeping in a rented bed and eating from a furnished table like a drummer, he had also made a considerable cash loan, security and interest not specified, to a resident of the village, and before the last of the cotton was ginned it was generally known that any sum between twenty-five cents and ten dollars could be borrowed from him at any time, if the borrower agreed to pay enough for the accommodation. In the next spring Tull, in Jefferson with a drove of cattle for shipping on the railroad, came to see Ratliff, who was sick in bed in the house which he owned and which his widowed sister kept for him, with a recurrent old gall-bladder trouble. Tull told him of a considerable herd of scrub cattle which had passed the winter in pasture on the farm which Snopes's father had rented from the Varners for another year —a herd which, by the time Ratliff had been carried to a Memphis hospital and operated on and returned home and once more took an interest in what went on about him, had increased gradually and steadily and then overnight vanished, its disappearance coincident with the appearance of a herd of good Herefords in a pasture on another place which Varner owned and kept himself as his home farm, as though transmogrified, translated complete and intact save for their altered appearance and obviously greater worth, it only later becoming known that the cattle had reached the pasture via a foreclosed lien nominally held by a Jefferson bank. Bookwright and Tull both came to see him and told him of this.

"Maybe they was in the bank vault all the time," Ratliff said weakly. "Who did Will say they belonged to?"

"He said they was Snopes's," Tull said. "He said, 'Ask that son-of-a-gun of Jody's.' "

"And did you?" Ratliff said.

"Bookwright did. And Snopes said, 'They're in Varner's pasture.' And Bookwright said, 'But Will says they are yourn.' And Snopes turned his head and spit and says, 'They're in Varner's pasture.' "

And Ratliff, ill, did not see this either. He only heard it second hand, though by that time he was mending, well enough to muse upon it, speculate, curious, shrewd, and inscrutable himself, sitting up now in a chair propped with pillows in a window where he could watch the autumn begin, feel the bright winy air of October noons: How one morning in that second spring a man named Houston, heeled by a magnificent grave blue-ticked Walker hound, led a horse up to the blacksmith shop and saw, stooping over the forge and trying to start a fire in it with liquid from a rusty can, a stranger—a young, well-made, muscle-bound man who, turning, revealed an open equable face beginning less than an inch below his hairline, who said, "Howdy. I cant seem to get this here fire started. Everytime I put this here coal oil onto it, it just goes further out. Watch." He prepared to pour from the can again.

"Hold on," Houston said. "Is that coal oil you've got?"

"It was setting on that ere ledge yonder," the other said. "It looks like the kind of a can coal oil would be in. It's a little rusty, but I never heard tell of even rusty coal oil that wouldn't burn before." Houston came and took the can from him and sniffed it. The other watched him. The splendid hound sat in the doorway and watched them both. "It dont smell exactly like coal oil, does it?"

"—t," Houston said. He set the can back on the sooty ledge above the forge. "Go on. Haul that mud out. You'll have to start over. Where's Trumbull?" Trumbull was the smith who had been in the shop for almost twenty years, until this morning.

"I dont know," the other said. "Wasn't nobody here when I come."

"What are you doing here? Did he send you?"

"I dont know," the other said. "It was my cousin hired me. He told me to be here this morning and get the fire started

And tend to the business till he come. But everytime I put that ere coal oil——"

"Who is your cousin?" Houston said. At that moment a gaunt aged horse came up rapidly, drawing a battered and clattering buggy one of whose wheels was wired upright by two crossed slats, which looked as if its momentum alone held it intact and that the instant it stopped it would collapse into kindling. It contained another stranger—a frail man none of whose garments seemed to belong to him, with a talkative weasel's face—who halted the buggy, shouting at the horse as if they were a good-sized field apart, and got out of the buggy and came into the shop, already (or still) talking.

"Morning, morning," he said, his little bright eyes darting. "Want that horse shod, hey? Good, good: save the hoof and save all. Good-looking animal. Seen a considerable better one in a field a piece back. But no matter; love me, love my horse, beggars cant be choosers, if wishes were horseflesh we'd all own thoroughbreds. What's the matter?" he said to the man in the apron. He paused, though still he seemed to be in violent motion, as though the attitude and position of his garments gave no indication whatever of what the body within them might be doing—indeed, if it were still inside them at all. "Aint you got that fire started yet? Here." He darted to the ledge; he seemed to translate himself over beneath it without increasing his appearance of violent motion at all, and had taken the can down and sniffed at it and then prepared to empty it onto the coals in the forge before anyone could move. Then Houston intercepted him at the last second and took the can from him and flung it out the door.

"I just finished taking that damn hog piss away from him," Houston said. "What the hell's happened here? Where's Trumbull?"

"Oh, you mean the fellow that used to be here," the newcomer said. "His lease has done been cancelled. I'm leasing the shop now. My name's Snopes. I. O. Snopes. This here's my young cousin, Eck Snopes. But it's the old shop, the old stand; just a new broom in it."

"I don't give a damn what his name is," Houston said. "Can he shoe a horse?" Again the newcomer turned upon the man in the apron, shouting at him as he had shouted at the horse:

"All right. All right. Get that fire started." After watching a moment, Houston took charge and they got the fire going. "He'll pick it up though," the newcomer said. "Just give him time. He's handy with tools, even though he aint done no big sight of active blacksmithing. But give a dog a good name and you dont need to hang him. Give him a few days to practise up and he'll shoe a horse quick as Trumbull or any of them."

"I'll shoe this one," Houston said. "Just let him keep pumping that bellows. He looks like he ought to be able to do that without having to practise." Nevertheless, the shoe shaped and cooled in the tub, the newcomer darted in again. It was as if he took not only Houston but himself too by complete surprise—that weasel-like quality of existing independent of his clothing so that although you could grasp and hold that you could not restrain the body itself from doing what it was doing until the damage had been done—a furious already dissipating concentration of energy vanishing the instant after the intention took shape, the newcomer darting between Houston and the raised hoof and clapping the shoe onto it and touching the animal's quick with the second blow of the hammer on the nail and being hurled, hammer and all, into the shrinking-tub by the plunging horse which Houston and the man in the apron finally backed into a corner and held while Houston jerked nail and shoe free and flung them into the corner and backed the horse savagely out of the shop, the hound rising and resuming its position quietly at proper heeling distance behind the man. "And you cal tell Will Varner—if he cares a damn, which evidently he dont," Houston said, "that I have gone to Whiteleaf to have my horse shod."

The shop and the store were just opposite, only the road between. There were several men already on the gallery, who watched Houston, followed by the big quiet regal dog, lead the horse away. They did not even need to cross the road to see one of the strangers, because presently the smaller and older one crossed to the store, in the clothes which would still appear not to belong to him on the day they finally fell off his body, with his talkative pinched face and his bright darting eyes. He mounted the steps, already greeting them. Still talking, he entered the store, his voice voluble and rapid and meaningless like something talking to itself about nothing in a deserted cavern. He came out again, still talking: "Well, gentlemen, off with the old and on with the new. Competition is the life of trade, and though a chain aint no stronger than its weakest link, I dont think you'll find the boy yonder no weak reed to have to lean on once he catches onto it. It's the old shop, the old stand; it's just a new broom in it and maybe you cant teach a old dog new tricks but you can teach a new young willing one anything. Just give him time; a penny on the waters pays interest when the flood turns. Well, well; all pleasure and no work, as the fellow says, might make Jack so sharp he might cut his-self. I bid you good morning, gentlemen." He went on and got into the buggy, still talking, now to the man in the shop and now to the gaunt horse, all in one breath, without any break to indicate to the hearers which he addressed at any time. He drove away, the men on the gallery looking after him, completely expressionless. During the day they crossed to the shop, one by one, and looked at the second stranger—the quiet empty open face which seemed to have been a mere afterthought to the thatching of the skull, like the binding of a rug, harmless. A man brought up a wagon with a broken hound. The new smith even repaired it, though it took him most of the forenoon, working steadily but in a dreamlike state in which what actually lived inside him apparently functioned somewhere else, paying no heed to and having no interest in, not even in the money he would earn, what his hands were doing; busy, thick-moving, getting nowhere seemingly though at last the job was finished. That afternoon Trumbull, the old smith, appeared. But if they had waited about the store to see what would happen when he arrived who until last night anyway must have still believed himself the incumbent, they were disappointed. He drove through the village with his wife, in a wagon loaded with household goods. If he even looked toward his old shop nobody saw him do it—an old man though still hale, morose and efficient, who would have invited no curiosity even before yesterday. They never saw him again.

A few days later they learned that the new smith was living in the house where his cousin (or whatever the relationship was: nobody ever knew for certain) Flem lived, the two of them sleeping together in the same bed. Six months later the smith had married one of the daughters of the family where the two of them boarded. Ten months after that he was pushing a perambulator (once—or still—Will Varner's, like the cousin's saddle) about the village on Sundays, accompanied by a five- or six-year-old boy, his son by a former wife which the village did not know either he had ever possessed—indicating that there was considerably more force and motion to his private life, his sex life anyway, than would appear on the surface of his public one. But that all appeared later. All they saw now was that they had a new blacksmith—a man who was not lazy, whose intentions were good and who was accommodating and unfailingly pleasant and even generous, yet in whom there was a definite limitaion of physical co-ordination beyond which design and plan and pattern all vanished, disintegrated into dead components of pieces of wood and iron straps and vain tools.

Two months later Flem Snopes built a new blacksmith shop in the village. He hired it done, to be sure, but he was there most of the day, watching it going up. This was not only the first of his actions in the village which he was ever seen in physical juxtaposition to, but the first which he not only admitted but affirmed, stating calmly and flatly that he was doing it so that people could get decent work done again. He bought completely new equipment at cost price through the store and hired the young farmer who during the slack of planting and harvesting time had been Trumbull's apprentice. Within a month the new shop had got all the trade which Trumbull had had and three months after that Snopes had sold the new shop—smith clientele and goodwill and new equipment—to Varner, receiving in return the old equipment in the old shop, which he sold to a junk man, moved the new equipment to the old shop and sold the new building to a farmer for a cowshed, without even having to pay himself to have it moved, leaving this kinsman now apprentice to the new smith—at which point even Ratliff had lost count of what profit Snopes might have made. But I reckon I can guess the rest of it, he told himself, sitting, a little pale but otherwise well, in his sunny window. He could almost see it—in the store, at night, the door barred on the inside and the lamp burning above the desk where the clerk sat, chewing steadily, while Jody Varner stood over him, in no condition to sit down, with a good deal more in his eyes than had been in them last fall, shaking, trembling, saying in a shaking voice: "I want to make one pure and simple demand of you and I want a pure and simple Yes and No for a answer: How many more is there? How much longer is this going on? Just want is it going to cost me to protect one goddamn barn full of hay?"

2

He had been sick and he showed it as, the buckboard once more with a new machine in the dog-kennel box and the little sturdy team fat and slick with the year's idleness hitched in an adjacent alley, he sat at the counter of a small side-street restaurant in which he owned a sleeping partner's half interest, with a cup of coffee at his hand and in his pocket a contract to sell fifty goats to a Northerner who had recently established a goat-ranch in the western part of the county. It was actually a subcontract which he had purchased at the rate of twenty-five cents a goat from the original contractor who held his from the Northerner at seventy-five cents a goat and was about to fail to complete. Ratliff bought the subcontract because he happened to know of a herd of some fifty-odd goats in a little-travelled section near Frenchman's Bend village which the original contractor had failed to find and which Ratliff was confident he could acquire by offering to halve his profit with the owner of them.

He was on his way to Frenchman's Bend now, though he had not started yet and did not know just when he would start. He had not seen the village in a year now. He was looking forward to his visit not only for the pleasure of the shrewd dealing which far transcended mere gross profit, but with the sheer happiness of being out of bed and moving once more at free will, even though a little weakly, in the sun and air which men drank and moved in and talked and dealt with one another—a pleasure no small part of which lay in the fact that he had not started yet and there was absolutely nothing under heaven to make him start until he wanted to. He did not still feel weak, he was merely luxuriating in that supremely gutful lassitude of convalescence in which time, hurry, doing, did not exist, the accumulating seconds and minutes and hours to which in its well state the body is slave both waking and sleeping, now reversed and time now the lip-server and mendicant to the body's pleasure instead of the body thrall to time's headlong course. So he sat, thin, the fresh clean blue shirt quite loose upon him now, yet looking actually quite well, the smooth brown of his face not pallid but merely a few shades lighter, cleaner-looking; emanating in fact a sort of delicate robustness like some hardy odorless infrequent wodland plant blooming into the actual heel of winter's snow, nursing his coffee cup in one thin hand and telling three or four listeners about his operation in that shrewd humorous voice which would require a good deal more than just illness to other than merely weaken its volume a little, when two men entered. They were Tull and Bookwright. Bookwright had a stock whip rolled about its handle and thrust into the back pocket of his overalls.

"Howdy, boys," Ratliff said. "You're in early."

"You mean late," Bookwright said. He and Tull went to the counter.

"We just got in last night with some cattle to ship today," Tull said. "So you was in Memphis. I thought I'd missed you."

"We all missed him," Bookwright said. "My wife aint mentioned nobody's new sewing machine in almost a year. What was it that Memphis fellow cut outen you anyway?"

"My pocketbook," Ratliff said. "I reckon that's why he put me to sleep first."

"He put you to sleep first to keep you from selling him a sewing machine or a bushel of harrow teeth before he could get his knife open," Bookwright said. The counterman came and slid two plates of bread and butter before them.

"I'll have steak," Tull said.

"I wont," Bookwright said. "I been watching the dripping sterns of steaks for two days now. Let alone running them back out of corn fields and vegetable patches. Bring me some ham and a half a dozen fried eggs." He began to eat the bread, wolfing it. Ratliff turned slightly on his stool to face them.

"So I been missed," he said. "I would a thought you folks would a had so many new citizens in Frenchman's Bend by now you wouldn't a missed a dozen sewing-machine agents. How many kinfolks has Flem Snopes brought in to date? Is it two more, or just three?"

"Four," Bookwright said shortly, eating.

"Four?" Ratliff said. "That's that blacksmith—I mean, the one that uses the blacksmith shop for his address until it's time to go back home and eat again—what's his name? Eck. And that other one, the contractor, the business executive——"

"He's going to be the new school professor next year," Tull said mildly. "Or so they claim."

"No no," Ratliff said. "I'm talking about them Snopeses. That other one. I.O. That Jack Houston throwed into the water tub that day in the blacksmith shop."

"That's him," Tull said. "They claim he's going to teach the school next year. The teacher we had left all of a sudden just after Christmas. I reckon you never heard about that neither."

But Ratliff wasn't listening to this. He wasn't thinking about the other teacher. He stared at Tull, for the moment surprised out of his own humorous poise. "What?" he said. "Teach the school? That fellow? That Snopes? The one that came to the shop that day that Jack Houston— Here, Odum," he said; "I been sick, but sholy it aint affected my ears that much."

Bookwright didn't answer. He had finished his bread; he leaned and took a piece from Tull's plate. "You aint eating it," he said. "I'll tell him to bring some more in a minute."

"Well," Ratliff said. "I'll be damned. By God, I knowed

there was something wrong with him soon as I saw him. That was it. He was standing in front of the wrong thing—a blacksmith shop or a plowed field. But teaching the school. I just hadn't imagined that yet. But that's it, of course. He has found the one and only place in the world or Frenchman's Bend either where he not only can use them proverbs of hisn all day long but he will be paid for doing it. Well," he said. "So Will Varner has caught that bear at last. Flem has grazed up the store and he has grazed up the blacksmith shop and now he is starting in on the school. That just leaves Will's house. Of course, after that he will have to fall back on you folks, but that house will keep him occupied for a while because Will——"

"Hah!" Bookwright said shortly. He finished the slice of bread he had taken from Tull's plate and called to the counterman: "Here. Bring me a piece of pie while I'm waiting."

"What kind of pie, Mr Bookwright?" the counterman said.

"Eating pie," Bookwright said.

"—because Will might be a little hard to dislodge outen the actual house," Ratliff went on. "He might even draw the line there altogether. So maybe Flem will have to start in on you folks sooner than he had figured on——"

"Hah," Bookwright said again, harsh and sudden. The counterman slid the pie along to him. Ratliff looked at him.

"All right," Ratliff said. "Hah what?"

Bookwright sat with the wedge of pie poised in his hand before his mouth. He turned his fierce dark face toward Ratliff. "I was sitting on the sawdust pile at Quick's mill last week. His fireman and another nigger were shovelling the chips over toward the boiler, to fire with. They were talking. The fireman wanted to borrow some money, said Quick wouldn't let him have it. 'Go to Mr Snopes at the store,' the other nigger says. 'He will lend it to you. He lent me five dollars over two years ago and all I does, every Saturday night I goes to the store and pays him a dime. He aint even mentioned that five dollars.'" Then he turned his head and bit into the pie, taking a little less than half of it. Ratliff watched him with a faint quizzical expression which was almost smiling.

"Well well well," he said. "So he's working the top and the bottom both at the same time. At that rate it will be a while yet before he has to fall back on you ordinary white folks in the middle." Bookwright took another huge bite of the pie. The counterman brought his and Tull's meal and Bookwright crammed the rest of the pie into his mouth. Tull began to cut his steak neatly into bites as though for a child to eat it. Ratliff watched them. "Aint none of you folks out there done nothing about it?" he said.

"What could we do?" Tull said. "It aint right. But it aint none of our business."

"I believe I would think of something if I lived there," Ratliff said.

"Yes," Bookwright said. He was eating his ham as he had the pie. "And wind up with one of them bow ties in place of your buckboard and team. You'd have room to wear it."

"Sho now," Ratliff said. "Maybe you're right." He stopped looking at them now and raised his spoon, but lowered it again. "This here cup seems to have a draft in it," he said to the counterman. "Maybe you better warm it up a little. It might freeze and bust, and I would have to pay for the cup too." The counterman swept the cup away and refilled it and slid it back. Ratliff spooned sugar into it carefully, his face still wearing that faint expression which would have been called smiling for lack of anything better. Bookwright had mixed his six eggs into one violent mess and was now eating them audibly with a spoon. He and Tull both ate with expedition, though Tull even contrived to do that with almost niggling primness. They did not talk, they just cleaned their plates and rose and went to the cigar case and paid their bills.

"Or maybe them tennis shoes," Bookwright said. "He aint wore them in a year now.—No," he said. "If I was you I would go out there nekkid in the first place. Then you wont notice the cold coming back."

"Sho now," Ratliff said mildly. After they left he drank his coffee again, sipping it without haste, talking again to the three or four listeners, finishing the story of his operation. Then he rose too and paid for his coffee, scrupulously, and put on his overcoat. It was now March but the doctor had told him to wear it, and in the alley now he stood for a while beside the buckboard and the sturdy little horses overfat with idleness and sleek with new hair after their winter coats, looking quietly at the dog-kennel box where, beneath the cracked paint of their fading and incredible roses, the women's faces smiled at him in fixed and sightless invitation. It would need painting again this year; he must see to that. It will have to be something that will burn, he thought. And in his name. Known to be in his name. Yes, he thought, if my name was Will Varner and my partner's name was Snopes I believe I would insist that some part of our partnership at least, that part of it that will burn anyway, would be in his name. He walked on slowly, buttoned into the overcoat. It was the only one in sight. But then the sick grow well fast in the sun; perhaps when he returned to town he would no longer need it. And soon he would not need the sweater beneath it either—May and June, the summer, the long good days of heat. He walked on, looking exactly as he always had save for the thinness and the pallor, pausing twice to tell two different people that yes, he felt all right now, the Memphis doctor had evidently cut the right thing out whether by accident or design, crossing the Square now beneath the shaded marble gaze of the Confederate soldier, and so into the courthouse and the Chancery Clerk's office, where he found what he sought—some two hundred acres of land, with buildings, recorded to Flem Snopes.

Toward the end of the afternoon he was sitting in the halted buckboard in a narrow back road in the hills, reading the name on a mailbox. The post it sat on was new, but the box was not. It was battered and scarred; at one time it had apparently been crushed flat as though by a wagon wheel and straightened again, but the crude lettering of the name might have been painted on it yesterday. It seemed to shout at him, all capitals, MINKSNOPES, sprawling, without any spacing between the two words, trailing off and uphill and over the curve of the top to include the final letters. Ratliff turned in beside it—a rutted lane now; at the end of it a broken-backed cabin of the same two rooms which were scattered without number through these remote hill sections which he travelled. It was built on a hill; below it was a foul muck-trodden lot and a barn leaning away downhill as though a human breath might flatten it. A man was emerging from it, carrying a milk pail, and then Ratliff knew that he was being watched from the house itself though he had seen no one. He pulled the team up. He did not get down. "Howdy," he said. "This Mr. Snopes? I brought your machine."

"Brought my what?" the man in the lot said. He came through the gate and set the pail on the end of the sagging gallery. He was slightly less than medium height also but thin, with a single line of heavy eyebrow. But it's the same eyes, Ratliff thought.

"Your sewing machine," he said pleasantly. Then he saw from the corner of his eye a woman standing on the gallery—a big-boned hard-faced woman with incredible yellow hair, who had emerged with a good deal more lightness and quickness than the fact that she was barefoot would have presaged. Behind her were two towheaded children. But Ratliff did not look at her. He watched the man, his expression bland courteous and pleasant.

"What's that?" the woman said. "A sewing machine?"

"No," the man said. He didn't look at her either. He was approaching the buckboard. "Get on back in the house." The woman paid no attention to him. She came down from the gallery, moving again with that speed and co-ordination which her size belied. She stared at Ratliff with pale hard eyes.

"Who told you to bring it here?" she said.

Now Ratliff looked at her, still bland, still pleasant. "Have I done made a mistake?" he said. "The message come to me in Jefferson, from Frenchman's Bend. It said Snopes. I taken it to mean you, because if your . . . cousin?" Neither of them spoke, staring at him. "Flem. If Flem had wanted it, he would have waited till I got there. He knowed I was due there tomorrow. I reckon I ought to made sho." The woman laughed harshly, without mirth.

"Then take it on to him. If Flem Snopes sent you word about anything that cost more than a nickel it wasn't to give away. Not to his kinfolks anyhow. Take it on to the Bend."

"I told you to go in the house," the man said. "Go on." The woman didn't look at him. She laughed harshly and steadily, staring at Ratliff.

"Not to give away," she said. "Not the man that owns a hundred head of cattle and a barn and pasture to feed them in his own name." The man turned and walked toward her. She turned and began to scream at him, the two children watching Ratliff quietly from behind her skirts as if they were deaf or as if they lived in another world from that in which the woman screamed, like two dogs might. "Deny it if you can!" she cried at the man. "He'd let you rot and die right here and glad of it, and you know it! Your own kin you're so proud of because he works in a store and wears a necktie all day! Ask him to give you a sack of flour even and see what you get. Ask him! Maybe he'll give you one of his old neckties someday so you can dress like a Snopes too!" The man walked steadily toward her. He did not even speak again. He was the smaller of the two of them; he walked steadily toward her with a curious sidling deadly, almost deferential, air until she broke, turned swiftly and went back toward the house, the herded children before her still watching Ratliff over their shoulders. The man approached the buckboard.

"You say the message came from Flem?" he said.

"I said it come from Frenchman's Bend," Ratliff said. "The name mentioned was Snopes."

"Who was it seems to done all this mentioning about Snopes?"

"A friend," Ratliff said pleasantly. "He seems to made a mistake. I ask you to excuse it. Can I follow this lane over to the Whiteleaf Bridge road?"

"If Flem sent you work to leave it here, suppose you leave it."

"I just told you I thought I had made a mistake and ask you to excuse it," Ratliff said. "Does this lane——"

"I see," the other said. "That means you aim to have a little cash down. How much?"

"You mean on the machine?"

"What do you think I am talking about?"

"Ten dollars," Ratliff said. "A note for twenty [illegible] months. That's gathering-time."

"Ten dollars? With the message you got from——"

"We aint talking about messages now," Ratliff said. "We're talking about a sewing machine."

"Make it five."

"No," Ratliff said pleasantly.

"All right," the other said, turning. "Fix up your note." He went back to the house. Ratliff got out and went to the rear of the buckboard and opened the dog kennel's door and drew from beneath the new machine a tin dispatch box. It contained a pen, a carefully corked ink bottle, a pad of note forms. He was filling in the note when Snopes returned, reappeared at his side. As soon as Ratliff's pen stopped Snopes slid the note toward himself and took the pen from Ratliff's hand and dipped it and signed the note, all in one continuous motion, without even reading it, and shoved the note back to Ratliff and took something from his pocket which Ratliff did not look at yet because he was looking at the signed note, his face perfectly expressionless. He said quietly,

"This is Flem Snopes's name you have signed."

"All right," the other said. "Then what?" Ratliff looked at him. "I see. You want my name on it too, so one of us anyway cant deny it has been signed. All right." He took the note and wrote again on it and passed it back. "And here's your ten dollars. Give me a hand with the machine." But Ratliff did not move again, because it was not money but another paper which the other had given him, folded, dog-eared and soiled. Opened, it was another note. It was dated a little more than three years ago, for ten dollars with interest, payable on demand one year after date of execution, to *Isaac Snopes or bearer*, and signed *Flem Snopes*. It was indorsed on the back (and Ratliff recognised the same hand which had just signed the two names to the first note) to *Mink Snopes*, by *Isaac Snopes (X) his mark*, and beneath that and still in the same hand and blotted (or dried at least), to *V.K. Ratliff*, by *Mink Snopes*, and Ratliff looked at it quite quietly and quite soberly for almost a minute. "All right," the other said.

"Me and Flem are his cousins. Our grandma left us all three ten dollars a piece. We were to get it when the least of us—that was him—come twenty-one. Flem needed some cash and he borrowed his from him on this note. Then he needed some cash a while back and I bought Flem's note from him. Now if you want to know what color his eyes are or anything else, you can see for yourself when you get to Frenchman's Bend. He's living there now with Flem."

"I see," Ratliff said. "Isaac Snopes. He's twenty-one, you say?"

"How could he have got that ten dollars to lend Flem if he hadn't been?"

"Sho," Ratliff said. "Only this here aint just exactly a cash ten dollars——"

"Listen," the other said. "I dont know what you are up to and I dont care. But you aint fooling me any more than I am fooling you. If you were not satisfied Flem is going to pay that first note, you wouldn't have taken it. And if you aint afraid of that one, why are you afraid of this one, for less money, on the same machine, when this one has been collectible by law for more than two years? You take these notes on to him down yonder. Just hand them to him. Then you give him a message from me. Say 'From one cousin that's still scratching dirt to keep alive, to another cousin that's risen from scratching dirt to owning a herd of cattle and a hay barn. To owning cattle and a hay barn.' Just say that to him. Better keep on saying it over to yourself on the way down there so you will be sure not to forget it."

"You dont need to worry," Ratliff said. "Does this road lead over to Whiteleaf Bridge?"

He spent that night in the home of kin people (he had been born and raised not far away) and reached Frenchman's Bend the next afternoon and turned his team into Mrs Littlejohn's lot and walked down to the store, on the gallery of which apparently the same men who had been there when he saw it last a year ago were still sitting, including Bookwright. "Well, boys," he said. "A quorum as usual, I see."

"Bookwright says it was your pocketbook that Memphis fellow cut outen you," one said. "No wonder it taken you a year to get over it. I'm just surprised you didn't die when you reached back and found it gone."

"That's when I got up," Ratliff said. "Otherwise I'd a been laying there yet." He entered the store. The front of it was empty but he did not pause, not even long enough for his contracted pupils to have adjusted themselves to the obscurity, as he might have been expected to. He went on to the counter, saying pleasantly, "Howdy, Jody. Howdy, Flem. Dont bother; I'll get it myself." Varner, standing beside the desk at which the clerk sat, looked up.

"So you get well, hah," he said.

"I got busy," Ratliff said, going behind the counter and opening the store's single glassed-in case which contained a jumble of shoestrings and combs and tobacco and patent medicines and cheap candy. "Maybe that's the same thing." He began to choose sticks of the striped gaudy candy with care, choosing and rejecting. He did not once look toward the rear of the store, where the clerk at the desk had never looked up at all. "You know if Uncle Ben Quick is at home or not?"

"Where would he be?" Varner said. "Only I thought you sold him a sewing machine two-three years back."

"Sho," Ratliff said, rejecting a stick of candy and substituting another one for it. "That's why I want him to be at home: so his folks can look after him when he faints. I'm going to buy something from him this time."

"What in thunder has he got you had to come all the way out here to buy?"

"A goat," Ratliff said. He was counting the candy sticks into a sack now.

"A what?"

"Sho," Ratliff said. "You wouldn't think it, would you? But there aint another goat in Yoknapatawpha and Grenier County both except them of Uncle Ben's."

"No I wouldn't," Varner said. "But what's curioser than that is what you want with it."

"What does a fellow want with a goat?" Ratliff said. He moved to the cheese cage and put a coin into the cigar box. "To pull a wagon with. You and Uncle Will and Miss Maggie all well, I hope."

"Ah-h-h!" Varner said. He turned back to the desk. But Ratliff had not paused to see him do it. He returned to the gallery, offering his candy about.

"Doctor's orders," he said. "He'll probably send me another bill now for ten cents for advising me to eat a nickel's worth of candy. I dont mind that though. What I mind is the order he give me to spend so much time setting down." He looked now, pleasant and quizzical, at the men sitting on the bench. It was fastened against the wall, directly beneath one of the windows which flanked the door, a little longer than the window was wide. After a moment a man on one end of the bench rose.

"All right," he said. "Come on and set down. Even if you wasn't sick you will probably spend the next six months pretending like you was."

"I reckon I got to get something outen that seventy-five dollars it cost me," Ratliff said. "Even if it aint no more than imposing on folks for a while. Only you are fixing to leave me setting in a draft. You folks move down and let me set in the middle." They moved and made room for him in the middle of the bench. He sat now directly before the open window. He took a stick of his candy himself and began to suck it, speaking in the weak thin penetrating voice of recent illness: "Yes sir. I'd a been in that bed yet if I hadn't a found that pocketbook gone. But it wasn't till I got up that I got sho enough scared. I says to myself, here I been laying on my back for a year now and I bet some enterprising fellow has done come in and flooded not only Frenchman's Bend but all Yoknapatawpha County too with new sewing machines. But the Lord was watching out for me. I be dog if I had hardly got outen bed before Him or somebody had done sent me a sheep just like He done to save Isaac in the Book. He sent me a goat-rancher."

"A what?" one said.

"A goat-rancher. You never heard of a goat-rancher. Because wouldn't nobody in this country think of it. It would take a Northerner to do that. This here one thought of it away up yonder in Massachusetts or Boston or Ohio and here he come all the way down to Mississippi with his hand grip bulging with greenback money and bought him up two thousand acres of as fine a hill-gully and rabbit-grass land as ever stood on one edge about fifteen miles west of Jefferson and built him a ten-foot practically waterproof fence around it and was just getting ready to start getting rich, when he run out of goats."

"Shucks," another said. "Never nobody in the world ever run out of goats."

"Besides," Bookwright said, suddenly and harshly, "if you want to tell them folks at the blacksmith shop about it too, why dont we all just move over there."

"Sho now," Ratliff said. "You fellow dont know how good a man's voice feels running betwixt his teeth until you have been on your back where folks that didn't want to listen could get up and go away and you couldn't follow them." Nevertheless he did lower his voice a little, thin, clear, anecdotal, unhurried: "This one did. You got to keep in mind he is a Northerner. They does things different from us. If a fellow in this country was to set up a goat-ranch, he would do it purely and simply because he had too many goats already. He would just declare his roof or his front porch or his parlor or wherever it was he couldn't keep the goats out of a goat-ranch and let it go at that. But a Northerner dont do it that way. When he does something, he does it with a organised syndicate and a book of printed rules and a gold-filled diploma from the Secretary of State at Jackson saying for all men to know by these presents, greeting, that them twenty thousand goats or whatever it is, is goats. He dont start off with goats or a piece of land either. He starts off with a piece of paper and a pencil and measures it all down setting in the library—so many goats to so many acres and so much fence to hold them. Then he writes off to Jackson and gets his diploma for that much land and fence and goats and he buys the land first so he can have something to build the fence on, and he builds the fence around it so nothing cant get outen it, and then he goes out to buy some things not to get outen the fence. So everything was going just fine at first. He picked out land that even the Lord hadn't never thought about starting a goat-ranch on and bought it without hardly no trouble at all except finding the folks it belonged to and making them understand it was actual money he was trying to give them, and that fence practically taken care of itself because he could set in one place in the middle of it and pay out the money for it. And then he found he had done run out of goats. He combed this country up and down and backwards and forwards to find the right number of goats to keep that gold diploma from telling him to his face he was lying. But he couldn't do it. In spite of all he could do, he still lacked fifty goats to take care of the rest of that fence. So now it aint a goat-ranch; it's a insolvency. He's either got to send that diploma back, or get them fifty goats from somewhere. So here he is, done come all the way down here from Boston, Maine, and paid for two thousand acres of land and built forty-four thousand feet of fence around it, and now the whole blame pro-jeck is hung up on that passel of goats of Uncle Ben Quick's because they aint another goat betwixt Jackson and the Tennessee line apparently."

"How do you know?" one said.

"Do you reckon I'd a got up outen bed and come all the way out here if I hadn't?" Ratliff said.

"Then you better get in that buckboard right now and go and make yourself sure," Bookwright said. He was sitting against a gallery post, facing the window at Ratliff's back. Ratliff looked at him for a moment, pleasant and inscrutable behind his faint constant humorous mask.

"Sho," he said. "He's had them goats a good while now. I reckon he'll be still telling me I cant do this and must do that for the next six months, not to mention sending me bills for it"—changing the subject so smoothly and completely that, as they realised later, it was as if he had suddenly produced a signboard with Hush in red letters on it, glancing easily and pleasantly upward as Varner and Snopes came out. Snopes did not speak. He went on across the gallery and descended the steps. Varner locked the door. "Aint you closing early, Jody?" Ratliff said.

"That depends on what you call late," Varner said shortly. He went on after the clerk.

"Maybe it is getting toward supper time," Ratliff said.

"Then if I was you I'd go eat it and then go and buy my goats," Bookwright said.

"Sho now," Ratliff said. "Uncle Ben might have a extra dozen or so by tomorrow. Howsomedever—" He rose and buttoned the overcoat about him.

"Go buy your goats first," Bookwright said. Again Ratliff looked at him, pleasant, impenetrable. He looked at the others. None of them were looking at him.

"I figure I can wait," he said. "Any of you fellows eating at Mrs Littlejohn's?" Then he said, "What's that?" and the others saw what he was looking at—the figure of a grown man but barefoot and in scant faded overalls which would have been about right for a fourteen-year-old boy, passing in the road below the gallery, dragging behind him on a string a wooden block with two snuff tins attached to its upper side, watching over his shoulder with complete absorption the dust it raised. As he passed the gallery he looked up and Ratliff saw the face too—the pale eyes which seemed to have no vision in them at all, the open drooling mouth encircled by a light fuzz of golden virgin beard.

"Another one of them," Bookwright said, in that harsh short voice. Ratliff watched the creature as it went on—the thick thighs about to burst from the overalls, the mowing head turned backward over its shoulder, watching the dragging block.

"And yet they tell us we was all made in His image," Ratliff said.

"From some of the things I see here and there, maybe he was," Bookwright said.

"I don't know as I would believe that, even if I knowed it was true," Ratliff said. "You mean he just showed up here one day?"

"Why not?" Bookwright said. "He aint the first."

"Sho," Ratliff said. "He would have to be somewhere." The creature, opposite Mrs Littlejohn's now, turned in the gate.

"He sleeps in her barn," another said. "She feeds him. He does some work. She can talk to him somehow."

"Maybe she's the one that was then," Ratliff said. He

turned; he still held the end of the stick of candy. He put it into his mouth and wiped his fingers on the skirt of his overcoat. "Well, how about supper?"

"Go buy your goats," Bookwright said. "Wait till after that to do your eating."

"I'll go tomorrow," Ratliff said. "Maybe by then Uncle Ben will have another fifty of them even." Or maybe the day after tomorrow, he thought, walking on toward the brazen sound of Mrs Littlejohn's supper-bell in the winy chill of the March evening. So he will have plenty of time. Because I believe I done it right. I had to trade not only on what I think he knows about me, but on what he must figure I know about him, as conditioned and restricted by that year of sickness and abstinence from the science and pastime of skullduggery. But it worked with Bookwright. He done all he could to warn me. He went as far and even further than a man can let hisself go in another man's trade.

So tomorrow he not only did not go to see the goat-owner, he drove six miles in the opposite direction and spent the day trying to sell a sewing machine he did not even have with him. He spent the night there and did not reach the village until midmorning of the second day, halting the buckboard before the store, to one of the gallery posts of which Varner's roan horse was tied. So he's even riding the horse now, he thought. Well well well. He did not get out of the buckboard. "One of you fellows mind handing me a nickel's worth of candy?" he said. "I might have to bribe Uncle Ben through one of his grandchillen." One of the men entered the store and fetched out the candy. "I'll be back for dinner," he said. "Then I'll be ready for another needy young doc to cut at again."

His destination was not far: a little under a mile to the river bridge, a little more than a mile beyond it. He drove up to a neat well-kept house with a big barn and pasture beyond it; he saw the goats. A hale burly old man was sitting in his stocking feet on the veranda, who roared, "Howdy, V. K. What in thunder are you fellows up to over at Varner's?"

Ratliff did not get out of the buckboard. "So he beat me," he said.

"Fifty goats," the other roared. "I've heard of a man paying a dime to get shut of two or three, but I never in my life heard of a man buying fifty."

"He's smart," Ratliff said. "If he bought fifty of anything he knowed beforehand he was going to need exactly that many."

"Yes, he's smart. But fifty goats. Hell and sulphur. I still got a passel left, bout one hen-house full, say. You want them?"

"No," Ratliff said. "It was just them first fifty."

"I'll give them to you. I'll even pay you a quarter to get the balance of them outen my pasture."

"I thank you," Ratliff said. "Well, I'll just charge this to social overhead."

"Fifty goats," the other said. "Stay and eat dinner."

"I thank you," Ratliff said. "I seem to done already wasted too much time eating now. Or sitting down doing something, anyway." So he returned to the village—that long mile then the short one, the small sturdy team trotting briskly and without synchronization. The roan horse still stood before the store and the men still sat and squatted about the gallery, but Ratliff did not stop. He went on to Mrs Littlejohn's and tied his team to the fence and went and sat in the veranda, where he could see the store. He could smell food cooking in the kitchen behind him and soon the men on the store's gallery began to rise and disperse, noonward, though the saddled roan still stood there. Yes, he thought, He has passed Jody. A man takes your wife and all you got to do to ease your feelings is to shoot him. But your horse.

Mrs Littlejohn spoke behind him: "I didn't know you were back. You going to want some dinner, aint you?"

"Yessum," he said. "I want to step down to the store first. But I wont be long." She went back into the house. He took the two notes from his wallet and separated them, putting one into his inside coat pocket, the other into the breast pocket of his shirt, and walked down the road in the March noon, treading the noon-impacted dust, breathing the unbreathing suspension of the meridian, and mounted the steps and crossed the now deserted gallery stained with tobacco and scarred with knives. The store, the interior, was like a cave, dim, cool, smelling of cheese and leather; it needed a moment for his eyes to adjust themselves. Then he saw the gray cap, the white shirt, the minute bow tie. The face looked up at him, chewing. "You beat me," Ratliff said. "How much?" The other turned his head and spat into the sand-filled box beneath the cold stove.

"Fifty cents," he said.

"I paid twenty-five for my contract," Ratliff said. "All I aim to get is seventy-five. I could tear the contract up and save hauling them to town."

"All right," Snopes said. "What'll you give?"

"I'll trade you this for them," Ratliff said. He drew the first note from the pocket where he had segregated it. And he saw it—an instant, a second of a new and completer stillness and immobility touch the blank face, the squat soft figure in the chair behind the desk. For that instant even the jaw had stopped chewing, though it began again almost at once. Snopes took the paper and looked at it. Then he laid it on the desk and turned his head and spat into the sand-box.

"You figure this note is worth fifty goats," he said. It was not a question, it was a statement.

"Yes," Ratliff said. "Because there is a message goes with it. Do you want to hear it?"

The other looked at him, chewing. Otherwise he didn't move, he didn't even seem to breathe. After a moment he said, "No." He rose, without haste. "All right," he said. He took his wallet from his hip and extracted a folded paper and gave it to Ratliff. It was Quick's bill-of-sale for the fifty goats. "Got a match?" Snopes said. "I dont smoke." Ratliff gave him the match and watched him set fire to the note and hold it, blazing, then drop it still blazing into the sand-box and then crush the carbon to dust with his toe. Then he looked up; Ratliff had not moved. And now just for another instant Ratliff believed he saw the jaw stop. "Well?" Snopes said. "What?" Ratliff drew the second note from his pocket. And then he knew that the jaw had stopped chewing. It did not move at all during the full minute while the broad impenetrable face hung suspended like a balloon above the soiled dog-eared paper, from back then front again. The face looked at

Ratliff again with no sign of life in it, not even breathing, as if the body which belonged to it had learned somehow to use over and over again its own suspirations. "You want to collect this too," he said. He handed the note back to Ratliff. "Wait here," he said. He crossed the room to the rear door and went out. What, Ratliff thought. He followed. The squat reluctant figure was going on, in the sunlight now, toward the fence to the livery lot. There was a gate in it. Ratliff watched Snopes pass through the gate and go on across the lot, toward the barn. Then something black blew in him, a suffocation, a sickness, nausea. They should have told me! he cried to himself. Somebody should have told me! Then, remembering: Why, he did! Bookwright did tell me. He said Another one. It was because I have been sick, was slowed up, that I didn't— He was back beside the desk now. He believed he could hear the dragging block long before he knew it was possible, though presently he did hear it as Snopes entered and turned, moving aside, the block thumping against the wooden step and the sill, the hulking figure in the bursting overalls blotting the door, still looking back over its shoulder, entering, the block thumping and scraping across the floor until it caught and lodged behind the counter leg where a three-year-old child would have stooped and lifted it clear though the idiot himself merely stood jerking fruitlessly at the string and beginning a wet whimpering moaning at once pettish and concerned and terrified and amazed until Snopes kicked the block free with his toe. They came on to the desk where Ratliff stood—the mowing and bobbing head, the eyes which at some instant, some second once, had opened upon, been vouchsafed a glimpse of, the Gorgon-face of that primal injustice which man was not intended to look at face to face and had been blasted empty and clean forever of any thought, the slobbering mouth in its mist of soft gold hair. "Say what your name is," Snopes said. The creature looked at Ratliff, bobbing steadily, drooling. "Say it," Snopes said, quite patiently. "Your name."

"Ike H-mope," the idiot said hoarsely.

"Say it again."

"Ike H-mope." Then he began to laugh, though almost at

once it stopped being laughing and Ratliff knew that it had never been laughing, cachinnant, sobbing, already beyond the creature's power to stop it, galloping headlong and dragging breath behind it like something still alive at the galloping heels of a cossack holiday, the eyes above the round mouth fixed and sightless.

"Hush," Snopes said. "Hush." At last he took the idiot by the shoulder, shaking him until the sound began to fall, bubbling and gurgling away. Snopes led him toward the door, pushing him on ahead, the other moving obediently, looking backward over his shoulder at the block with its two raked snuff tins dragging at the end of the filthy string, the block about to lodge again behind the same counter leg though this time Snopes kicked it free before it stopped. The hulking shape—the backlooking face with its hanging mouth and pointed faun's ears, the bursting overalls drawn across the incredible female thighs—blotted the door again and was gone. Snopes closed the door and returned to the desk. He spat again into the sand-box. "That was Isaac Snopes," he said. "I'm his guardian. Do you want to see the papers?"

Ratliff didn't answer. He looked down at the note where he had laid it on the desk when he returned from the door, with that same faint, quizzical, quiet expression which his face had worn when he looked at his coffee cup in the restaurant four days ago. He took up the note, though he did not look at Snopes yet. "So if I pay him his ten dollars myself, you will take charge of it as his guardian. And if I collect the ten dollars from you, you will have the note to sell again. And that will make three times it has been collected. Well well well." He took another match from his pocket and extended it and the note to Snopes. "I hear tell you said once you never set fire to a piece of money. This here's your chance to see what it feels like." He watched the second note burn too and drift, still blazing, onto the stained sand in the box, curling into carbon which vanished in its turn beneath the shoe.

He descended the steps, again into the blaze of noon upon the pocked quiet dust of the road; actually it was not ten minutes later. Only thank God men have done learned how to forget quick what they aint brave enough to try to cure, he told himself, walking on. The empty road shimmered with mirage, the pollen-roiled chiaroscuro of spring. Yes, he thought, I reckon I was sicker than I knowed. Because I missed it, missed it clean. Or maybe when I have et I will feel better. Yet, alone in the dining room where Mrs Littlejohn had set a plate for him, he could not eat. He could feel what he had thought was appetite ebbing with each mouthful becoming heavy and tasteless as dirt. So at last he pushed the plate aside and onto the table he counted the five dollars profit he had made—the thirty-seven-fifty he would get for the goats, less the twelve-fifty his contract had cost him, plus the twenty of the first note. With a chewed pencil stub he calculated the three years' interest on the ten-dollar note, plus the principal (that ten dollars would have been his commission on the machine, so it was no actual loss anyway) and added to the five dollars the other bills and coins—the frayed banknotes, the worn coins, the ultimate pennies. Mrs Littlejohn was in the kitchen, where she cooked what meals she sold and washed the dishes too, as well as caring for the rooms in which they slept who ate them. He put the money on the table beside the sink. "That what's-his-name, Ike. Isaac. They tell me you feed him some. He dont need money. But maybe——"

"Yes," she said. She dried her hands on her apron and took the money and folded the bills carefully about the silver and stood holding it. She didn't count it. "I'll keep it for him. Dont you worry. You going on to town now?"

"Yes," he said. "I got to get busy. No telling when I will run into another starving and eager young fellow that aint got no way to get money but to cut meat for it." He turned, then paused again, not quite looking back at her, with that faint quizzical expression on his face that was smiling now, sardonic, humorous. "I got a message I would like to get to Will Varner. But it dont matter especially."

"I'll give it to him," Mrs Littlejohn said. "If it aint too long I will remember it."

"It dont matter," Ratliff said. "But if you happen to think of it. Just tell him Ratliff says it aint been proved yet neither. He'll know what it means."

"I'll try to remember it," she said.

He went out to the buckboard and got into it. He would not need the overcoat now, and next time he would not even have to bring it along. The road began to flow beneath the flickering hooves of the small hickory-tough horses. I just never went far enough, he thought. I quit too soon. I went as far as one Snopes will set fire to another Snopes's barn and both Snopeses know it, and that was all right. But I stopped there. I never went on to where that first Snopes will turn around and stomp the fire out so he can sue that second Snopes for the reward and both Snopeses know that too.

3

Those who watched the clerk now saw, not the petty dispossession of a blacksmith, but the usurpation of an heirship. At the next harvest the clerk not only presided at the gin scales but when the yearly settling of accounts between Varner and his tenants and debtors occurred, Will Varner himself was not even present. It was Snopes who did what Varner had never even permitted his son to do—sat alone at the desk with the cash from the sold crops and the accountbooks before him and cast up the accounts and charged them off and apportioned to each tenant his share of the remaining money, one or two of them challenging his figures as they had when he first entered the store, on principle perhaps, the clerk not even listening, just waiting in his soiled white shirt and the minute tie, with his steady thrusting tobacco and his opaque still eyes which they never knew whether or not were looking at them, until they would finish, cease; then, without speaking a word, taking pencil and paper and proving to them that they were wrong. Now it was not Jody Varner who would come leisurely to the store and give the clerk directions and instructions and leave him to carry them out; it was the ex-clerk who would enter the store, mounting the steps and jerking his head at the men on the gallery exactly as Will Varner himself would do, and enter the store, from which presently the sound of his voice would come, speaking with matter-of-fact succinctness to the bull-goaded bafflement of the man who once had been his employer and who still seemed not to know just exactly what had happened to him. Then Snopes would depart, to be seen no more that day, for Will Varner's old fat white horse had a companion now. It was the roan which Jody had used to ride, the white and the roan now tied side by side to the same fence while Varner and Snopes examined fields of cotton and corn or herds of cattle or land boundaries, Varner cheerful as a cricket and shrewd and bowel-less as a tax-collector, idle and busy and Rabelaisian; the other chewing his steady tobacco, his hands in the pockets of the disreputable bagging gray trousers, spitting now and then his contemplative bullet-like globules of chocolate saliva. One morning he came to the village carrying a brand-new straw suitcase. That evening he carried it up to Varner's house. A month after that Varner bought a new runabout buggy with bright red wheels and a fringed parasol top, which, the fat white horse and the big roan in new brass-studded harness and the wheels glinting in vermilion and spokeless blurs, swept all day long along back country roads and lanes while Varner and Snopes sat side by side in outrageous paradox above a spurting cloud of light dust, in a speeding aura of constant and invincible excursion. And one afternoon in that same summer Ratliff again drove up to the store, on the gallery of which was a face which he did not recognise for a moment because he had only seen it once before and that two years ago, though only for a moment for almost at once he said, "Howdy. Machine still running good?" and sat looking with an expression quite pleasant and absolutely impenetrable at the fierce intractable face with its single eyebrow, thinking *Fox? cat? oh yes, mink.*

"Howdy," the other said. "Why not? Aint you the one that claims not to sell no other kind?"

"Sholy," Ratliff said, still quite pleasant, impenetrable. He got out of the buckboard and tied it to a gallery post and mounted the steps and stood among the four men who sat and squatted about the gallery. "Only it aint quite that, I would put it. I would say, folks names Snopes dont buy no other kind." Then he heard the horse and turned his head and saw it, coming up fast, the fine hound running easily and strongly beside it as Houston pulled up, already dismounting, and dropped the loose reins over its head as a Western rider does and mounted the steps and stopped before the post against which Mink Snopes squatted.

"I reckon you know where that yearling is," Houston said.

"I can guess," Snopes said.

"All right," Houston said. He was not shaking, trembling, any more than a stick of dynamite does. He didn't even raise his voice. "I warned you. You know the law in this country. A man must keep his stock up after ground's planted, or take the consequences."

"I would have expected you to have fences that would keep a yearling up," Snopes said. Then they cursed each other, hard and brief and without emphasis, like blows or pistol-shots, both speaking at the same time and neither moving, the one still standing in the middle of the steps, the other still squatting against the gallery post. "Try a shotgun," Snopes said. "That might keep it up." Then Houston went on into the store and those on the gallery stood or squatted quietly, the man with his single eyebrow no less quiet than any, until Houston came out again and passed without looking at any of them and mounted and galloped off, the hound following again, strong, high-headed, indefatigable, and after another moment or so Snopes rose too and went up the road on foot. Then one leaned and spat carefully over the gallery-edge, into the dust, and Ratliff said,

"I don't quite understand about that fence. I gathered it was Snopes's yearling in Houston's field."

"It was," the man who had spat said. "He lives on a piece of what used to be Houston's land. It belongs to Will Varner now. That is, Varner foreclosed on it about a year ago."

"That is, it was Will Varner Houston owed the money to," a second said. "It was the fences on that he was talking about."

"I see," Ratliff said. "Just conversational remarks. Unnecessary."

"It wasn't losing the land that seems to rile Houston," a third said. "Not that he dont rile easy."

"I see," Ratliff said again. "It's what seems to happened to it since. Or who it seems Uncle Will has rented it to. So Flem's got some more cousins still. Only this here seems to be a different kind of Snopes like a cotton-mouth is a different kind of snake." So that wasn't the last time this one is going to make his cousin trouble, he thought. But he did not say it, he just said, absolutely pleasant, easy, inscrutable: "I wonder where Uncle Will and his partner would be about now. I aint learned the route good yet like you folks."

"I passed them two horses and the buggy tied to the Old Frenchman fence this morning," the fourth man said. He too leaned and spat carefully over the gallery-edge. Then he added, as if in trivial afterthought: "It was Flem Snopes that was setting in the flour barrel."

BOOK TWO

Eula

CHAPTER ONE

When Flem Snopes came to clerk in her father's store, Eula Varner was not quite thirteen. She was the last of the sixteen children, the baby, though she had overtaken and passed her mother in height in her tenth year. Now, though not yet thirteen years old, she was already bigger than most grown women and even her breasts were no longer the little, hard, fiercely-pointed cones of puberty or even maidenhood. On the contrary, her entire appearance suggested some symbology out of the old Dionysic times—honey in sunlight and bursting grapes, the writhen bleeding of the crushed fecundated vine beneath the hard rapacious trampling goat-hoof. She seemed to be not a living integer of her contemporary scene, but rather to exist in a teeming vacuum in which her days followed one another as though behind sound-proof glass, where she seemed to listen in sullen bemusement, with a weary wisdom heired of all mammalian maturity, to the enlarging of her own organs.

Like her father, she was incorrigibly lazy, though what was in him a constant bustling cheerful idleness was in her an actual force impregnable and even ruthless. She simply did not move at all of her own volition, save to and from the table and to and from bed. She was late in learning to walk. She had the first and only peramublator the countryside had ever seen, a clumsy expensive thing almost as large as a dog-cart. She remained in it long after she had grown too large to straighten her legs out. When she reached the stage where it almost took the strength of a grown man to lift her out of it, she was graduated from it by force. Then she began to sit in chairs. It was not that she insisted upon being carried when she went anywhere. It was rather as though, even in infancy, she already knew there was nowhere she wanted to go, nothing new or novel at the end of any progression, one place like another anywhere and everywhere. Until she was five and six, when she did have to go anywhere because her mother declined to leave her at home while she herself was absent, she would be carried by their Negro manservant. The three of them would be seen passing along the road—

Mrs Varner in her Sunday dress and shawl, followed by the Negro man staggering slightly beneath his long, dangling, already indisputably female burden like a bizarre and chaperoned Sabine rape.

She had the usual dolls. She would place them in chairs about the one in which she sat, and they would remain so, none with either more or less of the semblance of life than any other. Finally her father had his blacksmith make her a miniature of the perambulator in which she had spent her first three years. It was crude and heavy also, but it was the only doll perambulator anyone in that country had ever seen or even heard of. She would place all the dolls in it and sit in a chair beside it. At first they decided it was mental backwardness, that she merely had not yet reached the maternal stage of female adulthood in miniature, though they soon realised that her indifference to the toy was that she would have to move herself to keep it in motion.

She grew from infancy to the age of eight in the chairs, moving from one to another about the house as the exigencies of sweeping and cleaning house and eating meals forced her to break cover. At her mother's insistence, Varner continued to have the blacksmith make miniatures of housekeeping implements—like brooms and mops, a small actual stove—hoping to make a sport, a game, of utility, all of which, singly and collectively, was apparently no more to her than the tot of cold tea to the old drunkard. She had no playmates, no inseparable girl companion. She did not want them. She never formed one of those violent, sometimes short-lived intimacies in which two female children form embattled secret cabal against their masculine coevals and the mature world too. She did nothing. She might as well still have been a foetus. It was as if only half of her had been born, that mentality and body had somehow become either completely separated or hopelessly involved; that either only one of them had ever emerged, or that one had emerged, itself not accompanied by, but rather pregnant with, the other. "Maybe she's fixing to be a tomboy," her father said.

"When?" Jody said—a spark, a flash, even though born of enraged exasperation. "At the rate she's going at it, there aint a acorn that will fall in the next fifty years that wont grow up and rot down and be burnt for firewood before she'll ever climb it."

When she was eight, her brother decided she should start to school. Her parents had intended that she should start someday, perhaps mainly because Will Varner was, with the nominal designation of Trustee, the principal mainstay and arbiter of the school's existence. It was, as the other parents of the countryside considered it, actually another Varner enterprise, and sooner or later Varner would have insisted that his daughter attend it, for a while at least, just as he would have insisted upon collecting the final odd cents of an interest calculation. Mrs Varner did not particularly care whether the daughter went to school or not. She was one of the best housewives in the county and was indefatigable at it. She derived an actual physical pleasure which had nothing at all to do with mere satisfaction in husbandry and forehandedness, from the laying-away of ironed sheets and the sight of packed shelves and potato cellars and festooned smoke-house rafters. She did not read herself, though at the time of her marriage she had been able to read a little. She did not practise it much then and during the last forty years she had lost even that habit, preferring now to be face to face with the living breath of event, fiction or news either, and being able to comment and moralise upon it. So she saw no need for literacy in women. Her conviction was that the proper combining of food ingredients lay not on any printed page but in the taste of the stirring spoon, and that the housewife who had to wait until she had been to school to know how much money she had left after subtracting from it what she had spent, would never be a housewife.

It was the brother, Jody, who emerged almost violently in her eighth summer as erudition's champion, and three months later came bitterly to regret it. He did not regret that it had been himself who had insisted that she go to school. His regret was that he was still convinced, and knew that he would remain convinced, of the necessity of that for which he now paid so dear a price. Because she refused to walk to school. She did not object to attending it, to being in school, she just declined to walk to it. It was not far. It was not a half mile from the Varner home. Yet during the five years she attended it, which, if it had been computed in hours based upon what she accomplished while there, would have been measured not in years or even months but in days, she rode to and from it. While other children living three and four and five times the distance walked back and forth in all weathers, she rode. She just calmly and flatly refused to walk. She did not resort to tears and she did not even fight back emotionally, let alone physically. She just sat down, where, static, apparently not even thinking, she emanated an outrageous and immune perversity like a blooded and contrary filly too young yet to be particularly valuable, though which in another year or so would be, and for which reason its raging and harried owner does not dare whip it. Her father immediately and characteristically washed his hands of the business. "Let her stay at home then," he said. "She aint going to lift her hand here either, but at least maybe she will learn something about housekeeping from having to move from one chair to another to keep out of the way of it. All we want anyway is to keep her out of trouble until she gets old enough to sleep with a man without getting me and him both arrested. Then you can marry her off. Maybe you can even find a husband that will keep Jody out of the poorhouse too. Then we will give them the house and store and the whole shebang and me and you will go to that world's fair they are talking about having in Saint Louis, and if we like it by God we will buy a tent and settle down there."

But the brother insisted that she go to school. She still declined to walk there, sitting supine and female and soft and immovable and not even thinking and apparently not even listening either, while the battle between her mother and brother roared over her tranquil head. So at last the Negro man who had used to carry her when her mother went visiting would bring up the family surrey and drive her the half mile to school and would be waiting there with the surrey at noon and at three oclock when school dismissed. This lasted about two weeks. Mrs Varner stopped it because it was too wasteful, like the firing up a twenty-gallon pot to make a bowl of soup would be wasteful. She delivered an ultimatum; if Jody wanted his sister to go to school, he would have to see that she got there himself. She suggested that, since he rode his horse to and from the store every day anyhow, he might carry Eula to and from school behind him, the daughter sitting there again, neither thinking nor listening while this roared and concussed to the old stalemate, sitting on the front porch in the mornings with the cheap oilcloth book-satchel they had bought her until her brother rode the horse up to the gallery-edge and snarled at her to come and mount behind him. He would carry her to the school and go and fetch her at noon and carry her back afterward and be waiting when school was out for the day. This lasted for almost a month. Then Jody decided that she should walk the two hundred yards from the schoolhouse to the store and meet him there. To his surprise, she agreed without protest. This lasted for exactly two days. On the second afternoon the brother fetched her home at a fast single-foot, bursting into the house and standing over his mother in the hall and trembling with anger and outrage, shouting. "No wonder she agreed so easy and quick to walk to the store and meet me!" he cried. "If you could arrange to have a man standing every hundred feet along the road, she would walk all the way home! She's just like a dog! Soon as she passes anything in long pants she begins to give off something. You can smell it! You can smell it ten feet away!"

"Fiddlesticks," Mrs Varner said. "Besides, dont worry me with it. It was you insisted she had to go to school. It wasn't me. I raised eight other daughters, I thought they turned out pretty well. But I am willing to agree that maybe a twenty-seven-year-old bachelor knows more about them than I do. Anytime you want to let her quit school, I reckon your pa and me wont object. Did you bring me that cinnamon?"

"No," Jody said. "I forgot it."

"Try to remember it tonight. I'm already needing it."

So she no longer began the homeward journey at the store. Her brother would be waiting for her at the schoolhouse. It had been almost five years now since this sight and become an integral part of the village's life four times a day and five days a week—the roan horse bearing the seething and angry man and the girl whom, even at nine and ten and eleven, there was too much—too much of leg, too much of breast, too much of buttock; too much of mammalian female meat which, in conjunction with the tawdry oilcloth receptacle that was obviously a grammar-grade book-satchel, was a travesty and paradox on the whole idea of education. Even while sitting behind her brother on the horse, the inhabitant of that meat seemed to lead two separate and distinct lives as infants in the act of nursing do. There was one Eula Varner who supplied blood and nourishment to the buttocks and legs and breasts; there was the other Eula Varner who merely inhabited them, who went where they went because it was less trouble to do so, who was comfortable there but in their doings she intended to have no part, as you are in a house which you did not design but where the furniture is all settled and the rent paid up. On the first morning Varner had put the horse into a fast trot, to get it over with quick, but almost at once he began to feel the entire body behind him, which even motionless in a chair seemed to postulate an invincible abhorrence of straight lines, jiggling its component boneless curves against his back. He had a vision of himself transporting not only across the village's horizon but across the embracing proscenium of the entire inhabited world like the sun itself, a kaleidoscopic convolution of mammalian ellipses. So he would walk the horse. He would have to, his sister clutching the cross of his suspenders or the back of his coat with one hand and holding the book-satchel with the other, passing the store where the usual quota of men would be squatting and sitting, past Mrs Littlejohn's veranda where there would usually be an itinerant drummer or horse-trader—and Varner now believing, convinced, that he knew why they were there too, the real reason why they had driven twenty miles from Jefferson—and so up to the school where the other children in overalls and coarse calico and cast-off adult shoes as often as not when they wore shoes at all, where already gathered after walking three and four and five times the distance. She would slide off the horse and her brother would sit for a moment longer, seething, watching the back which already used its hips to walk with as women used them, and speculate with raging impotence whether to call the school-teacher (he was a man) outside at once and have it out with him, warn or threaten or even use his fists, or whether to wait until that happened which he, Varner, was convinced must occur. They would repeat that at one oclock and in the reverse direction at twelve and three, Varner riding on a hundred yards up the road to where, hidden by a copse, a fallen tree lay. The Negro manservant had felled it one night while he sat the horse and held the lantern; he would ride up beside it, snarling fiercely to her the third time she mounted from it: "God damn it, cant you try to get on it without making it look like the horse is twenty feet tall?"

He even decided one day that she should not ride astride. anymore. This lasted one day, until he happened to look aside and so behind him and saw the incredible length of outrageously curved dangling leg and the bare section of thigh between dress and stocking-top looking as gigantically and profoundly naked as the dome of an observatory. And his rage was only intensified by the knowledge that she had not deliberately exposed it. He knew that she simply did not care, doubtless did not even know it was exposed, and if she had known, would not have gone to the trouble to cover it. He knew that she was sitting even on the moving horse exactly as she would in a chair at home, and, as he knew, inside the schoolhouse itself, so that he wondered at times in his raging helplessness how buttocks as constantly subject to the impact of that much steadily increasing weight could in the mere act of walking seem actually to shout aloud that rich mind- and will-sapping fluid softness; sitting, even on the moving horse, secret and not even sullen, bemused with that whatever it was which had nothing to do with flesh, meat, at all; emanating that outrageous quality of being, existing, actually on the outside of the garments she wore and not only being unable to help it but not even caring.

She attended the school from her eighth year until shortly after Christmas in her fourteenth. She would undoubtedly have completed that year and very probably the next one or two, learning nothing, except that in January of that year the school closed. It closed because the teacher vanished. He disappeared overnight, with no word to anyone. He neither collected his term's salary nor removed his meagre and monklike personal effects from the fireless rented lean-to room in which he had lived for six years.

His name was Labove. He came from the adjoining county, where Will Varner himself had discovered him by sheer chance. The incumbent, the Professor at that time, was an old man bibulous by nature, who had been driven still further into his cups by the insubordination of his pupils. The girls had respect neither for his ideas and information nor for his ability to convey them; the boys had no respect for his capacity, not to teach them but to make them obey and behave or even be civil to him—a condition which had long since passed the stage of mere mutiny and had become a kind of bucolic Roman holiday, like the baiting of a mangy and toothless bear.

Thus everyone, including the Professor, knew that he would not be there next term. But nobody minded especially whether the school functioned next year or not. They owned it. They had built the schoolhouse themselves and paid the teacher and sent their children to it only when there was no work for them to do at home, so it only ran between harvest-time and planting—from mid-October through March. Nothing had been done yet about replacing the Professor until one day in the summer Varner happened to make a business trip into the next county, was benighted, and was invited to pass the night in a bleak puncheon-floored cabin on a barren little hill farm. When he entered the house he saw, sitting beside the cold hearth and sucking a foul little clay pipe, an incredibly old woman wearing a pair of stout-looking man's shoes slightly unorthodox or even a little bizarre in appearance. But Varner paid no attention to them until he heard a clattering scraping noise behind him and turned and saw a girl of about ten, in a tattered though quite clean gingham dress and a pair of shoes, exactly like those of the old lady—if anything, even a little larger. Before he departed the next morning Varner had seen three more pairs of the same shoes, by which time he had discovered that they resembled no other shoes he had ever seen or even heard of. His host told him what they were.

"What?" Varner said. "Football shoes?"

"It's a game," Labove said. "They play it at the University." He explained. It was the eldest son. He was not at home now, off working at a sawmill to earn money to return to the University, where he had been for one summer normal term and then half of the following academic term. It was then that the University played the game out of which the shoes had come. The son had wanted to learn to be a school-teacher, or so he said when he left for the University the first time. That is, he wanted to go to the University. The father saw no point in it. The farm was clear and would belong to the son someday and it had always made them a living. But the son insisted. He could work at mills and such and save enough to attend the summer terms and learn to be a teacher anyway, since this was all they taught in the summer sessions. He would even be back home in the late summer in time to help finish the crop. So he earned the money —"Doing harder work than farming too," the elder Labove said. "But he was almost twenty-one. I couldn't have stood in his way even if I would have."—and enrolled for the summer session, which would last eight weeks and so would have had him back home in August but did not do so. When September arrived, he still had not returned. They did not know for certain where he was, though they were not worried so much as annoyed, concerned, even a little outraged that he should have deserted them with the remaining work on the crop—the picking and ginning of the cotton, the gathering and cribbing of the corn—to be done. In mid-September the letter came. He was going to stay on longer at the University, through the fall. He had a job there; they must gather the crops without him. He did not say what kind of a job it was and the father took it for granted as being another sawmill, since he would never have associated any sort of revenue-producing occupation with going to school, and they did not hear from him again until in October, when the first package arrived. It contained two pair of the curious cleated shoes. A third pair came early in November. The last two came just after Thanksgiving, which made five pair, although there were seven in the family. So they all used them indiscriminately, anyone who found a pair available, like umbrellas, four pair of them that is, Labove explained. The old lady (she was the elder Labove's grandmother) had fastened upon the first pair of emerge from the box and would let no one else wear them at all. She seemed to like the sound the cleats made on the floor when she sat in a chair and rocked. But that still left four pair. So now the children could go shod to school, removing the shoes when they reached home for whoever else needed to go outdoors. In January the son came home. He told them about the game. He had been playing it all that fall. They let him stay at the University for the entire fall term for playing it. The shoes were provided them free of charge to play it in.

"How did he happen to get six pairs?" Varner asked.

Labove did not know that. "Maybe they had a heap of them on hand that year," he said. They had also given the son a sweater at the University, a fine heavy warm dark blue sweater with a big red M on the front of it. The great-grandmother had taken that too, though it was much too big for her. She owuld wear it on Sundays, winter and summer, sitting beside him on the seat of the churchward wagon on the bright days, the crimson accolade of the color of courage and fortitude gallant in the sun, or on the bad days, sprawled and quiet but still crimson, still brave, across her shrunken chest and stomach as she sat in her chair and rocked and sucked the dead little pipe.

"So that's where he is now," Varner said. "Playing the football."

No, Labove told him. He was at the sawmill now. He had calculated that by missing the current summer term and working instead, he could save enough money to stay on at the University even after they stopped letting him stay to play the football, thus completing a full year in the regular school instead of just the summer school in which they only taught people how to be school-teachers.

"I thought that's what he wanted to be," Varner said.

"No," Labove said. "That was all he could learn in the summer school. I reckon you'll laugh when you hear this. He says he wants to be Governor."

"Sho now," Varner said.

"You'll laugh, I reckon."

"No," Varner said. "I aint laughing. Governor. Well well well. Next time you see him, if he would consider putting off the governor business for a year or two and teach school, tell him to come over to the Bend and see me."

That was in July. Perhaps Varner did not actually expect Labove to come to see him. But he made no further effort to fill the vacancy, which he certainly could not have forgotten about. Even apart from his obligation as Trustee, he would have a child of his own ready to start to school within another year or so. One afternoon in early September he was lying with his shoes off in the barrel-stave hammock slung between two trees in his yard, when he saw approaching on foot across the yard the man whom he had never seen before but knew at once—a man who was not thin so much as actually gaunt, with straight black hair coarse as a horse's tail and high Indian cheekbones and quiet pale hard eyes and the long nose of thought but with the slightly curved nostrils of pride and the thin lips of secret and ruthless ambition. It was a forensic face, the face of invincible conviction in the power of words as a principle worth dying for if necessary. A thousand years ago it would have been a monk's, a militant fanatic who would have turned his uncompromising back upon the world with actual joy and gone to a desert and passed the rest of his days and nights calmly and without an instant's self-doubt battling, not to save humanity about which he would have cared nothing, for whose sufferings he would have had nothing but contempt, but with his own fierce and unappeasable natural appetites.

"I came to tell you I cant teach for you this year," he said. "I haven't got time. I've got things fixed now so I can stay at the University the whole year."

Varner did not rise. "That's just one year. What about next year?"

"I have arranged about the sawmill too. I am going back to it next summer. Or something else."

"Sho," Varner said. "I been thinking about it some myself. Because the school here dont need to open until first of November. You can stay at Oxford until then and play your game. Then you can come and open the school and get it started. You can bring your books here from the University and keep up with the class and on the day you have to play the game again you can go back to Oxford and play it and let them find out whether you have kept up in the books or not or whether you have learned anything or whatever they would need to know. Then you could come back to the school; even a day or two wont matter. I will furnish you a horse that can make the trip in eight hours. It ain't but forty miles to Oxford from here. Then, when the time comes for the examination in January your pa was telling me about, you can shut up the school here and go back and stay until you are through with them. Then you can close the school here in March and go back for the rest of the year, until the last of next October if you wanted. I dont reckon a fellow that really wanted to would have much trouble keeping up with his class just forty miles away. Well?"

For some time now Varner knew that the other no longer saw him though he had not moved and his eyes were still open. Labove stood quite still, in a perfectly clean white shirt which had been washed so often that it now had about the texture of mosquito netting, in a coat and trousers absolutely clean too and which were not mates and the coat a little too small for him and which Varner knew were the only ones he owned and that he owned them only because he believed, or had been given to understand, that one could not wear overalls to a University classroom. He stood there enveloped in no waking incredulous joy and hope but in that consuming fury, the gaunt body not shaped by the impact of its environment but as though shrunken and leaned by what was within it, like a furnace. "All right," he said. "I'll be here the first of November." He was already turning away.

"Dont you want to know what your pay will be?"

"All right," Labove said, pausing. Varner told him. He

(Varner) had not moved in the hammock, his home-knit socks crossed at the ankles.

"That game," he said. "Do you like to play it?"

"No," Labove said.

"I hear it aint much different from actual fighting."

"Yes," Labove said, again shortly, paused, courteous and waiting, looking at the lean shrewd shoeless old man prone and profoundly idle in the hammock, who seemed to have laid upon him already the curse of his own invincibile conviction of the absolute unimportance of this or any other given moment or succession of them, holding him there and forcing him to spend time thinking about what he had never told anyone and did not intend to talk about since it did not matter now. It began just before the end of the summer term a year ago. He had intended to return home at the end of the term, as he had told his father he would, to help finish the crop. But just before the term ended he found a job. It was practically dropped into his lap. There would be two or three weeks yet before the cotton would be ready to pick and gin and he was already settled where he could stay on until the middle of September at little additional expense. So most of what the work would bring him would be clear profit. He took the job. It was grading and building a football field. He didn't know then what a football field was and he did not care. To him it was merely an opportunity to earn so much additional money each day and he did not even stop his shovel when he would speculate now and then with cold sardonicism on the sort of game the preparation of ground for which demanded a good deal more care and expense both than the preparing of that same ground to raise a paying crop on; indeed, to have warranted that much time and money for a crop, a man would have had to raise gold at least. So it was still sardonicism and not curiosity when in September and before the field was finished, it began to be used, and he discovered that the young men engaged upon it were not even playing the game but just practising. He would watch them at it. He was probably watching them more closely or at least more often than he was aware and with something in his face, his eyes, which he did not know was there too, because one afternoon one of them (he had already discovered that the game had a paid teacher) said to him, "You think you can do it better, do you? All right. Come here." That night he sat on the front steps of the coach's house in the dry dusty September darkness, still saying No quietly and patiently.

"I aint going to borrow money just to play a game on," he said.

"You wont have to, I tell you!" the coach said. "Your tuition will be paid. You can sleep in my attic and you can feed my horse and cow and milk and build the fires and I will give you your meals. Dont you understand?" It could not have been his face because that was in darkness, and he did not believe it had been in his voice. Yet the coach said, "I see. You don't believe it."

"No," he said. "I dont believe anybody will give me all that just for playing a game."

"Will you try it and see? Will you stay here and do it until somebody comes to you and asks you for money?"

"Will I be free to go when they do?"

"Yes," the coach said. "You have my word." So that night he wrote his father he would not be home to help finish the harvest and if they would need an extra hand in his place he would send money. And they gave him a uniform and on that afternoon, as on the one before when he had still worn the overalls in which he had been working, one of the other players failed to rise at once and they explained that to him—how there were rules for violence, he trying patiently to make this distinction, understand it: "But how can I carry the ball to that line if I let them catch me and pull me down?"

He didn't tell this. He just stood beside the hammock, in the clean unmatching garments, composed and grave, answering Yes or No briefly and quietly to Varner's questions while it recapitulated, ran fast and smooth and without significance now in his memory, finished and done and behind him, meaning nothing, the fall itself going fast, dreamlike and telescoped. He would rise in the icy attic at four oclock and build fires in the houses of five different faculty members and return to feed and milk. Then the lectures, the learning and wisdom distilled of all man had ever thought, plumbed, the ivied walls and monastic rooms impregnated with it, abundant, no limit save that of the listener's capacity and thirst; the afternoons of practice (soon he was excused from this on alternate days, which afternoons he spent raking leaves in the five yards), the preparing of coal and wood against tomorrow's fires. Then the cow again and then in the overcoat which the coach had given him he sat with his books beneath the lamp in his fireless garret until he went to sleep over the printed page. He did this for five days, up to the Saturday's climax when he carried a trivial contemptible obloid across fleeing and meaningless white lines. Yet during these seconds, despite his contempt, his ingrained conviction, his hard and spartan heritage, he lived, fiercely free—the spurning earth, the shocks, the hard breathing and the grasping hands, the speed, the rocking roar of massed stands, his face even then still wearing the expression of sardonic not-quite-belief. And the shoes. Varner was watching him, his hands beneath his head. "Them shoes," Varner said. It was because I never did really believe it was going to last until the next Saturday, Labove could have answered. But he did not, he just stood, his hands quiet at his sides, looking at Verner. "I reckon they always had a plenty of them on hand," Varner said.

"They bought them in lots. They kept all sizes on hand."

"Sho now," Varner said. "I reckon all a fellow had to do was just to say his old pair didn't fit good or had got lost."

Labove did not look away. He stood quietly facing the man in the hammock. "I knew what the shoes cost. I tried to get the coach to say what a pair was worth. To the University. What a touchdown was worth. Winning was worth."

"I see. You never taken a pair except when you beat. And you sent five pairs home. How many times did you play?"

"Seven," Labove said. "One of them nobody won."

"I see," Varner said. "Well, I reckon you want to get on back home before dark. I'll have that horse ready by November."

Labove opened the school in the last week of October. Within that week he had subdued with his fists the state of mutiny which his predecessor had bequeathed him. On Friday night he rode the horse Varner had promised him the forty-odd miles to Oxford, attended morning lectures and played a football game in the afternoon, slept until noon Sunday and was on his pallet bed in the unheated lean-to room in Frenchman's Bend by midnight. It was in the house of a widow who lived near the school. He owned a razor, the unmatching coat and trousers he stood in, two shirts, the coach's overcoat, a Coke, a Blackstone, a volume of Mississippi Reports, an original Horace and a Thucydides which the classics professor, in whose home he had built the morning fires, had given him at Christmas, and the brightest lamp the village had ever seen. It was nickel, with valves and pistons and gauges; as it sat on ths plank table it obviously cost more than everything else he owned lumped together and people would come in from miles away at night to see the fierce still glare it made.

By the end of that first week they all knew him—the hungry mouth, the insufferable humorless eyes, the intense ugly blue-shaved face like a composite photograph of Voltaire and an Elizabethan pirate. They called him Professor too even though he looked what he was—twenty-two—and even though the school was a single room in which pupils ranging in age from six to the men of nineteen whom he had had to meet with his fists to establish his professorship, and classes ranging from bald abc's to the rudiments of common fractions were jumbled together. He taught them all and everything. He carried the key to the building in his pocket as a merchant carries the key to his store. He unlocked it each morning and swept it, he divided the boys by age and size into water-carrying and wood-cutting details and by precept, bullying, ridicule and force saw that they did it, helping them at times not as an example but with a kind of contemptuous detached physical pleasure in burning up his excess energy. He would ruthlessly keep the older boys after school, standing before the door and barring it and beating them to the open windows when they broke for these. He forced them to climb with him to the roof and replace shingles and such which heretofore Varner, as Trustee, had seen to after the teacher had nagged and complained to him enough. At night passers would see the fierce dead glare of the patent lamp beyond the lean-to window where he would be sitting over the books which he did not love so much as he believed that he must read, compass and absorb and wring dry with something of that same contemptuous intensity with which he chopped firewood, measuring the turned pages against the fleeing seconds of irrecovable time like the implacable inching of a leaf worm.

Each Friday afternoon he would mount the wiry strong hammer-headed horse in Varner's lot and ride to where the next day's game would be played or to the railroad which would get him there, sometimes arriving only in time to change into his uniform before the whistle blew. But he was always back at the school on Monday morning, even though on some occasions it meant he had spent only one night—Saturday—in bed between Thursday and Monday. After the Thanksgiving game between the two State colleges, his picture was in a Memphis paper. He was in the uniform and the picture (to the people in the village, and for that reason) would not have looked like him. But the name was his and that would have been recognised, except that he did not bring the paper back with him. They did not know what he did on those week-ends, except that he was taking work at the University. They did not care. They had accepted him, and although his designation of professor was a distinction, it was still a woman's distinction, functioning actually in a woman's world like the title of reverend. Although they would not have actually forbidden him the bottle, they would not have drunk with him, and though they were not quite as circumspect in what they said before him as they would have been with the true minister, if he had responded in kind he might have found himself out of a position when the next term began and he knew it. This distinction he accepted in the spirit offered and even met it more than halfway, with that same grim sufficiency, not pride quite and not quite actual belligerence, grave and composed.

He was gone for a week at the time of the mid-term examinations at the University. He returned and hounded Varner into clearing a basketball court. He did a good deal of the work himself, with the older boys, and taught them the game. At the end of the next year the team had beaten every team they could find to play against and in the third year, himself one of the players, he carried the team to Saint Louis, where, in overalls and barefoot, they won a Mississippi Valley tournament against all comers.

When he brought them back to the village, he was through. In three years he had graduated, a master of arts and a bachelor of laws. He would leave the village now for the last time—the books, the fine lamp, the razor, the cheap reproduction of an Alma-Tadema picture which the classics professor had given him on the second Christmas—to return to the University to his alternating academic and law classes, one following another from breakfast time to late afternoon. He had to read in glasses now, leaving one class to walk blinking painfully against the light to the next, in the single unmatching costume he owned, through throngs of laughing youths and girls in clothes better than he had ever seen until he came here, who did not stare through him so much as they did not see him at all any more than they did the poles which supported the electric lights which until he arrived two years ago he had never seen before either. He would move among them and look with the same expression he would wear above the cleat-spurned fleeing lines of the football field, at the girls who had apparently come there to find husbands, the young men who had come there for what reason he knew not.

Then one day he stood in a rented cap and gown among others and received the tightly-rolled parchment scroll no larger than a rolled calendar yet which, like the calendar, contained those three years—the spurned cleat-blurred white lines, the nights on the tireless horse, the other nights while he had sat in the overcoat and with only the lamp for heat, above spread turning pages of dead verbiage. Two days after that he stood with his class before the Bench in an actual courtroom in Oxford and was admitted to the Bar, and it was finished. He made one that night at a noisy table in the hotel dining room, at which the Judge presided, flanked by the law professors and the other legal sponsors. This was the anteroom to that world he had been working to reach for three years now—four, counting that first one when he could not yet see his goal. He had only to sit with that fixed expression and wait until the final periphrase died, was blotted by the final concussion of palms, and rise and walk out of the room and on, his face steady in the direction he had chosen to set it, as it had been for three years now anyway, not faltering, now looking back. And he could not do it. Even with that already forty miles of start toward freedom and (he knew it, said it) dignity and self-respect, he could not do it. He must return, drawn back into the radius and impact of an eleven-year-old girl who, even while sitting with veiled eyes against the sun like a cat on the schoolhouse steps at recess and eating a cold potato, postulated that ungirdled quality of the very goddesses in his Homer and Thucydides: of being at once corrupt and immaculate, at once virgins and the mothers of warriors and of grown men.

On that first morning when her brother had brought her to the school, Labove had said to himself: No. No. Not here. Dont leave her here. He had taught the school for only one year, a single term of five months broken by the weekly night ride to Oxford and return and the two-weeks' gap of the mid-term examinations in January, yet he had not only extricated it from the chaos in which his predecessor had left it, he had even coerced the curriculum itself into something resembling order. He had no assistant, there was not even a partition in the single room, yet he had segregated the pupils according to capacity into a routine which they not only observed but he had finally come to believe in. He was not proud of it, he was not even satisfied. But he was satisfied that it was motion, progress, if not toward increasing knowledge to any great extent, at least toward teaching order and discipline. Then one morning he turned from the crude blackboard and saw a face eight years old and a body of fourteen with the female shape of twenty, which on the instant of crossing the threshold brought into the bleak, ill-lighted, poorly-heated room dedicated to the harsh functioning of Protestant primary education a moist blast of spring's liquorish corruption, a pagan triumphal prostration before the supreme primal uterus.

He took one look at her and saw what her brother would doubtless be the last to discern. He saw that she not only was not going to study, but there was nothing in books here or anywhere else that she would ever need to know, who had been born already completely equipped not only to face and combat but to overcome anything the future could invent to meet her with. He saw a child whom for the next two years he was to watch with what he thought at first was only rage, already grown at eight, who apparently had reached and passed puberty in the foetus, who, tranquil bemused and not even sullen, obedient to whatever outside compulsion it had been had merely transferred from one set of walls to another that quality of static waiting through and beneath the accumulating days of burgeoning and unhurryable time until whatever man it was to be whose name and face she probably had neither seen nor heard yet, would break into and disperse it. For five years he was to watch her, fetched each morning by the brother and remain just as he had left her, in the same place and almost in the same position, her hands lying motionless for hours on her lap like two separate slumbering bodies. She would answer "I dont know" when her attention was finally attracted at last, or, pressed, "I never got that far." It was as if her muscles and flesh too were even impervious to fatigue and boredom or as if, the drowsing maidenhead symbol's self, she possessed life but not sentience and merely waited until the brother came, the jealous seething eunuch priest, and removed her.

She would arrive each morning with the oilcloth satchel in which if she carried anything else beside the baked sweet potatoes which she ate at recess, Labove did not know it. By merely walking down the aisle between them she would transform the very wooden desks and benches themselves into a grove of Venus and fetch every male in the room, from the children just entering puberty to the grown men of nineteen and twenty, one of whicm was already a husband and father, who could turn ten acres of land between sunup and sundown, springing into embattled rivalry, importunate each for precedence in immolation. Sometimes on Friday nights there would be parties in the schoolhouse, where the pupils would play the teasing games of adolescence under his supervision. She would take no part in them, yet she would dominate them. Sitting beside the stove exactly as she had sat during the hours of school, inattentive and serene amid the uproar of squeals and trampling feet, she would be assaulted simultaneously beneath a dozen simultaneous gingham or calico dresses in a dozen simultaneous shadowy nooks and corners. She was neither at the head nor at the foot of her class, not because she declined to study on the one hand and not because she was Varner's daughter on the other and Varner ran the school, but because the class she was in ceased to have either head or foot twenty-four hours after she entered it. Within the year there even ceased to be any lower class for her to be promoted from, for the reason that she would never be at either end of anything in which blood ran. It would have but one point, like a swarm of bees, and she would be that point, that center, swarmed over and importuned yet serene and intact and apparently even oblivious, tranquilly abrogating the whole long sum of human thinking and suffering which is called knowledge, education, wisdom, at once supremely unchaste and inviolable: the queen, the matrix.

He watched that for two years, still with what he thought was only rage. He would graduate at the end of the second year, take his two degrees. He would be done then, finished. His one reason for having taken the school would be cancelled and discharged. His aim and purpose would be gained at the price it had cost him, not the least of which was riding that horse forty miles at night to and from the University, since after his dirt-farmer tradition and heritage, he did not ride a horse for fun. Then he could go on, quit the village and never lay eyes upon it again. For the first six months he believed he was going to do that and for the next eighteen he still told himself he was. This was especially easy not only to tell himself but to believe too while he was away from the village during the last two months of the spring term at the University and the following eight weeks of the summer term into which he was crowding by sections his fourth academic year, then the eight weeks of what the school called his vacation, which he spent at the sawmill although he did not need the money now, he could graduate without it, but it would be that much more in his pocket when he passed through the last door and faced the straight hard road with nothing between him and his goal save himself; then the six fall weeks when each Saturday afternoon the spurned white lines fled beneath him and the hysteric air screamed and roared and he for those fleet seconds and despite himself did live, fierce, concentrated, even though still not quite believing it.

Then one day he discovered that he had been lying to himself for almost two years. It was after he had returned to the University in the second spring and about a month before he would graduate. He had not formally resigned from the school, though when he left the village a month ago he believed it was for the last time, considering it understood between Varner and himself that he was teaching the school only to enable himself to finish at the University. So he believed he had quitted the village for the last time. The final examinations were only a month away, then the Bar examination and the door would be open to him. There was even the promise of a position in the profession he had chosen. Then one afternoon, he had no warning at all, he had entered the dining room of his boarding house for the evening meal when the landlady came and said, "I have a treat for you. My sister's husband brought them to me," and set a dish before him. It was a single baked sweet potato, and while the landlady cried, "Why, Mr Labove, you are sick!" he managed to rise and leave the room. In his room at last it seemed to him that he must go at once, start now, even on foot. He could see her, even smell her, sitting there on the school steps, eating the potato, tranquil and chewing and with that terrible quality of being not only helplessly and unawares on the outside of her clothing, but of being naked and not even knowing it. He knew now that it was not on the school steps but in his mind that she had contantly been for two years now, that it had not been rage at all but terror, and that the vision of that gate which he had held up to himself as a goal was not a goal but just a point to reach, as the man fleeing a holocaust runs not for a prize but to escape destruction.

But he did not really give up then, though for the first time he said the words. I will not go back. It had not been necessary to say them before because until now he had believed he was going on. But at least he could still assure himself aloud that he would not, which was something and which got him on through the graduation and the Bar initiation and banquet too. Just before the ceremony he had been approached by one of his fellow neophytes. After the banquet they were going to Memphis, for further and informal celebrating. He knew what that meant: drinking in a hotel room and then, for some of them at least, a brothel. He declined, not because he was a virgin and not because he did not have the money to spend that way but because up to the very last he still believed, still had his hill-man's purely emotional and foundationless faith in education, the white magic of Latin degrees, which was an actual counterpart of the old monk's faith in his wooden cross. Then the last speech died into the final clapping and scraping of chairs; the door was open and the road waited and he knew he would not take it. He went to the man who had invited him to Memphis and accepted. He descended with the group from the train in the Memphis station and asked quietly how to find a brothel. "Hell, man," the other said. "Restrain yourself. At least let's go through the formality of registering at the hotel." But he would not. He went alone to the address given him. He knocked firmly at the equivocal door. This would not help him either. He did not expect it to. His was that quality lacking which no man can ever be completely brave or completely craven: the ability to see both sides of the crisis and visualise himself as already vanquished—itself inherent with its own failure and disaster. At least it wont be my virginity that she is going to scorn, he told himself. The next morning he borrowed a sheet of cheap ruled tablet paper (the envelope was pink and had been scented onçe) from his companion of the night, and wrote Varner that he would teach the school for another year.

He taught it for three more years. By then he was the monk indeed, the bleak schoolhouse, the little barren village, was his mountain, his Gethsemane and, he knew it, his Golgotha too. He was the virile anchorite of old time. The heatless lean-to room was his desert cell, the thin pallet bed on the puncheon floor the couch of stones on which he would lie prone and sweating in the iron winter nights, naked, rigid, his teeth clenched in his scholar's face and his legs haired-over like those of a faun. Then day would come and he could rise and dress and eat the food which he would not even taste. He had never paid much attention to what he ate anyway, but now he would not always know that he had eaten it. Then he would go and unlock the school and sit behind his desk and wait for her to walk down the aisle. He had long since thought of marrying her, waiting until she was old enough and asking for her in marriage, attempting to, and had discarded that. In the first place, he did not want a wife at all, certainly not yet and probably not ever. And he did not want her as a wife, he just wanted her one time as a man with a gangrened hand or foot thirsts after the axe-stroke which will leave him comparatively whole again. But he would have paid even this price to be free of his obsession, only he knew that this could never be, not only because her father would never agree to it, but because of her, that quality in her which absolutely abrogated the exchange value of any single life's promise or capacity for devotion, the puny asking-price of any one man's reserve of so-called love. He could almost see the husband which she would someday have. He would be a dwarf, a gnome, without glands or desire, who would be no more a physical factor in her life than the owner's name on the fly-leaf of a book. There it was again, out of the books again, the dead defacement of type which had already betrayed him: the crippled Vulcan to that Venus, who would not possess her but merely own her by the single strength which power gave, the dead power of money, wealth, gewgaws, baubles, as he might own, not a picture, statue: a field, say. He saw it: the fine land rich and fecund and foul and eternal and impervious to him who claimed title to it, oblivious, drawing to itself tenfold the quantity of living seed its owner's whole life could have secreted and compounded, producing a thousandfold the harvest he could ever hope to gather and save.

So that was out. Yet still he stayed on. He stayed for the privilege of waiting until the final class was dismissed and the room was empty so that he could rise and walk with his calm damned face to the bench and lay his hand on the wooden plank still warm from the impact of her sitting or even kneel and lay his face to the plank, wallowing his face against it, embracing the hard unsentient wood, until the heat was gone. He was mad. He knew it. There would be times now when he did not even want to make love to her but wanted to hurt her, see blood spring and run, watch that serene face warp to the indelible mark of terror and agony beneath his own; to leave some indelible mark of himself on it and then watch it even cease to be a face. Then he would exorcise that. He would drive it from him, whereupon their positions would reverse. It would now be himself importunate and prostrate before that face which, even though but fourteen years old, postulated a weary knowledge which he would never attain, a surfeit, a glut of all perverse experience. He would be as a child before that knowledge. He would be like a young girl, a maiden, wild distracted and amazed, trapped not by the seducer's maturity and experience but by blind and ruthless forces inside herself which she now realised she had lived with for years without even knowing they were there. He would grovel in the dust before it, panting: "Show me what to do. Tell me. I will do anything you tell me, anything, to learn and know what you know." He was mad. He knew it. He knew that sooner or later something was going to happen. And he knew too that, whatever it would be, he would be the vanquished, even though he did not know yet what the one crack in his armor was and that she would find it unerringly and instinctively and without ever being aware that she had been in deadly danger. Danger? he thought, cried. Danger? Not to her: to me. I am afraid of what I might do, not because of her because there is nothing I or any man could do to her that would hurt her. It's because of what it will do to me.

Then one afternoon he found his axe. He continued to hack in almost an orgasm of joy at the dangling nerves and tendons of the gangrened member long after the first bungling blow. He had heard no sound. The last football had ceased and the door had closed for the last time. He did not hear it open again, yet something caused him to raise his wallowing face from the bench. She was in the room again, looking at him. He knew that she was not only recognised the place at which he knelt, but that she knew why. Possibly at that instant he believed she had known all the time, because he knew at once that she was neighter frightened nor laughing at him, that she simply did not care. Nor did she know that she was now looking at the face of a potential homicide. She merely released the door and came down the aisle toward the front of the room where the stove sat. "Jody aint come yet," she said. "It's cold out there. What are you doing down there?"

He rose. She came steadily on, carrying the oilcloth satchel which she had carried for five years now and which he knew she had never opened outside of the schoolhouse save to put into it the cold poatoes. He moved toward her. She stopped, watching him. "Dont be afraid," he said. "Don't be afraid."

"Afraid?" she said. "Of what?" She took one step back, then no more, watching his face. She was not afraid. She aint got that far either, he thought; and then something furious and cold, of repudiation and bereavement both, blew in him though it did not show in his face which was even smiling a little, tragic and sick and damned.

"That's it," he said. "That's the trouble. You are not afraid. That's what you have got to learn. That's one thing I am going to teach you, anyway." He had taught her something else, though he was not fo find it out for a minute or so yet. She had indeed learned one thing during the five years in school and was presently to take and pass an examination on it. He moved toward her. She still stood her ground. Then he had her. He moved as quickly and ruthlessly as if she had a football or as if he had the ball and she stood between him and the final white line which he hated and must reach. He caught her, hard, the two bodies hurling together violently because she had not even moved to avoid him, let alone to begin resisting yet. She seemed to be momentarily mesmerised by a complete inert soft surprise, big, immobile, almost eye to eye with him in height, the body which seemed always to be on the outside of its garments, which without even knowing it apparently had made a priapic hullabaloo of that to which, at the price of three years of sacrifice and endurance and flagellation and unceasing combat with his own implacable blood, he had bought the privilege of dedicating his life, as fluid and muscleless as a miraculous intact milk.

Then the body gathered itself into furious and silent resistance which even then he might have discerned to be neither fright nor even outrage but merely surprise and annoyance. She was strong. He had expected that. He had wanted that, he had been waiting for it. They wrestled furiously. He was still smiling, even whispering. "That's it," he said. "Fight it. Fight it. That's what it is: a man and a woman fighting each other. The hating. To kill, only to do it in such a way that the other will have to know forever afterward he or she is dead. Not even to lie quiet dead because forever afterward there will have to be two in that grave and those two can never again lie quiet anywhere together and neither can ever lie anywhere alone and be quiet until he or she is dead." He held her loosely, the better to feel the fierce resistance of bones and muscles, holding her just enough to keep her from actually reaching his face. She had made no sound, although her brother, who was never late in calling for her, must by now be just outside the building. Labove did not think of this. He would not have cared probably. He held her loosely, still smiling, whispering his jumble of fragmentary Greek and Latin verse and American-Mississippi obscenity, when suddenly she managed to free one of her arms, the elbow coming up hard under his chin. It caught him off-balance; before he regained it her other hand struck him a full-armed blow in the face. He stumbled backward, struck a bench and went down with it and partly beneath it. She stood over him, breathing deep but not panting and not even dishevelled.

"Stop pawing me," she said. "You old headless horseman Ichabod Crane."

After the sound of her feet and the closing door had ceased, he could hear the cheap clock which he had brought back with him from his room at the University, loud in the silence, with a tiny sound like minute shot being dropped into a can, though before he could begin to get up the door opened again and, sitting on the floor, he looked up at her as she came back down the aisle. "Where's my——" she said. Then she saw it, the book-satchel, and lifted it from the floor and turned again. Heheard the door again. So she hasn't told him yet, he thought. He knew the brother too. He would not have waited to take her home first, he would have come in at once, vindicated at last after five years of violent and unsupported conviction. That would be something, anyway. It would not be penetration, true enough, but it would be the same flesh, the same warm living flesh in which the same blood ran, under impact at least—a paroxysm, an orgasm of sorts, a katharsis, anyway—something. So he got up and went to his desk and sat down and squared the clock-face (it sat at an oblique angle, so he could see it from the point before the recitation bench where he usually stood) toward him. He knew the distance between the school and the Varner home and he had ridden that horse back and forth to the University enough to calculate time in horse-distance. He will gallop back too, he thought. So he measured the distance the minute hand would have to traverse and sat watching it as it crept toward the mark. Then he looked up at the only comparatively open space in the room, which still had the stove in it, not to speak of the recitation bench. The stove could not be moved, but the bench could. But even then. . . . Maybe he had better meet the brother outdoors, or someone might get hurt. Then he thought that that was exactly what he wanted: for somebody to get hurt, and then he asked himself quietly, Who? and answered himself: I dont know. I dont care. So he looked back at the clock-face. Yet even when a full hour had passed he still could not admit to himself that the final disaster had befallen him. He is lying in ambush for me with the pistol, he thought. But where? What ambush? What ambush could he want better than here? already seeing her entering the room again tomorrow morning, tranquil, untroubled, not even remembering, carrying the cold potato which at recess she would sit on the sunny steps and eat like one of the unchaste and perhaps even anonymously pregnant immortals eating bread of Paradise on a sunwise slope of Olympus.

So he rose and gathered up the books and papers which, with the clock, he carried to his barren room each afternoon and fetched back the next morning, and put them into the desk drawer and closed it and with his handkerchief he wiped off the desk top, moving without haste yet steadily, his face calm, and wound the clock and set it back on the desk. The overcoat which the football coach had given him six years ago hung on its nail. He looked at it for a moment, though presently he went and got it and even put it on and left the room, the now deserted room in which there were still and forever would be too many people; in which, from that first day when her brother had brought her into it, there had been too many people, who would make one too many forever after in any room she ever entered and remained in long enough to expel breath.

As soon as he emerged, he saw the roan horse tied to the post before the store. Of course, he thought quietly. Naturally he would not carry a pistol around with him, and it would not do him any good hidden under a pillow at home. Of course. That's it. That's where the pistol will be; telling himself that perhaps the brother even wanted witnesses, as he himself wanted them, his face tragic and calm now, walking on down the road toward the store. That will be proof, he cried silently. Proof in the eyes and beliefs of living men that that happened which did not. Which will be better than nothing, even though I am not here to know men believe it.

Which will be fixed in the beliefs of living men forever and ever ineradicable, since one of the two alone who know different will be dead.

It was a gray day, of the color and texture of iron, one of those wordless days of a plastic rigidity too dead to make or release snow even, in which even light did not alter but seemed to appear complete out of nothing at dawn and would expire into darkness without graduation. The village was lifeless—the shuttered and silent gin and blacksmith shop, the weathered store: the motionless horse alone postulating life and that not because it moved but because it resembled something known to be alive. But they would be inside the store. He could see them—the heavy shoes and boots, the overalls and jumper coats bulging over the massed indiscriminate garments beneath—planted about the box of pocked sand in which the stove, squatting, radiated the strong good heat which had an actual smell, masculine, almost monastic—a winter's concentration of unwomaned and deliberate tobacco-spittle annealing into the iron flanks. The good heat: he would enter it, not out of the bleak barren cold but out of life, mounting steps and walking through a door and out of living. The horse raised its head and looked at him as he passed it. But not you, he said to it. You've got to stand outside, stand here and remain intact for the blood to contrive to run through. I dont. He mounted the steps, crossing the heel-gnawed planks of the gallery. On the closed door was tacked a paper placard advertising a patent medicine, half defaced—the reproduction of a portrait, smug, bearded, successful, living far away and married, with children, in a rich house and beyond the reach of passion and blood's betrayal and not even needing to be dead to be embalmed with spaced tacks, ubiquitous and immortal in ten thousand fading and tattered effigies on ten thousand weathered and paintless doors and walls and fences in all the weathers of rain and ice and summer's harsh heat, about the land.

Then, with his hand already on the knob to turn it, he stopped. Once—it was one of the football trips of course, he had never ridden in a train otherwise save on that night visit to Memphis—he had descended onto a bleak station platform. There was a sudden commotion about a door. He heard a man cursing, shouting, a Negro ran out the door, followed by a shouting white man. The Negro turned, stooping, and as the onlookers scattered the white man shot the Negro in the body with a blunt pistol. He remembered how the Negro, clutching his middle, dropped onto his face then suddenly flopped over onto his back, actually appearing to elongate himself, to add at least a yard to his stature; the cursing white man was overpowered and disarmed, the train whistled once and began to draw away, a uniformed trainman breaking out of the crowd and running to overtake it and still looking back from the moving step. And he remembered how he shoved himself up, instinctively using his football tactics to make a place, where he looked down upon the Negro lying rigid on his back, still clutching his middle, his eyes closed and his face quite peaceful. Then there was a man—a doctor or an officer, he did not know—kneeling over the Negro. He was trying to draw the Negro's hands away. There was no outward show of resistance; the forearms and hands at which the doctor or officer was tugging merely seemed to have become iron. The Negro's eyes did not open nor his peaceful expression alter; he merely said: "Look out, white folks. I awready been shot." But they unclasped his hands at last, and he remembered the peeling away of the jumper, the overalls, a ragged civilian coat beneath which revealed itself to have been a long overcoat once, the skirts cut away at the hips as with a razor; beneath that a shirt and a pair of civilian trousers. The waist of them was unbuttoned and the bullet rolled out onto the platform, bloodless. He released the doorknob and removed the overcoat and hung it over his arm. At least I wont make a failure with one of us, he thought, opening the door, entering. At first he believed the room was empty. He saw the stove in its box of pocked sand, surrounded by the nail kegs and unpended boxes; he even smelled the rank scorch of recent spitting. But no one sat there, and when a moment later he saw the brother's thick humorless surly face staring at him over the desk, for an instant he felt rage and outrage. He believed that Varner had cleared the room, sent them all away deliberately in order to deny him that last vindication, the ratification of success which he had come to buy with his life; and suddenly he knew a furious disinclination, even a raging refusal, to die at all. He stooped quickly aside, already dodging, scrabbling about him for some weapon as Varner's face rose still further above the desk top like a bilious moon.

"What in hell are you after?" Varner said. "I told you two days ago that window sash aint come yet."

"Window sash?" Labove said.

"Nail some planks over it," Varner said. "Do you expect me to make a special trip to town to keep a little fresh air out of your collar?"

Then he remembered it. The panes had been broken out during the Christmas holidays. He had nailed boards over them at the time. He did not remember doing it. But then he did not remember being told about the promised sash two days ago, let alone asking about it. And now he stopped remembering the window at all. He rose quietly and stood, the overcoat over his arm; now he did not even see the surly suspicious face anymore. Yes, he thought quietly; Yes. I see. She never told him at all. She didn't even forget to. She doesn't even know anything happened that was worth mentioning. Varner was still talking; apparently someone had answered him:

"Well, what do you want, then?"

"I want a nail," he said.

"Get it, then." The face had already disappeared beyond the desk. "Bring the hammer back."

"I wont need the hammer," he said. "I just want a nail."

The house, the heatless room in which he had lived for six years now with his books and his bright lamp, was between the store and the school. He did not even look toward it when he passed. He returned to the schoolhouse and closed and locked the door. With a fragment of brick he drove the nail into the wall beside the door and hung the key on the nail. The schoolhouse was on the Jefferson road. He already had the overcoat with him.

CHAPTER TWO

1

Through that spring and through the long succeeding summer of her fourteenth year, the youths of fifteen and sixteen and seventeen who had been in school with her and others who had not, swarmed like wasps about the ripe peach which her full damp mouth resembled. There were about a dozen of them. They formed a group, close, homogeneous, and loud, of which she was the serene and usually steadily and constantly eating axis, center. There were three or four girls in the group, lesser girls, though if she were deliberately using them for foils, nobody knew it for certain. They were smaller girls, even though mostly older. It was though that abundance which had invested her cradle, not content with merely overshadowing them with the shape of features and texture of hair and skin, must also dwarf and extinguish them ultimately with sheer bulk and mass.

They were together at least once a week and usually oftener. They would meet at the church on Sunday mornings and sit together in two adjacent pews which presently became their own by common consent of the congregation and authorities, like a class or an isolation place. They met at the community parties which would be held in the now empty schoolhouse, which was to be used for nothing else for almost two years before another teacher was installed. They arrived in a group, they chose one another monotonously in the two-sing games, the boys clowning and ruthless, loud. They might have been a masonic lodge set suddenly down in Africa or China, holding a weekly meeting. They departed together, walking back down the star- or moonlit road in a tight noisy clump, to leave her at her father's gate before dispersing. If the boys had been sparring for opportunities to walk home with her singly, nobody knew that either because she was never known to walk home singly from anywhere or to walk anywhere anyhow when she could help it.

They would meet again at the singings and baptisings and picnics about the country. It was election year and after the last of the planting and the first of the laying-by of the crops, there were not only the first-Sunday all-day singings and baptisings, but the vote-rousing picnics as well. The Varner surrey would be seen now week after week among the other tethered vehicles at country churches or on the edge of groves within which the women spread a week's abundance of cold food on the long plank tables while the men stood beneath the raised platforms on which the candidates for the county offices and the legislature and Congress spoke, and the young people in groups or pairs moved about the grove or, in whatever of seclusion the girls could be enticed into, engaged in the clumsy horseplay of adolescent courtship or seduction. She listened to no speeches and set no tables and did no singing. Instead, with those two or three or four lesser girls she sat, nucleus of that loud frustrated group; the nucleus, the center, the centrice; here as at the school parties of last year, casting over them all that spell of incipient accouchement while refusing herself to be pawed at, preserving even within that aura of license and invitation in which she seemed to breathe and walk—or sit rather—a ruthless chastity impervious even to the light precarious balance, the actual overlapping, of Protestant religious and sexual excitement. It was as if she really knew what instant, moment, she was reserved for, even if not his name and face, and was waiting for that moment rather than merely for the time for the eating to start, as she seemed to be.

They would meet again at the homes of the girls. This would be by prearrangement without doubt, and doubtless contrived by the other girls, though if she were aware that they invited her so that the boys would come, nobody ever divined this from her behavior either. She would make visits of overnight or of two and three days with them. She was not allowed to attend the dances which would be held in the village schoolhouse or in other schoolhouses or country stores at night. She had never asked permission; it had rather been violently refused her by her brother before anyone knew whether she was going to ask it or not. The brother did not object to the house visits though. He even fetched her back and forth on the horse as he had used to do to and from the school and for the same reason he would not let her walk from the school to the store to meet him, still seething and grimly outraged and fanatically convinced of what he believed he was battling against, riding for miles, the oilcloth book-satchel containing the nightgown and the toothbrush which her mother compelled her to bring held in the same hand which clutched the cross of his suspenders, the soft mammalian rubbing against his back and the steady quiet sound of chewing and swallowing in his ear, stopping the horse at last before the house she had come to visit and snarling at her, "Cant you stop eating that damn potato long enough to get down and let me go back to work?"

In early September the annual County Fair was held in Jefferson. She and her parents went to town and lived for four days in a boarding house. The youths and the three girls were already there waiting for her. While her father looked at livestock and farm tools and her mother bustled cheerful and martinettish among ranked cans and jars and decorated cakes, she moved all day long in the hem-lengthened dresses she had worn last year to school and surrounded by her loud knot of loutish and belligerent adolescents, from shooting gallery to pitch game to pop stand, usually eating something, or time after time without even dismounting and still eating, rode, her long Olympian legs revealed halfway to the thigh astride the wooden horses of merry-go-rounds.

By her fifteenth year they were men. They were the size of men and doing the work of grown men at least—eighteen and nineteen and twenty, who in that time and country should have been thinking of marriage and, for her sake anyway, looking toward the other girls; for their own sakes, almost any other girl. But they were not thinking of marriage. There were about a dozen of them too, who at some moment, instant, during that second spring which her brother still could not definitely put his finger on, had erupted into her placid orbit like a stampede of wild cattle, trampling ruthlessly aside the children of last summer's yesterday. Luckily for her brother, the picnics were not as frequent this year as during the election summer, because he went with the family now in the surrey—the humorless seething raging man in his hot bagging broadcloth and collarless glazed shirt who now, as if in a kind of unbelieving amazement, did not even snarl at her anymore. He had nagged Mrs Varner into making her wear corsets. He would grasp her each time he saw her outside the house, in public or alone, and see for himself if she had them on.

Although the brother declined to attend the singings and baptisings, he had badgered the parents into standing in his stead then. So the young men had what might be called a free field only on Sundays. They would arrive in a body at the church, riding up on horses and mules taken last night from the plow and which would return to the plow with tomorrow's sun, and wait for the Varner surrey to arrive. That was all the adolescent companions of last year ever saw of her now—that glimpse of her between the surrey and the church door as she moved stiff and awkward in the corset and the hem-lengthened dress of last year's childhood, seen for an instant then hidden by the crowding surge of those who had dispossessed them. Within another year it would be the morning's formal squire in a glittering buggy drawn by a horse or mare bred for harness, and the youths of this year would be crowded aside in their turn. But that would be next year; now it was a hodge-podge though restrained into something like decorum or at least discretion by the edifice and the day, a leashed turmoil of lust like so many lowering dogs after a scarce-fledged and apparently unawares bitch, filing into the church to sit on a back bench where they could watch the honey-colored head demure among those of her parents and brother.

After church the brother would be gone, courting himself, it was believed, and through the long drowsing afternoons the trace-galled mules would doze along the Varner fence while their riders sat on the veranda, doggedly and vainly sitting each other out, crass and loud and baffled and raging not at one another but at the girl herself who apparently did not care whether they stayed or not, apparently not even aware that the sitting-out was going on. Older people, passing, would see them—the half dozen or so bright Sunday shirts with pink or lavender sleeve-garters, the pomaded hair above the shaved sunburned necks, the polished shoes, the hard loud faces, the eyes filled with the memory of a week of hard labor in fields behind them and knowledge of another week of it ahead; among them the girl, the centrice here too—the body of which there was simply too much dressed in the clothing of childhood, like a slumberer washed out of Paradise by a night flood and discovered by chance passers and covered hurriedly with the first garment to hand, still sleeping. They would sit leashed and savage and loud and wild at the vain galloping seconds while the shadows lengthened and the frogs and whippoorwills began and the fireflies began to blow and drift above the creek. Then Mrs Varner would come bustling out, talking, and still talking herd them all in to eat the cold remains of the heavy noon meal beneath the bug-swirled lamp, and they would give up. They would depart in a body, seething and decorous, to mount the patient mules and horses and ride in furious wordless amity to the creek ford a half mile away and dismount and hitch the horses and mules and with bare fists fight silently and savagely and wash the blood off in the water and mount again and ride their separate ways, with their skinned knuckles and split lips and black eyes and for the time being freed even of rage and frustration and desire, beneath the cold moon, across the planted land.

By the third summer the trace-galled mules had given way to the trotting horses and the buggies. Now it was the youths, the outgrown and discarded of last year, who waited about the churchyard on Sunday mornings to watch in impotent and bitter turn their own dispossession—the glittering buggy powdered only lightly over with dust, drawn by a bright mare or horse in brass-studded harness, driven by the man who owned them both—a man grown in his own right and never again to be haled from an attic bed in an iron dawn to milk cows or break land not his own, by a father who still held over him legally and sometimes physically too the power to bind and loose. Beside him would be the girl who last year, after a fashion at least, had been their own and who had outgrown them, escaped them like the dead summer itself, who had learned at last to walk without proclaiming the corsets beneath the dresses of silk in which she looked, not like a girl of sixteen dressed like twenty, but a woman of thirty dressed in the garments of her sixteen-year-old sister.

At one time in the spring, for an afternoon and evening, to be exact, there were four buggies. The fourth one belonged to a drummer, rented. He appeared in the village by accident one day, having lost his way and blundered upon Frenchman's Bend to ask directions without even knowing there was a store there, in a battered rig which a Jefferson livery stable rented to travelling men. He saw the store and stopped and tried to sell the clerk, Snopes, a bill of goods and got nowhere quickly. He was a youngish city man with city ways and assurance and insistence. He had presently wormed from the usual loungers on the gallery who the actual owner of the store was and where he lived, and went on to Varner's house and doubtless knocked and was or was not admitted, since that was all they knew then. Two weeks later he was back, in the same rig. This time he did not even try to sell the Varners anything; it was learned later that he had taken supper at the Varner house. That was Tuesday. On Friday he returned. He was now driving the best turnout which the Jefferson stable had—a runabout and a fair horse—and he not only wore a necktie, he had on the first white flannel trousers Frenchman's Bend ever saw. They were the last ones too, and they were not there long: he ate supper with the Varners and that evening he drove the daughter to a dance in a schoolhouse about eight miles away, and vanished. Someone else brought the daughter home and at daylight the next morning the hostler found the rented horse and buggy tied to the stable door in Jefferson and that afternoon the night station agent told of a frightened and battered man in a pair of ruined ice-cream pants who had bought a ticket on the early train. The train was going south, though it was understood that the drummer lived in Memphis, where it was later learned he had a wife and family, but about this nobody in Frenchman's Bend either knew or cared.

That left three. They were constant, almost in rotation, week and week and Sunday and Sunday about, last summer's foreclosed bankrupts waiting at the church to watch him of that morning lift her out of the buggy. They still waited there to look at her exposed leg when she got back into it, or, a lowering clot further along the road, they would stand suddenly out of the undergrowth as the buggy swept past to shout vicious obscenity after it out of the spinning and choking dust. At some time during the afternoon one or two or three of them would pass the Varner house, to see without looking at them the horse and buggy hitched to the fence and Will Varner napping in his wooden hammock in its small grove in the yard and the closed blinds of the parlor windows beyond, shuttered after the local fashion, against the heat. They would lurk in the darkness, usually with a jug of white hill whiskey, just beyond the light-radius of the homes or stores or school buildings within the lamplit doors and windows of which the silhouettes of dancing couples moved athwart the whine and squeal of fiddles. Once they charged yelling from a clump of shadow beside the moonlit road, upon the moving buggy, the mare rearing and plunging, the driver standing up in the buggy and slashing at them with the whip and laughing at them as they ducked and dodged. Because it was not the brother, it was this dead last summer's vain and raging jetsam, who divined or at least believed that there had never been but one buggy all the time. It was almost a year now since Jody had ceased to wait for her in the hall until she came out, dressed, the buggy waiting, to grasp her arm and exactly as he would have felt the back of a new horse for old saddle sores, grimly explore with his hard heavy hand to see if she had the corset on or not.

This buggy belonged to a man named McCarron who lived about twelve miles from the village. He was the only child of a widow, herself the only child of a well-to-do landowner. Motherless, she had eloped at nineteen with a handsome, ready-tongued, assured and pleasant man who had come into the country without specific antecedents and no definite past. He had been there about a year. His occupation seemed to be mainly playing poker in the back rooms of country stores or the tack rooms of stables, and winning, though perfectly honestly; there had never been any question of that. All the women said he would make a poor husband. The men said that only a shotgun would ever make him a husband of any sort, and most of them would have declined him as a son-in-law even on those terms, because he had that about him which loved the night—not the night's shadows, but the bright hysteric glitter-glare which made them, the perversity of unsleeping. Nevertheless, Alison Hoake climbed out a second-storey window one night. There was no ladder, no drain-pipe, no rope of knotted sheets. They said she jumped and McCarron caught her in his arms and they vanished for ten days and returned, McCarron walking, his fine teeth exposed though the rest of his face took no part in the smile, into the room where old Hoake had sat for ten days now with a loaded shotgun across his lap.

To everyone's surprise, he made not only a decent husband, but son-in-law too. He knew little about farming and did not pretend to like it, nevertheless he served as his father-in-law's overseer, carrying out the old man's verbatim instructions like a dictaphone record would have of course, but having himself the gift of getting along well with, and even dominating somewhat, all men not as ready of tongue as he, though it was actually his jolly though lightly-balanced temper and his reputation as a gambler which got him the obedience of the Negro field hands even more than his position as the son-in-law or even his proved prowess with a pistol. He even stayed home at night and quit the poker-playing. In fact, later nobody could decide for certain if the cattle-buying scheme had not been the father-in-law's instead of his. But within a year, by which time he was a father himself, he was buying up cattle and taking them in droves overland to the railroad and Memphis every two or three months. This went on for ten years; by which time the father-in-law had died and left the property to his grandson. Then McCarron made his last trip. Two nights later one of his drovers galloped up to the house and waked his wife. McCarron was dead, and the countryside never did know much about that either, shot in a gambling house apparently. His wife left the nine-year-old boy with the Negro servants and went in the farm wagon and fetched her husband's body home and buried it on the oak and cedar knoll beside her father and mother. Shortly after that a rumor, a tale of a brief day or two, went about that a woman had shot him. But that died; they only said to one another, "So that's what he was doing all the time," and there remained only the legend of the money and jewels he was supposed to have won during the ten years and fetched home at night and, with his wife's help, bricked up in one of the chimneys of the house.

The son, Hoake, at twenty-three looked older. This was his father's assurance in his face which was bold and handsome too. It was also a little swaggering and definitely spoiled though not vain so much as intolerant, which his father's face had not been. It also lacked humor and equability and perhaps intelligence too, which his father's face had not lacked, but which that of the man who sat for ten days after his daughter's elopement with a load shotgun on his lap, probably did. He grew up with a Negro lad for his sole companion. They slept in the same room, the Negro on a pallet on the floor, until he was ten years old. The Negro was a year older. When they were six and seven, he conquered the Negro with his fists in fair fight. Afterward he would pay the Negro out of his pocket money at a standard rate fixed between them, for the privilege of whipping the Negro, not severely, with a miniature riding crop.

At fifteen his mother sent him to a military boarding school. Precocious, well-co-ordinated and quick to learn whatever he saw was to his benefit, he acquired enough credits in three years to enter college. His mother chose an agricultural college. He went there and spent a whole year in the town without even matriculating while his mother believed he was passing his freshman work. The next fall he did matriculate, remained five months and was given the privilege of withdrawing from the school following a scandalous denouement involving the wife of a minor instructor. He returned home and spent the next two years ostensibly overseeing the plantation which his mother now ran. This meant that he spent some part of the day riding about it in the dress boots of his military school days which still fitted his small feet and which were the first riding boots the countryside had ever seen. Five months ago he happened by chance to ride through Frenchman's Bend village and saw Eula Varner,

This was he against whom, following the rout of the Memphis drummer, the youths of last summer's trace-galled mules rose in embattled concert to defend that in which apparently they and the brother both had no belief, even though they themselves had failed signally to disprove it, as knights before them have probably done. A scout of two or three would lurk about the Varner fence to watch the buggy depart and find which road it would take. They would follow or precede it to whatever plank-trampling fiddle-impregnated destination, to wait there with the jug of raw whiskey and follow it back home or toward home—the long return through night-time roads across the mooned or unmooned sleeping land, the mare's feet like slow silk in the dust as a horse moves when the reins are wrapped about the upright whip in its dashboard socket, the fords into which the unguided mare would step gingerly down and stop unchidden and drink, nuzzling and blowing among the broken reflections of stars, raising its dripping muzzle and maybe drinking again or maybe just blowing into the water as a thirst-quenched horse will. There would be no voice, no touch of rein to make it move on; anyway, it would be standing there too long, too long, too long. One night they charged the moving buggy from the roadside shadows and were driven off by the whip because they had no concerted plan but were moved by a spontaneous combustion of rage and grief. A week after that, the horse and buggy tied to the Varner fence, they burst with yells and banging pans around the corner of the dark veranda, McCarron presently strolling composedly out, not from the porch but from the clump of trees where Varner's wooden hammock hung, and called upon two or three of them by name and cursed them in a pleasant, drawling, conversational voice and dared any two of them to meet him down the road. They could see the pistol hanging in his hand against his flank.

Then they gave him formal warning. They could have told the brother but they did not, not because the brother would more than likely have turned upon the informers with physical violence. Like the teacher Labove, they would have welcomed that, they would have accepted that with actual joy.

As with Labove, it would at least have been the same living flesh warm under furious impact, bruising, scoriating, springing blood, which, like Labove, was what they actually desired now whether they knew it or not. It was because they were already insulated against acceptance of the idea of telling him by the fact that their rage would be wasted then upon the agent of their vengeance and not the betrayer; they would have met the profferer of a mortal affronting and injury with their hands bound up in boxing gloves. So they sent McCarron a formal warning in writing with their names signed. One of them rode the twelve miles to his mother's house one night and fastened the notice to the door. The next afternoon McCarron's Negro, a grown man too now, brought the five separate answers and escaped from them at last, bloody about the head but not seriously hurt.

Yet for almost another week he foiled them. They were trying to take him when he was in the buggy alone, either before he had reached the Varner house or after he had left it. But the mare was too fast for them to overtake, and their spiritless plow-animals would not stand ground and halt the mare, and they knew from the previous attempt that if they tried to stop the mare on foot, he would ride them down, standing up in the buggy with the slashing whip and his hard bare jeering teeth. Besides, he had the pistol, they had learned enough about him to know that he had never been without it since he turned twenty-one. And there was still the matter to be settled between him and the two who had beaten his Negro messenger.

So they were forced at last to ambush him at the ford with Eula in the buggy when the mare stopped to drink. Nobody ever knew exactly what happened. There was a house near the ford, but there were no yells and shouts this time, merely abrasions and cuts and missing teeth on four of the five faces seen by daylight tomorrow. The fifth one, the other of the two who had beaten the Negro, still lay unconscious in the nearby house. Someone found the butt of the buggy whip. It was clotted with dried blood and human hair and later, years later, one of them told that it was the girl who had wielded it, springing from the buggy and with the reversed whip beating three of them back while her companion used the reversed pistol-butt against the wagon-spoke and the brass knuckles of the other two. That was all that was ever known, the buggy reaching the Varner house not especially belated. Will Varner, in his nightshirt and eating a piece of cold peach pie with a glass of buttermilk in the kitchen, heard them come up from the gate and onto the veranda, talking quietly, murmuring as she and her young men did about what her father believed was nothing, and on into the house, the hall, and on to the kitchen door. Varner looked up and saw the bold handsome face, the pleasant hard revelation of teeth which would have been called smiling at least, though it was not particularly deferent, the swelling eye, the long welt down the jaw, the hanging arm flat against the side. "He bumped into something," the daughter said.

"I see he did," Varner said. "He looks like it kicked him too."

"He wants some water and a towel," she said. "It's over yonder," she said, turning; she did not come into the kitchen, the light. "I'll be back in a minute." Varner heard her mount the stairs and move about in her room overhead but he paid no further attention. He looked at McCarron and saw that the exposed teeth were gritted rather than smiling, and he was sweating. After he saw that, Varner paid no more attention to the face either.

"So you bumped into something," he said. "Can you get that coat off?"

"Yes," the other said. "I did it catching my mare. A piece of scantling."

"Serve you right for keeping a mare like that in a wood-shed," Varner said. "This here arm is broke."

"All right," McCarron said. "Aint you a veterinary? I reckon a man aint so different from a mule."

"That's correct," Varner said. "Usually he aint got quite as much sense." The daughter entered. Varner had heard her on the stairs again, though he did not notice that she now wore another dress from that in which she had left the house. "Fetch my whiskey jug," he said. It was beneath his bed, where it stayed. She fetched it down. McCarron sat now with his bared arm flat on the kitchen table. He fainted once, erect in the chair, but not for long. After that it was only the fixed teeth and the sweat until Varner had done. "Pour him another drink and go wake Sam to drive him home," Varner said. But McCarron would not, either be driven home or go to bed where he was. He had a third drink from the jug and he and the girl went back to the veranda and Varner finished his pie and milk and carried the jug back upstairs and went to bed.

It was not the father and not even the brother, who for five or six years now had actually been supported upright and intact in breathing life by an idea which had not even grown through the stage of suspicion at all but had sprung fullblown as a conviction only the more violent for the fact that the most unremitting effort had never been able to prove it, whom divination descended upon. Varner took a drink himself from the jug and shoved it back under the bed where a circle of dust marked the place where it had sat for years, and went to sleep. He entered his accustomed state of unsnoring and childlike slumber and did not hear his daughter mount the stairs, to remove this time the dress which had her own blood on it. The mare, the buggy, was gone by then, though McCarron fainted in it again before he reached home. The next morning the doctor found that, although the break had been properly set and splinted, nevertheless it had broken free since, the two bone-ends telescoping, and so had to be set again. But Varner did not know that—the father, the lean pleasant shrewd unillusioned man asleep in the bed above the whiskey jug twelve miles away, who, regardless of what error he might have made in the reading of the female heart in general and his daughter's in particular, had been betrayed at the last by failing to anticipate that she would not only essay to, but up to a certain point actually support, with her own braced arm from underneath, the injured side.

Three months later, when the day came for the delicate buggies and the fast bright horses and mares to be seen no more along the Varner fence, Will Varner himself was the last to discover it. They and the men who drove them were gone, vanished overnight, not only from Frenchman's Bend but from the country itself. Although one of the three knew certainly one who was guilty, and the other two knew collectively two who were not, all three of them fled, secretly and by back roads probably, with saddle-bags or single hurried portmanteaus for travelling fast. One of them went because of what he believed the Varner men would do. The other two fled because they knew that the Varners would not do it. Because the Varners too would know by now from the one incontrovertible source, the girl herself, that two of them were not guilty, and so those two would thus be relegated also to the flotsam of a vain dead yesterday of passionate and eternal regret and grief, along with the impotent youths who by badgering them also, along with him who had been successful, had conferred upon them likewise blindly and unearned the accolade of success. By fleeing too, they put in a final and despairing bid for the guilt they had not compassed, the glorious shame of the ruin they did not do.

So when the word went quietly from house to house about the country that McCarron and the two others had vanished and that Eula Varner was in what everyone else but her, as it presently appeared, called trouble, the last to learn of it was the father—this man who cheerfully and robustly and undeviatingly declined to accept any such theory as female chastity other than as a myth to hoodwink young husbands with just as some men decline to believe in free tariff or the efficacy of prayer; who, as it was well known, had spent and was still spending no inconsiderable part of his time proving to himself his own contention, who at the present moment was engaged in a liaison with the middle-fortyish wife of one of his own tenants. He was too old, he told her baldly and plainly, to be tomcatting around at night, about his own house or any other man's. So she would meet him in the afternoons, on pretence of hunting hen-nests, in a thicket beside the creek near her house, in which sylvan Pan-hallowed retreet, the fourteen-year-old boy whose habit it was to spy on them told, Varner would not even remove his hat. He was the last to hear about it, waked where he slept in his sock feet in the wooden hammock, by the peremptory voice of his wife, hurrying, lean, loose-jointed and still not quite awake, in his stockings across the yard and into the hall where Mrs Varner, in a loose old wrapper and the lace boudoir cap in which she took her afternoon naps, shouted at him in an immediate irate voice above the uproar of his son's voice from the daughter's room upstairs: "Eula's got a baby. Go up there and knock that fool in the head."

"Got a what?" Varner said. But he did not pause. He hurried on, Mrs Varner following, up the stairs and into the room in which for the last day or two the daughter had remained more or less constantly, not even coming down for meals, suffering from what, if Varner had thought about it at all, he would have judged merely a stomach disorder from eating too much, possibly accumulated and suddenly and violently retroactive after sixteen years of visceral forbearance and outragement. She sat in a chair beside the window in her loosened hair and a bright near-silk negligee she had ordered recently from a Chicago mail-order house. Her brother stood over her, shaking her arm and shouting: "Which one was it? Tell me which one!"

"Stop shoving me," she said. "I dont feel good." Again Varner did not pause. He came between them and thrust Jody back.

"Let her alone," he said. "Get on out of here." Jody turned on Varner his suffused face.

"Let her alone?" he said. He laughed fiercely, with no mirth, his eyes pale, popping and enraged. "That's what's the matter now! She's done been let alone too damn much already! I tried. I knowed what was coming. I told both of you five years ago. But no. You both knew better. And now see what you got! See what's happened! But I'll make her talk. by God, I'll find out who it was. And then I——"

"All right," Varner said. "What's happened?" For a moment, a minute almost, Jody appeared to be beyond speech. He glared at Varner. He looked as though only a supreme effort of will kept him from bursting where he stood.

"And he asks me what's happened," he said at last, in an amazed and incredulous whisper. "He asks me what's happened." He whirled; he jerked one hand upward in a gesture of furious repudiation and, Varner following, rushed upon

Mrs Varner, who had just reached the door, her hand upon her fleshy now heaving breast and her mouth open for speech as soon as breath returned. Jody weighed two hundred pounds and Mrs Varner, although not much over five feet tall, weighed almost as much. Yet he managed somehow to run past her in the door, she grasping at him as Varner, eel-like, followed. "Stop the fool!" she shouted, following again as Varner and Jody thundered back down the stairs and into the ground-floor room which Varner still called his office though for the last two years now the clerk, Snopes, had slept on a cot in it, where Varner now overtook Jody bending over the open drawer of the clumsy (and now priceless, though Varner did not know it) walnut secretary which had belonged to Varner's grandfather, scrabbling a pistol from among the jumble of dried cotton bolls and seed pods and harness buckles and cartridges and old papers which it contained. Though the window beside the desk the Negress, the cook, could be seen running across the back yard toward her cabin, her apron over her head, as Negroes do when trouble starts among the white people. Sam, the man, was following, though slower, looking back at the house, when both Varner and Jody saw him at the same time.

"Sam! Saddle my horse!" Jody roared.

"You Sam!" Varner shouted. They both grasped the pistol now, the four hands now apparently hopelessly inextricable in the open drawer. "Dont touch that horse! Come back here this minute!" Mrs Varner's feet were now pounding in the hall. The pistol came free of the drawer, they stepped back, their hands locked and tangled, to see her now in the door, her hand still at her heaving breast, her ordinarily cheerful opinionated face suffused and irate.

"Hold him till I get a stick of stove-wood," she gasped. "I'll fix him. I'll fix both of them. Turning up pregnant and yelling and cursing here in the house when I am trying to take a nap!"

"All right," Varner said. "Go and get it." She went out; she seemed to have been sucked violently out of the door by her own irate affrontment. Varner wrenched the pistol free and hurled Jody (he was quite strong, incredibly wiry and quick for all his sixty years, though he had cold intelligence for his ally where the son had only blind rage) back into the desk and went and threw the pistol into the hall and slammed the door and turned the key and came back, panting a little but not much. "What in hell are you trying to do?" he said.

"Nothing!" Jody cried. "Maybe you dont give a damn about your name, but I do. I got to hold my head up before folks even if you aint."

"Hah," Varner said. "I aint noticed you having any trouble holding it up. You have just about already got to where you cant get it far enough down to lace your own shoes." Jody glared at him, panting.

"By God," he said, "maybe she wont talk but I reckon I can find somebody that will. I'll find all three of them. I'll——"

"What for? Just out of curiosity to find out for certain just which of them was and wasn't diddling her?" Again for a long moment Jody could not speak at all. He stood against the desk, huge, bull-goaded, impotent and outraged, actually suffering, not from lese-Varner but from frustration. Mrs Varner's heavy stockinged feet pounded again in the hall; she began now to hammer at the door with the stick of wood.

"You, Will!" she shouted. "Open this door!"

"You mean you aint going to do *nothing?*" Jody said. "Not anything?"

"Do what?" Varner said. "To who? Dont you know them damn tomcats are halfway to Texas now? Where would you be about now, if it was you? Where would I be, even at my age, if I was footloose enough to prowl any roof I wanted to and could get in when I did? I know damn well where, and so would you—right where they are and still lathering horsemeat." He went to the door and unlocked it, though the steady irate tattoo of Mrs Varner's stick was so loud that she apparently did not hear the key turn at all. "Now you go on out to the barn and set down until you cool off. Make Sam dig you some worms and go fishing. If this family needs any head-holding-up done, I'll tend to it myself." He turned the knob. "Hell and damnation, all this hullabaloo and uproar because one confounded running bitch finally foxed herself.

What did you expect—that she would spend the rest of her life just running water through it?"

That was Saturday afternoon. On the next Monday morning the seven men squatting about the gallery of the store saw the clerk, Snopes, coming on foot down the road from Varner's house, followed by a second man who was carrying a suitcase. The clerk not only wore the gray cloth cap and the minute tie but a coat too, and then they saw that the suitcase which the second man carried was the straw one which Snopes had carried new to Varner's house one afternoon a year ago and left there. Then they began to look at the man who was carrying it. They saw that the clerk was heeled as by a dog by a man a little smaller than himself but shaped exactly like him. It was as though the two of them were merely graded by perspective. At first glance even the two faces were identical, until the two of them mounted the steps. Then they saw that the second face was a Snopes face right enough, differing from the other only by that unpredictable variation within the iron kinship to which they had become accustomed—in this case a face not smaller than the other exactly but closer, the features plucked together at the center of it not by some inner impulse but rather from the outside, as though by a single swift gesture of the fingers of one hand; a face quick and bright and not derisive exactly, but profoundly and incorrigibly merry behind the bright, alert, amoral eyes of a squirrel or a chipmunk.

They mounted the steps and crossed the gallery, carrying the suitcase. Snopes jerked his head at them exactly as Will Varner himself did it, chewing; they entered the store. After a while three more men came out of the blacksmith shop opposite, so there were a dozen of them about within sight of the gallery when, an hour later, the Varner surrey came up. The Negro, Sam, was driving. Beside him in front was the tremendous battered telescope bag which Mr and Mrs Varner had made their honeymoon to Saint Louis with and which all travelling Varners had used since, even the daughters marrying, sending it back empty, when it would seem to be both symbol and formal notice of moonset, the mundane return, the valedictory of bright passion's generous impulsive abandon, as the printed card had been of its hopeful dawn. Varner, in the back seat with his daughter, called a general greeting, short, perfectly inflectionless, unreadable. He did not get out, and those on the gallery looked quietly once and then away from the calm beautiful mask beside him beneath the Sunday hat, the veil, above the Sunday dress, even the winter coat, seeing without looking at him as Snopes came out of the store, carrying the straw suitcase, and mounted to the front seat beside the telescope bag. The surrey moved on. Snopes turned his head once and spat over the wheel. He had the straw suitcase on his knees like the coffin of a baby's funeral.

The next morning Tull and Bookwright returned from Jefferson, where they had delivered another drove of cattle to the railroad. By that night the countryside knew the rest of it —how on that Monday afternoon Varner and his daughter and his clerk had visited his bank, where Varner had cashed a considerable check. Tull said it was for three hundred dollars. Bookwright said that meant a hundred and fifty then, since Varner would discount even his own paper to himself fifty percent. From there they had gone to the courthouse, to the Chancery Clerk's office, where a deed to the Old Frenchman place was recorded to Flem and Eula Varner Snopes. A Justice of the Peace had a desk in the Circuit Clerk's office, where they bought the license.

Tull blinked rapidly, telling it. He coughed. "The bride and groom left for Texas right after the ceremony," he said.

"That makes five," a man named Armstid said. "But they say Texas is a big place."

"It's beginning to need to be," Bookwright said. "You mean six."

Tull coughed. He was still blinking rapidly. "Mr. Varner paid for it too," he said.

"Paid for what too?" Armstid said.

"The wedding license," Tull said.

2

She knew him well. She knew him so well that she never had to look at him anymore. She had known him ever since her fourteenth summer, when the people said that he had "passed" her brother. They did not say it to her. She would not have heard them. She would not have cared. She saw him almost every day, because in her fifteenth summer he began to come to the house itself, usually after supper, to sit with her father on the veranda, not talking but listening, spitting his tobacco neatly over the railing. Sometimes on Sunday afternoons he would come and squat against a tree beside the wooden hammock where her father lay in his stockings, still not talking and still chewing; she would see him there from where she sat on the veranda surrounded by her ravening crowd of that year's Sunday beaux. By then she had learned to recognise the mute hissing of his tennis shoes on the veranda planks; without rising or even turning her head she would call toward the interior of the house: "Papa, here's that man," or, presently, "the man,"—"papa, here's the man again," though sometimes she said Mr Snopes, saying it exactly as she would have said Mr Dog.

In the next summer, her sixteenth, she not only did not look at him, she never saw him again because he now lived in the same house, eating at the same table, using her brother's saddle horse to attend to his and her father's interminable business. He would pass her in the hall where her brother held her, dressed to go out to the waiting buggy, while his hard raging hand explored to see if she had the corset on, and she would not see him. She faced him across the table to eat twice a day because she ate her own breakfast in the kitchen, at whatever midmorning hour her mother finally got her up, though once she was awake it was no further trouble to get her down to the table; harried at last from the kitchen by the Negress or her mother, the last half-eaten biscuit in her hand and her face unwashed and looking, in the rich deshabille of her loose hair and the sloven and not always clean garments she had groped into between bed and breakfast table, as if she had just been surprised from a couch of illicit love by a police raid, she would meet and pass him returning to his noon meal, in the hall, and he had never been. And so one day they clapped her into her Sunday clothes and put the rest of her things—the tawdry mail-order negligees and nightgowns, the big cheap flimsy shoes and what toilet things she had—into the tremendous bag and took her to town in the surrey and married her to him.

Ratliff was in Jefferson that Monday afternoon too. He saw the three of them cross the Square from the bank to the courthouse and followed them. He walked past the door to the Chancery Clerk's office and saw them inside; he could have waited and seen them go from there to the Circuit Clerk's office and he could have witnessed the marriage, but he did not. He did not need to. He knew what was happening now and he had already gone on to the station, there waiting an hour before the train was due, and he was not wrong; he saw the straw suitcase and the big telescope bag go into the vestibule, in that juxtaposition so more paradoxical and bizarre; he saw the calm beautiful mask beneath the Sunday hat once more beyond a moving window, looking at nothing, and that was all. If he had lived in Frenchman's Bend itself during that spring and summer, he would have known no more—a little lost village, nameless, without grace, forsaken, yet which wombed once by chance and accident one blind seed of the spendthrift Olympian ejaculation and did not even know it, without tumescence conceived, and bore—one bright brief summer, concentric, during which three fairly well-horsed buggies stood in steady rotation along a picket fence or spun along adjacent roads between the homes and the crossroads stores and the schoolhouses and churches where people gathered for pleasure or at least for escape, and then overnight and simultaneously were seen no more; then eccentric: buggies gone, vanished—a lean, loose-jointed, cotton-socked, shrewd, ruthless old man, the splendid girl with her beautiful masklike face, the froglike creature which barely reached her shoulder, cashing a check, buying a license, taking a train—a word, a single will to believe born of envy and old deathless regret, murmured from cabin to cabin above the washing pots and the sewing, from wagon to horseman in roads and lanes or from rider to halted plow in field furrows; the word, the dream and wish of all male under sun capable of harm—the young who only dreamed yet of the ruins they were still incapable of; the sick and the maimed sweating in sleepless beds, impotent for the harm they willed to do; the old, now-glandless earth-creeping, the very buds and blossoms, the garlands of whose yellowed triumphs had long fallen into the profitless dust, embalmed now and no more dead to the living world if they were sealed in buried vaults, behind the impregnable matronly calico of others' grandchildren's grandmothers—the word, with its implications of lost triumphs and defeats of unimaginable splendor—and which best: to have that word, that dream and hope for future, or to have had need to flee that word and dream, for past. Even one of the actual buggies remained. Ratliff was to see it, discovered a few months afterward, standing empty and with propped shafts in a stable shed a few miles from the village, gathering dust; chickens roosted upon it, steadily streaking and marring the once-bright varnish with limelike droppings, until the next harvest, the money-time, when the father of its late driver sold it to a Negro farmhand, after which it would be seen passing through the village a few times each year, perhaps recognised, perhaps not, while its new owner married and began to get a family and then turn gray, spilling children, no longer glittering, its wheels wired upright in succession by crossed barrel slaves until staves and delicate wheels both vanished, translated apparently in motion at some point into stout, not new, slightly smaller wagon wheels, giving it a list, the list too interchangeable, ranging from quarter to quarter between two of its passing appearances behind a succession of spavined and bony horses and mules in wire- and rope-patched harness, as if its owner had horsed it ten minutes ago out of a secret boneyard for this particular final swan-song's apotheosis which, woefully misinformed as to its own capacities, was each time not the last.

But when he at last turned his little tough team toward Frenchman's Bend again, Bookwright and Tull had long since returned home and told it. It was now September. The cotton was open and spilling into the fields; the very air smelled of it. In field after field as he passed along the pickers, arrested in stooping attitudes, seemed fixed amid the constant surf of bursting bolls like piles in surf, the long, partly-filled sacks streaming away behind them like rigid frozen flags. The air was hot, vivid and breathless—a final fierce concentration of the doomed and dying summer. The feet of the small horses twinkled rapidly in the dust and he sat, loose and easy to the motion, the reins loose in one hand, inscrutable of face, his eyes darkly impenetrable, quizzical and bemused, remembering, still seeing them—the bank, the courthouse, the station; the calm beautiful mask seen once more beyond a moving pane of glass, then gone. But that was all right, it was just meat, just gal-meat he thought, and God knows there was a plenty of that, yesterday and tomorrow too. Of course there was the waste, not wasted on Snopes but on all of them, himself included— Except was it waste? he thought suddenly, seeing the face again for an instant as though he had recalled not only the afternoon but the train too—the train itself, which had served its day and schedule and so, despite the hard cars, the locomotive, no more existed. He looked at the face again. It had not been tragic, and now it was not even damned, since from behind it there looked out only another mortal natural enemy of the masculine race. And beautiful: but then, so did the highwayman's daggers and pistols make a pretty shine on him, and now as he watched, the lost calm face vanished. It went fast; it was as if the moving glass were in retrograde, it too merely a part, a figment, of the concentric flotsam and jetsam of the translation, and there remained only the straw bag, the minute tie, the constant jaw:

Until at last, baffled, they come to the Prince his-self. 'Sire,' they says. 'He just wont. We cant do nothing with him.'

'What?' the Prince hollers.

'He says a bargain is a bargain. That he swapped in good faith and honor, and now he has come to redeem it, like the law says. And we cant find it,' they says. 'We done looked everywhere. It wasn't no big one to begin with nohow, and we was specially careful in handling it. We sealed it up in a asbestos matchbox and put the box in a separate compartment to itself. But when we opened the compartment, it was gone. The matchbox was there and the seal wasn't broke. But there wasn't nothing in the matchbox but a little kind of

dried-up smear under one edge. And now he has come to redeem it. But how can we redeem him into eternal torment without his soul?'

'Damn it,' the Prince hollers. 'Give him one of the extra ones. Aint there souls turning up here every day, banging at the door and raising all kinds of hell to get in here, even bringing letters from Congressmen, that we never even heard of? Give him one of them.'

'We tried that,' they says. 'He wont do it. He says he dont want no more and no less than his legal interest according to what the banking and civil laws states in black and white is hisn. He says he has come prepared to meet his bargain and signature, and he sholy expects you of all folks to meet yourn.'

'Tell him he can go then. Tell him he had the wrong address. That there aint nothing on the books here against him. Tell him his note was lost—if there ever was one. Tell him we had a flood, even a freeze.'

'He wont go, not without his——'

'Turn him out. Eject him.'

'How?' they says. 'He's got the law.'

'Oho,' the Prince says. 'A sawmill advocate. I see. All right,' he says. 'Fix it. Why bother me?' And he set back and raised his glass and blowed the flames offen it like he thought they was already gone. Except they wasn't gone.

'Fix what?' they says.

'His bribe!' the Prince hollers. 'His bribe! Didn't you just tell me he come in here with his mouth full of law? Did you expect him to hand you a wrote-out bill for it?'

'We tried that,' they says. 'He wont bribe.'

Then the Prince set up there and sneered at them with his sharp bitter tongue and no talkback, about how likely what they thought was a bribe would be a cash discount with maybe a trip to the Legislature throwed in, and them standing there and listening and taking it because he was the Prince. Only there was one of them that had been there in the time of the Prince's pa. He used to dandle the Prince on his knee when the Prince was a boy; he even made the Prince a little pitchfork and learned him how to use it prac-

tising on Chinees and Dagoes and Polynesians, until his arms would get strong enough to handle his share of white folks. He didn't appreciate this and he drawed his-self up and he looked at the Prince and he says,

'Your father made, unreproved, a greater failure. Though maybe a greater man tempted a greater man.'

'Or you have been reproved by a lesser,' the Prince snaps back. But he remembered them old days too, when the old fellow was smiling fond and proud of his crude youthful inventions with BB size lava and brimstone and such, and bragging to the old Prince at night about how the boy done that day, about what he invented to do to that little Dago or Chinee that even the grown folks hadn't thought of yet. So he apologised and got the old fellow smoothed down, and says, 'What did you offer him?'

'The gratifications.'

'And——?'

'He has them. He says that for a man that only chews, any spittoon will do.'

'And then?'

'The vanities.'

'And——?'

'He has them. He brought a gross with him in the suitcase, specially made up for him outen asbestos, with unmeltable snaps.'

'Then what does he want?' the Prince hollers. 'What does he want? Paradise?' And the old one looks at him and at first the Prince thinks it's because he aint forgot that sneer. But he finds out different.

'No,' the old one says. 'He wants hell.'

And now for a while there aint a sound in that magnificent kingly hall hung about with the proud battle-torn smokes of the old martyrs but the sound of frying and the faint constant screams of authentic Christians. But the Prince was the same stock and blood his pa was. In a flash the sybaritic indolence and the sneers was gone; it might have been the old Prince his-self that stood there. 'Bring him to me,' he says. 'Then leave us.'

So they brought him in and went away and closed the

door. His clothes was still smoking a little, though soon he had done brushed most of it off. He come up to the Throne, chewing, toting the straw suitcase.

'Well?' the Prince says.

He turned his head and spit, the spit frying off the floor quick in a little blue ball of smoke. 'I come about that soul,' he says.

'So they tell me,' the Prince says. 'But you have no soul.'

'Is that my fault?' he says.

'Is it mine?' the Prince says. 'Do you think I created you?'

'Then who did?' he says. And he had the Prince there and the Prince knowed it. So the Prince set out to bribe him his-self. He named over all the temptations, the gratifications, the satieties; it sounded sweeter than music the way the Prince fetched them up in detail. But he didn't even stop chewing, standing there holding the straw suitcase. Then the Prince said, 'Look yonder,' pointing at the wall, and there they was, in order and rite for him to watch, watching his-self performing them all, even the ones he hadn't even thought about inventing to his-self yet, until they was done, the last unimaginable one. And he just turned his head and spit another scorch of tobacco onto the floor and the Prince flung back on the Throne in very exasperation and baffled rage.

'Then what do you want?' the Prince says. 'What do you want? Paradise?'

'I hadn't figured on it,' he says. 'Is it yours to offer?'

'Then whose is it?' the Prince says. And the Prince knowed he had him there. In fact, the Prince knowed he had him all the time, ever since they had told him how he had walked in the door with his mouth already full of law; he even leaned over and rung the fire-bell so the old one could be there to see and hear how it was done, then he leaned back on the Throne and looked down at him standing there with his straw suitcase, and says, 'You have admitted and even argued that I created you. Therefore your soul was mine all the time. And therefore when you offered it as security for this note, you offered that which you did not possess and so laid yourself liable to——'

'I have never disputed that,' he says.

'—criminal action. So take your bag and—' the Prince says. 'Eh?' the Prince says. 'What did you say?'

'I have never disputed that,' he says.

'What?' the Prince says. 'Disputed what?' Except that it dont make any noise, and now the Prince is leaning forward, and now he feels that ere hot floor under his knees and he can feel his-self grabbing and hauling at his throat to get the words out like he was digging potatoes outen hard ground. 'Who are you?' he says, choking and gasping and his eyes a-popping up at him setting there with that straw suitcase on the Throne among the bright, crown-shaped flames. 'Take Paradise!' the Prince screams. 'Take it! Take it!' And the wind roars up and the dark roars down and the Prince scrabbling across the floor, clawing and scrabbling at that locked door, screaming. . . .

BOOK THREE

The Long Summer

CHAPTER ONE

1

Sitting in the halted buckboard, Ratliff watched the old fat white horse emerge from Varner's lot and come down the lane beside the picket fence, surrounded and preceded by the rich sonorous organ-tones of its entrails. So he's back to the horse again, he thought. He's got to straddle his legs at least to keep on moving. So he had to pay that too. Not only the deed to the land and the two-dollar wedding license and them two tickets to Texas and the cash, but the riding in that new buggy with somebody to do the driving, to get that patented necktie out of his store and out of his house. The horse came up and stopped, apparently of its own accord, beside the buckboard in which Ratliff sat neat, decorous, and grave like a caller in a house of death.

"You must have been desperate," he said quietly. He meant no insult. He was not even thinking of Varner's daughter's shame or of his daughter at all. He meant the land, the Old Frenchman place. He had never for one moment believed that it had no value. He might have believed this if anyone else had owned it. But the very fact that Varner had ever come into possession of it and still kept it, apparently making no effort to sell it or do anything else with it, was proof enough for him. He declined to believe that Varner ever had been or ever would be stuck with anything; that if he acquired it, he got it cheaper than anyone else could have, and if he kept it, it was too valuble to sell. In the case of the Old Frenchman place he could not see why this was so, but the fact that Varner had bought it and still had it was sufficient. So when Varner finally did let it go, Ratliff believed it was because Varner had at last got the price for which he had been holding it for twenty years, or at least some sufficient price, whether it was in money or not. And when he considered who Varner had relinquished possession to, he believed that the price had been necessity and not cash.

Varner knew that Ratliff was thinking it. He sat the old horse and looked down at Ratliff, the little hard eyes beneath their bushy rust-colored brows glinting at the man who was a good deal nearer his son in spirit and intellect and physical appearance too than any of his own get. "So you think pure liver aint going to choke that cat," he said.

"Maybe with that ere little piece of knotted-up string in it?" Ratliff said.

"What little piece of knotted-up string?"

"I dont know," Ratliff said.

"Hah," Varner said. "You going my way?"

"I reckon not," Ratliff said. "I'm going to mosey down to the store." Unless maybe he even feels he can set around it too again now, he thought.

"So am I," Varner said. "I got that damn trial this morning. That damn Jack Houston and that What's-his-name. Mink. About that durned confounded scrub yearling."

"You mean Houston sued him?" Ratliff said. *"Houston?"*

"No no. Houston just kept the yearling up. He kept it up all last summer and Snopes let him pasture and feed it all winter, and it run in Houston's pasture all this spring and summer too. Then last week for some reason he decided to go and get it. I reckon he figured to beef it. So he went to Houston's with a rope. He was in Houston's pasture, trying to catch it, when Houston come up and stopped him. He finally had to draw his pistol, he claims. He says Snopes looked at the pistol and said, 'That's what you'll need. Because you know I aint got one.' And Houston said all right, they would lay the pistol on a fence post and back off one post apiece on each side and count three and run for it."

"Why didn't they?" Ratliff said.

"Hah," Varner said shortly. "Come on. I want to get it over with. I got some business to tend to."

"You go on," Ratliff said. "I'll mosey on slow. I aint got no yearling calf nor trial neither today."

So the old fat clean horse (it looked always as if it had just come back from the dry-cleaner's; you could almost smell the benzine) moved on again, with a rich preliminary internal chord, going on along the gapped and weathered picket fence. Ratliff sat in the still-motionless buckboard and watched it and the lean, loose-jointed figure which, with the exception of the three-year runabout interval, had bestridden it, the same saddle between them, for twenty-five years, thinking how if, as dogs do, the white horse or his own two either had snuffed along the fence for yellow-wheeled buggies now, they would not have found them, thinking: And all the other two-legged feice in this country between thirteen ane eighty can pass here now without feeling no urge to stop and raise one of them against it. And yet those buggies were still there. He could see them, sense them. Something was; it was too much to have vanished that quickly and completely—the air polluted and rich and fine which had flowed over and shaped that abundance and munificence, which had done the hydraulic office to that almost unbroken progression of chewed food, which had held intact the constant impact of those sixteen years of sitting down: so why should not that body at the last have been the unscalable sierra, the rosy virginal mother of barricades for no man to conquer scot-free or even to conquer at all, but on the contrary to be hurled back and down, leaving no scar, no mark of himself (That ere child aint going to look no more like nobody this country ever saw than she did, he thought.)—the buggy merely a part of the whole, a minor and trivial adjunct, like the buttons on her clothing, the clothes themselves, the cheap beads which one of the three of them had given her. That would never have been for him, not even at the prime summer peak of what he and Varner both would have called his tomcatting's heyday. He knew that without regret or grief, he would not have wanted it to be (It would have been like giving me a pipe organ, that never had and never would know any more than how to wind up the second-hand music box I had just swapped a mailbox for, he thought.) and he even thought of the cold and froglike victor without jealousy: and this not because he knew that, regardless of whatever Snopes had expected or would have called what it was he now had, it would not be victory. What he felt was outrage at the waste, the useless squandering; at a situation intrinsically and inherently wrong by any economy, like building a log dead-fall and baiting it with a freshened heifer to catch a rat; or no, worse: as though the gods themselves had funnelled all the concentrated bright wet-slanted unparadised June onto a breeding pismires. Beyond the white horse, beyond ... orner of the picket fence, the faint, almost overgrown lane turned off which led to the Old Frenchman place. The horse attempted to turn into it until Varner hauled it roughly back. Not to mention the poorhouse, Ratliff thought, But then, he wouldn't have been infested. He shook his own reins slightly. "Boys," he said, "advance."

The team, the buckboard, went on in the thick dust of the spent summer. Now he could see the village proper—the store, the blacksmith shop, the metal roof of the gin with a thin rapid shimmer of exhaust above the stack. It was now the third week in September; the dry, dust-laden air vibrated steadily to the rapid beat of the engine, though so close were the steam and the air in temperature that no exhaust was visible but merely a thin feverish shimmer of mirage. The very hot, vivid air, which seemed to be filled with the slow laborious plaint of laden wagons, smelled of lint; wisps of it clung among the dust-stiffened roadside weeds and small gouts of cotton lay imprinted by hoof- and wheel-marks into the trodden dust. He could see the wagons too, the long motionless line of them behind the patient, droop-headed mules, waiting to advance a wagon-length at a time, onto the scales and then beneath the suction pipe where Jody Varner would now be again, what with a second new clerk in the store—the new clerk exactly like the old one but a little smaller, a little compacter, as if they had both been cut with the same die but in inverse order to appearance, the last first and after the edges of the die were dulled and spread a little—with his little, full, bright-pink mouth like a kitten's button and his bright, quick, amoral eyes like a chipmunk and his air of merry and incorrigible and unflagging conviction of the inherent constant active dishonesty of all men, including himself.

Jody Varner was at the scales; Ratliff craned his turkey's neck in passing and saw the heavy bagging broadcloth, the white collarless shirt with a yellow halfmoon of sweat at each armpit, the dusty, lint-wisped black hat. So I reckon maybe everybody is satisfied now, he thought. Or everybody except one, he added to himself because before he reached the store

Will Varner came out of it and got onto the white horse which someone had just untied and held for him, and on the gallery beyond Ratliff now saw the eruption of men whose laden wagons stood along the road opposite, waiting for the scales, and as he drove up to the gallery in his turn, Mink Snopes and the other Snopes, the proverbist, the schoolteacher (he now wore a new frock coat which, for all its newness, looked no less like it belonged to him than the old one teacher, the two of them seeming to pass him in a whirling of in which Ratliff saw the intractable face now cold and still behind the single eyebrow; beside it the rodent's face of the teacher, the two of them seeming to pass him in a whirling of flung unco-ordinated hands and arms out of the new, black, swirling frock coat, the voice that, also like the gestures, seemed to be not servant but master of the body which supplied blood and wind to them:

"Be patient; Caesar never built Rome in one day; patience is the horse that runs steadiest; justice is the right man's bread but poison for the evil man if you give it time. I done looked the law up; Will Varner has misread it pure and simple. We'll take a appeal. We will—" until the other turned his furious face with its single violent emphasis of eyebrow upon him and said fiercely: "—t!" They went on. Ratliff moved up to the gallery. While he was tying his team, Houston came out, followed by the big hound, and mounted and rode away. Ratliff mounted to the gallery where now at least twenty men were gathered, Bookwright among them.

"The plaintiff seems to had legal talent," he said. "What was the verdict?"

"When Snopes pays Houston three dollars pasturage, he can get his bull," Quick said.

"Sho now," Ratliff said. "Wasn't this lawyer even allowed nothing by the court?"

"The lawyer was fined what looked like the considerable balance of one uncompleted speech," Bookwright said. "If that's what you want to know."

"Well well," Ratliff said. "Well well well. So Will couldn't do nothing to the next succeeding Snopes but stop him from talking. Not that any more would have done any good.

Snopes can come and Snopes can go, but Will Varner looks like he is fixing to snopes forever. Or Varner will Snopes forever—take your pick. What is it the fellow says: off with the old and on with the new; the old job at the old stand, maybe a new fellow doing the jobbing but it's the same old stern getting reamed out?" Bookwright was looking at him.

"If you would stand closer to the door, he could hear you a heap better," he said.

"Sholy," Ratliff said. "Big ears have little pitchers, the world beats a track to the rich man's hog-pen but it aint every family has a new layer, not to mention a prophet. Waste not want not, except that a full waist dont need no prophet to prophesy a profit and just whose." Now they were all watching him—the smooth, impenetrable face with something about the eyes and the lines beside the mouth which they could not read.

"Look here," Bookwright said. "What's the matter with you?"

"Why, nothing," Ratliff said. "What could be wrong with nothing nowhere nohow in this here best of all possible worlds? Likely the same folks that sells him the neckties will have a pair of long black stockings too. And any sign-painter can paint him a screen to set up alongside the bed to look like looking up at a wall full of store shelves of canned goods——"

"Here," Bookwright said.

"—so he can know to do what every man and woman that ever seen her between thirteen and Old Man Hundred-and-One McCallum has been thinking about for twenty-nine days now. Of course, he could fix it with a shed roof to climb up on and a window to crawl through too. But that aint neccessary; that aint his way. No sir. This here man aint no trifling eave-cat. This here man—" A little boy of eight or ten came up, trotting, in overalls, and mounted the steps and gave them a quick glance out of eyes as blue and innocent as periwinkles and trotted intently into the store. "—this here man that all he needs is just to set back there in the store until after a while one comes in to get a nickel's worth of lard, not buy it: come and ax Mr Snopes for it, and he gives it to her and writes in a book about it and her not knowing no more about what he wrote in that book and why than she does how that ere lard got into that tin bucket with the picture of a hog on it that even she can tell is a hog, and he puts the bucket back and puts the book away and goes and shuts the door and puts the bar up and she has done already went around behind the counter and laid down on the floor because maybe she thinks by now that's what you have to do, not to pay for the lard because that's done already been wrote down in the book, but to get out of that door again—" The new clerk appeared suddenly among them. He bounced out of the store, his features all seeming to hasten into the center of his face in a fierce depthless glare of bright excitement, the little periwinkle-eyed boy trotting intently around him and on down the steps without waiting.

"All right, boys," the clerk said rapidly, tensely. "He's started. You better hurry. I cant go this time. I got to stay here. Kind of make a swing around from the back so old Littlejohn cant see you. She's done already begun to look cross-eyed." Five or six men had already risen, with a curious, furtive, defiant sort of alacrity. They began to leave the gallery. The little boy was now tortting indefatigably along the fence which encloded the end of Mrs Littlejohn's lot.

"What's this?" Ratliff said.

"Come on, if you aint seen it yet," one of the departing men said.

"Seen what?" Ratliff said. He looked about at the ones who had not risen. Bookwright was one of them. He was whittling steadily and deeply into a stick of white pine, his face lowered.

"Go on, go on," a second said behind the man who had paused on the steps. "It'll be over before we get there." The group went on then. Ratliff watched them too hurry along Mrs Littlejohn's lot fence after the little boy, still with that curiously furtive defiance.

"What's this you all have got here now?" he said.

"Go and see it," Bookwright said harshly. He did not look up from his knife. Ratliff looked at him.

"Have you seen it?"

"No."

"You going to?"

"No."

"You know what it is?"

"Go on and see it," Bookwright said again, harshly and violently.

"It looks like I'll have to, since aint nobody going to tell me," Ratliff said. He moved toward the steps. The group was now well on ahead, hurrying along the fence. Ratliff began to descend. He was still talking. He continued to talk as he went down the steps, not looking back; nobody could have told whether he was actually talking to the men behind him or not, if he was talking to anyone or not: "—goes and puts the bar up on the inside and comes back and this here black brute from the field with the field sweat still drying on her that she dont know it's sweat she smells because she aint never smelled nothing else, just like a mule dont know it's mule he smells for the same reason, and the one garment to her name and that's the one she's laying there on the floor behind the counter in and looking up past him at them rows of little tight cans with fishes and devils on them that she dont know what's on the inside either because she aint never had the dime or the fifteen cents that even if he was to give her the nickel, not to mention the lard she come after, she would have after the next two or three times she come after lard, but just heard somewhere one day the name of what folks said was inside them, laying there and looking up at them every time his head would get out of the way long enough, and says, 'Mr Snopes, whut you ax fer dem sardines?' "

2

As winter became spring and the spring itself advanced, he had less and less of darkness to flee through and from. Soon it was dark only when he left the barn, backed carefully, with one down-groping foot, from the harness-room where his quilt-and-straw bed was, and turned his back on the long rambling loom of the house where last night's new drummer-faces snored on the pillows of the beds which he had now learned to make as well as Mrs Littlejohn could; by April it was the actual thin depthless suspension of false dawn itself, in which he could already see and know himself to be an entity solid and cohered in visibility instead of the uncohered all-sentience of fluid and nerve-springing terror alone and terribly free in the primal sightless inimicality. That was gone now. Now the terror existed only during that moment after the false dawn, that interval's second between it and the moment which birds and animals know: when the night at last succumbs to day; and then he would begin to hurry, trot, not to get there quicker but because he must get back soon, without fear and calmly now in the growing visibility, the gradation from gray through primrose to the morning's ultimate gold, to the brow of the final hill, to let himself downward into the creekside mist and lie in the drenched myriad waking life of grasses and listen for her approach.

Then he would hear her, coming down the creekside in the mist. It would not be after one hour, two hours, three; the dawn would be empty, the moment and she would not be, then he would hear her and he would lie drenched in the wet grass, serene and one and indivisible in joy, listening to her approach. He would smell her; the whole mist reeked with her; the same malleate hands of mist which drew along his prone drenched flanks palped her pearled barrel too and shaped them both somewhere in immediate time, already married. He would not move. He would lie amid the waking instant of earth's teeming life, the motionless fronds of water-heavy grasses stooping into the mist before his face in black, fixed curves, along each parabola of which the marching drops held in minute magnification the dawn's rosy miniatures, smelling and even tasting the rich, slow, warm barn-reek milk-reek, the flowing immemorial female, hearing the slow planting and the plopping suck of each deliberate cloven mud-spreading hoof, invisible still in the mist loud with its hymeneal choristers.

Then he would see her; the bright thin horns of morning, of sun, would blow the mist away and reveal her, planted, blond, dew-pearled, standing in the parted water of the ford, blowing into the water the thick, warm, heavy, milk-laden breath; and lying in the drenched grasses, his eyes now blind with sun, he would wallow faintly from thigh to thigh, making a faint, thick, hoarse moaning sound. Because he cannot make one with her through the day's morning and noon and evening. It is not that he must return to work. There is no work, no travail, no muscular and spiritual reluctance to overcome, constantly war against; yesterday was not, tomorrow is not, today is merely a placid and virginal astonishment at the creeping ridge of dust and trash in front of the broom, at sheets coming smooth and taut at certain remembered motions of the hands—a routine grooved, irkloss; a firm gentle compelling hand, a voice to hold and control him through joy out of kindness as a dog is taught and held.

It is because he can go no further. He tried it. It was the third time he lay and waited for her; the mist blew away and he saw her and this time there was no today even—no beds to return to, no hand, no voice: he repudiated fidelity and even habit. He rose and approached her, speaking to her, his hand extended. She raised her head and looked at him and scrambled up the further bank, out of the water. He followed, stepping gingerly down into the water, and began to cross, lifting his feet high at each step, moaning a little, urgent and concerned yet not to alarm her more. He fell once, at full length into the water, making no effort to catch himself, vanishing completely with one loud cry and rising again, streaming, his breath already indrawn to cry again. But he stopped the cry, speaking to her instead, and climbed out onto the bank and approached her again, his hand extended. This time she ran, rushed on a short distance and turned, her head lowered; she whirled and rushed away again before his hand touched her, he following, speaking to her, urgent and cajoling. Finally she broke back past him and went back to the ford. She ran faster than he could; trotting, moaning, he watched the vain stippling of leaf-shadows as they fled across the intact and escaping shape of love as the recrossed the creek and galloped on up the path for a short way, where once more the stopped to graze.

He ceased to moan. He hurried back to the creek and began to cross it, lifting his feet high out of the water at each step as if he expected each time to find solidity there, or perhaps at each step did not know whether he would or not. This time he did not fall. but as soon as he climbed the bank, she moved again, on up the path, not galloping now but purposefully, so that he once more had to run, once more steadily losing ground, moaning again now with that urgent and now alarmed and bewildered amazement. She was now retracing the path by which she had appeared that morning and all the other mornings. Probably he did not even know it, was paying no attention at all to where he was going, seeing nothing but the cow; perhaps he did not even realise they were in the lot, even when she went on across it and entered the milking shed which she had left less than an hour ago, though he probably knew generally where she would come from each morning, since he knew most of the adjacent countryside and was never disoriented: objects became fluid in darkness but they did not alter in place and juxtaposition. Perhaps he did not even comprehend that she was in her stable, in any stable, but only that she had stopped at last, ceased to flee at last, because at once he stopped the alarmed and urgent moaning and followed her into the shed, speaking to her again, murmurous, drooling, and touched her with his hand. She whirled; possibly he saw, not that she could not, but only that she did not flee. He touched her again, his hand, his voice, thin and hungry with promise. Then he was lying on his back, her heels were still thudding against the plank wall beside his head and then the dog was standing over him and an instant later the man was hauling him savagely to his feet by the slack of his shirt. Then he was outside the shed while Houston still clutched him by the shirt and cursed in what he could not know was not rage but angry exasperation. The dog stood a few feet away, watching.

"Ike H-mope," he said. "Ike H-mope."

"Ike hell," Houston said, cursing, shaking him. "Go on!" he said. "Git!" He spoke to the dog. "Take him out of here. Easy, now." Now the dog shouted at him. It did not move yet, it merely shouted once; it was as if it said "Boo!" and, still moaning, trying now to talk to the man with his blasted eyes, he moved on toward the still-open gate which he had just entered. Now the dog moved too, just behind him. He looked back at the shed, the cow; he tried again to speak to the man with his eyes, moaning, drooling, when the dog shouted at him again, once, taking one pace toward him but no more, whereupon he gave the dog one terrified glance and broke, trotting toward the gate. The dog shouted again, three times in rapid succession, and he cried now, hoarse and abject, running now, the thick reluctant hips working with a sort of abject and hopeless unco-ordination. "Easy, now!" Houston shouted. He did not hear. He heard only the feet of the dog just behind him. He ran heavily, bellowing.

So now he can go no further. He can lie in the grass and wait for her and hear her and then see her when the mist parts, and that is all. So he would rise from the grass and stand, still swaying faintly from side to side and making the faint, hoarse sound. Then he would turn and mount the hill, stumbling a little because his eyes were still full of sun yet. But his bare feet would know the dust of the road, and in it again, he would begin to trot again, hurrying, still moaning, his shadow shortening on the dust ahead and the mounting sun warm on his back and already drying the dust on his damp overalls; and so back to the house, the littered rooms and the unmade beds. Soon he would be sweeping again, stopping only occasionally to make the hoarse sound of bafflement and incredulous grieving, then watching again with peaceful and absorbed astonishment the creeping ridge of dust and trash before the moving broom. Because even while sweeping he would still see her, blond among the purpling shadows of the pasture, not fixed amid the suppurant tender green but integer of spring's concentrated climax, by it crowned, garlanded.

He was upstairs sweeping when he saw the smoke. He knew exactly where it was—the hill, the sedge-and-brier overgrown hill beyond the creek. Although it was three miles away, he can even see her backing away before the flames and hear her bellowing. He began to run where he stood, carrying the broom. He ran blundering at the wall, the high small window through which he had seen the smoke, which he could not have passed through even if he could have taken the eighteen-foot drop to the earth, as a moth or a trapped bird might. Then the corridor door was facing him and without pausing he ran to it and through it, still carrying the broom, and on down the corridor toward the stairs, when Mrs Littlejohn emerged from a second bedroom and stopped him. "You, Isaac," she said. "You, Isaac." She did not raise her voice and she did not touch him, yet he stopped, moaning, the empty eyes striving at her, picking his feet up in turn like a cat standing on something hot. Then she put her hand out and took him by the shoulder and turned him and he went obediently back up the corridor and into the room again, moaning; he even made a stroke or two with the broom before he saw the smoke again through the window. This time he found the corridor door almost at once, though he did not approach it. Instead he stood for a moment, looking at the broom in his hands, whimpering, then at the bed, smooth and neat where he had just made it up, and he stopped whimpering and went to the bed and turned the covers back and put the broom into it, the straw end on the pillow like a face, and drew the covers up smooth again, tucking them about the broom with that paradoxical unco-ordinated skill and haste, and left the room.

He made no sound now. He did not move on tiptoe, yet he went down the corridor with astonishing silence and celerity; he had reached the stairs and begun to descend before Mrs Littlejohn could have emerged from the other room. At first, three years ago, he would not try to descend them. He had ascended them alone; nobody ever knew if he had walked or crawled up, or if perhaps he had mounted them without realising he was doing so, altering his position in altitude, depth perception not functioning in reverse. Mrs Littlejohn had gone to the store. Someone passing the house heard him and when she returned there were five or six people in the hall, looking up at where he clung to the rail at the top step, his eyes shut, bellowing. He still clung to the rail, bellowing and tugging back, when she tried to break his grip and draw him downward. He stayed upstairs three days while she carried food to him and people would come in from miles away and say, "Aint you got him down yet?" before she finally coaxed him to attempt to descend. And even then it took several minutes, while faces gathered in the lower hall to watch as the firm, gentle, unremitting hand, the cold, grim, patient voice, drew him, clinging to the rail and bellowing, step by step downward. For a while after that he would fall down them each time he tried to descend. He would know he was going to fall; he would step blindly and already moaning onto nothing and plunge, topple, sprawling and bumping, terrified not by pain but by amazement, to lie at last on the floor of the lower hall, bellowing, his blasted eyes staring aghast and incredulous at nothing.

But at last he learned to negotiate them. Now he merely slowed a little before stepping, not confidently quite but not with alarm, off onto that which at each successive step, was not quite space; was almost nothing but at each advancing instant, not quite was, and hurried on through the lower hall and into the back yard, where he paused again and began to sway from side to side and moan, his empty face now filled with baffled bewilderment. Because he could not see the smoke from here and now all he remembers is the empty dawn-hill from which he will let himself downward into the creekside mist to wait for her, and it is wrong now. Because he stands in sun, visible—himself, earth, trees, house—already cohered and fixed in visibility; no darkness to flee through and from, and this is wrong. So he stood, baffled, moaning and swaying for a time, then he moved again, across the yard to the lot gate. He had learned to open it too. He turned the catch and the gate vanished from between its two posts; he passed through and after a moment he found the gate where it had swung to against the fence and closed it and turned the latch and went on across the sun-glared lot, moaning, and entered the hallway of the stable.

Because of his sun-contracted pupils, he could not see at once. But then, it always was dark when he entered the stable on his way to bed, so at once he ceased to moan and went straight to the door to the harness-room, moving now with actual assurance, and grasped the door-jamb with both hands and raised his foot to the step, and, his down-groping foot already on the ground, he backed out of darkness and into visibility, turning, visibility roaring soundless down about him, establishing him intact and cohered in it and already trotting, running, toward the crest where he will let himself downward into the creekside mist to lie and wait for her, on across the lot and through the spread place in the wire fence. His overalls snagged on the wire but he ripped free, making no sound now, and into the road, running, his thick female thighs working, his face, his eyes, urgent and alarmed.

When he reached the hill three miles away, he was still trotting; when he turned from the road and mounted to the crest of the hill and saw the smoke beyond the creek, he made the hoarse, aghast sound again and ran on down the hill and through the now-dry grass in which at dawn he had lain, and to the creek, the ford. He did not hesitate. He ran full-tilt off the bank and onto the rimpled water, continuing to run even after he began to fall, plunging face-down into the water, completely submerged, and rose, streaming, knee-deep, bellowing. He lifted one foot above the surface and stepped forward as though onto a raised floor and took another step running before he fell. This time his outflung hands touched the further bank and this time when he rose he actually heard the cow's voice, faint and terrified, from beyond the smokepall on the other hill. He raised one foot above the surface and ran again. When he fell this time he lay on dry land. He scrambled up and ran in his sodden overalls, across the pasture and on up the other hill, on whose crest and smokepall lay without wind, grading from blue to delicate mauve and lilac and then copper beneath the meridional sun.

A mile back he had left the rich, broad, flat river-bottom country and entered the hills—a region which topographically was the final blue and dying echo of the Appalachian Mountains. Chickasaw Indians had owned it, but after the Indians it had been cleared where possible for cultivation, and after the Civil War, forgotten save by small peripatetic sawmills which had vanished too now, their sites marked only by the mounds of rotting sawdust which were not only their gravestones but the monuments of a people's heedless greed. Now it was a region of scrubby second-growth pine and oak among which dogwood bloomed until it too was cut to make cotton spindles, and old fields where not even a trace of furrow showed any more, gutted and gullied by forty years of rain and frost and heat into plateaus choked with rank sedge and briers loved of rabbits and quail coveys, and crumbling ravines striated red and white with alternate sand and clay. It was toward one of these plateaus that he now ran, running in ashes without knowing it since the earth here had had time to cool, running among the blackened stubble of last year's sedge dotted with small islands of this year's incombustible green and the blasted heads of tiny blue-and-white daisies, and so onto the crest of the hill, the plateau.

The smoke lay like a wall before him; beyond it he could hear the steady terrified bellowing of the cow. He ran into the smoke toward the voice. The earth was now hot to his feet. He began to snatch them quickly up; he cried once himself, hoarse and amazed, whereupon, as though in answer, the smoke, the circumambience itself, screamed back at him. The sound was everywhere, above and beneath, funnelling downward at him; he heard the hooves and as he paused, his breath indrawn, the horse appeared, materialised furiously out of the smoke, monstrous and distorted, wild-eyed and with tossing mane, bearing down upon him. He screamed too. For an instant they yelled face to face, the wild eyes, the yellow teeth, the long gullet red with ravening gleeful triumph, stooping at him and then on as the horse swerved without breaking, the wind, the fierce dragon-reek of its passage, blasting at his hair and garments; it was gone. He ran again toward the cow's voice. When he heard the horse behind him again he did not even look back. He did not even scream again. He just ran, running, as again the earth, the smoke, filled and became thunderous with the hard, rapid hoofbeats and again the intolerable voice screamed down at him and he flung both arms about his head and fell sprawling as the wind, the dragon-reek, blasted at him again as the maddened horse soared over his prone body and vanished once more.

He scrambled up and ran. The cow was quite near now and now he saw the fire—a tender, rosy, creeping thread low in the smoke between him and the location of the cow's voice. Each time his feet touched the earth now he gave a short shriek like an ejaculation, trying to snatch his foot back before it could have taken his weight, then turning immediately in aghast amazement to the other foot which he had for the moment forgotten, so that presently he was not progressing at all but merely moving in one spot, like a dance, when he heard the horse coming at him again. He screamed. His voice and that of the horse became one voice, wild, furious and without hope, and he ran into and through the fire and burst into air, sun, visibility again, shedding flames which sucked away behind him like a tattered garment. The cow stood at the edge of a ravine about ten feet away, facing the fire, her head lowered, bellowing. He had just time to reach her and turn, his body intervened and his arms about his head, as the frantic horse burst out of the smoke and bore down upon them.

It did not even swerve. It took off almost without gathering, at full stride. The teeth, the wild eyes, the long red gullet, stooped at him, framed out of a swirled rigidity of forelock and mane, the entire animal floating overhead in monstrous deliberation. The air was filled with furious wings and the four crescent-glints of shod hooves as, still screaming, the horse vanished beyond the ravine's lip, sucking first the cow and then himself after it as though by the violent vacuum of its passing. Earth became perpendicular and fled upward—the yawn of void without even the meretricious reassurance of graduated steps. He made no sound as the three of them plunged down the crumbling sheer, at the bottom of which the horse rolled to its feet without stopping and galloped on down the ditch and where he, lying beneath the struggling and bellowing cow, received the violent relaxing of her fear-constricted bowels. Overhead, in the down draft of the ravine, the last ragged flame tongued over the lip, tip-curled, and vanished, swirled off into the windless stain of pale smoke on the sunny sky.

At first he couldn't do anything with her at all. She scrambled to her feet, facing him, her head lowered, bellowing. When he moved toward her, she whirled and ran at the crumbling sheer of the slope, scrambling furiously at the vain and shifting sand as though in a blind paroxysm of shame, to escape not him alone but the very scene of the ouragement of privacy where she had been sprung suddenly upon and without warning from the dark and betrayed and outraged by her own treacherous biological inheritance, he following again, speaking to her, trying to tell her how this violent violation of her maiden's delicacy is no shame, since such is the very iron imperishable warp of the fabric of love. But she would not hear. She continued to scrabble at the shifting rise, until at last he set his shoulder to the hams and heaved forward. Striving together, they mounted for a yard or so up the slope, the sand shifting and fleeing beneath their feet, before momentum and strength were spent and, locked together and motionless, they descended once more to the floor of the ditch, planted and fixed ankle-deep in a moving block of sand like two effigies on a float. Again, his shoulder to her hams, they rushed at the precipice and up it for a yard or more before the treacherous footing completely failed. He spoke to her, exhortative; they made a supreme effort. But again the earth fled upward; footing, sand and all plucked violently from beneath them and rushed upward into the pale sky still faintly stained with smoke, and once more they lay inextricable and struggling on the floor of the ravine, he once more underneath, until, bellowing and never ceasing her mad thrashing, the cow scrambled up and galloped on down the ditch as the horse had done, vanishing before he could get to his feet to follow.

The ravine debouched onto the creek. Almost at once he was in the pasture again, though possibly he did not realise it, seeing only the cow as she galloped on ahead. Possibly at the moment he did not even recognise the ford at once, even when the cow, slowing, walked down into the water and stopped and drank and he ran up, slowing too, moaning, urgent but not loud, not to send her once more into flight. So he approaches the bank, stilling his voice now, picking his feet up and putting them down again in one spot, his singed and scorched face urgent and tense. But she does not move, and at last he steps down into the water, onto the water, forgetting again that it will give under his weight, crying once again not so much in surprise as in alarm lest he alarm her, and steps again forward onto the receptive solid, and touches her. She does not even stop drinking; his hand has lain on her flank for a second or two before she lifts her dripping muzzle and looks back at him, once more maiden meditant, shame-free.

Houston found them there. He came across the pasture on the horse, bareback, galloping, the hound following, and saw the thick squatting shape in the water behind the cow, clumsily washing her legs with a broken willow branch. "Is she all right?" he shouted, speaking to the horse to slow it since he did not even have a hackamore: "Whoa. Whoa. Ho now. Ho now, damn you.—Why in hell didn't you try to catch the horse?" he shouted. "He might have broke—" Then the other, squatting in the water, turned his scorched face and Houston recognised him. He began to curse, checking the horse with his hand in its mane, already flinging his leg over and sliding down before the horse stopped, cursing with that fretted exasperation which was not anger, rage. He came to the creek, the hound following, and stooped and caught up a dried limb left from last winter's flood water and slashed the cow savagely with it and flung the broken end after her as she sprang forward and scrambled up the further bank. "Git!" Houston shouted. "Git on home, you damn whore!" The cow galloped on a few steps, then stopped and began to graze. "Take her home," Houston said to the dog. Without moving, only raising its head, the hound bayed once. The cow jerked her head up and trotted again, and he in the creek made again his faint hoarse sound, rising too as the hound rose. But the dog did not even cross the creek, it did not even hurry; it merely followed the bank until it came opposite the cow and bayed again, once, contemptuous and peremptory. This time the cow went off at a gallop, back up the creek toward the lot, the hound following on its side of the creek. They went ouf of sight so. Twice more at invervals the hound bayed, one time, as though it merely shouted "Boo!" each time the cow prepared to stop.

He stood in the water, moaning. Now he actually bellowed himself, not loud, just amazed. When Houston and the dog came up he had looked around, at first at the dog. His mouth had opened to cry then, but insisted there had come into his face an expression almost intelligent in its foolish fatuity, which, when Houston began to curse, faded and became one of incredulity, amazement, and which was still incredulous and bereft as he stood in the water, moaning, while Houston on the bank looked at the stained foul front of his overalls, cursing with that baffled exasperation, saying, "Jesus Christ. Jesus Christ.—Come here," he said. "Get out of there;" gesturing his arm savagely. But the other did not move, moaning, looking away up the creek where the cow had gone, until Houston came to the edge and leaned and caught him by the strap of his overalls and drew him roughly out of the water and, his nose wrinkled fiercely and still cursing, unfastened the straps and snatched the overalls down about his hips. "Step out!" Houston said. But he did not move until Houston jerked him, stumbling, out of the overalls, to stand in his shirt and nothing else, moaning faintly, though when Houston picked up the overalls gingerly by the strap and flung them into the creek, he cried again, once, hoarse, abject, not loud. "Go on," Houston said. "Wash them." He made violent washing motions in pantomine. But the other only looked at Houston, moaning, until Houston found another stick and twisted it into the overalls and soused and walloped them violently in the water, cursing steadily, and drew them out and, still using the stick, scrubbed them front-down on the grass. "There," he said. "Now git! Home! Home!" he shouted. "Stay there! Let her alone!" He had stopped moaning to watch Houston. Now he began to moan again, drooling, while Houston glared at him in baffled and raging exasperation. Then Houston took a handful of coins from his pocket and chose a fifty-cent piece and came and put it into his shirt pocket and buttoned the flap and went back to the horse, speaking to it until he touched it, grasped it by the mane, and vaulted onto its back. He had stopped moaning now, he just watched as, again without seeming to gather itself, just as when it had soared above him and the cow on the edge of the ravine an hour ago, the horse made two short circles under Houston's hand and then took the creek cleanly, already galloping, and was gone.

Then he began to moan again. He stood for a while, moaning, looking down at the shirt pocket which Houston had buttoned, fumbling at it. Then he looked at his soaked and wadded overalls on the ground beside him. After a while he stooped and picked them up. One leg was turned wrong-side-outward. He tried patiently for a while to put them on so, moaning. Then presently they came straight again and he got into them and fastened the straps and went to the creek and crossed, moving gingerly, raising his foot at each step as if he were mounting onto a raised floor, and climbed out and went back to the place where he had lain at each dawn for three months now, waiting for her. It was the same spot; he would return as exactly to it each time as a piston to its cylinder-head, and he stood there for a time, fumbling at the buttoned pocket, moaning. Then he went on up the hill; his feet knew the dust of the road again though perhaps he himself was unaware of it, possibly it was pure instinct functioning in the desolation of bereavement which carried him back toward the house which he had left that morning, because twice more in the first mile he stopped and fumbled at the buttoned pocket. Apparently he was not trying to unbutton the pocket without being able to do it, because presently he had the coin in his hand, looking at it, moaning. He was standing then on a plank bridge over a narrow, shallow, weed-choked ditch. He made no false motion with the hand which held the coin, he had made no motion of any kind, he was standing perfectly still at the moment, yet suddenly his palm was empty. The coin rang dully once on the dusty planks and perhaps glinted once, then vanished, though who to know what motion, infinitesimal and convulsive, of supreme repudiation there might have been, its impulse gone, vanished with the movement, because he even ceased to moan as he stood looking at his empty palm with quiet amazement, turning the hand over to look at the back, even raising and opening the other hand to look into it. Then—it was an effort almost physical, like childbirth—he connected two ideas, he progressed backward into time and recaptured an image by logical retrogression and fumbled into the shirt pocket again, peering into it, though only for a moment, as if he actually did not expect to find the coin there, though it was doubtless pure instinct which caused him to look down at the dusty planks on which he stood. And he was not moaning. He made no sound at all. He just stood there, looking at the planks, lifting his feet in turn; when he stepped off the bridge and into the ditch, he fell. You could not have told if he did step off intentionally or if he fell off, though it was doubtless a continuation of the instinct, the inherited constant awareness of gravity, which caused him to look under the bridge for the coin—if he were looking for it as he squatted in the weeds, bobbing his head faintly yet still making no sound. From then on he made no sound at all. He squatted for a time, pulling at the weeds, and now even the paradoxical dexterity was missing from his movements, even the dexterity which caused his hands to function at other times as though in spite of him; watching him you would have said he did not want to find the coin. And then you would have said, known, that he did not intend to find it; when after a time a wagon came up the road and crossed the bridge and the driver spoke to him, when he raised his face it was not even empty, it was unfathomable and profoundly quiet; when the man spoke his name, he did not even reply with the one sound which he knew, or at least was ever known to make, and that infallibly when anyone spoke to him.

He did not move until the wagon was out of sight, though he was not watching it. Then he rose and climbed back into the road. He was already trotting, back in the direction from which he had just come, treading his own tracks into the hot dust of the road beneath the May noon, back to where he would leave the road to mount the hill, and crossed the hill again and trotted down the slope to the creek. He passed the place where he would lie in the wet grass each dawn without even looking at it and turned on up the creek, trotting. It was then about two oclock Saturday afternoon. He could not have known that at that hour and day Houston, a childless widower who lived alone with the hound and a Negro man to cook for them both, would already be sitting on the gallery of Varner's store three miles away; he could not have thought that maybe Houston would not be at home. Certainly he did not pause to find out. He entered the lot, trotting, he went straight to the closed door of the shed. There was a halter hanging from a nail beside it. Perhaps he merely put his hand on the halter by chance in fumbling at the latch. But he put it on the cow properly, as he had seen it done.

At six oclock that afternoon they were five miles away. He did not know it was that distance. It did not matter; there is no distance in either space or geography, no prolongation of time for distance to exist in, no muscular fatigue to establish its accomplishment. They are moving not toward a destination in space but a destination in time, toward the pinnacle-keep of evening where morning and afternoon become one; the sleight hand of May shapes them both, not in the immediate, the soon, but in the now as, facing her, braced against the pull of the rope, he speaks to her implacable and compelling while she tugs back, shaking her head against the rope and bellowing. She had been doing this for the last half hour, drawn backward and barnward by the discomfort of her bag. but he held her, slacking the rope gradually until his other hand touched her, first her head then her neck, speaking to her until the resistance went out of her and she moved on again. They were in the hills now, among pines. Although the afternoon wind had fallen, the shaggy crests still made a constant murmuring sound in the high serene air. The trunks and the massy foliage were the harps and strings of afternoon; the barred inconstant shadow of the day's retrograde flowed steadily over them as they crossed the ridge and descended into shadow, into the azure bowl of evening, the windless well of night; the portcullis of sunset fell behind them. At first she would not let him touch her bag at all. Even then she kicked him once, but only because the hands were strange and clumsy. Then the milk came down, warm among his fingers and on his hands and wrists, making a thin sharp hissing on the earth.

There was a moon at that time. It waned nightly westward; juxtaposed to it, each dawn the morning star burned in fierce white period to the night, and he would smell the waking's instant as she would rise, hindquarters first, backing upward out of invisibility, attenuating then disseminating out of the nest-form of sleep, the smell of milk. Then he would rise too and tie the rope-end to a swinging branch and seek and find the basket by the smell of the feed which it contained last night, and depart. From the edge of the woods he would look back. She would be still invisible, but he could hear her; it was as though he can see her—the warm breath visible among the tearing roots of grass, the warm reek of the urgent milk a cohered shape amid the fluid and abstract earth.

The barn is less than a half mile away. Soon it looms, forthright and square upon the scroll and cryptogram of heaven. The dog meets him at the fence, not barking, furrowing invisibility somewhere between sight and sound, moving completely in neither. On the first morning it rushed at him, yapping furiously. He stopped then. Perhaps he remembered that other dog five miles away, but only for a moment, since such is succeeding's success, such is that about victory which out-odors the betraying stink of all past defeats: so that now it comes up to him already fawning, invisible and fluid about his walking legs, its warm wet limber tongue shaping for him out of invisibility his own swinging hand.

In the ammoniac density of the barn, filled with the waking dawn-sounds of horses and cattle, he cannot even sense space. But he does not hesitate. He finds the crib door and enters; his sightless hand which knows and remembers finds the feed-box. He sets the basket down and begins to fill it, working steadily and fast, spilling half of what his cupped hands raise, as on the two preceding mornings establishing between feed-box and basket the agent of his own betrayal. When he rises and faces the door, he can see it now, gray, lighter in tone yet paradoxically no more luminous, as if a rectangle of opaque glass had been set into nothing's self while his back was turned, to further confound obscurity. And now he becomes aware of the birds. The cattle-sounds are louder now, constant; he can actually see the dog waiting in the stable door and he knows that he should hurry, since he knows that soon someone will come to feed and milk. So he leaves the crib, pausing for a moment in the door before descending as though he were listening, breathing in the reek, the odor of cows and mares as the successful lover does that of a room full of women, his the victor's drowsing rapport with all anonymous faceless female flesh capable of love walking the female earth.

He and the dog recross the lot together in the negative dawn-washed cacophonous and loud with birds. He can see the fence now, where the dog leaves him. He climbs through the fence, hurrying now, carrying the basket awkwardly before him in both arms, leaving in the wet grass a dark fixed wake. Now he watches the recurrence of that which he discovered for the first time three days ago: that dawn, light, is not decanted onto earth from the sky, but instead is from the earth itself suspired. Roofed by the woven canopy of blind annealing grass-roots and the roots of trees, dark in the blind dark of time's slit and rich refuse—the constant and unslumbering anonymous worm-glut and the inextricable known bones—Troy's Helen and the nymphs and the snoring mitred bishops, the saviors and the victims and the kings—it wakes, upseeping, attrive in unaccountable creeping channels: first, root; then front by frond, from whose escaping tips like gas it rises and disseminates and stains the sleep-fast earth with drowsy insect-murmur; then, still upward-seeking, creeps the knitted bark of trunk and limb where, suddenly louder leaf by leaf and dispersive in diffusive sudden speed, melodious with the winged and jeweled throats, it upward bursts and fills night's globed negation with jonquil thunder. Far below, the gauzy hemisphere treads with herald-cock, and sty and pen and byre salute the day. Vanes on steeples groove the southwest wind, and fields for plowing, since sunset married to the bedded and unhorsed plow, spring into half-furrowed sight like the slumbering half-satiate sea. Then the sun itself: within the half-mile it overtakes him. The silent copper roar fires ned grass and flings long before him his shadow prone for the vain eluded treading; the earth mirrors his antic and constant frustration which soars up the last hill and, motionless in the void, hovers until he himself crests over, whereupon it drops an invisible bridge across the ultimate ebb of night and, still preceding him, leaps visible once more across the swale and touches the corpse itself, shortening into the nearing leafy wall, head: shoulders: hips: and then the trotting legs, until at last it stands upright upon the mazy whimple of the windy leaves for one intact inconstant instant before he runs into and through it.

She stands as he left her, tethered, chewing. Within the mind enoromus moist and pupilless globes he sees himself in twin miniature mirrored by the inscrutable abstraction; one with that which Juno might have looked out with, he watches himself contemplating what those who looked at Juno saw. He sets the basket before her. She begins to eat. The shifting shimmer of incessant leaves gives to her a quality of illusion as insubstantial as the prone negative of his late hurrying, but this too is not so: one blond touch stipulates and affirms both weight and mass out of the flowing shadow-maze; a hand's breadth of contact shapes her solid and whole out of the infinity of hope. He squats beside her and begins to draw the teats.

They eat from the basket together. He has eaten feed before—hulls and meal, and oats and raw corn and silage and pig-swill, never much at one time but more or less constantly while he is awake as birds do, eating not even very much of the filled plate which Mrs Littlejohn would set for him, leaving it less than half-emptied, then an hour later eating something else, anything else, things which the weary long record of shibboleth and superstition had taught his upright kind to call filth, neither liking nor disliking the taste of any thing save that of certain kinds of soil and the lime in old plaster and the dissolved ink in chewed nesspapers and the formic acid of stinging ants, making but one discrimination: he is herbivorous, even the life he eats in the life of plants. Then he removed the basket. It was not empty. It contained yet almost to the measured ounce exactly half of the original feed, but he takes it away from her, drags it from beneath the swinging muzzle which continues to chew out of the center of surprise, and hangs it over a limb, who is learning fast now, who has learned success and then precaution and secrecy and how to steal and even providence; who has only lust and greed and bloodthirst and a moral conscience to keep him awake at night, yet to acquire.

They go first to the spring. He found it on the first day—a brown creep of moisture in a clump of alder and beech, sunless, which wandered away without motion among the unsunned roots of other alders and willows. He cleaned it out and scooped a basin for it, which now at each return of light stood full and clear and leaf by leaf repeating until they lean and interrupt the green reflections and with their own drinking faces break each's mirroring, each face to its own shattered image wedded and annealed. Then he rises and takes up the rope, and they go on across the swale, toward the woods, and enter them.

Dawn is now over. It is now bald and forthright day. The sun is well up the sky. The air is still loud with birds, but the cries are no longer the mystery's choral strophe and antistrophe rising vertical among the leafed altars, but are earth-parallel, streaking the lateral air in prosaic busy accompaniment to the prosaic business of feeding. They dart in ceaseless arrowings, tinted and electric, among the pines whose shaggy crests murmur dry and incessant in the high day wind. Now he slacks the rope; from now until evening they will advance only as the day itself advances, no faster. They have the same destination: sunset. They pursue it as the sun itself does and within the compass of one single immutable horizon. They pace the ardent and unheeding sun, themselves unheeding and without ardor among the shadows of the soaring trunks which are the sun-geared ratchet-spokes which wheel the axled earth, powerful and without haste, up out of the caverns of darkness, through dawn and morning and mid-morning, and on toward and at last into the slowing neap of noon, the flood, the slack of peak and crown of light garlanding all within one single coronet the fallen and unregenerate seraphim. The sun is a yellow column, perpendicular. He bears it on his back as, stooping with that thick, reluctant unco-ordination of thigh and knee, he gathers first the armful of lush grass, then the flowers. They are the bright blatant wild daisies of flamboyant summer's spenthrift beginning. At times his awkward and disobedient hand, instead of breaking the stem, merely shuts about the escaping stalk and strips the flower-head into a scatter of ravished petals. But before he reaches the windless noon-bound shade in which she stands, he has enough of them. He has more than enough; if he had only gathered two of them, there would have been too many: he lays the plucked grass before her, then out of the clumsy fumbling of the hands there emerges, already in dissolution, the abortive diadem. In the act of garlanding, it disintegrates, rains down the slant of brow and chewing head; fodder and flowers become one inexhaustible rumination. From the sliding rhythm of the jaws depends one final blossom.

That afternoon it rained. It came without warning and it did not last long. He watched it for some time and without alarm, wanton and random and indecisive before it finally developed, concentrated, drooping in narrow unperpendicular bands in two or three different places at one time, about the horizon, like gauzy umbilical loops from the bellied cumulae, the sun-bellied ewes of summer grazing up the wind from the southwest. It was as if the rain were actually seeking the two of them, hunting them out where they stood amid the shade, finding them finally in a bright intransegent fury. The pine-snoring wind dropped, then gathered; in an anticlimax of complete vacuum the shaggy pelt of earth became overblown like that of a receptive mare for the rampant crash, the furuios brief fecundation which, still, rampant, seeded itself in flash and glare of noise and fury and then was gone, vanished; then the actual rain, from a sky already breaking as if of its own rich over-fertile weight, running in a wild lateral turmoil among the unrecovered leaves, not in drops but in needles of fiery ice which seemed to be not trying to fall but, immune to gravity, earthless, were merely trying to keep pace with the windy uproar which had begotten and foaled them, striking in thin brittle strokes through his hair and shirt and against his lifted face, each brief lance already filled with the glittering promise of its imminent cessation like the brief bright saltless tears of a young girl over a lost flower; then gone too, fled north and eastward beyond the chromatic arch of its own insubstantial armistice, leaving behind it the spent confetti of its carnival to gather and drip leaf by leaf and twig by twig then blade by blade of grass, to gather in murmurous runnels, releasing in mirrored repetition the sky which, glint by glint of fallen gold and blue, the falling drops had prisoned.

It was over at last. He takes up the rope again and they move out from beneath the tree and go on, moving no faster than before but for the first time since they entered the woods, with purpose. Because it is nearing sunset. Although the rain had not seemed to last long, yet now it is as if there had been something in that illogical and harmless sound and fury which abrogated even the iron schedule of grooved and immutable day as the abrupt unplumbable tantrum of a child, the very violence of which is its own invincible argument against protraction, can somehow seem to set the clock up. He is soaking wet. His overalls are heavy and dank and cold upon him—the sorry refuse, the scornful lees of glory—a lifeless chill which is no kin to the vivid wet of the living water which has carried into and still retains within the very mud, the boundless freedom of the golden air as that same air glitters in the leaves and branches which globe in countless minute repetition the intact and iridescent cosmos. They walk in splendor. Joined by the golden skein of the wet grass rope, they move in single file toward the ineffable effulgence, directly into the sun. They are still pacing it. They mount the final ridge. They will arrive together. At the same moment all three of them cross the crest and descend into the bowl of evening and are extinguished.

The rapid twilight effaces them from the day's tedious recording. Original, in the womb-dimension, the unavoidable first and the inescapable last, eyeless, they descend the hill. He finds the basket by smell and lifts it down from the limb and sets it before her. She nuzzles into it, blowing the sweet breath-reek into the sweetish reek of feed until they become indistinguishable with that of the urgent and unimpatient milk as it flows among and about his fingers, hands, wrists, warm and indivisible as the strong inexhaustible life ichor itself, inherently, of itself, renewing. Then he leaves the invisible basket where he can find it again at dawn, and goes to the spring. Now he can see again. Again his head interrupts, then replaces as once more he breaks with drinking the reversed drinking of his drowned and fading image. It is the well of days, the still and insatiable aperture of earth. It holds in tranquil paradox of suspended precipitation dawn, noon, and sunset; yesterday, today, and tomorrow—star-spawn and hieroglyph, the fierce white dying rose, then gradual and invincible speeding up to and into slack-flood's coronal of nympholept noon. Then ebb's afternoon, until at last the morning, noon, and afternoon flow back, drain the sky and creep leaf by voiceless leaf and twig and branch and trunk, descending, gathering frond by frond among the grass, still creeping downward in drowsy insect murmurs, until at last the complete all of light gathers about that still and tender mouth in one last expiring inhalation. He rises. The swale is constant with random and erratic fireflies. There is the one fierce evening star, though almost at once the marching constellations mesh and gear and wheel strongly on. Blond too in that gathered last of light, she owns no dimension against the lambent and undimensional grass. But she is there, solid amid the abstract earth. He walks lightly upon it, returning, treading lightly that frail inextricable canopy of the subterrene slumber—Helen and the bishops, the kings and the graceless seraphim. When he reaches her, she has already begun to lie down—first the forequarters, then the hinder ones, lowering herself in two distinct stages into the spent ebb of evening, nestling back into the nest-form of sleep, the mammalian attar. They lie down together.

3

It was after sunset when Houston returned home and missed the cow. He was a widower, without family. Since the death of his wife three or four years ago, the cow was the only female creature on the place, obviously. He even had a man cook, a Negro, who did the milking too, but on this Saturday the Negro had asked permission to attend a picnic of his race, promising to be back in plenty of time to milk and get supper too—a statement in which Houston naturally put no credence at all. Indeed, except for a certain monotonous recapitulation about the promise which finally began to impinge on him, he might not have returned home at all that night and so would not have missed the cow until the next day.

As it was, he returned home just after sunset, not for food, the presence or lack of which meant nothing to him, but to milk the cow, the prospect and necessity of which had been facing him and drawing nearer and nearer all afternoon. Because of this, he had drunk a little more than his customary Saturday afternoon quantity, which (a man naturally of a moody, though robustly and healthily so, habit) in conjunction with the savage fixation about females which the tragic circumstances of his bereavement had created in him, and the fact that not only must he return and establish once more physical contact with the female world which three years ago he had abjured but the time this would require would be that (the hour between sunset and dark) one of the entire day's hierarchy which he could least bear—when the presence of his dead wife and sometimes even that of the son which they had never had, would be everywhere about the house and the place—left him in no very predictable frame of mind when he went to the cowshed and found the cow gone.

He thought at first that she had merely continued to bump and butt at the door until the latch turned and allowed it to open. But even then he was surprised that the discomfort of her bag had not fetched her, waiting and even lowing, at the lot gate before he arrived. But she was not there, and cursing her (and himself for having neglected to close the gate which led to the creek pasture) he called the hound and took the path back to the creek. It was not yet full dark. He could (and did) see tracks, though when he did notice the prints of the man's bare feet, the cow's prints superposed, so he merely took the two sets of tracks to be six hours apart and not six feet. But primarily he did not bother with the tracks because he was convinced he knew where the cow was, even when the hound turned from the creek at the ford and bore away up the hill. He shouted it angrily back. Even when it paused and looked back at him in grave and intelligent surprise, he still acted out of that seething conviction born of drink and exasperation and the old strong uncompromising grief, shouting at the dog until it returned and then actually kicking it toward the ford and then following it across, where it now heeled him, puzzled and gravely alert, until he kicked at it again and drove it out ahead.

She was not in the pasture. Now he knew that she was not, and therefore had been led away; it was as though his very savageness toward the dog had recalled him to something like sanity. He recrossed the creek. He had in his hip pocket the weekly county paper which he had taken from his mailbox on his way to the village early in the afternoon. He rolled it into a torch. By its light he saw the prints of the idiot's feet and those of the cow where they had turned away at the ford and mounted the hill to the road, where the torch burned out, leaving him standing there in the early starlight (the moon had not risen yet) cursing again in that furious exasperation which was not rage but savage contempt and pity for all blind flesh capable of hope and grief.

He was almost a mile from his horse. What with the vain quartering of the pasture, he had already walked twice that distance, and he was boiling with that helpless rage at abstract circumstance which feeds on its own impotence, has no object to retaliate upon; it seemed to him that once more he had been victim of a useless and elaborate practical joke at the hands of the prime maniacal Risibility, the sole purpose of which had been to leave him with a mile's walk in darkness. But even if he could not actually punish, hurt, the idiot, at least he could put the fear, if not of God, at least of cow-stealing and certainly of Jack Houston, into him, so that in any event he, Houston, would not leave home each time from now on wondering whether or not the cow would be there when he returned. Yet, mounted at last and in motion again and the cool wind of motion drawing about him, he found that the grim icy rage had given way to an even more familiar sardonic humor, a little clumsy and heavy-footed perhaps, but indomitable and unconquerable above even the ruthless grief: so that long before he reached the village he knew exactly what he would do. He would cure the idiot forever more of coveting cows by the immemorial and unfailing method: he would make him feed and milk her; he would return home and ride back tomorrow morning and make him feed and milk again and then lead the cow back on foot to where he had found her. So he did not stop at Mrs Littlejohn's house at all. He turned into the lane and went on toward the lot; it was Mrs Littlejohn who spoke to him from the dense moonshade beside the fence: "Who's that?"

He stopped the horse. She aint even saw the dog, he thought. That was when he knew he was not going to say anything else to her either. He could see her now, tall, tall like a chimney and with little more shape, standing at the fence. "Jack Houston," he said.

"What you want?" she said.

"Thought I'd water my horse at your trough."

"Aint there water at the store any more?"

"I come from home."

"Oh," she said. "Then you aint—" She spoke in a harsh rush, stopping. Then he knew he was going to say more. He was saying it:

"He's all right. I saw him."

"When?"

"Before I left home. He was there this morning and again this evening. In my pasture. He's all right. I reckon he's taking a Saturday holiday too."

She grunted. "That nigger of yours go to the picnic?"

"Yessum."

"Then come on in and eat. There's some cold supper left."

"I done et." He began to turn the horse. "I wouldn't worry. If he's still there, I'll tell him to get to hell on home."

She grunted again. "I thought you was going to water your horse."

"That's a fact," he said. So he rode into the lot. He had to dismount and open the gate and close it and then open it and close it again in order to do so, and then mount again. She was still standing beside the fence but when he called goodnight in passing she did not answer.

He returned home. The moon was now high and full above the trees. He stabled the horse and crossed the blanched lot, passing the moony yawn of the empty cow-shed, and went on to the dark and empty and silver-roofed house and undressed and lay on the monklike iron cot where he now slept, the hound on the floor beside it, the moony square of the window falling across him as it had used to fall across both of them when his wife was alive and there was a bed there in place of the cot. He was not cursing now, and it was still not rage when at sunup he sat the horse in the road where he had lost the tracks last night. He looked down at the dust blandly inscrutable with the wheel- and hoof- and human-prints of a whole Saturday afternoon, where the very virginity of the idiot at hiding had seemed to tap at need an inexhaustible reservoir of cleverness as one who has never before needed courage can seem at need to find it, cursing, not with rage but with that savage contempt and pity for the weak, nerve-raddled, yet curiously indestructible flesh already doomed and damned before it saw light and breathed.

By that time the owner of the barn had already found in the crib the telltale ridge of spilled feed beginning at the feed-box and ending in a shelving crescent about the shape of the absent basket; presently he even discovered it was his own basket which was gone. He tracked the feet across the lot and lost them. But there was nothing else missing, not a great quantity of feed and the basket was an old one. He gathered up the spilled feed and put it back into the box and soon even his first burst of impotent wrath at the moral outrage, the crass violation of private property, evaporated, recurring only once or twice during the day as angry and exasperated puzzlement: so that on the second morning when he entered the crib and saw the mute ridge of spilled feed ending in that empty embracing crescent, he experienced a shocking bewilderment followed by a furious and blazing wrath like that of a man who, leaping to safety from in front of a runaway, slips on a banana skin. For that moment his state of mind was homicidal. He saw in this second flagrant abrogation of the ancient biblical edict (on which he had established existence, integrity, all) that man must sweat or have not, the same embattled moral point which he had fought singly and collectively with his five children for more than twenty years and in which battle, by being victorious, he had lost. He was a man past middle age, who with nothing to start with but sound health and a certain grim and puritanical affinity for abstinence and endurance, had made a fair farm out of the barren scrap of hill land which he had bought at less than a dollar an acre and married and raised a family on it and fed and clothed them all and even educated them after a fashion, taught them at least hard work, so that as soon as they became big enough to resist him, boys and girls too, they left home (one was a professional nurse, one a ward-heeler to a minor county politician, one a city barber, one a prostitute; the oldest had simply vanished completely) so that there now remained the small neat farm which likewise had been worked to the point of mute and unflagging mutual hatred and resistance but which could not leave him and so far had not been able to eject him but which possibly knew that it could and would outlast him, and his wife who possibly had the same, perhaps not hope for resisting, but maybe staff and prop for bearing and enduring.

He ran out of the barn, shouting her name. When she appeared in the kitchen door, he shouted at her to come and milk and ran on into the house and reappeared with a shotgun, and ran past her again in the barn, cursing her for her slowness, and bridled one of the mules and took up the gun and followed the tracks once more across the lot, to where they disappeared at the fence. But this time he did not quit, and presently he found them again—the dark, dragging wake still visible in the dew-heavy grass of his hayfield, crossing the field and entering the woods. Then he did lose them. But still he did not quit. He was too old fort his, too old certainly for such prolonged and panting rage and thirst for blood. He had eaten no breakfast yet, and at home there was that work waiting, the constant and unflagging round of repetitive nerve-and-flesh wearing labor by which alone that piece of earth which was his mortal enemy could fight him with, which he had performed yesterday and must perform again today and again tomorrow and tomorrow, alone and unassisted or else knock under to that very defeat which had been his barren victory over his children;—this until the day came when (he knew this too) he would stumble and plunge, his eyes still open and his empty hands stiffening into the shape of the plow-handles, into the furrow behind the plow, or topple into the weedy ditch, still clutching the brush-hook or the axe, this final victory marked by a cenotaph of coiling buzzards on the sky until some curious stranger happened there and found and buried what was left of him. Yet he went on. After a while he even found the tracks again, three of them in a sandy ditch where a branch ran, coming upon them more or less by chance since the last one he had seen was a mile away; he could have had no reason to believe they were even the right ones, though as it happened they were. But he did not for one moment doubt that they were the right ones. About the middle of the morning he even discovered whom the cow belonged to. He met Houston's Negro, also on a mule, in the woods. He told the Negro violently, even swinging the gun toward him, that he had seen no stray cow, there was no stray cow about there, and that this was his land although he owned nothing within three miles of where he stood unless it might have been the temporarily hidden feed-basket, and ordered the Negro to get off it and stay off.

He returned home. He had not given up; he now knew not only what he intended to do, but how to do it. He saw before him not mere revenge and reprisal, but redress. He did not want to surprise the thief; he wanted now to capture the cow and either collect a reward from its owner for returning it, or if the owner refused, resort to his legal rights and demand a pound fee on the cow as a stray—this, this legal dollar which would be little enough compensation, not for the time he had spent recovering the cow, but for the time he had lost from the endless round of that labor which he could not have hired done in his place, not because he could not pay for it but because no man in that country, white or black, would work for him at any price, and which he durst not permit to get the ascendancy of him or he would be lost. He did not even go to the house. He went straight to the field and put the mule into the plow which he had left in the furrow last night and plowed until his wife rang the bell at noon; he returned to the field after dinner and plowed on until dark.

He was in the barn, the mule already saddled and waiting in its stall, before moonset the next morning. He saw against the pallid lift of dawn the thick, bearlike figure enter with the basket and followed by his own dog, and enter the crib and then emerge, carrying the basket in both arms as a bear does, and hurry back across the lot, the dog still following. When he saw the dog he was suffused again by that almost unbearable rage. He had heard it on the first morning, but its uproar had ceased by the time he came good awake; now he understood why he had not heard it on the second and third mornings, and he knew now that even if the man did not look back and see him, if he now appeared from the barn the dog in all likelihood would bark at him. So when he did feel it safe to come out of the barn, there was nothing in sight but the dog, which stood peering through the fence after the thief, remaining unaware of his presence until he had actually kicked it, savage and raging, toward the house.

But the thief's dark wake lay again upon the dew-pearled grass of the pasture, though when he reached the woods he discovered that he had made the same error of underestimation which Houston had made: that there is perhaps something in passion too, as well as in poverty and innocence, which cares for its own. So he spent another half morning, breakfastless, seething with incredulous outrage, riding the green and jocund solitudes of the May woods, while behind him the dark reminder of his embattled and unremitting fields stood higher and higher in despotic portent. This time he even found the trail again—the stain of wasted milk on the earth (so close he was), the bent grass where the basket had sat while the cow fed from it. He should have found the basket itself hanging on the limb, since nobody had tried to conceal it. But he did not look that high, since he now had the cow's trail. He followed it, calm and contained and rigidly boiling, losing it and finding it and losing it again, on through the morning and into the access of noon—that concentration of light and heat which he could seem to feel raising not only the temperature of his blood but that of the very abstract conduits and tubes through which the current of his wrath had to flow. That afternoon though he discovered that the sun had nothing to do with it. He also stood beneath a tree while the thunderstorm crashed and glared and the furious cold rain drove at that flesh which cringed and shivered only on the outside, then galloped on in tearful and golden laughter across the glittering and pristine earth. He was then seven miles from home. There was an hour more of daylight. He had done perhaps four of the miles and the evening star had risen, when it occurred to him that the fugitives might just possibly return to the place where he had found the milk-stain on the earth. He went back there without hope. He was not even raging anymore.

He reached home about midnight, on foot, leading the mule and the cow. At first he had been afraid that the thief himself would escape. Then he had expected him to. Then for that half mile between the barn and the place where he had found them, he tried to drive away the creature which had started up from beside the cow with a hoarse, alarmed cry which he recognised, which still followed, moaning and blundering along in the darkness behind even when he would turn—a man too old for this, spent not so much by the long foodless day as by constant and unflagging rage—and shout at it, cursing. His wife was waiting at the lot gate with a lighted lantern. He entered, he handed the two halter-reins carefully to her and went and closed the gate carefully and stooped as an old man stoops and found a stick and then sprang, ran at the idiot, striking at it, cursing in a harsh spent panting voice, the wife following, calling him by name. "You stop!" she cried. "Stop it! Do you want to kill yourself?"

"Hah!" he said, panting, shaking. "I aint going to die for a few more miles yet. Go get the lock." It was a padlock. It was the only lock of any sort on the place. It was on the front gate, where he had put it the day after his last child left home. She went and got it while he still tried to drive the idiot from the lot. But he could not overtake the creature. It moved awkwardly and thickly, moaning and bubbling, but he could neither overtake it nor frighten it. It was somewhere behind him, just outside the radius of the lantern which his wife held, even while he locked the piece of chain through the door of the stall into which he had put the cow. The next morning when he unlocked the chain, the creature was inside the stall with the cow. It had even fed the cow, climbing back out and then back into the stall to do it, and for that five miles to Houston's place it still followed, moaning and slobbering, though just before they reached the house he looked back, and it was gone. He did not know just when it disappeared. Later, returning, with Houston's dollar in his pocket, he examined the road to see just where it had vanished. But he found no trace.

The cow was in Houston's lot less than ten minutes. Houston was at the house at the time; his immediate intention was to send the cow on by his Negro. But he countermanded this in the next breath and sent the man instead to saddle his horse, during which time he stood waiting, cursing again with that savage and bleak contempt which was not disgust nor rage. Mrs Littlejohn was putting her horse into the buggy when he led the cow into the lot, so he did not need to tell her himself, after all. They just looked at one another, not man and woman but two integers which had both reached the same ungendered peace even if by different roads. She drew the clean, knotted rag from her pocket. "I dont want money," he said roughly. "I just dont want to see her again."

"It's his," she said, extending the rag. "Take it."

"Where'd he get money?"

"I dont know. V. K. Ratliff gave it to me. It's his."

"I reckon it is, if Ratliff gave it up. But I still dont want it."

"What else could he do with it?" she said. "What else did he ever want?"

"All right," Houston said. He took the rag. He did not open it. If he had asked how much was in it, she could not have told him since she had never counted it either. Then he said, furious and still out of his calm rigid face: "God damn it, keep them both away from my place. Do you hear?"

That lot was beyond the house from the road; the rear wall of the stable was not in sight from either. It was not directly in view from anywhere in the village proper, and on this September forenoon Ratliff realised that it did not need to be. Because he was walking in a path, a path which he had not seen before, which had not been there in May. Then that rear wall came into his view, the planks nailed horizontally upon it, that plank at head-height prized off and leaning, the projecting nails faced carefully inward, against the wall and no more motionless than the row of backs, the row of heads which filled the gap. He knew not only what he was going to see but that, like Bookwright, he did not want to see it, yet, unlike Bookwright, he was going to look. He did look, leaning his face in between two other heads; and it was as though it were himself inside the stall with the cow, himself looking out of the blasted tongueless face at the row of faces watching him who had been given the wordless passions but not the specious words. When they looked around at him, he already held the loose plank, holding it as if he were on the point of striking at them with it. But his voice was merely sardonic, mild even, familiar, cursing as Houston had: not in rage and not even in outraged righteousness.

"I notice you come to have your look too," one said.

"Sholy," Ratliff said. "I aint cussing you folks. I'm cussing all of us," lifting the plank and fitting it back into the orifice. "Does he—What's his name? that new one? Lump.—does he make you pay again each time, or is it a general club ticket good for every performance?" There was a half-brick on the ground beside the wall. With it he drove the nails back while they watched him, the brick splitting and shaling, crumbling away onto his hands in fine dust—a dry, arid, pallid dust of the color of shabby sin and shame, not splendid, not magnificent like blood, and fatal. "That's all," he said. "It's over. This here engagement is completed." He did not wait to see if they were departing. He crossed the lot in the bright hazy glare of the September noon, and the back yard. Mrs Littlejohn was in the kitchen. Again like Houston, he did [illegible] to tell her.

"What do you think I think when I look out that window and watch them sneaking up along that fence?" she said.

"Only all you done was think," he said. "That new clerk," he said. "That Snopes encore. Launcelot," he said. "Lump. I remember his ma." He remembered her in life, as well as from inquiry—a thin, eager, plain woman who had never had quite enough to eat and showed it and did not even know that she had actually never had enough to eat, who taught school. Out of a moil of sisters and brothers fathered by a congenital failure who between a constant succession of not even successful petty-mercantile bankruptcies, begot on his whining and sluttish wife still more children whom he could not quite clothe and feed. Out of this, through one summer term at the State Teacher's College and into a one-room country school, and out of the school before the first year was done and into marriage with a man under indictment then because of a drummer's sample-case of shoes, all for the right foot, which had vanished from a railway baggage-room. And who brought with her into that marriage, as sole equipment and armament, the ability to wash and feed and clothe a swarm of brothers and sisters without ever enough food or clothing or soap to do it with, and a belief that there was honor and pride and salvation and hope too to be found for man's example between the pages of books, and who bore one child and named it Launcelot, flinging this quenchless defiance into the very jaws of the closing trap, and died. "Launcelot!" Ratliff cried. He did not even curse: not that Mrs Littlejohn would have minded, or perhaps even have heard him. "Lump! Just think of his shame and horror when he got big enough to realise what his ma had done to his family's name and pride so that he even had to take Lump for folks to call him in place of it! He pulled that plank off! At just exactly the right height! Not child-height and not woman-height: man-height! He just keeps that little boy there to watch and run to the store and give the word when it's about to start. Oh, he aint charging them to watch it yet, and that's what's wrong. That's what I dont understand.

What I am afraid of. Because if he, Lump Snopes, Launcelot Snopes . . . I said encore," he cried. "What I was trying to say was echo. Only what I meant was forgery." He ceased, having talked himself wordless, mute into baffled and aghast outrage, glaring at the man-tall, man-grim woman in the faded wrapper who stared as steadily back at him.

"So that's it," she said. "It aint that it is, that itches you. It's that somebody named Snopes, or that particular Snopes, is making something out of it and you dont know what it is. Or is it because folks come and watch? It's all right for it to be, but folks mustn't know it, see it."

"Was," he said. "Because it's finished now. I aint never disputed I'm a pharisee," he said. "You dont need to tell me he aint got nothing else. I know that. Or that I can sholy leave him have at least this much. I know that too. Or that besides, it aint any of my business. I know that too, just as I know that the reason I aint going to leave him have what he does have is simply because I am strong enough to keep him from it. I am stronger than him. Not righter. Not any better, maybe. But just stronger."

"How are you going to stop it?"

"I dont know. Maybe I even cant. Maybe I dont even want to. Maybe all I want is just to have been righteouser, so I can tell myself I done the right thing and my conscience is clear now and at least I can go to sleep tonight." But he seemed to be at no loss as to what to do next. He did stand for a time on Mrs Littlejohn's front steps, but he was only canvassing the possibilities—or rather, discarding the faces as he called them up: the fierce intractable one barred with the single eyebrow; the high one ruddy and open and browless as a segment of watermelon above the leather blacksmith's apron; that third one which did not belong to the frock coat so much as it appeared to be attached to it like a toy balloon by its string, the features of which seemed to be in a constant state of disorganised flight from about the long, scholarly, characterless nose as if the painted balloon-face had just been fetched in out of a violent and driving rain—Mink, Eck, I. O.; and then he began to think Lump again, cursing, driving his mind back to the immediate problem with an almost physical effort, though actually standing quite still on the top step, his face familiar and enigmatic, quiet, actually almost smiling, bringing the three possible faces once more into his mind's eye and watching them elide once more —the one which would not stay at all; the second which would never even comprehend what he was talking about; the third which in that situation would be like one of the machines in railway waiting-rooms, into which you could insert the copper coin or lead slug of impulse to action, and you would get something back in return, you would not know what, except that it would not be worth quite as much as the copper or the slug. He even thought of the older one, or at least the first one: Flem, thinking how this was probably the first time anywhere where breath inhaled and suspired and men established the foundations of their existences on the currency of coin, that anyone had ever wished Flem Snopes were here instead of anywhere else, for any reason, at any price.

It was now nearing noon, almost an hour since he had seen the man he sought emerge from the store. He made inquiries at the store; ten minutes later he turned from a lane, through a gate in a new wire fence. The house was new, one-storey, paintless. There were a few of the summer's flowers blooming on dustily into the summer's arid close, all red ones —cannas and geraniums—in a raw crude bed before the steps and in rusted cans and buckets along the edge of the porch. The same little boy was in the yard beyond the house, and a big, strong, tranquil-faced young woman opened the door to him, an infant riding her hip and another child peering from behind her skirt. "He's in his room, studying," she said. "Just walk right in."

The room also was unpainted, of tongue-and-groove planking; it looked and was as air-tight as a strong-box and not much larger, though even then he remarked how the odor of it was not a bachelor-uncle smell but was curiously enough that of a closet in which a middle-aged widow kept her clothes. At once he saw the frock coat lying across the bed's foot, because the man (he really was holding a book, and he wore spectacles) in the chair had given the opening door one alarmed look and sprang up and snatched up the coat and began to put it on. "Never mind," Ratliff said. "I aint going to stay long. This here cousin of yours. Isaac." The other finished getting into the coat, buttoning it hurriedly about the paper dickey he wore in place of a shirt (the cuffs were attached to the coat sleeves themselves) then removing the spectacles with that same flustered haste, as if he had hurried into the coat in order to remove the spectacles, so that for that reason Ratliff noticed that the frames had no lenses in them. The other was watching him with that intentness which he had seen before, which (the concentration and intelligence both) seemed actually to be no integral part either of the organs or the process behind them, but seemed rather to be a sort of impermanent fungus-growth on the surface of the eyeballs like the light down which children blow from the burrs of dandelion blooms. "About that cow," Ratliff said.

Now the features fled. They streamed away from the long nose which burlesqued ratiocination and firmness and even made a sort of crass Roman holiday of rationalised curiosity, fluid and flowing even about the fixed grimace of glee. Then Ratliff saw that the eyes were not laughing but were watching him and that there was something intelligently alert, or at least competent, behind them, even if it were not firm. "Aint he a sight now?" Snopes cackled, chortled. "I done often thought, since Houston give him that cow and Mrs Littlejohn located them in that handy stall, what a shame it is some of his folks aint running for office. Bread and circuses, as the fellow says, makes hay at the poll-box. I dont know of no cheaper way than Lump's got to get a man——"

"Beat," Ratliff said. He did not raise his voice, and he did not speak further than that one word. The other face did not change either: the long, still nose, the fixed grimace, the eyes which partook of the life of neither. After a moment Snopes said:

"Beat?"

"Beat," Ratliff said.

"Beat," the other said. If it were not intelligence, Ratliff told himself, it was a good substitute. "Except as it happens, I aint——"

"Why?" Ratliff said. "When Caesar's wife goes up to Will Varner next month to get that ere school job again, and he aint pure as a marble monument, what do you think is going to happen?" The face did not actually alter because the features were in a constant state of flux, having no relation to one another save that the same skull bore them, the same flesh fed them.

"Much obliged," Snopes said. "What do you figure we better do?"

"We aint going to do nothing," Ratliff said. "I dont want to teach school."

"But you'll help. After all, we was getting along all right until you come into it."

"No," Ratliff said harshly. "Not me. But I aim to do this much. I am going to stay here until I see if his folks are doing something about it. About letting them folks hang around that crack and watch, anyhow."

"Sholy," Snopes said. "That ere wont do. That's it. Flesh is weak, and it wants but little here below. Because sin's in the eye of the beholder; cast the beam outen your neighbors' eyes and out of sight is out of mind. A man cant have his good name drug in the alleys. The Snopes name has done held its head up too long in this country to have no such reproaches against it like stock-diddling."

"Not to mention that school," Ratliff said.

"Sholy. We'll have a conference. Family conference. We'll meet at the shop this afternoon."

When Ratliff reached the shop that afternoon, they were both there—the smith's apprentice and the school-teacher, and a third man: the minister of the village church—a farmer and a father; a harsh, stupid, honest, superstitious and upright man, out of no seminary, holder of no degrees, functioning neither within nor without any synod but years ago ordained minister by Will Varner as he decreed his school-teachers and commissioned his bailiffs. "It's all right," I. O. said when Ratliff entered. "Brother Whitfield has done solved it. Only——"

"I siad I knowed of a case before where it worked," the minister corrected. Then he told them—or the teacher did, that is:

"You take and beef the critter the fellow has done formed the habit with, and cook a piece of it and let him eat it. It's got to be a authentic piece of the same cow or sheep or whatever it is, and the fellow has got to know that's what he is eating; he cant be tricked nor forced to eating it, and a substitute wont work. Then he'll be all right again and wont want to chase nothing but human women. Only—" and now Ratliff noticed it—something in the diffusive face at once speculative and annoyed: "—only Mrs Littlejohn wont let us have the cow. You told me Houston give it to him."

"No I didn't," Ratliff said. "You told me that."

"But didn't he?"

"Mrs Littlejohn or Houston or your cousin will be the one to tell you that."

"Well, no matter. Anyway, she wont. And now we got to buy it from her. And what I cant understand is, she says she dont know how much, but that you do."

"Oh," Ratliff said. But now he was not looking at Snopes. He was looking at the minister. "Do you know it will work, Reverend?" he said.

"I know it worked once," Whitfield said.

"Then you have knowed it to fail."

"I never knowed it to be tried but that once," Whitfield said.

"All right," Ratliff said. He looked at the two others—cousins, nephew and uncle, whatever they were. "It will cost you sixteen dollars and eighty cents."

"Sixteen dollars and eighty cents?" I. O. said. "Hell fire." The little quick pale eyes darted from face to face between them. Then he turned to the minister. "Look here. A cow is a heap of different things besides the meat. Yet it's all that same cow. It's got to be, because it's some things that cow never even had when it was born, so what else can it be but the same thing? The horns, the hair. Why couldn't we take a little of them and make a kind of soup; we could even take a little of the actual living blood so it wouldn't be no technicality in it——"

"It was the meat, the flesh," the minister said. "I taken the whole cure to mean that not only the boy's mind but his insides too, the seat of passion and sin, can have the proof that the partner of his sin is dead."

"But sixteen dollars and eighty cents," I. O. said. He looked at Ratliff. "I dont reckon you aim to put up none of it."

"No," Ratliff said.

"And Mink aint, not to mention after that law verdict Will Varner put on him this morning," the other said fretfully. "And Lump. If anything, Lump is going to be put out considerable with what after all wasn't a whole heap of your business," he told Ratliff. "And Flem aint in town. So that leaves me and Eck here. Unless Brother Whitfield would like to help us out for moral reasons. After all, what reflects on one, reflects on all the members of a flock."

"But he dont," Ratliff said. "He cant. Come to think of it, I've heard of this before myself. It's got to be done by the fellow's own blood kin, or it wont work." The little bright quick eyes went constantly between his face and the minister's.

"You never said nothing about that," he said.

"I just told you what I know happened," Whitfield said. "I don't know how they got the cow."

"But sixteen-eighty," I. O. said. "Hell fire." Ratliff watched him—the eyes which were much shrewder than they appeared—not intelligent; he revised that: shrewd. Now he even looked at his cousin or nephew for the first time. "So it's me and you, Eck." And the cousin or nephew spoke for the first time.

"You mean we got to buy it?"

"Yes," I. O. said. "You sholy wont refuse a sacrifice for the name you bear, will you?"

"All right," Eck said. "If we got to." From beneath the leather apron he produced a tremendous leather purse and opened it and held it in one grimed fist as a child holds the paper sack which it is about to inflate with its breath. "How much?"

"I'm a single man, unfortunately," I. O. said. "But you got three children——"

"Four," Eck said. "One coming."

"Four. So I reckon the only way to figure it is to divide it according to who will get the most benefits from curing him. You got yourself and four children to consider. That will be five to one. So that will be I pay the one-eighty and Eck pays the fifteen because five goes into fifteen three times and three times five is fifteen dollars. And Eck can have the hide and the rest of the beef."

"But a beef and hide aint worth fifteen dollars," Eck said. "And even if it was, I dont want it. I dont want fifteen dollars worth of beef."

"It aint the beef and the hide. That's just a circumstance. It's the moral value we are going to get out of it."

"How do I need fifteen dollars worth of moral value when all you need is a dollar and eighty cents?"

"The Snopes name. Cant you understand that? That aint never been aspersed yet by no living man. That's got to be kept pure as a marble monument for your children to grow up under."

"But I still dont see why I got to pay fifteen dollars, when all you got to pay is——"

"Because you got four children. And you make five. And five times three is fifteen."

"I aint got but three yet," Eck said.

"Aint that just what I said? five times three? If that other one was already here, it would make four, and five times four is twenty dollars, and then I wouldn't have to pay anything."

"Except that somebody would owe Eck three dollars and twenty cents change," Ratliff said.

"What?" I. O. said. But he immediately turned back to his cousin or nephew. "And you got the meat and the hide," he said. "Cant you even try to keep from forgetting that?"

CHAPTER TWO

1

The woman Houston married was not beautiful. She had neither wit nor money. An orphan, a plain girl, almost homely and not even very young (she was twenty-four) she came to him out of the home of the remote kinswoman who had raised her, with the domestic skill of her country heritage and blood and training and a small trunk of neat, plain, dove-colored clothes and the hand-stitched sheets and towels and table-linen which she had made herself and an infinite capacity for constancy and devotion, and no more. And they were married and six months later she died and he grieved for her for four years in black, savage, indomitable fidelity, and that was all.

They had known one another all their lives. They were both only children, born of the same kind of people, on farms not three miles apart. They belonged to the same country congregation and attended the same one-room country school, where, although five years his junior, she was already one class ahead of him when he entered and, although he failed twice during the two years he attended it, she was still one class ahead of him when he quit, vanished, not only from his father's house but from the country too, fleeing even at sixteen the immemorial trap, and was gone for thirteen years and then as suddenly returned, knowing (and perhaps even cursing himself) on the instant he knew he was going to return, that she would still be there and unmarried; and she was.

He was fourteen when he entered the school. He was not wild, he was merely unbitted yet; not high-spirited so much as possessed of that strong lust, not for life, not even for movement, but for that fetterless immobility called freedom. He had nothing against learning; it was merely the confinement, the regimentation, which it entailed. He could competently run his father's farm, and his mother had taught him to write his name before she died at last and so gave up trying to compel his father to send him to the school which for four years at least he had contrived to avoid by playing his mother's spoiling fondness against the severity of his father's pride; he really enjoyed the increasing stint of responsibility and even work which his father set him as a training for manhood. But at last he outgeneralled himself with his own strategy: finally even his father admitted that there was nothing else about the farm for him to learn. So he entered school, not a paragon but a paradox. He was competent for citizenship before he could vote and capable of fatherhood before he learned to spell. At fourteen he was already acquainted with whiskey and was the possessor of a mistress—a Negro girl two or three years his senior, daughter of his father's renter—and so found himself submitting to be taught his abc's four and five and six years after his coevals and hence already too big physically for where he was; bulging in Lilliput, inevitably sophisticated, logically contemptuous, invincibly incorrigible, not deliberately intending to learn nothing but merely convinced that he would not, did not want and did not believe he needed to.

Afterward, it seemed to him that the first thing he saw when he entered the room was that bent, demure, simply-brown and straight-haired head. Still later, after he believed he had escaped, it seemed to him that it had been in his life always, even during those five years between his birth and hers; and not that she had contrived somehow to exist during those five years, but that he himself had not begun to exist until she was born, the two of them chained irrevocably from that hour and onward forever, not by love but by implacable constancy and invincible repudiation—on the one hand, that steadfast and undismayable will to alter and improve and remake; on the other, that furious resistance. It was not love —worship, prostration—as he knew it, as passion had manifested heretofore in an experience limited to be sure, yet not completely innocent. He would have accepted that, taken it as his due, calling himself submitting to it as he called himself submitting when he was really using that same quality which he called proffered slavedom in all the other women—his mother and his mistress—so far in his life. What he did not comprehend was that until now he had not known what true slavery was—that single constant despotic undeviating will of the enslaved not only for possession, complete assimilation, but to coerce and reshape the enslaver into the seemliness of his victimization. She did not even want him yet, not because she was too young yet but because apparently she had not found even in him the one suitable. It was as though she had merely elected him out of all the teeming earth, not as one competent to her requirements, but as one possessing the possibilities on which she would be content to establish the structure of her life.

She was trying to get him through school. Not out of it and apparently not even educated, any wiser; apparently just through it, grade by grade in orderly progression and at the appointed times for advancing from one to the next as people commonly do. At one time the thought occurred to him that what she perhaps wanted was to get him on and into the class of his age, where he should have been; that if she could do that, perhaps she would let him alone, to fail or not fail as his nature and character dictated. Perhaps she would have. Or perhaps she, who was fond enough to attempt it at all, was also wise enough to know that he not only would never reach the grade where he should have been but he would not even keep up with the one where he was, and more: that where he was did not even matter, that even failing did not matter so long as she had a hand too in the failing.

It was a feud, a gage, wordless, uncapitulating, between that unflagging will not for love or passion but for the married state, and that furious and as unbending one for solitariness and freedom. He was going to fail that first year. He expected to. Not only himself but the whole school knew it. She never even spoke directly to him, she would pass him on the playground without even looking at him, apparently ever seeing him, yet there would be, mute and inevitable on his desk, the apple or the piece of cake from her lunch-box, and secret in one of his books the folded sheet of problems solved or spelling corrected or sentences written out in the round, steadfast child's hand—the reward and promise which he spurned, the assistance which he repudiated, raging not because his integrity and gullibility had been attempted but because he could neither publicly express the scorn of the repudiation nor be sure that the private exposition—the wanton destruction of the food or the paper—had even registered upon that head bent, decorous, intent, in profile or three-quarters and sometimes in full rear, which he had never yet heard even pronounce his name. Then one day a boy not a third his size chanted a playground doggerel at him—not that Lucy Pate and Jack Houston were sweethearts, but that Lucy Pate was forcing Jack Houston to make the rise to the second grade. He struck the child as he would one of his own size, was immediately swarmed over by four older boys and was holding his furious own when his assailants gave back and she was beside him, flailing at his enemies with her school-satchel. He struck her as blindly and furiously as he had the little boy and flung her away. For the next two minutes he was completely berserk. Even after he was down, the four of them had to bind him up with a piece of fence wire in order to turn him loose and run.

So he won that first point. He failed. When he entered school the next fall, in the same grade and surrounded (a giant knee-deep in midgets) by a swarm of still smaller children, he believed that he had even escaped. The face was still there to be sure, and it looked no smaller, no more distant. But he now believed he saw it from beyond the additional abyss of yet another intervening grade. So he believed that he had taken the last point too, and the game; it was almost two months before he discovered that she too had failed in her last year's examinations.

Now something very like panic took possession of him. Because he also discovered that the scale and tone of the contest between them had altered. It was no more deadly; that was impossible. It had matured. Up to now, for all its deadly seriousness, it had retained something of childhood, something both illogical and consistent, both reasonable and bizarre. But now it had become a contest between adults; at some instant during that summer in which they had not even seen one another except among the congregation at church, the ancient worn glove of biological differentiation had been flung and raised. It was as if, mutually unaware yet at the same moment, they had looked upon the olden Snake, had eaten of the Tree with the will and capacity for assimilation but without the equipment, even if the lack of equipment were not true in his case. There were no more apples and cake now, there was only the paper, correct, inescapable and implacable, in the book or in his overcoat pocket or in the mailbox before his gate; he would submit his own blank paper at the written monthly tests and receive back that one bearing a perfect grade and written in that hand, even to the signature, which was coming more and more to look like his own. And always there was the face which still never addressed him nor even looked at him, bent, in profile or three-quarters, sober and undismayable. He not only looked at it all day, he carried it home with him at night, waking from sleep to meet it, still serene, still steadfast. He would even try to efface and exorcise it beyond that of the Negress paramour but it still remained, constant, serene, not reproachful nor even sad nor even angry, but already forgiving him before forgiveness had been dared or earned; waiting, tranquil, terrifying. Once during that year the frantic thought occurred to him of escaping her forever by getting beyond the reach of her assistance, of applying himself and making up the lost years, overhauling the class where he should have been. For a short time he even attempted it. But there was the face. He knew he could never pass it, not that it would hold him back, but he would have to carry it on with him in his turn, just as it had held him somehow in abeyance during those five years before she was even born; not only would he never pass it, he would not even ever overtake it by that one year, so that regardless of what stage he might reach it would still be there, one year ahead of him, inescapable and impervious to passing. So there was but one alternative. That was the old one: the movement not in retrograde since he could retrograde no further than the grade in which he already was, but of braking, clapping the invincible spike-heels of immobility into the fleeing and dizzy scope.

He did that. His mistake was in assuming a limitation to female ruthlessness. He watched his blank monthly test papers vanish into the teacher's hands and then return to him, perfectly executed even to his own name at the top, while the months passed and the final examination for promotion or not arrived. He submitted the blank sheets bearing nothing but his name and the finger-smudges where he had folded them and closed for the last time the books which he had not noon and through supper and into the evening itself. He was even managed to soil and walked out of the room, free save for the minor formality of being told by the teacher that he had failed. His conviction of freedom lasted through the afterundressing for bed, one leg already out of his trousers; without pause or falter he put the leg back into the trousers, already running, barefoot and shirtless, out of the house where his father was already asleep. The schoolhouse was not locked, though he had to break a lock to get into the teacher's desk. Yet all three of his papers were there, even to the same type of foolscap which he had submitted in blank—arithmetic, geography, the paragraph of English composition which, if he had not known he had submitted a blank one and if it had not been that he could neither pronounce nor recognise some of the words and could not understand all of what the ones he did know were talking about, he could not have sworn himself he had not written.

He returned home and got a few clothes and the pistol which he had owned for three years now, and waked his father, the two of them meeting for the last time in life in the summer lamplit midnight room—the determined and frightened youth and the fierce thin wiry man almost a head shorter, unshaven, with a wild flurry of gray hair, in a calf-length nightshirt, who gave him the contents of the worn wallet from the trousers flung across a nearby chair and, in iron spectacles now, wrote out the note for the amount, with interest, and made the son sign it. "All right," he said. "Go then, and be damned to you. You certainly ought to be enough kin to me to take care of yourself at sixteen. I was. But I'll bet you the same amount, by God, that you'll be hollering for help before six months." He went back past the schoolhouse and restored the papers, including the new set of blank ones; he would have repaired the broken lock if he could. And he even paid the bet, although he did not lose it. He sent the money back out of three times that sum won at dice one Saturday night a year later in the railroad construction camp in Oklahoma where he was a time-keeper.

He fled, not from his past, but to escape his future. It took him twelve years to learn you cannot escape either of them. He was in El Paso then, which was one end of his run as a locomotive fireman well up the service list toward an engine of his own, where he lived in the neat, small, urban house which he had rented for four years now, with the woman known to the neighborhood and the adjacent grocers and such as his wife, whom he had taken seven years ago out of a Galveston brothel. He had been a Kansas wheat-hand, he had herded sheep in New Mexico, he was again with a construction gang in Arizona and west Texas and then a longshoreman on the Galveston docks; if he were still fleeing, he did not know it because it had been years now since he had even remembered that he had forgotten the face. And when he proved that at least you cannot escape either past or future with nothing better than geography, he did not know that. (Geography: that paucity of invention, that fatuous faith in distance of man, who can invent no better means than geography for escaping; himself of all, to whom, so he believed he believed, geography had never been merely something to walk upon but was the very medium which the fetterless to- and fro-going required to breathe in.) And if he were merely being consistent in escaping from one woman by violating the skirts of another, as with his mother and the Negro girl of his adolescence, he did not know that, taking almost by force out of the house at daybreak the woman whom he had never seen until the previous midnight; there was a scene by gaslight between him and the curl-papered landlady as violent as if he were ravishing from the house an only daughter with an entailed estate.

They lived together for seven years. He went back to railroading and stuck with it and even came at last into the hierarchical current of seniority; he was mentally and spiritually, and with only an occasional aberration, physically faithful to her who in her turn was loyal, discreet, undemanding, and thrifty with his money. She bore his name in the boarding houses where they lived at first, then in the rented house in El Paso which they called home and were furnishing as they were able to buy furniture. Although she had never suggested it, he even thought of marrying her, so had the impact of the West which was still young enough then to put a premium on individuality, softened and at last abolished his inherited southern-provincial-Protestant fanaticism regarding marriage and female purity, the biblical Magdalen. There was his father, to be sure. He had not seen him since the night he left home and he did not expect to see him again. He did not think of his father as being dead, being any further removed than the old house in Mississippi where he had seen him last; he simply could not visualise them meeting anywhere else except in Mississippi, to which he could only imagine himself returning as an old man. But he knew what his father's reaction to his marriage with a once-public woman would be, and up to this time, with all that he had done and failed to do, he had never once done anything which he cound not imagine his father also doing, or at least condoning. Then he received the message that his father was dead (He received at the same time an offer from a neighbor for the farm. He did not sell it. At the time he did not comprehend why.) and so that was removed. But it had never actually existed anyway. He had already settled that as a matter purely between him and himself, long ago one night while the dim engine rocked through the darkness over the clucking rail-joints: "Maybe she was not much once, but neither was I. And for a right smart while now she has been better than I know myself to have been." Perhaps they would have a child after a while. He thought of waiting for that, letting that be the sign. At first that eventuality had never occurred to him—here again was the old mystical fanatic Protestant; the hand of God laying upon the sinner even after the regeneration: the Babylonian interdict by heaven forever against reproduction. He did not know just how much time, just what span of chastity, would constitute purgatorium and absolution, but he would imagine it—some instant, mystical still, when the blight of those nameless and faceless men, the scorched scars of merchandised lust, would be effaced and healed from the organs which she had prostituted.

But that time was past now, not the mystic moment when the absolvement would be discharged, but the hour, the day before the elapse of which he had thought she would have told him she was pregnant and they would have married. It was long past now. It would never be. And one night in that twelfth year, in the boarding house at the other end of his run where he spent the alternate nights, he took out the three-year-old offer for the farm and he knew why he had not accepted it. I'm going home, he told himself—no more than that, not why; not even seeing the face which up to the day he entered school he could not even have described and which now he could not even remember. He made his run back to El Paso the next day and drew the seven years' accumulation out of the bank and divided it into two equal parts. The woman who had been his wife for seven years glanced once at the money and then stood cursing him. "You are going to get married," she said. There were no tears; she just cursed him. "What do I want with money? Look at me. Do you think I will lack money? Let me go with you. There will be some town, some place close where I can live. You can come when you want to. Have I ever bothered you?"

"No," he said. She cursed him, cursing them both. If she would just touch me, hit me, make me mad enough to hit her, he thought. But that did not happen either. It was not him she cursed, any more than she could curse the woman she had never seen and whose face even he could not quite recall. So he divided his half of the money again—that money which he had been lucky with: not lucky in the winning or earning or finding, but lucky in having the vices and desiring the pleasures which left a fair balance of it after they had been fed and satisfied—and returned to Mississippi. But even then, it apparently took him still another year to admit that he did not want to escape that past and future. The countryside believed he had come back to sell the farm. Yet the weeks passed, and he did not. Spring came and he had made no preparations either to rent it or work it himself. He merely continued to live in the old pre-Civil War house which, although no mansion, owning no columns, had been too big for three, while month after month passed, still apparently on that vacation from the Texas railroad his father had already told them he worked for, alone, without companionship, meeting (when he met them at all) the contemporaries who remembered him from youth over casual drinks or cards and that not often. Occasionally he would be seen at the picnics during the summer, and each Saturday afternoon he would make one of the group on the gallery of Varner's store, talking a little, answering questions rather, about the West, not secret and reserved so much as apparently thinking in another tongue from that in which he listened and would presently have to answer. He was bitted now, even if it did not show so much yet. There was still the mark of space and solitude in his face, but fading a little, rationalised and corrupted even into something consciously alert even if it was not fearful; the beast, prime solitary and sufficient out of the wild fields, drawn to the trap and knowing it to be a trap, not comprehending why it was doomed but knowing it was, and not afraid now—and not quite wild.

They were married in January. His part of the Texas money was gone then, though the countryside still believed he was rich, else he could not have lived for a year without working and would not have married a penniless orphan. Since he had arrived home solvent, the neighborhood would be unalterably convinced forever that he was wealthy, just as it had been unalterably convinced at first that only beggary had brought him home. He borrowed money from Will Varner, on a portion of the land, to build the new house on a new site nearer the road. He bought the stallion too then, as if for a wedding present to her, though he never said so. Or if that blood and bone and muscles represented that polygamous and bitless masculinity which he had relinquished, he never said that. And if there were any among his neighbors and acquaintances—Will Varner or Ratliff perhaps—who discerned that this was the actual transference, the deliberate filling of the vacancy of his abdication, they did not say it either.

Three months after the marriage the house was finished and they moved into it, with a Negro woman to cook although the only other hired cook, white or black, in the country was Varner's. Then the countryside would call, the men to the lot to look at the stallion, the women to the house, the new bright rooms, the new furniture and equipment and devices for saving steps and labor whose pictures they would dream over in the mail-order catalogues. They would watch her moving among the new possessions, busy, indefatigable, in the plain, neat garments, the plain and simple hair, the plain face blooming now with something almost like beauty —not amazement at luck, not particularly vindication of will and faith, but just serene, steadfast and boldly rosy when they would remark how the house had been completed exactly in time to catch the moon's full of April through the window where the bed was placed.

Then the stallion killed her. She was hunting a missing hen-nest in the stable. The Negro man had warned her: "He's a horse, missy. But he's a man horse. You keep out of there." But she was not afraid. It was as if she had recognised that transubstantiation, that duality, and thought even if she did not say it: Nonsense. I've married him now. He shot the stallion, running first into the stall with the now frenzied animal with nothing but an open pocket knife, until the Negro grappled with him and persuaded him to wait for the pistol to be fetched from the house, and for four years and two months he had lived in the new house with the hound and the Negro man to cook for them. He sold the mare which he had bought for her, and the cow he owned then, and discharged the woman cook and gave away the chickens. The new furniture had been bought on installment. He moved it all into the barn at the old place where he was born and notified the merchant to come and get it. Then he had only the stove, the kitchen table he ate from, and the cot he had substituted for the bed beneath the window. The moon was full on that first night he slept on the cot too, so he moved the cot into another room and then against a north wall where the moon could not possibly reach him, and two nights later he even went and spent one night in the old house. But there he lost everything, not only peace but even fibred and durable grief for despair to set its teeth into.

So he returned to the new house. The moon was waning

then and would return only at monthly intervals, so that left only that single hour between sunset and full dark between its fulls, and weariness was an antidote for that. And weariness was cheap: he not only had the note he had given Will Varner for the loan, but there had been some trouble with the installment people who did not want to take the furniture back. So he farmed again, finding gradually how much he had forgotten about it. Thus, at times he would have actually forgotten that hour he dreaded until he would find himself entering it, walking into it, finding it suddenly upon him, drowning him with suffocation. Then that stubborn part of her and sometimes even of the son which perhaps next year they would have had would be everywhere about the house he had built to please her even though it was empty now of all the objects she had touched and used and looked at except the stove and the kitchen table and the one garment—not a nightgown or an undergarment, but the gingham dress which resembled the one in which he had first seen her that day at the school—and the window itself, so that even on the hottest evenings of summer he would sit in the sweltering kitchen while the Negro man cooked supper, drinking whiskey from a stone jug and tepid water from the cedar bucket and talking louder and louder, profane, intolerant, argumentative, with no challenge to be rebutted and no challenger to be vanquished and overcome.

But sooner or later the moon would wax again. There would be nights which were almost blank ones. Yet sooner or later that silver and blanched rectangle of window would fall once more, while night waxed into night then waned from night, as it had used to fall across the two of them while they observed the old country belief that the full moon of April guaranteed the fertilising act. But now there was no body beside his own for the moon to fall upon, and nothing for another body to have lain beside his own upon. Because the cot was too narrow for that and there was only the abrupt downward sheer of inky shadow in which only the invisible hound slept, and he would lie rigid, indomitable, and panting. "I dont understand it," he would say. "I dont know why. I wont ever know why. But You cant beat me. am strong as You are. You cant beat me."

He was still alive when he left the saddle. He had heard the shot, then an instant later he knew he must have felt the blow before he heard it. Then the orderly sequence of time as he had known it for thirty-three years became inverted. He seemed to feel the shock of the ground while he knew he was still falling and had not yet reached it, then he was on the ground, he had stopped falling, and remembering what he had seen of stomach-wounds he thought: If I dont get the hurting started quick, I am going to die. He willed to start it, and for an instant he could not understand why it did not start. Then he saw the blank gap, the chasm somewhere between vision and where his feet should have been, and he lay on his back watching the ravelled and shattered ends of sentience and will projecting into the gap, hair-light and worm-blind and groping to meet and fuse again, and he lay there trying to will the sentience to meet and fuse. Then he saw the pain blast light lightning across the gap. But it came from the other direction: not from himself outward, but inward toward himself out of all the identifiable lost earth. Wait, wait, he said. Just go slow at first, and I can take it. But it would not wait. It roared down and raised him, tossed and spun. But it would not wait for him. It would not wait to hurl him into the void, so he cried, "Quick! Hurry!" looking up out of the red roar, into the face which with his own was wedded and twinned forever now by the explosion of that ten-gauge shell—the dead who would carry the living into the ground with him; the living who must bear about the repudiating earth with him forever, the deathless slain—then, as the slanted barrels did not move: "God damn it, couldn't you even borrow two shells, you fumbling ragged—" and put the world away. His eyes, still open to the lost sun, glazed over with a sudden well and run of moisture which flowed down the alien and unremembering cheeks too, already drying, with a newness as of actual tears.

2

That shot was too loud. It was not only too loud for any shot, it was too loud for any sound, louder than any sound needed to be. It was as though the very capacity of space and echo for reproducing noise were leagued against him too in the vindication of his rights and the liquidation of his injuries, building up and building up about the thicket where he crouched and the dim faint road which ran beside it long after the gun-butt had shocked into his shoulder and the black powder smoke had reeked away and the horse had whirled, galloping, the empty stirrups clashing against the empty saddle. He had not fired the gun in four years; he had not even been certain that either two of the five shells he owned would explode. The first one had not; it was the second one—the vain click louder than thunderbolt, the furious need to realign and find the second trigger, then the crash which after the other deafening click he did not hear at all, the reek and stink of powder pressing him backward and downward into the thicket until for an instant he was physically off-balance, so that even if he could have made a second shot it would have been too late and the hound too was gone, leaving him betrayed here too, crouching behind the log, panting and trembling.

Then he would have to finish it, not in the way he wanted to but in the way he must. It was no blind, instinctive, and furious desire for flight which he had to combat and curb. On the contrary. What he would have liked to do would be to leave a printed placard on the breast itself: *This is what happens to the men who impound Mink Snopes's cattle,* with his name signed to it. But he could not, and here again, for the third time since he had pulled the trigger, was that conspiracy to frustrate and outrage his rights as a man and his feelings as a sentient creature. He must rise and quit the thicket and do what he had next to do, not to finish it but merely to complete the first step of what he had started, put into motion, who realised now that he had known already, before he heard the horse and raised the gun, that that would happen which had happened: that he had pulled trigger on an enemy but had only slain a corpse to be hidden. So he sat up behind the log and shut his eyes and counted slowly until the shaking stopped and the sound of the galloping horse and even the outrageous and incredible shot had died out of his ears and he could rise, carrying the slanted gun still loaded with the shell which had failed to explode, and emerge from the thicket, already hurrying. But even then it would be dusk before he reached home.

It was dusk. He emerged from the bottom and looked up the slope of his meagre and sorry corn and saw it—the paintless two-room cabin with an open hallway between and a lean-to kitchen, which was not his, on which he paid rent but not taxes, paying almost as much in rent in one year as the house had cost to build; not old, yet the roof of which already leaked and the weather-stripping had already begun to rot away from the wall planks and which was just like the one he had been born in which had not belonged to his father either, and just like the one he would die in if he died indoors—which he probably would even if in his clothes, repudiated without warning at some instant between bed and table or perhaps the door itself, by his unflagging furious heart-muscles—and it was just like the more than six others he had lived in since his marriage and like the twice that many more he knew he would live in before he did die and although he paid rent on this one he was unalterably convinced that his cousin owned it and he knew that this was as near as he would ever come to owning the roof over his head. Then he saw the two children in the yard before it, who even as he saw them, stood quickly up, watching him, then turned and scuttled toward the house. Then it seemed to him that he could see her also, standing in the open hallway almost exactly where she had stood eight hours before and watched his back where he sat over the cold hearth, oiling the gun with the bacon-drippings which was the only thing he owned that could be used for oil, which would not lubricate but in contact with the metal would congeal into a substance like soap, inherent with its own salty corrosion; standing there as if in all that time she had not moved, once more framed by an opening, though without the lamp, as she was standing in the savage lamplight, above the loud harsh voices of invisible men, in the open door of the mess-hall in that south Mississippi convict camp where he first saw her nine years ago. He stopped looking at the house; he had only glanced at it as it was, and mounted through the yellow and stunted stand of his corn, yellow and stunted because he had had no money to buy fertilizer to put beneath it and owned neither the stock nor the tools to work it properly with and had had no one to help him with what he did own in order to gamble his physical strength and endurance against his body's livelihood not only with ordinary climate but with the incredible spring of which the dry summer was the monstrous abortion, which had rained every day from the middle of May into July, as if the zodiac too had stacked cards against him. He mounted on among the bitten and fruitless stalks, carrying the gun which looked too big for him to carry or aim or dare to fire, which he had acquired seven years ago at the sacrifice of actual food and had acquired at all only because no other man would want it since it carried a shell too big to shoot at anything but a wild goose or a deer and too costly to shoot at anything but a man.

He did not look toward the house again. He went on past it and entered the rotting lattice which enclosed the well and leaned the gun against the wall and removed his shoes and drew a bucket of water and began to wash the shoes. Then he knew that she was behind him. He didn't look back, sitting on the rotted bench, small, in a faded clean shirt and patched overalls, tipping the bucket over the shoe and scrubbing at it with a corn cob. She began to laugh, harshly and steadily. "I told you this morning," she said. "I said, if you do, if you left here with that gun, I was going." He didn't look up, crouched over the wet shoe into which he had slipped his hand like a shoe-last, scrubbing at it with the cob. "Never you mind where. Dont you worry about where when they come for you." He didn't answer. He finished the first shoe and set it down and slipped his hand into the second one and tipped water from the bucket over it and began to scrub it. "Because it wont be far!" she cried suddenly, yet without raising her voice at all. "Because when they come to hang you, I'm going to be where I can see it!" Now he rose. He set the unfinished second shoe carefully down and laid the cob beside it and rose, small, almost a half head shorter than she, barefoot, moving toward her, not fast, sidling a little, his head bent and apparently not even looking at her as she stood in the gaping and broken entrance—the bleached hair darkening again at the roots since it had been a year now since there had been any money to buy more dye, the harshly and steadily laughing face watching him with a curious and expectant glitter in the eyes. He struck her across the mouth. He watched his hand, almost labored, strike across the face which did not flinch, beneath the eyes which did not even blink. "You damned little murdering bastard," she said past the bright sudden blood. He struck her again, the blood smearing between mouth and palm and then renewed, striking again with that slow gathering which was not deliberation but extreme and patiently indomitable and implacable weariness, and again. "Go," he said. "Go. Go."

He followed her, across the yard and into the hallway, though he did not enter the room. From the door he could see her, although the room itself was almost completely dark, against the small high square of the dusk-faint window. Then the match spurted and glared and steadied above the wick, and now she was framed in an opening by shadeless light and surrounded by the loud soundless invisible shades of the nameless and numberless men—that body which, even when he was actually looking at them, at times to him had never borne children, was anterior even to the two-dollar marriage which had not sanctified but sanctioned them, which each time he approached it, it was not garments intervening but the cuckolding shades which had become a part of his past too, as if he and not she had been their prone recipient; which despite the soiled and shapeless garments concealing it he would contemplate even from the cold starless night-periphery beyond both hatred and desire and tell himself: It's like drink. It's like dope to me. Then he saw the faces of the two children also, in the same flare of match and wick as if she had touched that single match to all three of them at the same time. They were sitting on the floor in the corner, not crouched, not hiding, just sitting there in the dark as they had been sitting doubtless ever since he had watched them scuttle toward the house when he came out of the bottom, looking at him with that same quality which he himself possessed: not abject but just still, with an old tired wisdom, acceptance of the immitigable discrepancy between will and capability due to that handicap of physical size in which none of the three of them had had any choice, turning from him to look without curiosity at the blood on their mother's face and watching quietly as she took a garment from a nail in the wall and spread it on the pallet bed and wrapped the other objects—the other garments, the single pair of half-size shoes which either child wore indiscriminately in cold weather, the cracked hand-glass, the wooden comb, the handleless brush—into it. "Come," she said. He moved aside and they passed him, the children huddled against her skirt and for a moment hidden from him as they emerged from the room, then visible again, moving on up the hallway before her, he following, keeping that same distance, stopping again at the entrance while they crossed the porch and descended the warped and rotting steps. When she paused on the ground beyond the steps he moved again, again with that invincible, that weary implacability, until he saw and stopped also and watched the larger child hurry across the yard, soundless and incorporeal in the dusk which was almost night now, and snatch something from the ground and return, clasping the object—a wooden block with the tops of four snuff tins nailed to it like wheels—to its breast. They went on. He did not follow further. He did not even appear to be looking at them as they passed through the broken gate.

He returned to the house and blew out the lamp, whereupon the dark became complete, as if the puny vanishing flame had carried along with it all that remained of day, so that when he returned to the well, it was by touch alone that he found the cob and the unfinished shoe and finished cleaning it. Then he washed the gun. When he first got it, when the gun was new, or new at least to him, he had had a cleaning rod for it. He had made it himself, of cane, chosen carefully and trimmed and scraped carefully and eyed neatly at the tip to take the greasy rag, and during the first year or so, when he had had money to buy powder and shot and caps to load the shells with and could hunt a little now and then, he had been no less particular in the care of the cleaning rod than of the gun because he had only bought the gun but the rod he had made. But the rod was gone now, he did not remember when nor know where, vanished along with the other accumulations of his maturity which had been dear to him too once, which he had shed somehow and somewhere along the road between the attaining of manhood and this hour when he found himself with nothing but an empty and foodless house which did not actually belong to him, and the gun, and that irremediable instant when the barrels had come level and true and his will had told his finger to contract, which nothing but his own death would ever efface from his memory. So he tipped water from the bucket over the gun and removed his shirt and wiped it dry and picked up the shoes and returned to the house and, without lighting the lamp again, stood in the dark at the cold stove and ate with his fingers from the pot of cold peas which sat on it and went and lay down, still in his overalls, on the pallet bed in the room which was empty at last even of the loud shades, lying flat on his back in the darkness with his eyes open and his arms straight beside him, thinking of nothing. Then he heard the sound.

At first he did not move; except for his regular and unhurried breathing, he might have been the corpse his attitude resembled, lying perfectly still while the first cry died away and the myriad night-silence came down and then indrew and the second cry came, ringing, deep, resonant and filled with grief. He did not move. It was as though he had been expecting it, waiting for it; had lain down and composed and emptied himself, not for sleep but to gather strength and will as distance runners and swimmers do, before assuming the phase of harried and furious endeavor which his life was about to enter, lying there for perhaps ten minutes while the long cries rang up from the dark bottom, as if he knew that those ten minutes were to be the last of peace. Then he rose. Still in the dark, he put on the still-damp shirt and the shoes he had just washed and from a nail behind the door he took down the new plow-line still looped in the coils in which his cousin, Varner's clerk, had knotted it two weeks ago, and left the house.

The night was moonless. He descended through the dry and invisible corn, keeping his bearing on a star until he reached the trees, against the black solidity of which fireflies winked and drifted and from beyond which came the booming and grunting of frogs and the howling of the dog. But once among them, he could not even see the sky anymore, though he realised then what he should have before: that the hound's voice would guide him. So he followed it, slipping and plunging in the mud and tripping and thrashing among the briers and tangled undergrowth and blundering against invisible tree trunks, his arm crooked to shield his face, sweating, while the steady cries of the dog drew nearer and nearer and broke abruptly off in mid-howl. He believed for an instant that he actually saw the phosphorescent glints of eyes although he had no light to reflect them, and suddenly and without knowing that he was going to do it, he ran toward where he had seen the eyes. He struck the next tree a shocking blow with his shoulder; he was hurled sideways but caught balance again, still plunging forward, his hands extended. He was falling now. If there's a tree in front of me now, he thought, it will be all. He actually touched the dog. He felt its breath and heard the click of its teeth as it slashed at him, springing away, leaving him on his hands and knees in the mud while the noise of its invisible flight crashed and ceased.

He was kneeling at the brink of the depression. He had only to rise and, half stooping, his arm still crooked to fend his face, step down into the ankle-deep ooze of sunless mud and rotting vegetation and follow it for another step or so to reach the brush-pile. He thrust the coiled plow-line into the bib of his overalls and stooped and began to drag away the slimed and rotten branches. Something gave a choked, infant-like cry, scrabbling among the sticks; it sprawled frantically across his foot as he kicked at it, telling himself: It's just a possum. It aint nothing but a possum, stooping again to the tangle of foul and sweating wood, lifting it away until he reached the body. He wiped his hands free of mud and slime on his shirt and overalls and took hold of the shoulders and began to walk backward, dragging it along the depression. It was not a ditch, it was an old logging road, choked with undergrowth and almost indistinguishable now, about two feet below the flat level of the bottom. He followed it for better than a mile, dragging the body which outweighed him by fifty pounds, pausing only to wipe his sweating hands from time to time on his shirt and to establish his whereabouts anew whenever he could find enough visible sky to distinguish the shapes of individual trees against.

Then he turned and dragged the body up out of the depression and went on for a hundred yars, still walking backward. He seemed to know exactly where he was, he did not even look over his shoulder until he released the body at last and stood erect and laid his hand upon what he sought—the shell of a once-tremendous pin oak, topless and about ten feet tall, standing in the clearing which the lightning bolt or age or decay or whatever it had been, had created. Two years ago he had lined a wild bee into it; the sapling which he had cut and propped against the shell to reach the honey was still in place. He took the plow-line from his breast and knotted one end about the body and removed his shoes and with the other end of the rope between his teeth, he climbed the sapling and straddled the rim of the shell and hand over hand hauled up the body which was half again as large as he, dragging it bumping and scraping up the trunk, until it lay like a half-filled sack across the lip. The knot in the rope had slipped tight. At last he took his knife and cut the rope and tumbled the body over into the shell. But it stopped almost at once, and only when it was too late did he realise that he should have reversed it. He shoved at it, probing about the shoulders, but it was not hung, it was wedged by one twisted arm. So he tied one end of the rope about the stub of a limb just below his foot and took a turn of the rope about his wrist and stood up on the wedged shoulders and began to jump up and down, whereupon without warning the body fled suddenly beneath him, leaving him dangling on the rope. He began to climb it, hand over hand, rasping off with his knuckles the rotten fibre of the wall so that a faint, constant, dry powder of decay filled his nostrils like snuff. Then he heard the stub crack, he felt the rope slip free and he leaped upward from nothing and got the finger-tips of one hand over the lip. But when his weight came down on it, a whole shard of the rotten shell carried away and he flung the other hand up but the shell crumbled beneath that one also and he climbed interminably, furiously perpetual and without gain, his mouth open for his panting breath and his eyes glaring at the remote September sky which had long since turned past midnight, until at last the wood stopped crumbling, leaving him dangling by his hands, panting, until he could pull himself up once more and straddle the rim. After a while he climbed down and lifted the propped sapling onto his shoulder and carried it fifteen or twenty yards beyond the edge of the clearing and returned and got his shoes. When he reached home dawn had already begun. He took off the muddy shoes and lay down on the pallet bed. Then, as if it had waited for him to lie down, the hound began to howl again. It seemed to him that he had even heard the intake of breath before the first cry came up from the bottom where it was still night, measured, timbrous, and prolonged.

His days and nights were now reversed. He would emerge from the bottom with the morning star or perhaps the actual sun and mount through the untended and abortive corn. He did not wash the shoes now. He would not always remove them, and he would make no fire but would eat standing from the pot of cold peas on the stove while they lasted and drank down to its dregs the pot of cold, stale coffee while it lasted, and when they were gone he would eat handsfull of raw meal from the almost empty barrel. For during the first day or so he would be hungry, since what he was doing now was harder than any work he had ever done, besides the excitement, the novelty. But after that it was not new anymore, and by then he realised it could have but one ending and so it would last forever, and he stopped being hungry. He would merely rouse, wake, to tell himself, You got to eat, and eating the raw meal (presently there was nothing in the barrel but the dried cake on the sides which he would scrape off with a knife-blade) which he did not want and apparently did not even need, as if his body were living on the incorrigible singleness of his will like so much fatty tissue. Then he would lie down on the pallet bed in his overalls and shoes on which the freshest and most recent caking of mud had not even begun to dry, still chewing and with the lengthening stubble about his mouth still full of meal grains and, as though in a continuation of the lying down, plunge not into oblivion but into an eyeless and tongueless interval of resting and recuperation like a man stepping deliberately into a bath, to wake as though to an alarm clock at the same afternoon hour, the continuity unbroken between the lying down and the opening of eyes again, since it was only the body which bore and would bear the burden which needed the rest. He would build a fire in the stove then, although there was nothing to cook save the scrapings from the meal barrel. But it was the hot drink he wanted, though there was no more coffee either. So he would fill the pot with water and heat it and drink the hot water sweetened with sugar, then in the splint chair on the porch he would watch the night, the darkness, emerge from the bottom and herd, drive, the sun gradually up the slope of the corn-patch which even in dusk stood no less barren and yellow than in sunlight, and at last take the house itself. Then the hound would begin and he would sit there for perhaps ten or fifteen minutes longer, as the holder of the annual commuter's ticket sits on his accustomed bench and continues to read his paper after the train has already whistled for the stop.

On the second afternoon when he waked a little boy was sitting on the front steps—the round-headed periwinkle-eyed son of his kinsman who operated Varner's blacksmith shop—though at the first sound of his feet on the floor the boy moved, so that when he reached the porch the boy was already on the ground beyond it and several feet away, looking back at him. "Uncle Lump says for you to come to the store," the boy said. "He says it's important." He didn't answer. He stood there with last night's mud now dried on the shoes and overalls and (so still had been his sleep) this morning's meal grains still clinging in the stubble around his mouth, until the boy turned and began to walk away and then began to run, looking back for an instant from the edge of the woods, then running on, vanishing. Still he didn't move and still there was nothing in his face. If it had been money, he could have brought it, he thought. Because it aint money. Not from them. And on the third morning he knew suddenly that someone was standing in the door watching him. He knew, even in the midst of the unreality which was not dream but a barren place where his mind, his will, stood like an unresting invincible ungrazing horse while the puny body which rode it renewed its strength, that it was not the boy now and that it was still morning, that he had not been asleep that long. They were hid here, watching me when I come up out of the bottom, he thought, trying to speak aloud to wake himself as he might have knelt to shake his own shoulder: Wake up. Wake up: until he waked, knowing at once that it was too late, not even needing the position of the window's shadow on the floor to tell him it was that same automatic hour of afternoon. He did not hurry. He started the fire and set the pot on to heat and scooped a handfull of meal scrapings from the barrel and ate it, chewing the splinters out of it, spitting them, rubbing them from his lips with his hand. In doing so, he discovered the meal already clinging in his beard and he ate that too, wiping the grains from either side with his fingers across his chewing mouth. Then he drank the cup of sweetened water and went out into the yard. The tracks were there. He knew the sheriff's—the heavy, deep, deliberate prints, even in the rainless summer's parched earth, of those two hundred and forty pounds of flesh which wore the metal shield smaller than a playing card, on which he had gambled not only his freedom but perhaps his obliteration too, followed by those of its satellites. He saw the prints of the hands and the crawling knees where one of them had searched back and forth beneath the floor while he was sleeping on top of it; he found leaning against the wall inside the stable his own shovel with which they had cleared away the year's accumulation of mule-droppings to examine the earth beneath, and he found among the trees above the cabin the place where the surrey had stood. And still there was nothing in his face—no alarm, no terror, no dread; not even contempt or amusement—only the cold and incorrigible, the almost peaceful, intractability.

He returned to the house and took the shotgun from its corner. It was covered now almost completely over with a thin, snuff-colored frost of rust, as though the very tedious care of that first night's wiping had overreached itself, had transferred the water from the gun to the shirt then back from the shirt to the gun again. And it did not breech, break, but opened slowly to steady force, exposing the thick, chocolate-colored soap-like mass of congealed animal fat, so that at last he dismantled it and boiled water in the coffee pot and scalded the grease away and laid the dismembered sections along the edge of the back porch where the sun fell on them as long as there was sun. Then he reassembled it and loaded it with two of the three remaining shells and leaned it against the wall beside the chair, and again he watched the night emerge from the bottom and mount through the bitten corn, taking corn, taking the house itself at last and, still rising, become as two up-opening palms releasing the westward-flying ultimate bird of evening. Below him, beyond the corn, the fireflies winked and drifted against the breast of darkness; beyond, within, it the steady booming of the frogs was the steady pulse and beat of the dark heart of night, so that at last when the unvarying moment came—that moment as unvarying from one dusk to the next as the afternoon's instant when he would awake—the beat of that heart seemed to fall still too, emptying silence for the first deep cry of strong and invincible grief. He reached his hand backward and took up the gun.

This time he used the hound's voice for a bearing from the start. When he entered the bottom he thought about wind and paused to test it. But there was no wind, so he went straight on toward the howling, not fast now since he was trying for silence, yet not slow either since this would not take long and then he could return home and lie down before midnight, long before midnight, telling himself as he moved cautiously and steadily toward the howling: Now I can go back to sleeping at night again. The howling was quite near now. He slanted the gun forward, his thumb on the two hammers. Then the dog's voice stopped, again in mid-howl; again for an instant he saw the two yellow points of eyes before the gun-muzzle blotted them. In the glare of the explosion he saw the whole animal sharp in relief, leaping. He saw the charge strike and hurl it backward into the loud welter of following darkness. By an actual physical effort he restrained his finger before it contracted on the second trigger and with the gun still at his shoulder he crouched, holding his breath and glaring into the sightless dark while the tremendous silence which had been broken three nights ago when the first cry of the hound reached him and which had never once been restored, annealed, even while he slept, roared down about him and, still roaring, began to stiffen and set like cement, not only in his hearing but in his lungs, his breathing, inside and without him too, solidifying from tree-trunk to tree-trunk, among which the shattered echoes of the shot died away in strangling murmurs, caught in that cooling solidity before they had had time to cease. With the gun still cocked and presented, he advanced toward the place where he had seen the dog fall, panting through his bared clenched teeth, feeling about with his feet in the undergrowth. Then he realised suddenly that he had already passed the spot and that he was still advancing. He knew that he was about to start running and then he was running, blindly in the pitch darkness, speaking, hissing to himself: Stop. Stop. You'll bust your damn brains out. He stopped, panting. He got his bearings anew on a patch of sky, yet he forced himself to remain motionless until even the panting stopped. Then he let the hammer of the gun down and went on, walking now. Now he had the booming of the frogs to guide him, blending and fading then rising again in choral climax, each separate voice not a single note but an octave, almost a chord, in bass, growing louder and louder and nearer and nearer, then ceasing abruptly too into a second of frozen immobility followed by a swift random patter of small splashes like hands striking the water, so that when he saw the water it was already shattered into fluid ceaseless gleams across which reflected stars slid and vanished and recovered. He flung the gun. For an instant he saw it, spinning slowly. Then it splashed, not sinking but disintegrating among that shattered scurrying of broken stars.

When he reached home, it was not even midnight yet. Now he removed not only the shoes but the overalls too which had not passed his knees in seventy-two hours, and lay down on the pallet. But at once he knew he was not going to sleep, not because of the seventy-two hours' habit of reversed days and nights, not because of any twitching and jerking of spent and ungovernable nerves and muscles, but because of that silence which the first gunshot had broken and the second one had made whole again. So he lay again, rigid and composed on his back, his arms at his sides and his eyes open in the darkness and his head and lungs filled with that roaring silence across which the random and velvet-shod fireflies drifted and winked and beyond which the constant frogs pulsed and beat, until the rectangle of sky beyond the oblique door of the room and the open end of the hallway began to turn gray and then primrose, and already he could see three buzzards soaring in it. Now I must get up, he told himself; I will have to start staying up all day if I aim to begin sleeping again at night. Then he began to say, Wake up. Wake up, until he waked at last, with the yellow square of window-shaped sun lying once more on the floor where each unvarying afternoon it would lie. Resting upon the quilt not an inch from his face was a folded scrap of brown paper; when he rose, he found in the dust at the doorsill the print of the little boy's naked foot. The note was in pencil, on a scrap torn from a paper sack, unsigned: *Come on in here your wifes got some money for you* He stood, unshaven, in his shirt, blinking at it. Now I can go, he thought, and something began to happen in his heart. He raised his head, blinking almost painfully, looking for the first time in three days beyond the desolate and foodless cabin which symbolised the impasse his life had reached, into the limitless freedom of the sunny sky. He spoke aloud. "Now I can—" he said. Then he saw the buzzards. At dawn he had seen three. Now he might possibly have counted them, though he did not. He just watched the black concentric spiraling as if they followed an invisible funnel, disappearing one by one below the trees. He spoke aloud again. "It's the dog," he said, knowing it was not the dog. And it didn't matter. Because I'll be gone then, he thought. It was not that something lifted from his heart; it was as though he had become aware for the first time of the weight which lay on it.

It was almost sunset when, shaved and with the shoes and overalls washed again, he mounted to the empty gallery and entered the store. His kinsman was behind the open candy case, in the act of putting something into his mouth.

"Where—" he said.

The cousin closed the case, chewing. "You durned fool, I sent word to you two days ago to get away from there before that pussel-gutted Hampton come prowling around here with that surrey full of deputies. A nigger grabbling in that slough found that durn gun before the water even quit shaking."

"It's not mine," he said. "I have no gun. Where——"

"Hell fire, everybody knows it's yours. There aint another one of them old hammer-lock ten-gauge Hadleys in this country but that one. That's why I never told no lie about it, let alone that durn Hampton sitting right out there on that bench when the nigger come up the steps with it. I says, 'Sure it's Mink's gun. He's been hunting for it ever since last fall.' Then I turns to the nigger. 'What the hell you mean, you black son of a bitch,' I says, 'borrowing Mr Snopes's gun last fall to go squirl hunting and letting it fall in that ere slough and claiming you couldn't find it?' Here." The cousin stooped beneath the counter and rose and laid the gun on the counter. It had been wiped off save for a patch of now-dried mud on the stock.

He did not even look at it. "It's not mine," he said. "Where is——"

"But that's all right now. I fixed that in time. What Hampton expected was for me to deny it was yours. Then he would a had you. But I fixed that. I throwed the suspicion right onto the nigger fore Hampton could open his mouth. I figger about tonight or maybe tomorrow night I'll take a few of the boys and go to the nigger's house with a couple of trace chains or maybe a little fire under his feet. And even if he dont confess nothing, folks will hear that he has done been visited at night and there's too many votes out here for Hampton to do nothing else but take him on in and send him to the penitentiary, even if he cant quite risk hanging him, and Hampton knows it. So that's all right. Besides, what I sent you that first message for was about your wife."

"Yes," he said. "Where——"

"She's going to get you in trouble. She's done already got you in trouble. That's how come that durn vote-sucking sheriff noseying around out here. His nigger found the horse, with him and the dog both missing, but that was all right until folks begun to remember how she turned up here that same night, with them two kids and that bundle of clothes and blood still running out of her busted mouth until folks couldn't help but know you had run her out of the house. And even that might have been all right if she hadn't started in telling everybody that would listen that you never done it. Just a horse with a empty saddle; no body and no blood neither found yet, and here she is trying to help you by telling everybody she meets that you never done something that nobody knows for sure has even been done yet. Why in hell aint you got out of here? Didn't you have sense enough to do that the first day?"

"On what?" he said.

The cousin had been blinking rapidly at him. Now the little eyes stopped blinking. "On what?" he said. The other did not answer. He had not moved since he entered, small, immobile, in the middle of the floor opposite the entrance, through which the dying sunlight stained him from head to foot with a thin wash like diluted blood. "You mean you aint got any money? You mean to stand there and tell me he never had nothing in his pocket? Because I dont believe it. By God, I know better. I saw inside his purse that same morning. He never carried a cent less than fifty . . ." The voice ceased, died. Then it spoke in a dawning incredulous amazement and no louder than a whisper: "Do you mean to tell me you never even looked? *never even looked?*" The other did not answer. He might not have even heard, motionless, looking at nothing while the last of the copper light, mounting like rising water up his body, gathered for an instant in concentrated and dying crimson upon the calm and wavering and intractable mask of his face, and faded, and the dusk, the twilight, gathered along the ranked shelves and in the shadowy corners and the old strong smells of cheese and leather and kerosene, condensed and thickened among the rafters above his head like the pall of oblivion itself. The cousin's voice seemed to emerge from it, sourceless, unlocatable, without even the weight of breath to give it volume: "Where did you put him?" and again, the cousin outside the counter now, facing him, almost breast to breast with him, the fierce repressed breathing murmuring on his face now: "By God, he had at least fifty dollars. I know. I seen it. Right here in this store. Where did you——"

"No," he said.

"Yes."

"No." Their faces were not a foot apart, their breathing steady and audible. Then the other face moved back, larger than his, higher than his, beginning to become featureless in the fading light.

"All right," the cousin said. "I'm glad you dont need money. Because if you come to me expecting any, you'd just have to keep on expecting. You know what Will Varner pays his clerks. You know about how much any man working for Will Varner's wages could get ahead in ten years, let alone two months. So you wont even need that ten dollars your wife's got. So that'll be just fine, wont it?"

"Yes," he said. "Where——"

"Staying at Will Varner's." He turned at once and went toward the door. As he passed out of it the cousin spoke again out of the shadows behind him: "Tell her to ask Will or Jody to lend her another ten to go with that one she's already got."

Although it was not quite dark yet, there was already a light in the Varner house. He could see it even at this distance, and it was as if he were standing outside of himself, watching the distance steadily shorten between himself and the light. And then that's all, he thought. All them days and nights that looked like they wasn't going to have no end, come down to the space of a little piece of dusty road between me and a lighted door. And when he put his hand on Varner's gate, it was as if she had been waiting, watching the road for him. She came out of the front door, running, framed again for an instant by the lighted doorway as when he had first seen her that night at the lumber camp to which, even nine years afterward, he did not like to remember how, by what mischance, he had come. The feeling was no less strong now than it had ever been. He did not dread to remember it nor did he try not to, and not in remorse for the deed he had done, because he neither required nor desired absolution for that. He merely wished he did not have to remember the fiasco which had followed the act, contemptuous of the body or the intellect which had failed the will to do, not writhing with impotent regret on remembering it and not snarling, because he never snarled; but just cold, indomitable, and intractable. He had lived in a dozen different sorry and ill-made rented cabins as his father had moved from farm to farm, without himself ever having been more than fifteen or twenty miles away from any one of them. Then suddenly and at night he had had to leave the roof he called home and the only land and people and customs he knew, without even time to gather up anything to take with him, if there had been anything to take, nor to say farewell to anyone if there had been anyone to say farewell to, to find himself weeks later and still on foot, more than two hundred miles away. He was seeking the sea; he was twenty-three then, that young. He had never seen it; he did not know certainly just where it was, except that it was to the south. He had never thought of it before and he could not have said why he wanted to go to it—what of repudiation of the land, the earth, where his body or intellect had faulted somehow to the cold undeviation of his will to do—seeking what of that iodinic proffer of space and oblivion of which he had no intention of availing himself, would never avail himself, as if, by deliberately refusing to cut the wires of remembering, to punish that body and intellect which had failed him. Perhaps he was seeking only the proffer of this illimitable space and irremediable forgetting along the edge of which the contemptible teeming of his own earth-kind timidly seethed and recoiled, not to accept the proffer but merely to bury himself in this myriad anonymity beside the impregnable haven of all the drowned intact golden galleons and the unattainable deathless seamaids. Then, almost there and more than twenty-four hours without food, he saw a light and approached it and heard the loud voices and saw her framed in the open door, immobile, upright and unlistening, while those harsh loud manshouts and cries seemed to rise toward her like a roaring incense. He went no further. The next morning he was at work there, an axeman, without even knowing whom he was working for, asking only incidentally of the foreman who hired him and who told him bluntly that he was too small, too light, to swing his end of a cross-cut saw, what his wage would be. He had never seen convicts' stripes before either, so it was not with that first light but only after several succeeding ones that he learned where he was —a tract of wild-catted virgin timber in process of being logged by a roaring man of about fifty who was no taller than he was, with strong, short iron-gray hair and a hard prominent belly, who through political influence or bribery or whatever got his convict labor from the State for the price of their board and keep; a widower who had lost his wife years ago at the birth of their first child and now lived openly with a magnificent quadroon woman most of whose teeth were gold and who superintended the kitchen where other convicts did the actual work, in a separate house set among the plank-and-canvas barracks in which the convicts lived. The woman in the lighted door was that child. She lived in the same house with her father and the quadroon, in a separate wing with an entrance of its own, and her hair was black then—a splendid heavy mane of it which whatever present one out of foremen and armed guards and convict laborers, and himself in his turn, after his summons came and he had long since discovered the reason for the separate entrance, contributed to keep cut almost man-short with razors. It was strong and short and not fine, either in the glare of that first evening's lamp or in the next day's sunlight when, the axe lifted for the stroke, he turned and she was sitting a big, rangy, well-kept horse behind and above him, in overalls, looking at him not brazenly and not speculatively, but intently and boldly, as a bold and successful man would. That was what he saw: the habit of success—that perfect marriage of will and ability with a single undiffused object—which set her not as a feminine garment but as one as masculine as the overalls and her height and size and the short hair; he saw not a nympholept but the confident lord of a harem. She did not speak that time. She rode on, and now he discovered that that separate entrance was not used only at night. Sometimes she would ride past on the horse and stop and speak briefly to the foreman and ride on; sometimes the quadroon would appear on the horse and speak a name to the foreman and return, and the foreman would call that name and the man would drop his axe or saw and follow the horse. Then he, still swinging his axe and not even looking up, would seem to follow and watch that man enter the private door and then watch him emerge later and return to work—the nameless, the identical, highwayman, murderer, thief, among whom there appeared to be no favorites and no jealousy. That was to be his alone, apparently. But even before his summons came, he was resigned to the jealousy and cognizant of his fate. He had been bred by generations to believe invincibly that to every man, whatever his past actions, whatever depths he might have reached, there was reserved one virgin, at least for him to marry; one maidenhead, if only for him to deflower and destroy. Yet he not only saw that he must compete for mere notice with men among whom he saw himself not only as a child but as a child of another race and species, but that when he did approach her at last he would have to tear aside not garments alone but the ghostly embraces of thirty or forty men; and this not only once but each time and hence (he foresaw even then his fate) forever: no room, no darkness, no desert even ever large enough to contain the two of them and the constant stallion-ramp of those inexpugnable shades. Then his turn, his summons came at last, as he had known it would. He obeyed it with foreknowledge but without regret. He entered not the hot and quenchless bed of a barren and lecherous woman, but the fierce simple cave of a lioness—a tumescence which surrendered nothing and asked no quarter, and which made a monogamist of him forever, as opium and homicide do of those whom they once accept. That was early one afternoon, the hot sun of July falling through the shadeless and even curtainless windows open to all outdoors, upon a bed made by hand of six-inch unplaned timbers cross-braced with light steel cables, yet which nevertheless would advance in short steady skidding jerks across the floor like a light and ill-balanced rocking chair. Five months later they were married. They did not plan it. Never at any time afterward did he fail to affirm, even to himself, that the marriage had been no scheme or even intention of hers. What did it was the collapse of her father's enterprise, which even he had been able to see was inherent with its own inevitable bankruptcy which the crash of each falling tree brought one stick nearer. Afterward it seemed to him that that afternoon's bedding had been the signal for that entire furious edifice of ravished acres and shotgun houses and toiling men and mules which had been erected overnight and founded on nothing, to collapse overnight into nothing, back into the refuse—the sawdust heaps, the lopped dead limbs and tree-butts and all the grief of wood—of its own murdering. He had most of his five months' pay. They walked to the nearest county-seat and bought a license; the Justice of the Peace who sold it to them removed his chew of tobacco and, holding it damp in his hand, called in two passing men and pronounced them man and wife. They returned to his native country, where he rented a small farm on shares. They had a second-hand stove, a shuck mattress on the floor, the razor with which he still kept her hair cut short, and little else. At that time they needed little else. She said: "I've had a hundred men, but I never had a wasp before. That stuff comes out of you is rank poison. It's too hot. It burns itself and my seed both up. It'll never make a kid." But three years afterward it did. Five years later it had made two; and he would watch them as they approached across whatever sorry field or patch, fetching his cold meagre dinner or the jug of fresh water, or as they played with blocks of wood or rusted harness buckles or threadless and headless plow-bolts which even he could no longer use, in the dust before whatever rented porch he sat on while the sweat cooled out of him, and in a resurgence of the old hot quick invincible fury still as strong and fierce and brief as on the first time, he would think, By God, they better be mine. Then, quieter, on the pallet bed where she would already be asleep although his own spent body had not yet ceased to jerk and twitch, he would think how, even if they were not, it was the same thing. They served to shackle her too, more irrevocably than he himself was shackled, since on her fate she had even put the seal of a formal acquiescence by letting her hair grow out again and dyeing it.

She came down the walk, running heavily but fast. She reached it before he had finished opening it, flinging both him and the gate back as she ran through it and caught him by the front of his overalls. "No!" she cried, though her voice still whispered: "No! Oh God, what do you mean? You cant come in here!"

"I can go anywhere I want to," he said. "Lump said—" Then he tried to wrench free, but she had already released him and caught his arm and was hurrying, almost dragging him along the fence, away from the light. He wrenched at her grip again, setting his feet. "Wait," he said.

"You fool!" she said, in that harsh panting whisper: "You fool! Oh, God damn you! God damn you!" He began to struggle, with a cold condensed fury which did not seem quite able or perhaps ready to emerge yet from his body. Then he lashed suddenly out, still not at her but to break her grip. But she held him, with both hands now, as they faced each other. "Why didn't you go that night? God, I thought of course you were going to get out as soon as I left!" She shook him savagely, with no more effort than if he were a child. "Why didn't you? Why in hell didn't you?"

"On what?" he said. "Where? Lump said——"

"I know you didn't have any money, like I know you haven't had anything to eat except the dust in that barrel. You could have hidden! In the woods—anywhere, until I would have time to—God damn you! God damn you! If they would just let me do the hanging!" She shook him, her face bent to his, her hard, hot, panting breath on his face. "Not for killing him, but for doing it when you had no money to get away on if you ran, and nothing to eat if you stayed. If they'd just let me do it: hang you just enough to take you down and bring you to and hang you again just enough to cut you down and bring you to—" He slashed out again, viciously. But she had already released him, standing on one foot now, the other foot angled upward from the knee to meet her reaching hand. She took something from her shoe and put it into his hand. He knew at once what it was—a banknote, folded and refolded small and square and still warm with body-heat. And it was just one note. It's one dollar, he thought, knowing it was not. It was I. O. and Eck, he told himself, knowing it was not, just as he knew there was but one man in the country who would have ten dollars in one bill—or at the most, two men; now he even heard what his cousin had said as he walked out of the store fifteen minutes ago. He didn't even look toward his hand.

"Did you sell Will something for it, or did you just take it out of his pants while he was asleep? Or was it Jody?"

"What if I did? What if I can sell enough more of it tonight to get ten more? Only for God's sake dont go back to the house. Stay in the woods. Then tomorrow morning—" He did not move; she saw only the slight jerk of his hand and wrist—no coin to ring against his thumbnail or to make any sound among the dust-stiffened roadside weeds where gouts of dusty cotton clung. When he went on, she began to run after him. "Mink!" she said. He walked steadily on. She was at his shoulder, running, though he continued to walk. "For God's sake," she said. "For God's sake." Then she caught his shoulder and swung him to face her. This time he slashed free and sprang into the weeds, stooping, and rose with a stick lifted in his hand and walked toward her again with that patient and implacable weariness, until she turned. He lowered the stick, but he continued to stand there until he could no longer distinguish her, even against the pale dust of the road. Then he tossed the stick into the weeds and turned. The cousin was standing behind him. If the other had been smaller or he larger he would have stepped on him, walked him down. The other stepped aside and turned with him, the faint rasp of the repressed breathing at his shoulder.

"So you throwed that away too," the cousin said. He didn't answer. They went on side by side in the thick, ankle-deep dust. Their feet made no sound in it. "He had at least fifty dollars. I tell you I saw it. And you expect me to believe you aint got it." He didn't answer. They walked steadily on, not fast, like two people walking without destination or haste, for pleasure or exercise. "All right. I'm going to do what wouldn't no other man living do: I'm going to give you the benefit of the doubt that you aint got it, actually never looked. Now where did you put him?" He didn't answer nor pause. The cousin caught him by the shoulder, stopping him; now there was in the fierce baffled breathing, the whispering voice, not only the old amazement but a sort of cold and desperate outrage, like one trying to reach through a fleeing crisis to the comprehension of an idiot: "Are you going to let that fifty dollars lay there for Hampton and them deputies to split up between them?"

He struck the hand off. "Let me alone," he said.

"All right. I'll do this. I'll give you twenty-five dollars now. I'll go with you, all you got to do is hand me the wallet, sight unseen. Or hand me his pants, if you dont want to take it out of them. You wont even touch or even see the money." He turned to go on again. "All right. If you are too puke-stomached to do it yourself, tell me where it is. When I come back, I'll give you ten dollars, though a fellow that just throwed away a ten-dollar bill dont—" He walked on. Again the hand caught his shoulder and swung him about; the tense fierce voice murmured from nowhere and everywhere out of the breathless dark: "Wait. Listen. Listen good. Suppose I look up Hampton; he's been around here all day; he's probably still somewhere here tonight. Suppose I tell him I done recollected a mistake, that that gun wasn't lost last fall because you come in the store and bought a nickel's worth of powder just last week. Then you can explain how you was aiming to swap Houston the powder for the pound-fee on that yearling——"

This time he did not fling the hand off. He merely began to walk toward the other with that patient and invincible weariness which the other did not recognise, walking steadily toward the cousin as the other gave ground. His voice was not loud either; it was flat, absolutely toneless: "I ask you to let me alone," he said. "I dont tell you; I ask you to let me alone. Not for my sake. Because I'm tired. I ask you to let me alone." The other backed away before him, moving slightly faster, so that the distance between them increased. When he stopped, it continued to increase until he could no longer see the other and only the whisper, furious and outraged, came back:

"All right, you durn little tight-fisted murderer. See if you get away with it."

Approaching the village again, his feet made no sound in the dust and, in the darkness, seemingly no progress either, though the light in Mrs Littlejohn's kitchen window just beyond the store's dark bulk—the only light anywhere—drew steadily nearer. Just beyond it the lane turned off which led to his cabin four miles away. That's where I would have kept straight on, to Jeflerson and the railroad, he thought; and suddenly, now that it was too late, now that he had lost all hope of alternative between planned and intelligent escape and mere blind desperate harried fleeing and doubling through the swamp and jungle of the bottom like a spent and starving beast cut off from its den, he knew that for three days now he had not only hoped but had actually believed that opportunity to choose would be given him. And he had not only lost that privilege of choice, but due to the blind mischance which had permitted his cousin either to see or guess what was in the wallet, even the bitter alternative was deferred for another night. It began to seem to him now that that puny and lonely beacon not only marked no ultimate point for even desperate election but was the period to hope itself, and that all which remained to him of freedom lay in the shortening space between it and his advancing foot. I thought that when you killed a man, that finished it, he told himself. But it dont. It just starts then.

When he reached home, he did not enter it. Instead, he went around to the woodpile and got his axe and stood for a moment to examine the stars. It was not much past nine; he could allow himself until midnight. Then he circled the house and entered the corn-patch. Halfway down the slope he paused, listening, then he went on. He did not enter the bottom either; he stepped behind the first tree large enough to conceal him and leaned the axe carefully against it where he could find it again and stood there, motionless, breathing quietly, and listened to the heavy body running with hurried and cautious concern among the clashing cornstalks, the tense and hurried panting drawing rapidly nearer, then the quick indraw of breath when the other ran past the tree, checking, as he stepped out from behind it and turned back up the slope.

They went back through the corn, in single file and five feet apart. He could hear the clumsy body behind him stumbling and thrashing among the sibilant rows, and the breathing fierce, outraged, and repressed. His own passage made no noise, even in the trigger-set dryness of the corn, as if his body had no substance. "Listen," the cousin said. "Let's look at this thing like two reasonable . . ." They emerged from corn and crossed the yard and entered the house, still five feet apart. He went on to the kitchen and lit the lamp and squatted before the stove, preparing to start the fire. The cousin stood in the door, breathing heavily and watching while the other coaxed the chips into a blaze and took the coffee-pot from the stove and filled it from the water pail and set it back. "Aint you even got nothing to eat?" the cousin said. The other did not answer. "You got some feed corn, aint you? We could parch some of that." The fire was burning well now. The other laid his hand on the pot, though of course it had not even begun to be warm yet. The cousin watched the back of his head. "All right," he said. "Let's go get some of it."

The other removed his hand from the pot. He did not look back. "Get it," he said. "I'm not hungry." The cousin breathed in the door, watching the still, slanted face. His breath made a faint, steady, rasping sound.

"All right," he said. "I'll go to the barn and get some." He left the door and walked heavily down the hallway and onto the back porch and stepped down to the earth, already running. He ran frantically in the blind darkness and on tiptoe, around toward the front of the house and stopped, peering around the corner toward the front door, holding his breath, then ran again, on to the steps, where he could see into the hallway lighted faintly by the lamp in the kitchen, and paused again for an instant, crouched, glaring. The son of a bitch tricked me, he thought; He went out the back: and ran up the steps, stumbling heavily and recovering, and thundered down the hall to the kitchen door and saw, in the instant of passing it, the other standing beside the stove as he had left him, his hand again on the coffee-pot. The murdering little son of a bitch, he thought. I wouldn't have believed it. I wouldn't have believed a man would have to go through all this even for five hundred dollars.

But when he stood in the door again, save for the slightly increased rasp and tempo of his breathing, he might never have left it. He watched the other fetch to the stove a cracked china cup, a thick glass tumbler, a tin can containing a little sugar, and a spoon; when he spoke, he might have been talking to his employer's wife over a tea-table: "It's done made up its mind at last to get hot, has it?" The other did not answer. He filled the cup from the pot and spooned sugar into it and stirred it and stood beside the stove, turned three quarters from the cousin, his head bent, sipping from the cup. After a moment the cousin approached and filled the tumbler and put sugar into it and sipped, wry-faced, his features all seeming to flee from the tumbler's rim, upward, gathering, eyes, nose, even mouth, toward his forehead, as if the skin in which they were embedded was attached to his skull only at one point somewhere in the back. "Listen," the cousin said. "Just try to look at this thing like two reasonable people. There's that fifty dollars laying out there, not belonging to nobody. And you cant go and get it without taking me, because I aint going to let you. And I cant go get it without taking you, because I dont know where it's at. Yet here we are, setting around this house while every minute we waste is bringing that durn sheriff and them deputies just that much closer to finding it. It's just a matter of pure and simple principle. Aint no likes and dislikes about it. If I had my way, I'd keep all of it myself, the same as you would. But you cant and I cant. Yet here we are, setting here—" The other tilted the cup and drained it.

"What time is it?" he said. From the creased bulge of his waistband the cousin wrenched a dollar watch on a thong of greasy leather and looked at it and prized it back into the fob-pocket.

"Twenty-eight past nine. And it aint going to stay that forever. And I got to open the store at six oclock in the morning. And I got to walk five miles tonight before I can go to bed. But never mind that. Dont pay no attention to that, because there aint nothing personal in this because it is a pure and simple business matter. Think about your—" The other set the empty cup on the stove.

"Checkers?" he said.

"—self. You got— What?" The cousin stopped talking. He watched the other cross the room and lift from among the shadows in the corner a short, broad piece of plank. From the shelf above it he took another tin can and brought them to the table. The board was marked off with charcoal into alternate staggered squares; the can contained a handful of small china- and glass-fragments in two colors, apparently from a broken plate and a blue glass bottle. He laid the board beside the lamp and began to oppose the men. The cousin watched him, the tumbler arrested halfway to his mouth. For an instant he ceased to breathe. Then he breathed again. "Why, sholy," he said. He set the glass on the stove and drew up a chair opposite. Sitting, he seemed to be on the point of enveloping not only the chair but the table too in a collapsing mass of flabby and badly-filled flesh, like a collapsing balloon. "We'll play a nickel a game against that fifty dollars," he said. "All right?"

"Move," the other said. They began to play—the one with a cold and deadly deliberation and economy of moves, the other with a sort of clumsy speed and dash. It was that amateurish, that almost childlike, lack of premeditation and plan or even foresight of one who, depending on manipulation and not intellect in games of chance, finds himself involved in one where dexterity cannot avail, yet nevertheless attempting to cheat even at bald and simple draughts with an incredible optimism, an incorrigible dishonesty long since become pure reflex and probably now beyond his control, making his dashing and clumsy moves then withdrawing his closed fist to sit watching with his little intent unwinking eyes the still, wasted, down-looking face opposite, talking steadily about almost everything except money and death, the fist resting on the table-edge still closed about the pawn or the king's crown which it had palmed. The trouble with checkers is, he thought, It aint nothing but checkers. At the end of an hour he was thirteen games ahead.

"Make it a quarter," he said.

"What time is it?" the other said. The cousin wrung the watch from his waistband again and returned it.

"Four minutes to eleven."

"Move," the other said. They played on. The cousin was not talking now. He was keeping score now with a chewed pencil stub on the edge of the board. Thus when, thirty minutes later, he totted up the score, the pencil presented to his vision not a symbol but a sum complete with decimal and dollar mark, which seemed in the next instant to leap upward and strike comprehension with an impact almost audible; he became dead still, for an instant he did not breathe indeed, thinking rapidly: Hell fire. Hell fire. Of course he never caught me. He didn't want to. Because when I have won all of his share, he'll figure he wont need to risk going where it's at. So now he had to completely reverse his entire tactics. And now for the first time the crawling hands on the face of the watch which he now produced without being asked and laid face-up beside the board, assumed a definite significance. Because this here just cant go on forever, he thought in a resurgence of the impotent rage. It just cant. A man just cant be expected to go through much more of this even for all of fifty dollars. So he reversed himself. Whereupon it was as if even dishonesty had foresworn him. He would make the dashing, clumsy, calculated moves; he would sit back with his own pawn or king's crown in his fist now. Only now the other's thin hard hand would be gripping that wrist while the cold, flat, dead voice demonstrated how a certain pawn could not possibly have arrived at the square on which it suddenly appeared to be, and lived, or even rapping the knuckles of that gripped hand on the table until it disgorged. Yet he would attempt it again, with that baffled and desperate optimism and hope, and be caught again and then try it again, until at the end of the next hour his movements on the board were not even childlike, they were those of an imbecile or a blind person. And he was talking again now: "Listen. There's that fifty dollars that dont belong to nobody because he never had no kin, nobody to claim it. Just laying out there for the first man that comes along to——"

"Move," the other said. He moved a pawn. "No," the other said. "Jump." He made the jump. The other moved a second pawn.

"—and here you are needing money to keep from being hung maybe and you cant go and get it because I wont leave. And me that cant get up and go on home and get to bed so I can get up, and go to work tomorrow because you wont show me where that money's at——"

"Move," the other said. The cousin moved a pawn. "No," the other said. "Jump." The cousin took the jump. Then he watched the gaunt black-haired fingers holding the scrap of blue glass clear the board in five jumps.

"And now it's after midnight. It will be light in six hours. And Hampton and them durn deputies—" The cousin ceased. The other was now standing, looking down at him; the cousin rose quickly. They stared at one another across the table. "Well?" the cousin said. His breath began to make the harsh, tense, rasping sound again, not triumphant yet. "Well?" he said. "Well?" But the other was not looking at him, he was looking down, the face still, wasted, seemingly without life.

"I ask you to go," the other said. "I ask you to leave me alone."

"Sholy," the cousin said, his voice no louder than the other's. "Quit now? after I done gone through all this?" The other turned toward the door. "Wait," the cousin said. The other did not pause. The cousin blew out the lamp and overtook the other in the hallway. He was talking again, whispering now. "If you'd just listened to me six hours ago. We'd a done had it and been back, in bed, instead of setting up here half the night. Dont you see how it was tit for tat all the time? You had me and I had you, and couldn't neither— Where we going?" The other didn't answer. He went steadily on across the yard, toward the barn, the cousin following; again he heard just behind him the tense, fierce adenoidal breathing, the whispering voice: "Hell fire, maybe you dont want me to have half of it and maybe I dont want nobody to have half of it neither. But hell fire, aint just half of it better than to think of that durn Hampton and them deputies—" He entered the barn and opened the door to the crib and stepped up into it, the cousin stopping just outside the door behind him, and reached down from its nail in the wall a short, smooth white-oak stick eyed at the end with a loop of hemp rope—a twister which Houston had used with his stallion, which Snopes had found when he rented the foreclosed portion of Houston's farm from the Varners—and turned and struck all in one motion and dropped the cudgel and caught the heavy body as it fell so that its own weight helped to carry it into the crib and all he needed to do was to drag it on in until the feet cleared the door. He unbuckled a hame-string and the check-rein from his plow gear and bound the other's hands and feet and tore a strip from the tail of his shirt and made a gag with it.

When he reached the bottom, he could not find the tree behind which he had left the axe. He knew what was wrong. It was as though with the cessation of that interminable voice he had become aware not of silence but of elapsed time, that on the instant it had ceased he had retraced and resumed at the moment it began in the store at six oclock in the afternoon, and now he was six hours late. You're trying too hard, he told himself. You got to slow up. So he held himself still for the space of a hundred, trying to orient himself by looking back up the slope, to establish whether he was above or below the tree, to the right or left of it. Then he went back halfway through the corn and looked back at the bottom from there, trying to recognise by its shape and position the tree where he had left the axe, standing in the roar not of silence now but of time's friction. He thought of starting from some point which he knew was below the tree he sought and searching each tree as he came to it. But the sound of time was too loud, so when he began to move, to run, it was toward neither the bottom nor the cabin but across the slope, quartering, out of the corn and on into the road a half mile beyond his house.

He ran for another mile and came to another cabin, smaller and shabbier than his. It belonged to the Negro who had found the gun. There was a dog here, a mongrel terrier, a feice, not much larger than a cat and noisy as a calliope; at once it came boiling out from beneath the house and rushed toward him in shrill hysteria. He knew it and it should know him; he spoke to it to quiet it but it continued to yap, the sound seeming to come from a dozen different points out of the darkness before him until he ran suddenly at it, whereupon the shrill uproar faded rapidly back toward the house. He continued to run, on toward the woodpile which he knew too; the axe was there. As he caught it up a voice said from the dark cabin: "Who there?" He didn't answer. He ran on, the terrier still yapping behind him though from beneath the house now. Now he was in corn again, better than his. He ran on through it, descending, toward the bottom.

Before entering the bottom, he stopped and took his bearings on a star. He did not expect to find the tree from this point, it was the old sunken road he aimed for; once in that, he could orient himself again. His surest course, even though it would be longer, would be to skirt the bottom until he reached country he knew in the dark and strike in for the tree from there, but when he examined the sky to fix his bearing, he thought, It's after one oclock.

Yet, thirty minutes later, he had not found the road. He had been able to see the sky only intermittently, and not always the star he guided by then. But he believed he had not deviated much. Also, he had cautioned himself: You will expect to come onto it before you do; you will have to watch for that. But in this time he had travelled twice the distance in which he should have found it. When he realised, admitted at last that he was lost, it was with neither alarm nor despair, but rage. It was as though, like the cousin and his dishonesty two or three hours ago, ruthlessness likewise had repudiated the disciple who had flagged for a moment in ruthlessness; that it was that humanity which had caused him to waste three hours in hope that the cousin would tire and go away instead of striking the other over the head when he ran past the tree where he had lost the axe, which had brought him to this.

His first impulse was to run, not in panic but to keep ahead of that avalanche of accumulating seconds which was now his enemy. But he quelled it, holding himself motionless, his spent body shaking faintly and steadily with exhaustion, until he was satisfied his muscles would not be able to take him by surprise and run with him. Then he turned deliberately and carefully until he believed he was facing his back trail and the direction from which he had come, and walked forward. After a while he came to an opening in which he could see the sky. The star on which he had fixed his course when he entered the bottom was directly in front of him. And now it's after two oclock, he thought.

Now he began to run, or as fast as he dared, that is. He could not help himself. I got to find the road now, he thought. If I try to go back and start over, it will be daylight before I get out of the bottom. So he hurried on, stumbling and thrashing among the briers and undergrowth, one arm extended to fend himself from the trees, voiceless, panting, blind, the muscles about his eyelids strained and aching against the flat impenetrable face of the darkness, until suddenly there was no earth under his feet; he made another stride, running upon nothing, then he was falling and then he was on his back, panting. He was in the road. But he did not know where. But I aint crossed it, he thought. I am still on the west side of it. And now it's past two o'clock.

Now he was oriented again. By turning his back on the road and holding a straight course, he would reach the edge of the bottom. Then he would be able to ascertain where he was. When he found himself falling, he had flung the axe away. He hunted for it on his hands and knees and found it and climbed out of the road and went on. He did not run now. Now he knew that he dared not lose himself again. When, an hour later, he emerged from the bottom, it was at the corner of a corn-patch. It was his own; the bizarre erst-fluid earth became fixed and stable in the old solid dimensions and juxtapositions. He saw the squat roof-line of his own house, and running again, stumbling a little among the rows of whispering stalks, panting through his dry lips and his dry clenched teeth, he saw and recognised the tree behind which he had left the axe, and again it was as if he had retraced and resumed at some dead point in time and only time was lost. He turned and approached it, he was about to pass it when a thicker shadow detached itself from the other shadow, rising without haste, and the cousin's voice said, weakly and harshly: "Forgot your durned axe, hah? Here it is. Take it."

He had stopped with no sound, no ejaculation, no catch of breath. Except I better not use the axe, he thought, still, immobile, while the other breathed harshly above him and the harsh, weak, outraged voice went on: "You durn little fratricidal murderer, if I hadn't just about stood all one man can stand, for twenty-five dollars or twenty-five thousand either, I'd be a good mind to knock you in the head with it and tote you out and throw you into Hampton's surrey myself. And by God it aint your fault it wasn't Hampton instead of me sitting here waiting for you. Hell fire, you hadn't hardly got started good chuckling over them other twenty-five dollars you thought you had just got before Hampton and the whole durn mess of them was in that crib, untying me and throwing water in my face. And I lied for you again. I told them you had knocked me in the head and tied me up and robbed me and lit out for the railroad. Now just how much longer do you figure I aim to keep telling lies just to save your neck? Hah?—Well? What are we waiting for? For Hampton?"

"Yes," he said. "All right." But not the axe, he thought. He turned and went on, into the trees. The other followed him, right at his heels now, the fierce adenoidal breath, the weak, outraged voice almost over his head, so that when he stooped and groped with his hand about the ground at his feet, the other walked into him.

"What the hell you doing now? Have you lost the durn axe again? Find it and give it to me and then get on and show me where it's at before not only sunup but ever durn vote-sucking—" His hand touched and found a stick large enough. I cant see this time, so I got to be ready to hit twice, he thought, rising. He struck toward the harsh, enraged voice, recovering and striking again though one blow had been enough.

He knew where he was now. He needed no guide, though presently he knew that he had one and he went quite fast now, nosing into the thin taint of air, needing to go fast now. Because it's more than three oclock now, he thought, thinking: I had forgot that. It's like just about everything was in cahoots against one man killing another. Then he knew that he smelled it, because now there was no focal point, no guiding point, it was everywhere; he saw the opening, the topless shell of the blasted oak rising against the leaf-frayed patch of rainless sky. He squared himself away for proper distance by touching his hand against the shell and swung the axe. The entire head sank helve-deep into the rotten pith. He wrenched at it, twisting it free, and raised it again. Then—there was no sound, the darkness itself merely sighed and flowed behind him, and he tried to turn but it was too late—something struck him between the shoulders. He knew at once what it was. He was not surprised even, feeling the breath and hearing the teeth as he fell, turning, trying to raise the axe, hearing the teeth again at his throat and feeling the hot breath-reek as he hurled the hound temporarily back with his forearm and got onto his knees and got both hands on the axe. He could see its eyes now as it leaped the second time. They seemed to float toward him interminably. He struck at them, striking nothing; the axe-head yent into the ground, almost snatching him after it onto his face. This time when he saw the eyes, he was on his feet. He rushed at them, the axe lifted. He went charging on even after the eyes vanished, crashing and plunging in the undergrowth, stopping at last, the axe raised and poised, panting, listening, seeing and hearing nothing. He returned to the tree.

At the first stroke of the axe, the dog sprang again. He was expecting it. He did not bury the head this time and he had the axe raised and ready as he whirled. He struck at the eyes and felt the axe strike and leap spinning from his hands, and he sprang toward where the animal thrashed and groaned in the underbrush, leaping toward the sound, stamping furiously about him, pausing crouched, to listen, leaping toward another sound and stamping again, but again in vain. Then he got down on his hands and knees and crawled in widening circles about the tree, hunting the axe. When he found it at last he could see, above the jagged top of the shell, the morning star.

He chopped again at the base of the shell, stopping after each blow to listen, the axe already poised, his feet and knees braced to whirl. But he heard nothing. Then he began to chop steadily, the axe sinking helve-deep at each stroke as though into sand or sawdust. Then the axe sank, helve and all, into the rotten wood, he knew now it was not imagination he had smelled and he dropped the axe and began to tear at the shell with his hands, his head averted, his teeth bared and clenched, his breath hissing through them, freeing one arm momentarily to fling the hound back though it surged against him again, whimpering, and then thrust its head into the growing orifice out of which the foul air seemed to burst with an audible sound. "Get back, God damn you!" he panted as though he were speaking to a man, trying again to hurl the hound away; "give me room!" He dragged at the body, feeling it slough upon its bones as though it were too large for itself. Now the hound had its entire head and shoulders in the opening, howling.

When the body came suddenly free, he went over backward, lying on his back in the mud, the body across his legs, while the hound stood over it, howling. He got up and kicked at it. It moved back, but when he stooped and took hold of the legs and began to walk backward, the hound was beside him again. But it was intent on the body, and as long as they were in motion, it did not howl. But when he stopped to get his breath, it began to howl again and again he braced himself and kicked at it and this time as he did so he discovered that he was actually seeing the animal and that dawn had come, the animal visible now, gaunt, thin, with a fresh bloody gash across its face, howling. Watching it, he stooped and groped until his hand found a stick. It was foul with slime but still fairly sound. When the hound raised its head to howl again, he struck. The dog whirled; he saw the long scar of the gunshot running from its shoulder to its flank as it sprang at him. This time the stick took it fairly between the eyes. He picked up the ankles, facing forward now, and tried to run.

When he came out of the undergrowth and onto the river bank, the east was turning red. The stream itself was still invisible—a long bank of mist like cotton batting, beneath which the water ran. He stooped; once more he raised the body which was half again his size, and hurled it outward into the mist and, even as he released it, springing after it, catching himself back just before he followed it, seeing at the instant of its vanishing the sluggish sprawl of three limbs where there should have been four, and recovering balance to turn, already running as the pattering rush of the hound whispered behind him and the animal struck him in the back. It did not pause. On his hands and knees he saw it in midair like a tremendous wingless bird soar out and vanish into the mist. He got to his feet and ran. He stumbled and fell once and got up, running. Then he heard the swift soft feet behind him and he fell again and on his hands and knees again he watched it soar over him and turn in midair so that it landed facing him, its eyes like two cigar-coals as it sprang at him before he could rise. He struck at its face with his hands and got up and ran. They reached the stump together. The hound leaped at him again, slashing at his shoulder as he ducked into the opening he had made and groped furiously for the missing arm, the hound still slashing at his back and legs. Then the dog was gone. A voice said: "All right, Mink. We've got him. You can come out now."

The surrey was waiting among the trees behind his house, where he had found the marks of it two days ago. He sat with a deputy in the back seat, their inside wrists manacled together. The sheriff rode beside the other deputy, who drove. The driver swung the team around to return to Varner's store and the Jefferson highroad, but the sheriff stopped him. "Wait," the sheriff said and turned in the front seat—a tremendous man, neckless, in an unbuttoned waistcoat and a collarless starched shirt. In his broad heavy face his small, cold, shrewd eyes resembled two bits of black glass pressed into uncooked dough. He addressed both of them. "Where does this road come out at the other end?"

"Into the old Whiteleaf Bridge road," the deputy said. "That's fourteen miles. And you are still nine miles from Whiteleaf store then. And when you reach Whiteleaf store, you are still eight miles from Jefferson. It's just twenty-five miles by Varner's."

"I reckon we'll skip Varner's this time," the sheriff said. "Drive on, Jim."

"Sure," the deputy said. "Drive on, Jim. It wouldn't be our money we saved, it would just be the county's." The sheriff, turning to face forward again, paused and looked at the deputy. They looked at one another. "I said all right, didn't I?" the deputy said. "Drive on."

Through the rest of that morning and into noon they wound among the pine hills. The sheriff had a shoe box of cold food and even a stone jug of buttermilk wrapped in wet gunnysacks. They ate without stopping save to let the team drink at a branch which crossed the road. Then the road came down out of the hills and in the early afternoon they passed Whiteleaf store in the long broad rich flatlands lush with the fine harvest, the fired and heavy corn and the cotton-pickers still moving through the spilling rows, and he saw the men squatting and sitting on the gallery beneath the patent medicine and tobacco posters stand suddenly up. "Well, well," the deputy said. "There are folks here too that act willing to believe their name is Houston for maybe ten or fifteen minutes anyway."

"Drive on," the sheriff said. They went on, pacing in the thick, soft dust the long, parched summer afternoon, though actually they could not keep pace with it and presently the fierce sun slanted into the side of the surrey where he sat. The sheriff spoke now without turning his head or removing his cob pipe: "George, swap sides with him. Let him ride in the shade."

"I'm all right," he said. "It dont bother me." After a while it did not bother him, or it was no worse for him than for the others, because the road approached the hills again, rising and winding again as the long shadows of the pines wheeled slowly over the slow surrey in the now slanting sun; soon Jefferson itself would appear beyond the final valley, with the poised fierce ball of the sun dropping down beyond it, shining from directly ahead and almost level into the surrey, upon all their faces. There was a board on a tree, bearing a merchant's name above the legend *Jefferson 4 mi,* drawing up and then past, yet with no semblance of motion, and he moved his feet slightly and braced his inside elbow for the coming jerk and gathered and hurled himself feet foremost out of the moving surrey, snapping his arm and shoulder forward against the expected jerk but too late, so that even as his body swung out and free of the wheel his head slipped down into the V of the stanchion which supported the top and the weight and momentum of his whole body came down on his vised neck. In a moment now he would hear the bone, the vertebrae, and he wrenched his body again, kicking backward now toward where he believed the moving wheel would be, thinking, If I can just hook my foot in them spokes, something will have to give; lashing with his foot toward the wheel, feeling each movement of his body travel back to his neck as though he were attempting, in a cold fury of complete detachment, to see which would go first: the living bone or the dead metal. Then something struck him a terrific blow at the base of his neck and ceased to be a blow and became instead a pressure, rational and furious with deadly intent. He believed he heard the bone and he knew he heard the deputy's voice: "Break! God damn it, break! Break!" and he felt the surge of the surrey and he even seemed to see the sheriff leaning ovr the seat-back and grappling with the raging deputy; choking, gasping, trying to close his mouth and he could not, trying to roll his head from beneath the cold hard blow of the water and there was a bough over his head against the sunny sky, with a faint wind in the leaves, and the three faces. But after a while he could breathe again all right, and the faint wind of motion had dried the water from his face and only his shirt was a little damp, not a cool wind yet but just a wind free at last of the unendurable sun, blowing out of the beginning of dusk, the surrey moving now beneath an ordered overarch of sunshot trees, between the clipped and tended lawns where children shrieked and played in bright small garments in the sunset and the ladies sat rocking in the fresh dresses of afternoon and the men coming home from work turned into the neat painted gates, toward plates of food and cups of coffee in the long beginning of twilight.

They approached the jail from the rear and drove into the enclosed yard. "Jump," the sheriff said. "Lift him out."

"I'm all right," he said. But he had to speak twice before he made any sound, and even then it was not his voice. "I can walk."

After the doctor had gone, he lay on his cot. There was a small, high, barred window in the wall, but there was nothing beyond the window save twilight. Then he smelled supper cooking somewhere—ham and hot bread and coffee—and suddenly a hot, thin, salty liquid began to run in his mouth, though when he tried to swallow, it was so painful that he sat up, swallowing the hot salt, moving his neck and head rigidly and gingerly to ease the swallowing. Then a loud trampling of feet began beyond the barred door, coming rapidly nearer, and he rose and went to it and looked through the bars into the common room where the Negro victims of a thousand petty white man's misdemeanors ate and slept together. He could see the head of the stairs; the trampling came from it and he watched a disorderly clump of heads in battered hats and caps and bodies in battered overalls and broken shoes erupt and fill the foul barren room with a subdued uproar of scuffling feet and mellow witless singsong voices—the chain gang which worked on the streets, seven or eight of them, in jail for vagrancy or razor fights or shooting dice for ten or fifteen cents, freed of their shovels and rock hammers for ten hours at least. He held to the bars and looked at them. "It—" he said. His voice made no sound at all. He put his hand to his throat and spoke again, making a dry, croaking sound. The Negroes fell completely still, looking at him, their eyeballs white and still in the already fading faces. "I was all right," he said, "until it started coming to pieces. I could have handled that dog." He held his throat, his voice harsh and dry and croaking. "But the son of a bitch started coming to pieces on me."

"Who him?" one of the Negroes said. They whispered among themselves, murmuring. The white eyeballs rolled at him.

"I was all right," he said. "But the son of a bitch——"

"Hush, white man," the Negro said. "Hush. Dont be telling us no truck like that."

"I would have been all right," he said, harsh, whispering. Then his voice failed altogether again and he held to the bars with one hand, holding his throat with the other, while the Negroes watched him, huddled, their eyeballs white and still in the failing light. Then with one accord they turned and rushed toward the stairs and he heard the slow steps too and then he smelled the food, and he clung to the bars, trying to see the stairhead. Are they going to feed them niggers before they do a white man? he thought, smelling the coffee and the ham.

3

That was the fall before the winter from which the people as they became older were to establish time and date events. The summer's rainless heat—the blazing days beneath which even the oak leaves turned brown and died, the nights during which the ordered stars seemed to glare down in cold and lidless amazement at an earth being drowned in dust—broke at last, and for the three weeks of Indian summer the ardor-wearied earth, ancient Lilith, reigned, throned and crowned amid the old invincible courtesan's formal defunction. Through these blue and drowsy and empty days filled with silence and the smell of burning leaves and woodsmoke, Ratliff, passing to and fro between his home and the Square, would see the two small grimed hands, immobile and clasping loosely the bars of the jail window at a height not a great deal above that at which a child would have held them. And in the afternoons he would watch his three guests, the wife and the two children, entering or leaving the jail on their daily visit. On the first day, the day he had brought her home with him, she had insisted on doing some of the housework, all of it which his sister would permit, sweeping and washing dishes and chopping wood for fires which his nieces and nephews had heretofore done (and incidentally, in doing so, gaining their juvenile contempt too), apparently oblivious of the sister's mute and outraged righteousness, big yet not fat, actually slender as Ratliff realised at last in a sort of shocked and sober . . . not pity: rather, concern; usually barefoot, with the untidy mass of bleached hair long since turning back to dark at the roots, and the cold face in which there was something of a hard not-quite-lost beauty, though it may have been only an ingrained and ineradicable self-confidence or perhaps just toughness. Because the prisoner had refused not only bond (if he could have made one) but counsel. He had stood between two officers—small, his face like a mask of intractability carved in wood, wasted and almost skeleton-thin—before the committing magistrate, and he might not even have been present, hearing or perhaps not hearing himself being arraigned, then at a touch from one of the officers turning back toward the jail, the cell. So the case was pretermitted from sheer desuetude of physical material for formal suttee, like a half-cast play, through the October term of court, to the spring term next May; and perhaps three afternoons a week Ratliff would watch his guests as, the children dressed in cast-off garments of his nephews and nieces, the three of them entered the jail, thinking of the four of them sitting in the close cell rank with creosote and old wraiths of human excreta—the sweat, the urine, the vomit discharged of all the old agonies: terror, impotence, hope. Waiting for Flem Snopes, he thought. For Flem Snopes.

Then the winter, the cold, came. By that time she had a job. He had known as well as she that the other arrangement could not last, since in a way it was his sister's house, even if only by a majority of voting strength. So he was not only not surprised, he was relieved when she came and told him she was going to move. Then, as soon as she told him she was going to leave, something happened to him. He told himself that it was the two children. "That's all right about the job," he said. "That's fine. But you dont need to move. You'll have to pay board and lodging if you move. And you will need to save. You will need money."

"Yes," she said harshly. "I'll need money."

"Does he still think—" He stopped himself. He said, "You aint heard yet when Flem will be back, have you?" She didn't answer. He didn't expect her to. "You will need to save all you can," he said. "So you stay here. Pay her a dollar a week board for the children if that would make you feel better about it. I dont reckon a kid would eat more than four bits' worth in seven days. But you stay here."

So she stayed. He had given up his room to them and he slept with his oldest nephew. Her job was in a rambling shabby side-street boarding house with an equivocal reputation, named the Savoy Hotel. Her work began at daybreak and ended sometime after dark, sometimes well after dark. She swept and made the beds and did some of the cooking, since there was a Negro porter who washed the dishes and kept up the fires. She had her meals there and received three dollars a week. "Only she's going to keep her heels blistered running barefooted in and out of them horse-traders' and petty juries' and agents for nigger insurance's rooms all night long," a town wit said. But that was her affair. Ratliff knew nothing about that and cared less and, to his credit, believed even still less than that. So now he would not see her at all save on Sunday afternoons as, the children in the new overcoats which he had bought for them and the woman in his old one which she had insisted on paying him fifty cents for, they would enter the gate to the jail or perhaps emerge from it. That was when it occurred to him how not once had any of his kin—old Ab or the schoolmaster or the blacksmith or the new clerk—come in to see him. And if all the facts about that business was knowed, he thought, There's one of them that ought to be there in that cell too. Or in another one just like it, since you cant hang a man twice—granted of course that a Snopes carries the death penalty even for another Snopes.

There was snow on Thanksgiving and though it did not remain two days, it was followed early in December by an iron cold which locked the earth in a frozen rigidity, so that after a week or so actual dust blew from it. Smoke turned white before it left the chimney, unable to rise, becoming the same color as the misty sky itself in which all day long the sun stood pale as an uncooked biscuit and as heatless. Now they dont even need to have to not come in to see him, Ratliff told himself. For a man to drive them twenty miles in from Frenchman's Bend just on a errand of mercy, even a Snopes dont have to excuse himself from it. There was a windowpane now between the bars and the hands; they were not visible now, even if anyone had paused along before the jail to look for them. Instead he would be walking fast when he passed, hunched in his overcoat, holding his ears in turn with his yarn-mitted hands, his breath wisping about the crimson tip of his nose and his watering eyes and into the empty Square across which perhaps one country wagon moved, its occupants wrapped in quilts with a lighted lantern on the seat between them while the frosted windows of the stores seemed to stare at it without comprehension or regret like the faces of cataracted old men.

Christmas passed beneath that same salt-colored sky, without even any surface softening of the iron ground, but in January a wind set up out of the northwest and blew the sky clear. The sun drew shadows on the frozen ground and for three days patches of it thawed a little at noon, for an inch or so, like a spreading of butter or axle-grease; and toward noon people would emerge, like rats or roaches, Ratliff told himself, amazed and tentative, at the sun or at the patches of earth soft again out of an old, almost forgotten time, capable again of taking a footprint. "It wont freeze again tonight," they told one another. "It's clouding up from the southwest. It will rain and wash the frost out of the ground and we will be all right again." It did rain. The wind moved counter-clockwise into the east. "It will go through to the northwest again and freeze again. Even that would be better than snow," they told one another, even though the rain had already begun to solidify and by nightfall had become snow, falling for two days and dissolving into the mud as it fell until the mud itself froze at last and still the snow fell and stopped too finally and the windless iron cold came down upon it without even a heatless wafer of sun to preside above a dead earth cased in ice; January and then February, no movement anywhere save the low constant smoke and the infrequent people unable to stand up on the sidewalks creeping townward or homeward in the middle of the streets where no horse could have kept its feet, and no sound save the chopping of axes and the lonely whistles of the daily trains and Ratliff would seem to see them, black, without dimension and unpeopled and plumed with fading vapor, rushing without purpose through the white and rigid solitude. At home now, sitting over his own fire on those Sunday afternoons, he would hear the woman arrive for the children after dinner and put the new overcoats on them above the outgrown garments in which regardless of temperature they had gone to Sunday school (his sister saw to that) with the nephew and nieces who had discarded them; and he would think of the four of them sitting, huddled still in the coats, about the small ineffective sheet-iron stove which did not warm the cell but merely drew from the walls like tears the old sweat of the old agonies and despairs which had harbored there. Later they would return. She would never stay for supper, but once a month she would bring to him the eight dollars she had saved out of her twelve-dollar salary, and the other coins and bills (once she had nine dollars more) which he never asked how she had come by. He was her banker. His sister may or may not have known this, though she probably did. The sum mounted up. "But it will take a lot of weeks," he said. She didn't asnwer. "Maybe he might answer a letter," he said. "After all, blood is blood."

The freeze could not last forever. On the ninth of March it even snowed again and this snow even went away without turning to ice. So people could move about again, and one Saturday he entered the restaurant of which he was half owner and saw Bookwright sitting again before a plate containing a mass of jumbled food a good deal of which was eggs. They had not seen one another in almost six months. No greeting passed between them. "She's back home again," Bookwright said. "Got in last week."

"She gets around fast," Ratliff said. "I just saw her toting a scuttle of ashes out of the back door of the Savoy Hotel five minutes ago."

"I mean the other one," Bookwright said, eating. "Flem's wife. Will drove over to Mottstown and picked them up last week."

"Them?"

"Not Flem. Her and the baby."

So he has already heard, Ratliff thought. Somebody has done already wrote him. He said: "The baby. Well well. February, January, December, November, October, September, August. And some of March. It aint hardly big enough to be chewing tobacco yet, I reckon."

"It wouldn't chew," Bookwright said. "It's a girl."

So for a while he didn't know what to do, though it did not take him long to decide. Better now, he told himself. Even if she was ever hoping without knowing she was. He waited at home the next afternoon until she came for the children. "His wife's back," he said. For just an instant she did not move at all. "You never really expected nothing else, did you?" he said.

"No," she said.

Then even that winter was over at last. It ended as it had begun, in rain, not cold rain but loud fierce gusts of warm water washing out of the earth the iron enduring frost, the belated spring hard on its bright heels and all coming at once, pell mell and disordered, fruit and bloom and leaf, pied meadow and blossoming wood and the long fields shearing dark out of winter's slumber, to the shearing plow. The school was already closed for the planting year when he passed it and drove up to the store and hitched his team to the old familiar post and mounted among the seven or eight men squatting and lounging about the gallery as if they had not moved since he had looked back last at them almost six months ago. "Well, men," he said. "School's already closed I see. Chillen can go to the field now and give you folks a chance to rest."

"It's been closed since last October," Quick said. "Teacher quit."

"I. O.? Quit?"

"His wife come in one day. He looked up and saw her and lit out."

"His what?" Ratliff said.

"His wife," Tull siad. "Or so she claimed. A kind of big gray-colored woman with a——"

"Ah shucks," Ratliff said. "He aint married. Aint he been here three years? You mean his mother."

"No, no," Tull said. "She was young all right. She just had a kind of gray color all over. In a buggy. With a baby about six months old."

"A baby?" Ratliff said. He looked from face to face among them, blinking. "Look here," he said. "What's all this anyway? How'd he get a wife, let alone a baby six months old? Aint he been right here three years? Hell a mile, he aint been out of hearing long enough to done that."

"Wallstreet says they are his," Tull said.

"Wallstreet?" Ratliff said. "Who's Wallstreet?"

"That boy of Eck's."

"That boy about ten years old?' Ratliff blinked at Tull now. "They never had that panic until a year or two back. How'd a boy ten years old get to be named Wall street?"

"I dont know," Tull said.

"I reckon it's his all right," Quick said. "Leastways he taken one look at that buggy and he aint been seen since."

"Sho now," Ratliff said. "A baby is one thing in pants

that will make any man run, provided he's still got room enough to start in. Which it seems I. O. had."

"He needed room," Bookwright said in his harsh, abrupt voice. "This one could have held him, provided somebody just throwed I. O. down first and give it time to get a hold. It was bigger than he was already."

"It might hold him yet," Quick said.

"Yes," Tull said. "She just stopped long enough to buy a can of sardines and crackers. Then she druv on down the road in the same direction somebody told her I. O. had been going. He was walking. Her and the baby both et the sardines."

"Well, well," Ratliff said. "Them Snopeses. Well, well—" He ceased. They watched quietly as the Varner surrey came up the road, going home. The Negro was driving; in the back seat with her mother, Mrs Flem Snopes sat. The beautiful face did not even turn as the surrey drew abreast of the store. It passed in profile, calm, oblivious, incurious. It was not a tragic face: it was just damned. The surrey went on.

"Is he really waiting in that jail yonder for Flem Snopes to come back and get him out?" the fourth man said.

"He's still in jail," Ratliff said.

"But is he waiting for Flem?" Quick said.

"No," Ratliff said. "Because Flem aint coming back here until that trial is over and finished." Then Mrs Littlejohn stood on her veranda, ringing the dinner bell, and they rose and began to disperse. Ratliff and Bookwright descended the steps together.

"Shucks," Bookwright said. "Even Flem Snopes aint going to let his own blood cousin be hung just to save money."

"I reckon Flem knows it aint going to go that far. Jack Houston was shot from in front, and everybody knows he never went anywhere without that pistol, and they found it laying there in the road where they found the marks where the horse had whirled and run, whether it had dropped out of his hand or fell out of his pocket when he fell or not. I reckon Flem had done inquired into all that. And so he aint coming back until it's all finished. He aint coming back here where Mink's wife can worry him or folks can talk about him for leaving his cousin in jail. There's some things even a

Snopes wont do. I dont know just exactly what they are, but they's some somewhere."

Then Bookwright went on, and he untied the team and drove the buckboard on into Mrs Littlejohn's lot and unharnessed and carried the harness into the barn. He had not seen it since that afternoon in September either, and something, he did not know what, impelled and moved him; he hung the gear up and went on through the dim high ammoniac tunnel, between the empty stalls, to the last one and looked into it and saw the thick, female, sitting buttocks, the shapeless figure quiet in the gloom, the blasted face turning and looking up at him, and for a fading instant there was something almost like recognition even if there could have been no remembering, in the devastated eyes, and the drooling mouth slacking and emitting a sound, hoarse, abject, not loud. Upon the overalled knees Ratliff saw the battered wooden effigy of a cow such as children receive on Christmas.

He heard the hammer before he reached the shop. The hammer stopped, poised; the dull, open, healthy face looked up at him without either surprise or interrogation, almost without recognition. "Howdy, Eck," Ratliff said. "Can you pull the old shoes off my team right after dinner and shoe them again? I got a trip to make tonight."

"All right," the other said. "Any time you bring them in."

"All right," Ratliff said. "That boy of yours. You changed his name lately, aint you?" The other looked at him, the hammer poised. On the anvil the ruby tip of the iron he was shaping faded slowly. "Wall street."

"Oh," the other said. "No, sir. It wasn't changed. He never had no name to speak of until last year. I left him with his grandma after my first wife died, while I was getting settled down; I was just sixteen then. She called him after his grandpa, but he never had no actual name. Then last year after I got settled down and sent for him, I thought maybe he better have a name. I. O. read about that one in the paper. He figured if we named him Wallstreet Panic it might make him get rich like the folks that run that Wallstreet panic."

"Oh," Ratliff said. "Sixteen. And one kid wasn't enough to settle you down. How many did it take?"

"I got three."

"Two more beside Wallstreet. What——"

"Three more besides Wall," the other said.

"Oh," Ratliff said. The other waited a moment. Then he raised the hammer again. But he stopped it and stood looking at the cold iron on the anvil and laid the hammer down and turned back to the forge. "So you had to pay all that twenty dollars," Ratliff said. The other looked back at him. "For that cow last summer."

"Yes. And another two bits for that ere toy one."

"You bought him that too?"

"Yes. I felt sorry for him. I thought maybe any time he would happen to start thinking, that ere toy one would give him something to think about."

BOOK FOUR

The Peasants

CHAPTER ONE

1

A little while before sundown the men lounging about the gallery of the store saw, coming up the road from the south, a covered wagon drawn by mules and followed by a considerable string of obviously alive objects which in the levelling sun resembled vari-sized and -colored tatters torn at random from large billboards—circus posters, say—attached to the rear of the wagon and inherent with its own separate and collective motion, like the tail of a kite.

"What in the hell is that?" one said.

"It's a circus," Quick said. They began to rise, watching the wagon. Now they could see that the animals behind the wagon were horses. Two men rode in the wagon.

"Hell fire," the first man—his name was Freeman—said. "It's Flem Snopes." They were all standing when the wagon came up and stopped and Snopes got down and approached the steps. He might have departed only this morning. He wore the same cloth cap, the minute bow tie against the white shirt, the same gray trousers. He mounted the steps.

"Howdy, Flem," Quick said. The other looked briefly at all of them and none of them, mounting the steps. "Starting you a circus?"

"Gentlemen," he said. He crossed the gallery; they made way for him. Then they descended the steps and approached the wagon, at the tail of which the horses stood in a restive clump, larger than rabbits and gaudy as parrots and shackled to one another and to the wagon itself with sections of barbed wire. Calico-coated, small-bodied, with delicate legs and pink faces in which their mismatched eyes rolled wild and subdued, they huddled, gaudy motionless and alert, wild as deer, deadly as rattlesnakes, quiet as doves. The men stood at a respectful distance, looking at them. At that moment Jody Varner came through the group, shouldering himself to the front of it.

"Watch yourself, doc," a voice said from the rear. But it was already too late. The nearest animal rose on its hind legs with lightning rapidity and struck twice with its forefeet at

Varner's face, faster than a boxer, the movement of its surge against the wire which held it travelling backward among the rest of the band in a wave of thuds and lunges. "Hup, you broom-tailed hay-burning sidewinders," the same voice said. This was the second man who had arrived in the wagon. He was a stranger. He wore a heavy densely black moustache, a wide pale hat. When he thrust himself through and turned to herd them back from the horses they saw, thrust into the hip pockets of his tight jeans pants, the butt of a heavy pearl-handled pistol and a florid carton such as small cakes come in. "Keep away from them, boys," he said. "They've got kind of skittish, they aint been rode in so long."

"Since when have they been rode?" Quick said. The stranger looked at Quick. He had a broad, quite cold, wind-gnawed face and bleak cold eyes. His belly fitted neat and smooth as a peg into the tight trousers.

"I reckon that was when they were rode on the ferry to get across the Mississippi River," Varner said. The stranger looked at him. "My name's Varner," Jody said.

"Hipps," the other said. "Call me Buck." Across the left side of his head, obliterating the tip of that ear, was a savage and recent gash gummed over with a blackish substance like axle-grease. They looked at the scar. Then they watched him remove the carton from his pocket and tilt a gingersnap into his hand and put the gingersnap into his mouth, beneath the moustache.

"You and Flem have some trouble back yonder?" Quick said. The stranger ceased chewing. When he looked directly at anyone, his eyes became like two pieces of flint turned suddenly up in dug earth.

"Back where?" he said.

"Your nigh ear," Quick said.

"Oh," the other said. "That." He touched his ear. "That was my mistake. I was absent-minded one night when I was staking them out. Studying about something else and forgot how long the wire was." He chewed. They looked at his ear. "Happen to any man careless around a horse. Put a little axle-dope on it and you wont notice it tomorrow though. They're pretty lively now, lazing along all day doing nothing.

It'll work out of them in a couple of days." He [illegible] another gingersnap into his mouth, chewing. "Don't you believe they'll gentle?" No one answered. They looked at the ponies, grave and noncommittal. Jody turned and went back into the store. "Them's good, gentle ponies," the stranger said. "Watch now." He put the carton back into his pocket and approached the horses, his hand extended. The nearest one was standing on three legs now. It appeared to be asleep. Its eyelid drooped over the cerulean eye; its head was shaped like an ironing-board. Without even raising the eyelid it flicked its head, the yellow teeth cropped. For an instant it and the man appeared to be inextricable in one violence. Then they became motionless, the stranger's high heels dug into the earth, one hand gripping the animal's nostrils, holding the horse's head wrenched half around while it breathed in hoarse, smothered groans. "See?" the stranger said in a panting voice, the veins standing white and rigid in his neck and along his jaw. "See? All you got to do is handle them a little and work hell out of them for a couple of days. Now look out. Give me room back there." They gave back a little. The stranger gathered himself then sprang away. As he did so, a second horse slashed at his back, severing his vest from collar to hem down the back exactly as the trick swordsman severs a floating veil with one stroke.

"Sho now," Quick said. "But suppose a man dont happen to own a vest."

At that moment Jody Varner, followed by the blacksmith, thrust through them again. "All right, Buck," he said. "Better get them on into the lot. Eck here will help you." The stranger, the severed halves of the vest swinging from either shoulder, mounted to the wagon seat, the blacksmith following.

"Get up, you transmogrified hallucinations of Job and Jezebel," the stranger said. The wagon moved on, the tethered ponies coming gaudily into motion behind it, behind which in turn the men followed at a respectful distance, on up the road and into the lane and so to the lot gate behind Mrs Littlejohn's. Eck got down and opened the gate. The wagon passed through but when the ponies saw the fence the herd surged backward against the wire which attached it to the wagon, standing on its collective hind legs and then trying to turn within itself, so that the wagon moved backward for a few feet until the Texan, cursing, managed to saw the mules about and so lock the wheels. The men following had already fallen rapidly back. "Here, Eck," the Texan said. "Get up here and take the reins." The blacksmith got back in the wagon and took the reins. Then they watched the Texan descend, carrying a looped-up blacksnake whip, and go around to the rear of the herd and drive it through the gate, the whip snaking about the harlequin rumps in methodical and pistol-like reports. Then the watchers hurried across Mrs Littlejohn's yard and mounted to the veranda, one end of which overlooked the lot.

"How you reckon he ever got them tied together?" Freeman said.

"I'd a heap rather watch how he aims to turn them loose," Quick said. The Texan had climbed back into the halted wagon. Presently he and Eck both appeared at the rear end of the open hood. The Texan grasped the wire and began to draw the first horse up to the wagon, the animal plunging and surging back against the wire as though trying to hang itself, the contagion passing back through the herd from animal to animal until they were rearing and plunging again against the wire.

"Come on, grab a holt," the Texan said. Eck grasped the wire also. The horses laid back against it, the pink faces tossing above the back-surging mass. "Pull him up, pull him up," the Texan said sharply. "They couldn't get up here in the wagon even if they wanted to." The wagon moved gradually backward until the head of the first horse was snubbed up to the tail-gate. The Texan took a turn of the wire quickly about one of the wagon stakes. "Keep the slack out of it," he said. He vanished and reappeared, almost in the same second, with a pair of heavy wire-cutters. "Hold them like that," he said, and leaped. He vanished, broad hat, flapping vest, wire-cutters and all, into a kaleidoscopic maelstrom of long teeth and wild eyes and slashing feet, from which presently the horses began to burst one by one like partridges flushing, each wearing a necklace of barbed wire. The first one crossed the lot at top speed, on a straight line. It galloped into the fence without any diminution whatever. The wire gave, recovered, and slammed the horse to earth where it lay for a moment, glaring, its legs still galloping in air. It scrambled up without having ceased to gallop and crossed the lot and galloped into the opposite fence and was slammed again to earth. The others were now freed. They whipped and whirled about the lot like dizzy fish in a bowl. It had seemed like a big lot until now, but now the very idea that all that fury and motion should be transpiring inside any one fence was something to be repudiated with contempt, like a mirror trick. From the ultimate dust the stranger, carrying the wire-cutters and his vest completely gone now, emerged. He was not running, he merely moved with a light-poised and watchful celerity, weaving among the calico rushes of the animals, feinting and dodging like a boxer until he reached the gate and crossed the yard and mounted to the veranda. One sleeve of his shirt hung only at one point from his shoulder. He ripped it off and wiped his face with it and threw it away and took out the paper carton and shook a gingersnap into his hand. He was breathing only a little heavily. "Pretty lively now," he said. "But it'll work out of them in a couple of days." The ponies still streaked back and forth through the growing dusk like hysterical fish, but not so violently now.

"What'll you give a man to reduce them odds a little for you?" Quick said. The Texan looked at him, the eyes bleak, pleasant and hard above the chewing jaw, the heavy moustache. "To take one of them off your hands?" Quick said.

At that moment the little periwinkle-eyed boy came along the veranda, saying, "Papa, papa; where's papa?"

"Who you looking for, sonny?" one said.

"It's Eck's boy," Quick said. "He's still out yonder in the wagon. Helping Mr Buck here." The boy went on to the end of the veranda, in diminutive overalls—a miniature replica of the men themselves.

"Papa," he said. "Papa." The blacksmith was still leaning from the rear of the wagon, still holding the end of the severed wire. The ponies, bunched for the moment, now slid past the wagon, flowing, stringing out again so that they appeared to have doubled in number, rushing on; the hard rapid light patter of unshod hooves came out of the dust. "Mamma says to come on to supper," the boy said.

The moon was almost full then. When supper was over and they had gathered again along the veranda, the alteration was hardly one of visibility even. It was merely a translation from the lapidary-dimensional of day to the treacherous and silver receptivity in which the horses huddled in mazy camouflage, or singly or in pairs rushed, fluid, phantom, and unceasing, to huddle again in mirage-like clumps from which came high abrupt squeals and the vicious thudding of hooves.

Ratliff was among them now. He had returned just before supper. He had not dared take his team into the lot at all. They were now in Bookwright's stable a half mile from the store. "So Flem has come home again," he said. "Well, well, well. Will Varner paid to get him to Texas, so I reckon it aint no more than fair for you fellows to pay the freight on him back." From the lot there came a high thin squeal. One of the animals emerged. It seemed not to gallop but to flow, bodiless, without dimension. Yet there was the rapid light beat of hard hooves on the packed earth.

"He aint said they was his yet," Quick said.

"He aint said they aint neither," Freeman said.

"I see," Ratliff said. "That's what you are holding back on. Until he tells you yhether they are his or not. Or maybe you can wait until the auction's over and split up and some can follow Flem and some can follow that Texas fellow and watch to see which one spends the money. But then, when a man's done got trimmed, I dont reckon he cares who's got the money."

"Maybe if Ratliff would leave here tonight, they wouldn't make him buy one of them ponies tomorrow," a third said.

"That's a fact," Ratliff said. "A fellow can dodge a Snopes if he just starts lively enough. In fact, I dont believe he would have to pass more than two folks before he would have another victim intervened betwixt them. You folks aint going to buy them things sho enough, are you... answered. They sat on the steps, their backs against the veranda posts, or on the railing itself. Only Ratliff and Quick sat in chairs, so that to them the others were black silhouettes against the dreaming lambence of the moonlight beyond the veranda. The pear tree across the road opposite was now in full and frosty bloom, the twigs and branches springing not outward from the limbs but standing motionless and perpendicular above the horizontal boughs like the separate and upstreaming hair of a drowned woman sleeping upon the uttermost floor of the windless and tideless sea.

"Anse McCallum brought two of them horses back from Texas once," one of the men on the steps said. He did not move to speak. He was not speaking to anyone. "It was a good team. A little light. He worked it for ten years. Light work, it was."

"I mind it," another said. "Anse claimed he traded fourteen rifle cartridges for both of them, didn't he?"

"It was the rifle too, I heard," a third said.

"No, it was just the shells," the first said. "The fellow wanted to swap him four more for the rifle too, but Anse said he never needed them. Cost too much to get six of them back to Mississippi."

"Sho," the second said. "When a man dont have to invest so much into a horse or a team, he dont need to expect so much from it." The three of them were not talking any louder, they were merely talking among themselves, to one another, as if they sat there alone. Ratliff, invisible in the shadow against the wall, made a sound, harsh, sardonic, not loud.

"Ratliff's laughing," a fourth said.

"Dont mind me," Ratliff said. The three speakers had not moved. They did not move now, yet there seemed to gather about the three silhouettes something stubborn, convinced, and passive, like children who have been chidden. A bird, a shadow, fleet and dark and swift, curved across the moonlight, upward into the pear tree and began to sing; a mockingbird.

"First one I've noticed this year," Freeman said.

"You can hear them along Whiteleaf every night," the first man said. "I heard one in February. In that snow. Singing in a gum."

"Gum is the first tree to put out," the third said. "That was why. It made it feel like singing, fixing to put out that way. That was why it taken a gum."

"Gum first to put out?" Quick said. "What about willow?"

"Willow ain't a tree," Freeman said. "It's a weed."

"Well, I dont know what it is," the fourth said. "But it aint no weed. Because you can grub up a weed and you are done with it. I been grubbing up a clump of willows outen my spring pasture for fifteen years. They are the same size every year. Only difference is, it's just two or three more trees every time."

"And if I was you," Ratliff said, "that's just exactly where I would be come sunup tomorrow. Which of course you aint going to do. I reckon there aint nothing under the sun or in Frenchman's Bend neither that can keep you folks from giving Flem Snopes and that Texas man your money. But I'd sholy like to know just exactly who I was giving my money to. Seems like Eck here would tell you. Seems like he'd do that for his neighbors, dont it? Besides being Flem's cousin, him and that boy of his, Wallstreet, helped that Texas man tote water for them tonight and Eck's going to help him feed them in the morning too. Why, maybe Eck will be the one that will catch them and lead them up one at a time for you folks to bid on them. Aint that right, Eck?"

The other man sitting on the steps with his back against the post was the blacksmith. "I dont know," he said.

"Boys," Ratliff said, "Eck knows all about them horses. Flem's told him, how much they cost and how much him and that Texas man aim to get for them, make off of them. Come on, Eck. Tell us." The other did not move, sitting on the top step, not quite facing them, sitting there beneath the successive layers of their quiet and intent concentrated listening and waiting.

"I dont know," he said. Ratliff began to laugh. He sat in the chair, laughing while the others sat or lounged upon the steps and the railing, sitting beneath his laughing as Eck had sat beneath their listening and waiting. Ratliff ceased laughing. He rose. He yawned, quite loud.

"All right. You folks can buy them critters if you want to. But me, I'd just as soon buy a tiger or a rattlesnake. And if Flem Snopes offered me either one of them, I would be afraid to touch it for fear it would turn out to be a painted dog or a piece of garden hose when I went up to take possession of it. I bid you one and all goodnight." He entered the house. They did not look after him, though after a while they all shifted a little and looked down into the lot, upon the splotchy, sporadic surge and flow of the horses, from among which from time to time came an abrupt squeal, a thudding blow. In the pear tree the mockingbird's idiot reiteration pulsed and purled.

"Anse McCallum made a good team outen them two of hisn," the first man said. "They was a little light. That was all."

When the sun rose the next morning a wagon and three saddled mules stood in Mrs Littlejohn's lane and six men and Eck Snopes's son were already leaning on the fence, looking at the horses which huddled in a quiet clump before the barn door, watching the men in their turn. A second wagon came up the road and into the lane and stopped, and then there were eight men beside the boy standing at the fence, beyond which the horses stood, their blue-and-brown eyeballs rolling alertly in their gaudy faces. "So this here is the Snopes circus, is it?" one of the newcomers said. He glanced at the faces, then he went to the end of the row and stood beside the blacksmith and the little boy. "Are them Flem's horses?" he said to the blacksmith.

"Eck dont know who them horses belong to any more than we do," one of the others said. "He knows that Flem come here on the same wagon with them, because he saw him. But that's all."

"And all he will know," a second said. "His own kin will be the last man in the world to find out anything about Flem Snopes's business."

"No," the first said. "He wouldn't even be that. The first man Flem would tell his business to would be the man that was left after the last man died. Flem Snopes dont even tell himself what he is up to. Not if he was laying in bed with himself in a empty house in the dark of the moon."

"That's a fact," a third said. "Flem would trim Eck or any other of his kin quick as he would us. Aint that right, Eck?"

"I dont know," Eck said. They were watching the horses, which at that moment broke into a high-eared, stiff-kneed swirl and flowed in a patchwork wave across the lot and brought up again, facing the men along the fence, so they did not hear the Texan until he was among them. He wore a new shirt and another vest a little too small for him and he was just putting the paper carton back into his hip pocket.

"Morning, morning," he said. "Come to get an early pick, have you? Want to make me an offer for one or two before the bidding starts and runs the prices up?" They had not looked at the stranger long. They were not looking at him now, but at the horses in the lot, which had lowered their heads, snuffing into the dust.

"I reckon we'll look a while first," one said.

"You are in time to look at them eating breakfast, anyhow," the Texan said. "Which is more than they done without they staid up all night." He opened the gate and entered it. At once the horses jerked their heads up, watching him. "Here, Eck," the Texan said over his shoulder, "two or three of you boys help me drive them into the barn." After a moment Eck and two others approached the gate, the little boy at his father's heels, though the other did not see him until he turned to shut the gate.

"You stay out of here," Eck said. "One of them things will snap your head off same as a acorn before you even know it." He shut the gate and went on after the others, whom the Texan had now waved fanwise outward as he approached the horses which now drew into a restive huddle, beginning to mill slightly, watching the men. Mrs Littlejohn came out of the kitchen and crossed the yard to the woodpile, watching the lot. She picked up two or three sticks of wood and paused watching the lot again. Now there were two more men standing at the fence.

"Come on, come on," the Texan said. "They wont hurt you. They just aint never been in under a roof before."

"I just as lief let them stay out here, if that's what they want to do," Eck said.

"Get yourself a stick—there's a bunch of wagon stakes against the fence yonder—and when one of them tries to rush you, bust him over the head so he will understand what you mean." One of the men went to the fence and got three of the stakes and returned and distributed them. Mrs Littlejohn, her armful of wood complete now, paused again halfway back to the house, looking into the lot. The little boy was directly behind his father again, though this time the father had not discovered him yet. The men advanced toward the horses, the huddle of which began to break into gaudy units turning inward upon themselves. The Texan was cursing them in a loud steady cheerful voice. "Get in there, you banjo-faced jack rabbits. Dont hurry them, now. Let them take their time. Hi! Get in there. What do you think that barn is—a law court maybe? Or maybe a church and somebody is going to take up a collection on you?" The animals fell slowly back. Now and then one feinted to break from the huddle, the Texan driving it back each time with skillfully thrown bits of dirt. Then one at the rear saw the barn door just behind it but before the herd could break the Texan snatched the wagon stake from Eck and, followed by one of the other men, rushed at the horses and began to lay about the heads and shoulders, choosing by unerring instinct the point animal and striking it first square in the face then on the withers as it turned and then on the rump as it turned further, so that when the break came it was reversed and the entire herd rushed into the long open hallway and brought up against the further wall with a hollow, thunderous sound like that of a collapsing mine-shaft. "Seems to have held all right," the Texan said. He and the other man slammed the half-length doors and looked over them into the tunnel of the barn, at the far end of which the ponies were now a splotchy phantom moiling punctuated by crackings of wooden partitions and the dry reports of hooves which gradually died away. "Yep, it held all right," the Texan said. The other two came to the doors and looked over them. The little boy came up beside his father now, trying to see through a crack, and Eck saw him.

"Didn't I tell you to stay out of here?" Eck said. "Dont you know them things will kill you quicker than you can say scat? You go and get outside of that fence and stay there."

"Why dont you get your paw to buy you one of them, Wall?" one of the men said.

"Me buy one of them things?" Eck said. "When I can go to the river anytime and catch me a snapping turtle or a moccasin for nothing? You go on, now. Get out of here and stay out." The Texan had entered the barn. One of the men closed the doors after him and put the bar up again and over the top of the doors they watched the Texan go on down the hallway, toward the ponies which now huddled like gaudy phantoms in the gloom, quiet now and already beginning to snuff experimentally into the long lipworn trough fastened against the rear wall. The little boy had merely gone around behind his father, to the other side, where he stood peering now through a knot-hole in a plank. The Texan opened a smaller door in the wall and entered it, though almost immediately he reappeared.

"I dont see nothing but shelled corn in here," he said. "Snopes said he would send some hay up here last night."

"Wont they eat corn either?" one of the men said.

"I don't know," the Texan said. "They aint never seen any that I know of. We'll find out in a minute though." He disappeared, though they could still hear him in the crib. Then he emerged once more, carrying a big double-ended feedbasket, and retreated into the gloom where the parti-colored rumps of the horses were now ranged quietly along the feeding trough. Mrs Littlejohn appeared once more, on the veranda this time, carrying a big brass dinner bell. She raised it to make the first stroke. A small commotion set up among the ponies as the Texan approached but he began to speak to them at once, in a brisk loud unemphatic mixture of cursing and cajolery, disappearing among them. The men at the door heard the dry rattling of the corn-pellets into the trough, a sound broken by a single snort of amazed horror. A plank cracked with a loud report; before their eyes the depths of the hallway dissolved in loud fury, and while they stared over the doors, unable yet to begin to move, the entire interior exploded into mad tossing shapes like a downrush of flames.

"Hell fire," one of them said. "Jump!" he shouted. The three turned and ran frantically for the wagon, Eck last. Several voices from the fence were now shouting something but Eck did not even hear them until, in the act of scrambling madly at the tail gate, he looked behind him and saw the little boy still leaning to the knot-hole in the door which in the next instant vanished into matchwood, the knot-hole itself exploding from his eye and leaving him, motionless in the diminutive overalls and still leaning forward a little until he vanished utterly beneath the towering parti-colored wave full of feet and glaring eyes and wild teeth which, overtopping, burst into scattering units, revealing at last the gaping orifice and the little boy still standing in it, unscathed, his eye still leaned to the vanished knot-hole.

"Wall!" Eck roared. The little boy turned and ran for the wagon. The horses were whipping back and forth across the lot, as if while in the barn they had once more doubled their number; two of them rushed up quartering and galloped all over the boy again without touching him as he ran, earnest and diminutive and seemingly without progress, though he reached the wagon at last, from which Eck, his sunburned skin now a sickly white, reached down and snatched the boy into the wagon by the straps of his overalls and slammed him face down across his knees and caught up a coiled hitching-rope from the bed of the wagon.

"Didn't I tell you to get out of here?" Eck said in a shaking voice. "Didn't I tell you?"

"If you're going to whip him, you better whip the rest of us too and then one of us can frail hell out of you," one of the others said.

"Or better still, take the rope and hang that durn fellow yonder," the second said. The Texan was now standing in the wrecked door of the barn, taking the gingersnap carton from his hip pocket. "Before he kills the rest of Frenchman's Bend too."

"You mean Flem Snopes," the first said. The Texan tilted the carton above his other open palm. The horses still rushed and swirled back and forth but they were beginning to slow now, trotting on high, stiff legs, although their eyes were still rolling whitely and various.

"I misdoubted that damn shell corn all along," the Texan said. "But at least they have seen what it looks like. They cant claim they aint got nothing out of this trip." He shook the carton over his open hand. Nothing came out of it. Mrs Littlejohn on the veranda made the first stroke with the dinner bell; at the sound the horses rushed again, the earth of the lot becoming vibrant with the light dry clatter of hooves. The Texan crumpled the carton and threw it aside. "Chuck wagon," he said. There were three more wagons in the lane now and there were twenty or more men at the fence when the Texan, followed by his three assistants and the little boy, passed through the gate. The bright cloudless early sun gleamed upon the pearl butt of the pistol in his hip pocket and upon the bell which Mrs Littlejohn still rang, peremptory, strong, and loud.

When the Texan, picking his teeth with a splintered kitchen match, emerged from the house twenty minutes later, the tethered wagons and riding horses and mules extended from the lot gate to Varner's store, and there were more than fifty men now standing along the fence beside the gate, watching him quietly, a little covertly, as he approached, rolling a little, slightly bowlegged, the high heels of his carved boots printing neatly into the dust. "Morning, gents," he said. "Here, bud," he said to the little boy, who stood slightly behind him, looking at the protruding butt of the pistol. He took a coin from his pocket and gave it to the boy. "Run to the store and get me a box of gingersnaps." He looked about at the quiet faces, protuberant, sucking his teeth. He rolled the match from one side of his mouth to the other without touching it. "You boys done made your picks, have you? Ready to start her off, hah?" They did not answer. They were not looking at him now. That is, he began to have the feeling that each face had stopped looking at him the second before his gaze reached it. After a moment Freeman said: "Aint you going to wait for Flem?"

"Why?" the Texan said. Then Freeman stopped looking at him too. There was nothing in Freeman's face either. There was nothing, no alteration, in the Texan's voice. "Eck, you done already picked out yours. So we can start her off when you are ready."

"I reckon not," Eck said. "I wouldn't buy nothing I was afraid to walk up and touch."

"Them little ponies?" the Texan said. "You helped water and feed them. I bet that boy of yours could walk up to any one of them."

"He better not let me catch him," Eck said. The Texan looked about at the quiet faces, his gaze at once abstract and alert, with an impenetrable surface quality like flint, as though the surface were impervious or perhaps there was nothing behind it.

"Them ponies is gentle as a dove, boys. The man that buys them will get the best piece of horseflesh he ever forked or druv for the money. Naturally they got spirit; I aint selling crowbait. Besides, who'd want Texas crowbait anyway, with Mississippi full of it?" His stare was still absent and unwinking; there was no mirth or humor in his voice and there was neither mirth nor humor in the single guffaw which came from the rear of the group. Two wagons were now drawing out of the road at the same time, up to the fence. The men got down from them and tied them to the fence and approached. "Come up, boys," the Texan said. "You're just in time to buy a good gentle horse cheap."

"How about that one that cut your vest off last night?" a voice said. This time three or four guffawed. The Texan looked toward the sound, bleak and unwinking.

"What about it?" he said. The laughter, if it had been laughter, ceased. The Texan turned to the nearest gatepost and climbed to the top of it, his alternate thighs deliberate and bulging in the tight trousers, the butt of the pistol catching and losing the sun in pearly gleams. Sitting on the post, he looked down at the faces along the fence which were attentive, grave, reserved and not looking at him. "All right," he said. "Who's going to start her off with a bid? Step right up; take your pick and make your bid, and when the last one is sold, walk in that lot and put your rope on the best piece of horseflesh you ever forked or druv for the money. There aint a pony there that aint worth fifteen dollars. Young, sound, good for saddle or work stock, guaranteed to outlast four ordinary horses; you couldn't kill one of them with a axle-tree—" There was a small violent commotion at the rear of the group. The little boy appeared, burrowing among the motionless overalls. He approached the post, the new and unbroken paper carton lifted. The Texan leaned down and took it and tore the end from it and shook three or four of the cakes into the boy's hand, a hand as small and almost as black as that of a coon. He held the carton in his hand while he talked, poniting out the horses with it as he indicated them. "Look at that one with the three stocking-feet and the frost-bit ear; watch him now when they pass again. Look at that shoulder-action; that horse is worth twenty dollars of any man's money. Who'll make me bid on him to start her off?" His voice was harsh, ready, forensic. Along the fence below him the men stood with, buttoned close in their overalls, the tobacco-sacks and worn purses, the sparse silver and frayed bills hoarded a coin at a time in the cracks of chimneys or chinked into the logs of walls. From time to time the horses broke and rushed with purposeless violence and huddled again, watching the faces along the fence with wild mismatched eyes. The lane was full of wagons now. As the others arrived they would have to stop in the road beyond it and the occupants came up the lane on foot. Mrs Littlejohn came out of her kitchen. She crossed the yard, looking toward the lot gate. There was a blackened wash pot set on four bricks in the corner of the yard. She built a fire beneath the pot and came to the fence and stood there for a time, her hands on her hips and the smoke from the fire drifting blue and slow behind her. Then she turned and went back into the house. "Come on, boys," the Texan said. "Who'll make me a bid?"

"Four bits," a voice said. The Texan did not even glance toward it.

"Or, if he dont suit you, how about that fiddle-head horse without no mane to speak of? For a saddle pony, I'd rather have him than that stocking-foot. I heard somebody say fifty cents just now. I reckon he meant five dollars, didn't he? Do I hear five dollars?"

"Four bits for the lot," the same voice said. This time there were no guffaws. It was the Texan who laughed, harshly, with only his lower face, as if he were reciting a multiplication table.

"Fifty cents for the dried mud offen them, he means," he said. "Who'll give a dollar more for the genuine Texas cockle-burrs?" Mrs Littlejohn came out of the kitchen, carrying the sawn half of a wooden hogshead which she set on a stump beside the smoking pot, and stood with her hands on her hips, looking into the lot for a while without coming to the fence this time. Then she went back into the house. "What's the matter with you boys?" the Texan said. "Here, Eck, you been helping me and you know them horses. How about making me a bid on that wall-eyed one you picked out last night? Here. Wait a minute." He thrust the paper carton into his other hip pocket and swung his feet inward and dropped, cat-light, into the lot. The ponies, huddled, watched him. Then they broke before him and slid stiffly along the fence. He turned them and they whirled and rushed back across the lot; whereupon, as though he had been waiting his chance when they should have turned their backs on him, the Texan began to run too, so that when they reached the opposite side of the lot and turned, slowing to huddle again, he was almost upon them. The earth became thunderous; dust arose, out of which the animals began to burst like flushed quail and into which, with that apparently unflagging faith in his own invulnerability, the Texan rushed. For an instant the watchers could see them in the dust—the pony backed into the angle of the fence and the stable, the man facing it, reaching toward his hip. Then the beast rushed at him in a sort of fatal and hopeless desperation and he struck it between the eyes with the pistol-butt and felled it and leaped onto its prone head. The pony recovered almost at once and paweh itself to its knees and heaved at its prisoned head and fought itself up, dragging the man with it; for an instant in the dust the watchers saw the man free of the earth and in violent lateral motion like a rag attached to the horse's head. Then the Texan's feet came back to earth and the dust blew aside and revealed them, motionless, the Texan's sharp heels braced into the ground, one hand gripping the pony's forelock and the other its nostrils, the long evil muzzle wrung backward over its scarred shoulder while it breathed in labored and hollow groans. Mrs Littlejohn was in the yard again. No one had seen her emerge this time. She carried an armful of clothing and a metal-ridged washboard and she was standing motionless at the kitchen steps, looking into the lot. Then she moved across the yard, still looking into the lot, and dumped the garments into the tub, still looking into the lot. "Look him over, boys," the Texan panted, turning his own suffused face and the protuberant glare of his eyes toward the fence. "Look him over quick. Them shoulders and—" He had relaxed for an instant apparently. The animal exploded again; again for an instant the Texan was free of the earth, though he was still talking: "—and legs you whoa I'll tear your face right look him over quick boys worth fifteen dollars of let me get a holt of who'll make me a bid whoa you blare-eyed jack rabbit, whoa!" They were moving now—a kaleidoscope of inextricable and incredible violence on the periphery of which the metal clasps of the Texan's suspenders sun-glinted in ceaseless orbit, with terrific slowness across the lot. Then the broad clay-colored hat soared deliberately outward; an instant later the Texan followed it, though still on his feet, and the pony shot free in mad, staglike bounds. The Texan picked up the hat and struck the dust from it against his leg, and returned to the fence and mounted the post again. He was breathing heavily. Still the faces did not look at him as he took the carton from his hip and shook a cake from it and put the cake into his mouth, chewing, breathing harshly. Mrs Littlejohn turned away and began to bail water from the pot into the tub, though after each bucketful she turned her head and looked into the lot again. "Now, boys," the Texan said. "Who says that pony ain't worth fifteen dollars? You couldn't buy that much dynamite for just fifteen dollars. There aint one of them cant do a mile in three minutes; turn them into pasture and they will board themselves; work them like hell all day and every time you think about it, lay them over the head with a single-tree and after a couple of days every jack rabbit one of them will be so tame you will have to put them out of the house at night like a cat." He shook another cake from the carton and ate it. "Come on, Eck," he said. "Start her off. How about ten dollars for that horse, Eck?"

"What need I got for a horse I would need a bear-trap to catch?" Eck said.

"Didn't you just see me catch him?"

"I seen you," Eck said. "And I dont want nothing as big as a horse if I got to wrastle with it every time it finds me on the same side of a fence it's on."

"All right," the Texan said. He was still breathing harshly, but now there was nothing of fatigue or breathlessness in it. He shook another cake into his palm and inserted it beneath his moustache. "All right. I want to get this auction started. I aint come here to live, no matter how good a country you folks claim you got. I'm going to give you that horse." For a moment there was no sound, not even that of breathing except the Texan's.

"You going to give it to me?" Eck said.

"Yes. Provided you will start the bidding on the next one." Again there was no sound save the Texan's breathing, and then the clash of Mrs Littlejohn's pail against the rim of the pot.

"I just start the bidding," Eck said. "I dont have to buy it lessen I aint over-topped." Another wagon had come up the lane. It was battered and paintless. One wheel had been repaired by crossed planks bound to the spokes with baling wire and the two underfed mules wore a battered harness patched with bits of cotton rope; the reins were ordinary cotton plow-lines, not new. It contained a woman in a shapeless gray garment and a faded sunbonnet, and a man in faded and patched though clean overalls. There was not room gon to draw out of the lane so the man left it standing where it was and got down and came forward—a thin man, not large, with something about his eyes, something strained and washed-out, at once vague and intense, who shoved into the crowd at the rear, saying,

"What? What's that? Did he give him that horse?"

"All right," the Texan said. "That wall-eyed horse with the scarred neck belongs to you. Now. That one that looks like he's had his head in a flour barrel. What do you say? Ten dollars?"

"Did he give him that horse?" the newcomer said.

"A dollar," Eck said. The Texan's mouth was still open for speech; for an instant his face died so behind the hard eyes. "A dollar?" he said. "One dollar? Did I actually hear that?"

"Durn it," Eck said. "Two dollars then. But I aint——"

"Wait," the newcomer said. "You, up there on the post." The Texan looked at him. When the others turned, they saw that the woman had left the wagon too, though they had not known she was there since they had not seen the wagon drive up. She came among them behind the man, gaunt in the gray shapeless garment and the sunbonnet, wearing stained canvas gymnasium shoes. She overtook the man but she did not touch him, standing just behind him, her hands rolled before her into the gray dress.

"Henry," she said in a flat voice. The man looked over his shoulder.

"Get back to that wagon," he said.

"Here, missus," the Texan said. "Henry's going to get the bargain of his life in about a minute. Here, boys, let the missus come up close where she can see. Henry's going to pick out that saddle-horse the missus has been wanting. Who says ten——"

"Henry," the woman said. She did not raise her voice. She had not once looked at the Texan. She touched the man's arm. He turned and struck her hand down.

"Get back to that wagon like I told you." The woman stood behind him, her hands rolled again into her dress. She was not looking at anything, speaking to anyone.

"He aint no more despair than to buy one of them things," she said. "And us not but five dollars away from the poorhouse, he aint no more despair." The man turned upon her with that curious air of leashed of dreamlike fury. The others lounged along the fence in attitudes gravely inattentive, almost oblivious. Mrs Littlejohn had been washing for some time now, pumping rhythmically up and down above the washboard in the sud-foamed tub. She now stood erect again, her soap-raw hands on her hips, looking into the lot.

"Shut your mouth and get back in that wagon," the man said. "Do you want me to take a wagon stake to you?" He turned and looked up at the Texan. "Did you give him that horse?" he said. The Texan was looking at the woman. Then he looked at the man; still watching him, he tilted the paper carton over his open palm. A single cake came out of it.

"Yes," he said.

"Is the fellow that bids in this next horse going to get that first one too?"

"No," the Texan said.

"All right," the other said. "Are you going to give a horse to the man that makes the first bid on the next one?"

"No," the Texan said.

"Then if you were just starting the auction off by giving away a horse, why didn't you wait till we were all here?" The Texan stopped looking at the other. He raised the empty carton and squinted carefully into it, as if it might contain a precious jewel or perhaps a deadly insect. Then he crumpled it and dropped it carefully beside the post on which he sat.

"Eck bids two dollars," he said. "I believe he still thinks he's bidding on them scraps of bob-wire they come here in instead of on one of the horses. But I got to accept it. But are you boys——"

"So Eck's going to get two horses at a dollar a head," the newcomer said. "Three dollars." The woman touched him again. He flung her hand off without turning and she stood again, her hands rolled into her dress across her flat stomach, not looking at anything.

"Misters," she said, "we got chaps in the house that never had shoes last winter. We aint got corn to feed the stock. We got five dollars I earned weaving by firelight after dark. And he aint no more despair."

"Henry bids three dollars," the Texan said. "Raise him a dollar, Eck, and the horse is yours." Beyond the fence the horses rushed suddenly and for no reason and as suddenly stopped, staring at the faces along the fence.

"Henry," the woman said. The man was watching Eck. His stained and broken teeth showed a little beneath his lip. His wrists dangled into fists below the faded sleeves of his shirt too short from many washings.

"Four dollars," Eck said.

"Five dollars!" the husband said, raising one clenched hand. He shouldered himself forward toward the gatepost. The woman did not follow him. She now looked at the Texan for the first time. Her eyes were a washed gray also, as though they had faded too like the dress and the sunbonnet.

"Mister," she said, "if you take that five dollars I earned my chaps a-weaving for one of them things, it'll be a curse on you and yours during all the time of man."

"Five dollars!" the husband shouted. He thrust himself up to the post, his clenched hand on a level with the Texan's knees. He opened it upon a wad of frayed banknotes and silver. "Five dollars! And the man that raises it will have to beat my head off or I'll beat hisn."

"All right," the Texan said. "Five dollars is bid. But dont you shake your hand at me."

At five oclock that afternoon the Texan crumpled the third paper carton and dropped it to the earth beneath him. In the copper slant of the leveling sun which fell also upon the line of limp garments in Mrs Littlejohn's back yard and which cast his shadow and that of the post on which he sat long across the lot where now and then the ponies still rushed in purposeless and tireless surges, the Texan straightened his leg and thrust his hand into his pocket and took out a coin and leaned down to the little boy. His voice was now hoarse, spent. "Here, bud," he said. "Run to the store and get me a box of gingersnaps." The men still stood along the fence, tireless, in their overalls and faded shirts. Flem Snopes was there now, appeared suddenly from nowhere, standing beside the fence with a space the width of three or four men on either side of him, standing there in his small yet definite isolation, chewing tobacco, in the same gray trousers and minute bow tie in which he had departed last summer but in a new cap, gray too like the other, but new, and overlaid with a bright golfer's plaid, looking also at the horses in the lot. All of them save two had been sold for sums ranging from three dollars and a half to eleven and twelve dollars. The purchasers, as they had bid them in, had gathered as though by instinct into a separate group on the other side of the gate, where they stood with their hands lying upon the top strand of the fence, watching with a still more sober intensity the animals which some of them had owned for seven and eight hours now but had not yet laid hands upon. The husband, Henry, stood beside the post on which the Texan sat. The wife had gone back to the wagon, where she sat gray in the gray garment, motionless, looking at nothing still; she might have been something inanimate which he had loaded into the wagon to move it somewhere, waiting now in the wagon until he should be ready to go on again, patient, insensate, timeless.

"I bought a horse and I paid cash for it," he said. His voice was harsh and spent too, the mad look in his eyes had a quality glazed now and even sightless. "And yet you expect me to stand around here till they are all sold before I can get my horse. Well, you can do all the expecting you want. I'm going to take my horse out of there and go home." The Texan looked down at him. The Texan's shirt was blotched with sweat. His big face was cold and still, his voice level.

"Take your horse then." After a moment Henry looked away. He stood with his head bent a little, swallowing from time to time.

"Aint you going to catch him for me?"

"It aint my horse," the Texan said in that flat still voice. After a while Henry raised his head. He did not look at the Texan.

"Who'll help me catch my horse?" he said. Nobody answered. They stood along the fence, looking quietly into the lot where the ponies huddled, already beginning to fade a little where the long shadow of the house lay upon them, deepening. From Mrs Littlejohn's kitchen the smell of frying ham came. A noisy cloud of sparrows swept across the lot and into a chinaberry tree beside the house, and in the high soft vague blue swallows stooped and whirled in erratic indecision, their cries like strings plucked at random. Without looking back, Henry raised his voice: "Bring that ere plow-line." After a time the wife moved. She got down from the wagon and took a coil of new cotton rope from it and approached. The husband took the rope from her and moved toward the gate. The Texan began to descend from the post, stiffly, as Henry put his hand on the latch. "Come on here," he said. The wife had stopped when he took the rope from her. She moved again, obediently, her hands rolled into the dress across her stomach, passing the Texan without looking at him.

"Dont you go in there, missus," he said. She stopped, not looking at him, not looking at anything. The husband opened the gate and entered the lot and turned, holding the gate open but without raising his eyes.

"Come on here," he said.

"Dont you go in there, missus," the Texan said. The wife stood motionless between them, her face almost concealed by the sunbonnet, her hands folded across her stomach.

"I reckon I better," she said. The other men did not look at her at all, at her or Henry either. They stood along the fence, grave and quiet and inattentive, almost bemused. Then the wife passed through the gate; the husband shut it behind them and turned and began to move toward the huddled ponies, the wife following in the gray and shapeless garment within which she moved without inference of locomotion, like something on a moving platform, a float. The horses were watching them. They clotted and blended and shifted among themselves, on the point of breaking through not breaking yet. The husband shouted at them. He began to curse them, advancing, the wife following. Then the huddle broke, the animals moving with high, stiff knees, circling the two people who turned and followed again as the herd flowed and huddled again at the opposite side of the lot.

"There he is," the husband said. "Get him into that corner." The herd divided; the horse which the husband had bought jolted on stiff legs. The wife shouted at it; it spun and poised, plunging, then the husband struck it across the face with the coiled rope and it whirled and slammed into the corner of the fence. "Keep him there now," the husband said. He shook out the rope, advancing. The horse watched him with wild, glaring eyes; it rushed again, straight toward the wife. She shouted at it and waved her arms but it soared past her in a long bound and rushed again into the huddle of its fellows. They followed and hemmed it again into another corner; again the wife failed to stop its rush for freedom and the husband turned and struck her with the coiled rope. "Why didn't you head him?" he said. "Why didn't you?" He struck her again; she did not move, not even to fend the rope with a raised arm. The men along the fence stood quietly, their faces lowered as though brooding upon the earth at their feet. Only Flem Snopes was still watching—if he ever had been looking into the lot at all, standing in his little island of isolation, chewing with his characteristic faint sidewise thrust beneath the new plaid cap.

The Texan said something, not loud, harsh and short. He entered the lot and went to the husband and jerked the uplifted rope from his hand. The husband whirled as though he were about to spring at the Texan, crouched slightly, his knees bent and his arms held slightly away from his sides, though his gaze never mounted higher than the Texan's carved and dusty boots. Then the Texan took the husband by the arm and led him back toward the gate, the wife following, and through the gate which he held open for the woman and then closed. He took a wad of banknotes from his trousers and removed a bill from it and put it into the woman's hand. "Get him into the wagon and get him on home," he said.

"What's that for?" Flem Snopes said. He had approached. He now stood beside the post on which the Texan had been sitting. The Texan did not look at him.

"Thinks he bought one of them ponies," the Texan said. He spoke in a flat still voice, like that of a man after a sharp run. "Get him on away, missus."

"Give him back that money," the husband said, in his lifeless, spent tone. "I bought that horse and I aim to have him if I got to shoot him before I can put a rope on him." The Texan did not even look at him.

"Get him on away from here, missus," he said.

"You take your money and I take my horse," the husband said. He was shaking slowly and steadily now, as though he were cold. His hands open and shut below the frayed cuffs of his shirt. "Give it back to him," he said.

"You dont own no horse of mine," the Texan said. "Get him on home, missus." The husband raised his spent face, his mad glazed eyes. He reached out his hand. The woman held the banknote in her folded hands across her stomach. For a while the husband's shaking hand merely fumbled at it. Then he drew the banknote free.

"It's my horse," he said. "I bought it. These fellows saw me. I paid for it. It's my horse. Here." He turned and extended the banknote toward Snopes. "You got something to do with these horses. I bought one. Here's the money for it. I bought one. Ask him." Snopes took the banknote. The others stood, gravely inattentive, in relaxed attitudes along the fence. The sun had gone now; there was nothing save violet shadow upon them and upon the lot where once more and for no reason the ponies rushed and flowed. At that moment the little boy came up, tireless and indefatigable still, with the new paper carton. The Texan took it, though he did not open it at once. He had dropped the rope and now the husband stooped for it, fumbling at it for some time before he lifted it from the ground. Then he stood with his head bent, his knuckles whitening on the rope. The woman had not moved. Twilight was coming fast now; there was a last mazy swirl of swallows against the high and changing azure. Then the Texan tore the end from the carton and tilted one of the cakes into his hand; he seemed to be watching the hand as it shut slowly upon the cake until a fine powder of snuff-colored dust began to rain from his fingers. He rubbed the hand carefully on his thigh and raised his head and glanced about until he saw the little boy and handed the carton back to him.

"Here, bud," he said. Then he looked at the woman, his voice flat, quiet again. "Mr Snopes will have your money for you tomorrow. Better get him in the wagon and get him on home. He dont own no horse. You can get your money tomorrow from Mr Snopes." The wife turned and went back to the wagon and got into it. No one watched her, nor the husband who still stood, his head bent, passing the rope from one hand to the other. They leaned along the fence, grave and quiet, as though the fence were in another land, another time.

"How many you got left?" Snopes said. The Texan roused; they all seemed to rouse then, returning, listening again.

"Got three now," the Texan said. "Swap all three of them for a buggy or a——"

"It's out in the road," Snopes said, a little shortly, a little quickly, turning away. "Get your mules." He went up on the lane. They watched the Texan enter the lot and cross it, the horses flowing before him but without the old irrational violence, as if they too were spent, vitiated with the long day, and enter the barn and then emerge, leading the two harnessed mules. The wagon had been backed under the shed beside the barn. The Texan entered this and came out a moment later, carrying a bedding-roll and his coat, and led the mules back toward the gate, the ponies huddled again and watching him with their various unmatching eyes, quietly now, as if they too realised there was not only an armistice between them at last but that they would never look upon each other again in both their lives. Someone opened the gate. The Texan led the mules through it and they followed in a body, leaving the husband standing beside the closed gate, his head still bent and the coiled rope in his hand. They passed the wagon in which the wife sat, her gray garment fading into the dusk, almost the same color and as still, looking at nothing; they passed the clothesline with its limp and unwinded drying garments, walking through the hot vivid smell of ham from Mrs Littlejohn's kitchen. When they reached the end of the lane they could see the moon, almost full, tremendous and pale and still lightless in the sky from which day had not quite gone. Snopes was standing at the end of the lane beside an empty buggy. It was the one with the glittering wheels and the fringed parasol top in which he and Will Varner had used to drive. The Texan was motionless too, looking at it.

"Well well well," he said. "So this is it."

"If it dont suit you, you can ride one of the mules back to Texas," Snopes said.

"You bet," the Texan said. "Only I ought to have a powder puff or at least a mandolin to ride it with." He backed the mules onto the tongue and lifted the breast-yoke. Two of them came forward and fastened the traces for him. Then they watched him get into the buggy and raise the reins.

"Where you heading for?" one said. "Back to Texas?"

"In this?" the Texan said. "I wouldn't get past the first Texas saloon without starting the vigilance committee. Besides, I aint going to waste all this here lace-trimmed top and these spindle wheels just on Texas. Long as I am this far, I reckon I'll go on a day or two and look-see them northern towns. Washington and New York and Baltimore. What's the short way to New York from here?" They didn't know. But they told him how to reach Jefferson.

"You're already headed right," Freeman said. "Just keep right on up the road past the schoolhouse."

"All right," the Texan said. "Well, remember about busting them ponies over the head now and then until they get used to you. You wont have any trouble with them then." He lifted the reins again. As he did so Snopes stepped forward and got into the buggy.

"I'll ride as far as Varner's with you," he said.

"I didn't know I was going past Varner's," the Texan said.

"You can go to town that way," Snopes said. "Drive on." The Texas shook the reins. Then he said,

"Whoa." He straightened his leg and put his hand into his pocket. "Here, bud," he said to the little boy, "run to the store and— Never mind. I'll stop and get it myself, long as I am going back that way. Well, boys," he said. "Take care of yourselves." He swung the team around. The buggy went on. They looked after it.

"I reckon he aims to kind of come up on Jefferson from behind," Quick said.

"He'll be lighter when he gets there," Freeman said. "He can come up to it easy from any side he wants."

"Yes," Bookwright said. "His pockets wont rattle." They went back to the lot; they passed on through the narrow way between the two lines of patient and motionless wagons, which at the end was completely closed by the one in which the woman sat. The husband was still standing beside the gate with his coiled rope, and now night had completely come. The light itself had not changed so much; if anything, it was brighter but with that other-worldly quality of moonlight, so that when they stood once more looking into the lot, the splotchy bodies of the ponies had a distinctness, almost a brilliance, but without individual shape and without depth—no longer horses, no longer flesh and bone directed by a principle capable of calculated violence, no longer inherent with the capacity to hurt and harm.

"Well, what are we waiting for?" Freeman said. "For them to go to roost?"

"We better all get our ropes first," Quick said. "Get your ropes everybody." Some of them did not have ropes. When they left home that morning, they had not heard about the horses, the auction. They had merely happened through the village by chance and learned of it and stopped.

"Go to the store and get some then," Freeman said.

"The store will be closed now," Quick said.

"No it wont," Freeman said. "If it was closed, Lump Snopes would a been up here." So while the ones who had come prepared got their ropes from the wagons, the others went down to the store. The clerk was just closing it.

"You all aint started catching them yet, have you?" he said. "Good; I was afraid I wouldn't get there in time." He opened the door again and amid the old strong sunless smells of cheese and leather and molasses he measured and cut off sections of plow-line for them and in a body and the clerk in the center and still talking, voluble and unlistened to, they returned up the road. The pear tree before Mrs Littlejohn's was like drowned silver now in the moon. The mockingbird of last night, or another one, was already singing in it, and they now saw, tied to the fence, Ratliff's buckboard and team.

"I thought something was wrong all day," one said. "Ratliff wasn't there to give nobody advice." When they passed down the lane, Mrs Littlejohn was in her back yard, gathering the garments from the clothesline; they could still smell the ham. The others were waiting at the gate, beyond which the ponies, huddled again, were like phantom fish, suspended apparently without legs now in the brilliant treachery of the moon.

"I reckon the best way will be for us all to take and catch them one at a time," Freeman said.

"One at a time," the husband, Henry, said. Apparently he had not moved since the Texan had led his mules through the gate, save to lift his hands to the top of the gate, one of them still clutching the coiled rope. "One at a time," he said. He began to curse in a harsh, spent monotone. "After I've stood around here all day, waiting for that—" He cursed. He began to jerk at the gate, shaking it with spent violence until one of the others slid the latch back and it swung open and Henry entered it, the others following, the little boy pressing close behind his father until Eck became aware of him and turned.

"Here," he said. "Give me that rope. You stay out of here."

"Aw, paw," the boy said.

"No sir. Them things will kill you. They almost done it this morning. You stay out of here."

"But we got two to catch." For a moment Eck stood looking down at the boy.

"That's right," he said. "We got two. But you stay close to me now. And when I holler run, you run. You hear me?"

"Spread out, boys," Freeman said. "Keep them in front of us." They began to advance across the lot in a ragged crescent-shaped line, each one with his rope. The ponies were now at the far side of the lot. One of them snorted; the mass shifted within itself but without breaking. Freeman, glancing back, saw the little boy. "Get that boy out of here," he said.

"I reckon you better," Eck said to the boy. "You go and get in the wagon yonder. You can see us catch them from there." The little boy turned and trotted toward the shed beneath which the wagon stood. The line of men advanced, Henry a little in front.

"Watch them close now," Freeman said. "Maybe we better try to get them into the barn first—" At that moment the huddle broke. It parted and flowed in both directions along the fence. The men at the ends of the line began to run, waving their arms and shouting. "Head them," Freeman said tensely. "Turn them back." They turned them, driving them back upon themselves again; the animals merged and spun in short, huddling rushes, phantom and inextricable. "Hold them now," Freeman said. "Dont let them get by us." The line advanced again. Eck turned; he did not know why—whether a sound, what. The little boy was just behind him again.

"Didn't I tell you to get in that wagon and stay there?" Eck said.

"Watch out, paw!" the boy said. "There he is! There's ourn!" It was the one the Texan had given Eck. "Catch him, paw!"

"Get out of my way," Eck said. "Get back to that wagon." The line was still advancing. The ponies milled, clotting, forced gradually backward toward the open door of the barn. Henry was still slightly in front, crouched slightly, his thin figure, even in the mazy moonlight, emanating something of that spent fury. The splotchy huddle of animals seemed to be moving before the advancing line of men like a snowball which they might have been pushing before them by some invisible means, gradually nearer and nearer to the black yawn of the barn door. Later it was obvious that the ponies were so intent upon the men that they did not realise the barn was even behind them until they backed into the shadow of it. Then an indescribable sound, a movement desperate and despairing, arose among them; for an instant of static horror men and animals faced one another, then the men whirled and ran before a gaudy vomit of long wild faces and splotched chests which overtook and scattered them and flung them sprawling aside and completely obliterated from sight Henry and the little boy, neither of whom had moved though Henry had flung up both arms, still holding his coiled rope, the herd sweeping on across the lot, to crash through the gate which the last man through it had neglected to close, leaving it slightly ajar, carrying all of the gate save the upright to which the hinges were nailed with them, and so among the teams and wagons which choked the lane, the teams springing and lunging too, snapping hitch-reins and tongues. Then the whole inextricable mass crashed among the wagons and eddied and divided about the one in which the woman sat, and rushed on down the lane and into the road, dividing, one half going one way and one half the other.

The men in the lot, except Henry, got to their feet and ran toward the gate. The little boy once more had not been touched, not even thrown off his feet; for a while his father held him clear of the ground in one hand, shaking him like a rag doll. "Didn't I tell you to stay in that wagon?" Eck cried. "Didn't I tell you?"

"Look out, paw!" the boy chattered out of the violent shaking. "There's ourn! There he goes!" It was the horse the Texan had given them again. It was as if they owned no other, the other one did not exist; as if by some absolute and instantaneous rapport of blood they had relegated to oblivion the one for which they had paid money. They ran to the gate and down the lane where the other men had disappeared. They saw the horse the Texan had given them whirl and dash back and rush through the gate into Mrs Littlejohn's yard and run up the front steps and crash once on the wooden veranda and vanish through the front door. Eck and the boy ran up onto the veranda. A lamp sat on a table just inside the door. In its mellow light they saw the horse fill the long hallway like a pinwheel, gaudy, furious and thunderous. A little further down the hall there was a varnished yellow melodeon. The horse crashed into it; it produced a single note, almost a chord, in bass, resonant and grave, of deep and sober astonishment; the horse with its monstrous and antic shadow whirled again and vanished through another door. It was a bedoom; Ratliff, in his underclothes and one sock and with the other sock in his hand and his back to the door, was leaning out the open window facing the lane, the lot. He looked back over his shoulder. For an instant he and the horse glared at one another. Then he sprang through the window as the horse backed out of the room and into the hall again and whirled and saw Eck and the little boy just entering the front door, Eck still carrying his rope. It whirled again and rushed on down the hall and onto the back porch just as Mrs Littlejohn, carrying an armful of clothes from the line and the washboard, mounted the steps.

"Get out of here, you son of a bitch," she said. She struck with the washboard: it divided neatly on the long mad face and the horse whirled and rushed back up the hall, where Eck and the boy now stood.

"Get to hell out of here, Wall!" Eck roared. He dropped to the floor, covering his head with his arms. The boy did not move, and for the third time the horse soared above the unwinking eyes and the unbowed and untouched head and onto the front veranda again just as Ratliff, still carrying the sock, ran around the corner of the house and up the steps. The horse whirled without breaking or pausing. It galloped to the end of the veranda and took the railing and soared outward, hobgoblin and floating, in the moon. It landed in the lot still running and crossed the lot and galloped through the wrecked gate and among the overturned wagons and the still intact one in which Henry's wife still sat, and on down the lane and into the road.

A quarter of a mile further on, the road gashed pallid and moony between the moony shadows of the bordering trees, the horse still galloping, galloping its shadow into the dust, the road descending now toward the creek and the bridge. It was of wood, just wide enough for a single vehicle. When the horse reached it, it was occupied by a wagon coming from the opposite direction and drawn by two mules already asleep in the harness and the soporific motion. On the seat were Tull and his wife, in splint chairs in the wagon behind them sat their four daughters, all returning belated from an all-day visit with some of Mrs Tull's kin. The horse neither checked nor swerved. It crashed once on the wooden bridge and rushed between the two mules which waked lunging in opposite direction in the traces, the horse now apparently scrambling along the wagon-tongue itself like a mad squirrel and scrabbling at the end-gate of the wagon with its forefeet as if it intended to climb into the wagon while Tull shouted at it and struck at its face with his whip. The mules were now trying to turn the wagon around in the middle of the bridge. It slewed and tilted, the bridge-rail cracked with a sharp report above the shrieks of the women; the horse scrambled at last across the back of one of the mules and Tull stood up in the wagon and kicked at its face. Then the front end of the wagon rose, flinging Tull, the reins now wrapped several times about his wrist, backward into the wagon bed among the overturned chairs and exposed stockings and undergarments of his women. The pony scrambled free and crashed again on the wooden planking, galloping again. The wagon lurched again; the mules had finally turned it on the bridge where there was not room for it to turn and were now kicking themselves free of the traces. When they came free, they snatched Tull bodily out of the wagon. He struck the bridge on his face and was dragged for several feet before the wrist-wrapped reins broke. Far up the road now, distancing the frantic mules, the pony faded on. While the five women still shrieked above Tull's unconscious body, Eck and the little boy came up, trotting, Eck still carrying his rope. He was panting. "Which way'd he go?" he said.

In the now empty and moon-drenched lot, his wife and Mrs Littlejohn and Ratliff and Lump Snopes, the clerk, and three other men raised Henry out of the trampled dust and carried him into Mrs Littlejohn's back yard. His face was blanched and stony, his eyes were closed, the weight of his head tauntened his throat across the protruding larynx; his teeth glinted dully beneath his lifted lip. They carried him on toward the house, through the dappled shade of the chinaberry trees. Across the dreaming and silver night a faint sound like remote thunder came and ceased. "There's one of them on the creek bridge," one of the men said.

"It's that one of Eck Snopes's," another said. "The one that was in the house." Mrs Littlejohn had preceded them into the hall. When they entered with Henry, she had already taken the lamp from the table and she stood beside an open door, holding the lamp high.

"Bring him in here," she said. She entered the room first and set the lamp on the dresser. They followed with clumsy scufflings and pantings and laid Henry on the bed and Mrs Littlejohn came to the bed and stood looking down at Henry's peaceful and bloodless face. "I'll declare," she said. "You men." They had drawn back a little, clumped, shifting from one foot to another, not looking at her nor at his wife either, who stood at the foot of the bed, motionless, her hands folded into her dress. "You all get out of here, V. K.," she said to Ratliff. "Go outside. See if you cant find something else to play with that will kill some more of you."

"All right," Ratliff said. "Come on boys. Aint no more horses to catch in here." They followed him toward the door, on tiptoe, their shoes scuffling, their shadows monstrous on the wall.

"Go get Will Varner," Mrs Littlejohn said. "I reckon you can tell him it's still a mule." They went out; they didn't look back. They tiptoed up the hall and crossed the veranda and descended into the moonlight. Now that they could pay attention to it, the silver air seemed to be filled with faint and sourceless sounds—shouts, thin and distant, again a brief thunder of hooves on a wooden bridge, more shouts faint and thin and earnest and clear as bells; once they even distinguished the words: "Whooey. Head him."

"He went through that house quick," Ratliff said. "He must have found another woman at home." Then Henry screamed in the house behind them. They looked back into the dark hall where a square of light fell through the bedroom door, listening while the scream sank into a harsh respiration: "Ah. Ah. Ah" on a rising note about to become screaming again. "Come on," Ratliff said. "We better get

Varner." They went up the road in a body, treading the moon-blanched dust in the tremulous April night murmurous with the moving of sap and the wet bursting of burgeoning leaf and bud and constant with the thin and urgent cries and the brief and fading bursts of galloping hooves. Varner's house was dark, blank and without depth in the moonlight. They stood, clumped darkly in the silver yard and called up at the blank windows until suddenly someone was standing in one of them. It was Flem Snopes's wife. She was in a white garment; the heavy braided club of her hair looked almost black against it. She did not lean out, she merely stood there, full in the moon, apparently blank-eyed or certainly not looking downward at them—the heavy gold hair, the mask not tragic and perhaps not even doomed: just damned, the strong faint lift of breasts beneath marblelike fall of the garment; to those below what Brunhilde, what Rhinemaiden on what spurious river-rock of papier-mâché, what Helen returned to what topless and shoddy Argos, waiting for no one. "Evening, Mrs Snopes," Ratliff said. "We want Uncle Will. Henry Armstid is hurt at Mrs Littlejohn's." She vanished from the window. They waited in the moonlight, listening to the faint remote shouts and cries, until Varner emerged, sooner than they had actually expected, hunching into his coat and buttoning his trousers over the tail of his nightshirt, his suspenders still dangling in twin loops below the coat. He was carrying the battered bag which contained the plumber-like tools with which he drenched and wormed and blistered and floated or drew the teeth of horses and mules; he came down the steps, lean and loose-jointed, his shrewd ruthless head cocked a little as he listened also to the faint bell-like cries and shouts with which the silver air was full.

"Are they still trying to catch them rabbits?" he said.

"All of them expect Henry Armstid," Ratliff said. "He caught his."

"Hah," Varner said. "That you, V. K.? How many did you buy?"

"I was too late," Ratliff said. "I never got back in time."

"Hah," Varner said. They moved on to the gate and into the road again. "Well, it's a good bright cool night for running them." The moon now high overhead, a pearled and mazy yawn in the soft sky, the ultimate ends of which rolled onward, whorl on whorl, beyond the pale stars and by pale stars surrounded. They walked in a close clump, tramping their shadows into the road's mild dust, blotting the shadows of the burgeoning trees which soared, trunk branch and twig against the pale sky, delicate and finely thinned. They passed the dark store. Then the pear tree came in sight. It rose in mazed and silver immobility like exploding snow; the mockingbird still sang in it. "Look at that tree," Varner said. "It ought to make this year, sho."

"Corn'll make this year too," one said.

"A moon like this is good for every growing thing outen earth," Varner said. "I mind when me and Mrs Varner was expecting Eula. Already had a mess of children and maybe we ought to quit then. But I wanted some more gals. Others had done married and moved away, and a passel of boys, soon as they get big enough to be worth anything, they aint got time to work. Got to set around store and talk. But a gal will stay home and work until she does get married. So there was a old woman told my mammy once that if a woman showed her belly to the full moon after she had done caught, it would be a gal. So Mrs Varner taken and laid every night with the moon on her nekid belly, until it fulled and after. I could lay my ear to her belly and hear Eula kicking and scrouging like all get-out, feeling the moon."

"You mean it actually worked sho enough, Uncle Will?" the other said.

"Hah," Varner said. "You might try it. You get enough women showing their nekid bellies to the moon or the sun either or even just to your hand fumbling around often enough and more than likely after a while there will be something in it you can lay your ear and listen to, provided something come up and you aint got away by that time. Hah, V.K.?" Someone guffawed.

"Dont ask me," Ratliff said. "I cant even get nowhere in time to buy a cheap horse." Two or three guffawed this time. Then they began to hear Henry's respirations from the house: "Ah. Ah. Ah." and they ceased abruptly, as if they had not been aware of their closeness to it. Varner walked on in front, lean, shambling, yet moving quite rapidly, though his head was still slanted with listening as the faint, urgent, indomitable cries murmured in the silver lambence, sourceless, at times almost musical, like fading bell-notes; again there was a brief rapid thunder of hooves on wooden planking.

"There's another one on the creek bridge," one said.

"They are going to come out even on them things, after all," Varner said. "They'll get the money back in exercise and relaxation. You take a man that aint got no other relaxation all year long except dodging mule-dung up and down a field furrow. And a night like this one, when a man aint old enough yet to lay still and sleep, and yet he aint young enough anymore to be tomcatting in and out of other folks' back windows, something like this is good for him. It'll make him sleep tomorrow night anyhow, provided he gets back home by then. If we had just knowed about this in time, we could have trained up a pack of horse-dogs. Then we could have held one of these field trials."

"That's one way to look at it, I reckon," Ratliff said. "In fact, it might be a considerable comfort to Bookwright and Quick and Freeman and Eck Snopes and them other new horse-owners if that side of it could be brought to their attention, because the chances are aint none of them thought to look at it in that light yet. Probably there aint a one of them that believes now there's any cure a-tall for that Texas disease Flem Snopts and that Dead-eye Dick brought here."

"Hah," Varner said. He opened Mrs Littlejohn's gate. The dim light still fell outward across the hall from the bedroom door; beyond it, Armstid was saying "Ah. Ah. Ah" steadily. "There's a pill for every ill but the last one."

"Even if there was always time to take it," Ratliff said.

"Hah," Varner said again. He glanced back at Ratliff for an instant, pausing. But the little hard bright eyes were invisible now; it was only the bushy overhang of the brows which seemed to concentrate downward toward him in writhen immobility, not frowning but with a sort of fierce risibility. "Even if there was time to take it. Breathing is a sight-draft dated yesterday."

At nine oclock on the second morning after that, five men were sitting or squatting along the gallery of the store. The sixth was Ratliff. He was standing up, and talking: "Maybe there wasn't but one of them things in Mrs Littlejohn's house that night, like Eck says. But it was the biggest drove of just one horse I ever seen. It was in my room and it was on the front porch and I could hear Mrs Littlejohn hitting it over the head with that washboard in the back yard all at the same time. And still it was missing everybody everytime. I reckon that's what that Texas man meant by calling them bargains: that a man would need to be powerful unlucky to ever get close enough to one of them to get hurt." They laughed, all except Eck himself. He and the little boy were eating. When they mounted the steps, Eck had gone on into the store and emerged with a paper sack, from which he took a segment of cheese and with his pocket knife divided it carefully into two exact halves and gave one to the boy and took a handful of crackers from the sack and gave them to the boy, and now they squatted against the wall, side by side and, save for the difference in size, identical, eating.

"I wonder what that horse thought Ratliff was," one said. He held a spray of peach bloom between his teeth. It bore four blossoms like miniature ballet skirts of pink tulle. "Jumping out windows and running indoors in his shirt-tail? I wonder how many Ratliffs that horse thought he saw."

"I dont know," Ratliff said. "But if he saw just half as many of me as I saw of him, he was sholy surrounded. Everytime I turned my head, that thing was just running over me or just swirling to run back over that boy again. And that boy there, he stayed right under it one time to my certain knowledge for a full one-and-one-half minutes without ducking his head or even batting his eyes. Yes sir, when I looked around and seen that varmint in the door behind me blaring its eyes at me, I'd a made sho Flem Snopes had brought a tiger back from Texas except I knowed that couldn't no just one tiger completely fill an entire room." They laughed again, quietly. Lump Snopes, the clerk, sitting in the only chair tilted back against the door-facing and partly blocking the entrance, cackled suddenly.

"If Flem had knowed how quick you fellows was going to snap them horses up, he'd a probably brought some tigers," he said. "Monkeys too."

"So they was Flem's horses," Ratliff said. The laughter stopped. The other three had open knives in their hands, with which they had been trimming idly at chips and slivers of wood. Now they sat apparently absorbed in the delicate and almost tedious movements of the knife-blades. The clerk had looked quickly up and found Ratliff watching him. His constant expression of incorrigible and mirthful disbelief had left him now; only the empty wrinkles of its remained about his mouth and eyes.

"Has Flem ever said they was?" he said. "But you town fellows are smarter than us country folks. Likely you done already read Flem's mind." But Ratliff was not looking at him now.

"And I reckon we'd a bought them," he said. He stood above them again, easy, intelligent, perhaps a little sombre but still perfectly impenetrable. "Eck here, for instance. With a wife and family to support. He owns two of them, though to be sho he never had to pay money for but one. I heard folks chasing them things up until midnight last night, but Eck and that boy aint been home a-tall in two days." They laughed again, except Eck. He pared off a bite of cheese and speared it on the knife-point and put it into his mouth.

"Eck caught one of hisn," the second man said.

"That so?" Ratliff said. "Which one was it, Eck? The one he give you or the one you bought?"

"The one he give me," Eck said, chewing.

"Well, well," Ratliff said. "I hadn't heard about that. But Eck's still one horse short. And the one he had to pay money for. Which is pure proof enough that them horses wasn't Flem's because wouldn't no man even give his own blood kin something he couldn't even catch." They laughed again, but they stopped when the clerk spoke. There was no mirth in his voice at all.

"Listen," he said. "All right. We done all admitted you are too smart for anybody to get ahead of. You never bought no horse from Flem or nobody else, so maybe it aint none of your business and maybe you better just leave it at that."

"Sholy," Ratliff said. "It's done already been left at that two night ago. The fellow that forgot to shut that lot gate done that. With the exception of Eck's horse. And we know that wasn't Flem's, because that horse was give to Eck for nothing."

"There's others besides Eck that aint got back home yet," the man with the peach spray said. "Bookwright and Quick are still chasing theirs. They was reported three miles west of Burtsboro Old Town at eight oclock last night. They aint got close enough to it yet to tell which one it belongs to."

"Sholy," Ratliff said. "The only new horse-owner in this country that could a been found without bloodhounds since whoever it was left that gate open two nights ago, is Henry Armstid. He's laying right there in Mrs Littlejohn's bedroom where he can watch the lot so that any time the one he bought happens to run back into it, all he's got to do is to holler at his wife and run out with the rope and catch it—" He ceased, though he said, "Morning, Flem," so immediately afterward and with no change whatever in tone, that the pause was not even discernible. With the exception of the clerk, who sprang up, vacated the chair with a sort of servile alacrity, and Eck and the little boy who continued to eat, they watched above their stilled hands as Snopes in the gray trousers and the minute tie and the new cap with its bright overplaid mounted the steps. He was chewing; he already carried a piece of white pine board; he jerked his head at them, looking at nobody, and took the vacated chair and opened his knife and began to whittle. The clerk now leaned in the opposite side of the door, rubbing his back against the facing. The expression of merry and invincible disbelief had returned to his face, with a quality watchful and secret.

"You're just in time," he said. "Ratliff here seems to be in a considerable sweat about who actually owned them horses." Snopes drew his knife-blade neatly along the board, the neat, surgeon-like silver curling before it. The others were whittling again, looking carefully at nothing, except Eck and the boy, who were still eating, and the clerk rubbing his back against the door-facing and watching Snopes with that secret and alert intensity. "Maybe you could put his mind at rest." Snopes turned his head slightly and spat, across the gallery and the steps and into the dust beyond them. He drew the knife back and began another curling sliver.

"He was there too," Snopes said. "He knows as much as anybody else." This time the clerk guffawed, chortling, his features gathering toward the center of his face as though plucked there by a hand. He slapped his leg, cackling.

"You might as well to quit," he said. "You cant beat him."

"I reckon not," Ratliff said. He stood above them, not looking at any of them, his gaze fixed apparently on the empty road beyond Mrs Littlejohn's house, impenetrable, brooding even. A hulking, half-grown boy in overalls too small for him, appeared suddenly from nowhere in particular. He stood for a while in the road, just beyond spitting-range of the gallery, with that air of having come from nowhere in particular and of not knowing where he would go next when he should move again and of not being troubled by that fact. He was looking at nothing, certainly not toward the gallery, and no one on the gallery so much as looked at him except the little boy, who now watched the boy in the road, his periwinkle eyes grave and steady above the bitten cracker in his halted hand. The boy in the road moved on, thickly undulant in the tight overalls, and vanished beyond the corner of the store, the round head and the unwinking eyes of the little boy on the gallery turning steadily to watch him out of sight. Then the little boy bit the cracker again, chewing. "Of course there's Mrs Tull," Ratliff said. "But that's Eck she's going to sue for damaging Tull against that bridge. And as for Henry Armstid——"

"If a man aint got gumption enough to protect himself, it's his own look-out," the clerk said.

"Sholy," Ratliff said, still in that dreamy, abstracted tone, actually speaking over his shoulder even. "And Henry Armstid, that's all right because from what I hear of the conversation that's taken place, Henry had already stopped owning that horse he thought was his before that Texas man left. And as for that broke leg, that wont put him out none because his wife can make his crop." The clerk had ceased to rub his back against the door. He watched the back of Ratliff's head, unwinking too, sober and intent; he glanced at Snopes who, chewing, was watching another sliver curl away from the advancing knife-blade, then he watched the back of Ratliff's head again.

"It wont be the first time she has made their crop," the man with the peach spray said. Ratliff glanced at him.

"You ought to know. This wont be the first time I ever saw you in their field, doing plowing Henry never got around to. How many days have you already given them this year?" The man with the peach spray removed it and spat carefully and put the spray back between his teeth.

"She can run a furrow straight as I can," the second said.

"They're unlucky," the third said. "When you are unlucky, it dont matter much what you do."

"Sholy," Ratliff said. "I've heard laziness called bad luck so much that maybe it is."

"He aint lazy," the third said. "When their mule died three or four years ago, him and her broke their land working time about in the traces with the other mule. They aint lazy."

"So that's all right," Ratliff said, gazing up the empty road again. "Likely she will begin right away to finish the plowing; the oldest gal is pretty near big enough to work with a mule, aint she? or at least to hold the plow steady while Mrs Armstid helps the mule?" He glanced again toward the man with the peach spray as though for an answer, but he was not looking at the other and he went on talking without any pause. The clerk stood with his rump and back pressed against the door-facing as if he had paused in the act of scratching, watching Ratliff quite hard now, unwinking. If Ratliff had looked at Flem Snopes, he would have seen nothing below the down-slanted peak of the cap save the steady motion of his jaws. Another sliver was curling with neat deliberation before the moving knife. "Plenty of time now because all she's got to do after she finishes washing Mrs Littlejohn's dishes and sweeping out the house to pay hers and Henry's board, is to go out home and milk and cook up enough vittles to last the children until tomorrow and feed them and get the littlest ones to sleep and wait outside the door until that biggest gal gets the bar up and gets into bed herself witht he axe——"

"The axe?" the man with the peach spray said.

"She takes it to bed with her. She's just twelve, and what with this country still more or less full of them uncaught horses that never belonged to Flem Snopes, likely she feels maybe she cant swing a mere washboard like Mrs Littlejohn can. —and then come back and wash up the supper dishes. And after that, not nothing to do until morning except to stay close enough where Henry can call her until it's light enough to chop the wood to cook breakfast and then help Mrs Littlejohn wash the dishes and make the beds and sweep while watching the road. Because likely any time now Flem Snopes will get back from wherever he has been since the auction, which of course is to town naturally to see about his cousin that's got into a little legal trouble, and so get that five dollars. 'Only maybe he wont give it back to me,' she says, and maybe that's what Mrs Littlejohn thought too, because she never said nothing. I could hear her——"

"And where did you happen to be during all this?" the clerk said.

"Listening," Ratliff said. He glanced back at the clerk, then he was looking away again, almost standing with his back to them. "—could hear her dumping the dishes into the pan like she was throwing them at it. 'Do you reckon he will give it back to me?' Mrs Armstid says. 'That Texas man give it to him and said he would. All the folks there saw him give Mr Snopes the money and heard him say I could get it from Mr Snopes tomorrow.' Mrs Littlejohn was washing the dishes now, washing them like a man would, like they was made out of iron. 'No,' she says. 'But asking him wont do no hurt.'—'If he wouldn't give it back, it aint no use to ask,' Mrs Armstid says.—'Suit yourself,' Mrs Littlejohn says. 'It's your money.' Then I couldn't hear nothing but the dishes for a while. 'Do you reckon he might give it back to me?' Mrs Armstid says. 'That Texas man said he would. They all heard him say it.'—'Then go and ask him for it,' Mrs Littlejohn says. Then I couldn't hear nothing but the dishes again.

'He wont give it back to me,' Mrs Armstid says.—'All right," Mrs Littlejohn says. 'Dont ask him, then.' Then I just heard the dishes. They would have two pans, both washing. 'You dont reckon he would, do you?' Mrs Armstid says. Mrs Littlejohn never said nothing. It sounded like she was throwing the dishes at one another. 'Maybe I better go and talk to Henry,' Mrs Armstid says.—'I would,' Mrs Littlejohn says. And I be dog if it didn't sound exactly like she had two plates in her hands, beating them together like these here brass bucket-lids in a band. 'Then Henry can buy another five-dollar horse with it. Maybe he'll buy one next time that will out and out kill him. If I just thought he would, I'd give him back that money, myself.'—'I reckon I better talk to him first.' Mrs Armstid says. And then it sounded just like Mrs Littlejohn taken up the dishes and pans and all and throwed the whole business at the cookstove—" Ratliff ceased. Behind him the clerk was hissing "Psst! Psst! Flem. Flem!" Then he stopped, and all of them watched Mrs Armstid approach and mount the steps, gaunt in the shapeless gray garment, the stained tennis shoes hissing faintly on the boards. She came among them and stood, facing Snopes but not looking at anyone, her hands rolled into her apron.

"He said that day he wouldn't sell Henry that horse," she said in a flat toneless voice. "He said you had the money and I could get it from you." Snopes raised his head and turned it slightly again and spat neatly past the woman, across the gallery and into the road.

"He took all the money with him when he left," he said. Motionless, the gray garment hanging in rigid, almost formal folds like drapery in bronze, Mrs Armstid appeared to be watching something near Snopes's feet, as though she had not heard him, or as if she had quitted her body as soon as she finished speaking and although her body, hearing, had received the words, they would have no life nor meaning until she returned. The clerk was rubbing his back steadily against the door-facing again, watching her. The little boy was watching her too with his unwinking ineffable gaze, but nobody else was. The man with the peach spray removed it and spat and put the twig back into his mouth.

"He said Henry hadn't bought no horse," she said. "He said I could get the money from you."

"I reckon he forgot it," Snopes said. "He took all the money away with him when he left." He watched her a moment longer, then he trimmed again at the stick. The clerk rubbed his back gently against the door, watching her. After a time Mrs Armstid raised her head and looked up the road where it went on, mild with spring dust, past Mrs Littlejohn's, beginning to rise, on past the not-yet-bloomed (that would be in June) locust grove across the way, on past the schoolhouse, the weathered roof of which, rising beyond an orchard of peach and pear trees, resembled a hive swarmed about by a cloud of pink-and-white bees, ascending, mounting toward the crest of the hill where the church stood among its sparse gleam of marble headstones in the sombre cedar grove where during the long afternoons of summer the constant mourning doves called back and forth. She moved; once more the rubber soles hissed on the gnawed boards.

"I reckon it's about time to get dinner started," she said.

"How's Henry this morning, Mrs Armstid?" Ratliff said. She looked at him, pausing, the blank eyes waking for an instant.

"He's resting, I thank you kindly," she said. Then the eyes died again and she moved again. Snopes rose from the chair, closing his knife with his thumb and brushing a litter of minute shavings from his lap.

"Wait a minute," he said. Mrs Armstid paused again, half-turning, though still not looking at Snopes nor at any of them. Because she cant possibly actually believe it, Ratliff told himself. Any more than I do. Snopes entered the store, the clerk, motionless again, his back and rump pressed against the door-facing as though waiting to start rubbing again, watched him enter, his head turning as the other passed him like the head of an owl, the little eyes blinking rapidly now. Jody Varner came up the road on his horse. He did not pass but instead turned in beside the store, toward the mulberry tree behind it where he was in the habit of hitching his horse. A wagon came up the road, creaking past. The man driving it lifted his hand; one or two of the men on the gallery lifted

theirs in response. The wagon went on. Mrs Ar
after it. Snopes came out of the door carrying a small striped paper bag and approached Mrs Armstid. "Here," he said. Her hand turned just enough to receive it. "A little sweetening for the chaps," he said. His other hand was already in his pocket, and as he turned back to the chair, he drew something from his pocket and handed it to the clerk, who took it. It was a five-cent piece. He sat down in the chair and tilted it back against the door again. He now had the knife in his hand again, already open. He turned his head slightly and spat again, neatly past the gray garment, into the road. The little boy was watching the sack in Mrs Armstid's hand. Then she seemed to discover it also, rousing.

"You're right kind," she said. She rolled the sack into the apron, the little boy's unwinking gaze fixed upon the lump her hands made beneath the cloth. She moved again. "I reckon I better get on and help with dinner," she said. She descended the steps, though as soon as she reached the level earth and began to retreat, the gray folds of the garment once more lost all inference and intimation of locomotion, so that she seemed to progress without motion like a figure on a retreating and diminishing float; a gray and blasted tree-trunk moving, somehow intact and upright, upon an unhurried flood. The clerk in the doorway cackled suddenly, explosively, chortling. He slapped his thigh.

"By God," he said, "you cant beat him."

Jody Varner, entering the store from the rear, paused in midstride like a pointing bird-dog. Then, on tiptoe, in complete silence and with astonishing speed, he darted behind the counter and sped up the gloomy tunnel, at the end of which a hulking, bear-shaped figure stooped, its entire head and shoulders wedged into the glass case which contained the needles and thread and snuff and tobacco and the stale gaudy candy. He snatched the boy savagely and viciously out; the boy gave a choked cry and struggled flabbily, cramming a final handful of something into his mouth, chewing. But he ceased to struggle almost at once and became slack and inert save for his jaws. Varner dragged him around the counter as the clerk entered, seemed to bounce suddenly into the store with a sort of alert concern. "You, Saint Elmo!" he said.

"Aint I told you and told you to keep him out of here?" Varner demanded, shaking the boy. "He's damn near eaten that candy-case clean. Stand up!" The boy hung like a half-filled sack from Varner's hand, chewing with a kind of fatalistic desperation, the eyes shut tight in the vast flaccid colorless face, the ears moving steadily and faintly to the chewing. Save for the jaw and the ears, he appeared to have gone to sleep chewing.

"You, Saint Elmo!" the clerk said. "Stand up!" The boy assumed his own weight, though he did not open his eyes yet nor cease to chew. Varner released him. "Git on home," the clerk said. The boy turned obediently to re-enter the store. Varner jerked him about again.

"Not that way," he said. The boy crossed the gallery and descended the steps, the tight overalls undulant and reluctant across his flabby thighs. Before he reached the ground, his hand rose from his pocket to his mouth; again his ears moved faintly to the motion of chewing.

"He's worse than a rat, aint he?" the clerk said.

"Rat, hell," Varner said, breathing harshly. "He's worse than a goat. First thing I know, he'll graze on back and work through that lace leather and them hame-strings and lap-links and ring-bolts and eat me and you and him all three clean out the back door. And then be damned if I wouldn't be afraid to turn my back for fear he would cross the road and start in on the gin and the blacksmith shop. Now you mind what I say. If I catch him hanging around here one more time, I'm going to set a bear-trap for him." He went out onto the gallery, the clerk following. "Morning, gentlemen," he said.

"Who's that one, Jody?" Ratliff said. Save for the clerk in the background, they were the only two standing, and now, in juxtaposition, you could see the resemblance between them—a resemblance intangible, indefinite, not in figure, speech, dress, intelligence; certainly not in morals. Yet it was there, but with this bridgeless difference, his hallmark of his fate upon him: he would become an old man; Ratliff too: but an old man who at about sixty-five would be caught and married by a creature not yet seventeen probably, who would for the rest of his life continue to take revenge upon him for her whole sex; Ratliff, never. The boy was moving without haste up the road. His hand rose again from his pocket to his mouth.

"That boy of I. O.'s," Varner said. "By God, I've done everything but put out poison for him."

"What?" Ratliff said. He glanced quickly about at the faces; for an instant there was in his own not only bewilderment but something almost like terror. "I thought—the other day you fellows told me— You said it was a woman, a young woman with a baby— Here now," he said. "Wait."

"This here's another one," Varner said. "I wish to hell he couldn't walk. Well, Eck, I hear you caught one of your horses."

"That's right," Eck said. He and the little boy had finished the crackers and cheese and he had sat for some time now, holding the empty bag.

"It was the one he give you, wasn't it?" Varner said.

"That's right," Eck said.

"Give the other one to me, paw," the little boy said.

"What happened?" Varner said.

"He broke his neck," Eck said.

"I know," Varner said. "But how?" Eck did not move. Watching him, they could almost see him visibly gathering and arranging words, speech. Varner, looking down at him, began to laugh steadily and harshly, sucking his teeth. "I'll tell you what happened. Eck and that boy finally run it into that blind lane of Freeman's, after a chase of about twenty-four hours. They figured it couldn't possibly climb them eight-foot fences of Freeman's so him and the boy tied their rope across the end of the lane, about three feet off the ground. And sho enough, soon as the horse come to the end of the lane and seen Freeman's barn, it whirled just like Eck figured it would and come helling back up that lane like a scared hen-hawk. It probably never even seen the rope at all. Mrs Freeman was watching from where she had run up onto the porch. She said that when it hit that rope, it looked just like one of these here great big Christmas pinwheels. But the one you bought got clean away, didn't it?"

"That's right," Eck said. "I never had time to see which way the other one went."

"Give him to me, paw," the little boy said.

"You wait till we catch him," Eck said. "We'll see about it then."

That afternoon Ratliff sat in the halted buckboard in front of Bookwright's gate. Bookwright stood in the road beside it. "You were wrong," Bookwright said. "He come back."

"He come back," Ratliff said. "I misjudged his . . . nerve aint the word I want, and sholy lack of it aint. But I wasn't wrong."

"Nonsense," Bookwright said. "He was gone all day yesterday. Nobody saw him going to town or coming back, but that's bound to be where he was at. Aint no man, I dont care if his name is Snopes, going to let his own blood kin rot in jail."

"He wont be in jail long. Court is next month, and after they send him to Parchman, he can stay outdoors again. He will even go back to farming, plowing. Of course it wont be his cotton, but then he never did make enough out of his own cotton to quite pay him for staying alive."

"Nonsense," Bookwright said. "I dont believe it. Flem aint going to let him go to the penitentiary."

"Yes," Ratliff said. "Because Flem Snopes has got to cancel all them loose-flying notes that turns up here and there every now and then. He's going to discharge at least some of them notes for good and all." They looked at one another—Ratliff grave and easy in the blue shirt, Bookwright sober too, black-browed, intent.

"I thought you said you and him burned them notes."

"I said we burned two notes that Mink Snopes gave me. Do you think that any Snopes is going to put all of anything on one piece of paper than can be destroyed by one match? Do you think there is any Snopes that don't know that?"

"Oh," Bookwright said. "Hah," he said, with no mirth. "I reckon you gave Henry Armstid back his five dollars too." Then Ratliff looked away. His face changed—something

fleeting, quizzical, but not smiling, his eyes di
was gone.

"I could have," he said. "But I didn't. I might have if I could just been sho he would buy something this time that would sho enough hill him, like Mrs Littlejohn said. Besides, I wasn't protecting a Snopes from Snopeses; I wasn't even protecting a people from a Snopes. I was protecting something that wasn't even a people, that wasn't nothing but something that dont want nothing but to walk and feel the sun and wouldn't know how to hurt no man even if it would and wouldn't want to even if it could, just like I wouldn't stand by and see you steal a meat-bone from a dog. I never made them Snopeses and I never made the folks that cant wait to bare their backsides to them. I could do more, but I wont. I wont, I tell you!"

"All right," Bookwright said. "Hook your drag up; it aint nothing but a hill. I said it's all right."

2

The two actions of Armstid pl. vs. Snopes, and Tull pl. vs. Eckrum Snopes (and anyone else named Snopes or Varner either which Tull's irate wife could contrive to involve, as the village well knew) were accorded a change of venue by mutual agreement and arrangement among the litigants. Three of the parties did, that is, because Flem Snopes flatly refused to recognise the existence of the suit against himself, stating once and without heat and first turning his head slightly aside to spit, "They wasn't none of my horses," then fell to whittling again while the baffled and helpless bailiff stood before the tilted chair with the papers he was trying to serve.

"What a opportunity for that Snopes family lawyer this would a been," Ratliff said when told about it. "What's his name? that quick-fatherer, the Moses with his mouth full of mottoes and his coat-tail full of them already half-grown retroactive sons? I dont understand yet how a man that has to spend as much time as I do being constantly reminded of them folks, still cant keep the names straight. I. O. That he never had time to wait. This here would be probably the one tried case in his whole legal existence where he wouldn't be bothered with no narrow-ideaed client trying to make him stop talking, and the squire presiding himself would be the only man in company with authority to tell him to shut up."

So neither did the Varner surrey nor Ratliff's buckboard make one among the wagons, the buggies, and the saddled horses and mules which moved out of the village on that May Saturday morning, to converge upon Whiteleaf store eight miles away, coming not only from Frenchman's Bend but from other directions too since by that time, what Ratliff had called 'that Texas sickness,' that spotted corruption of frantic and uncatchable horses, had spread as far as twenty and thirty miles. So by the time the Frenchman's Bend people began to arrive, there were two dozen wagons, the teams reversed and eased of harness and tied to the rear wheels in order to pass the day, and twice that many saddled animals already standing about the locust grove beside the store and the site of the hearing had already been transferred from the store to an adjacent shed where in the fall cotton would be stored. But by nine oclock it was seen that even the shed would not hold them all, so the palladium was moved again, from the shed to the grove itself. The horses and mules and wagons were cleared from it; the single chair, the gnawed table bearing a thick Bible which had the appearance of loving and constant use of a piece of old and perfectly-kept machinery and an almanac and a copy of Mississippi Reports dated 1881 and bearing along its opening edge a single thread-thin line of soilure as if during all the time of his possession its owner (or user) had opened it at only one page though that quite often, were fetched from the shed to the grove; a wagon and four men were dispatched and returned presently from the church a mile away with four wooden pews for the litigants and their clansmen and witnesses; behind these in turn the spectators stood—the men, the women, the children, sober, attentive, and neat, not in their Sunday clothes to be sure, but in the clean working garments donned that morning for the Saturday's diversion of sitting about the country stores or trips into the county seat, and in which they would return to the field on Monday morning and would wear all that week until Friday night came round again. The Justice of the Peace was a neat, small, plump old man resembling a tender caricature of all grandfathers who ever breathed, in a beautifully laundered though collarless white shirt with immaculate starch-gleaming cuffs and bosom, and steel-framed spectacles and neat, faintly curling white hair. He sat behind the table and looked at them—at the gray woman in the gray sunbonnet and dress, her clasped and motionless hands on her lap resembling a gnarl of pallid and drowned roots from a drained swamp; at Tull in his faded but absolutely clean shirt and the overalls which his womenfolks not only kept immaculately washed but starched and ironed also, and not creased through the legs but flat across them from seam to seam, so that on each Saturday morning they resembled the short pants of a small boy, and the sedate and innocent blue of his eyes above the month-old corn-silk beard which concealed most of his abraded face and which gave him an air of incredible and paradoxical dissoluteness, not as though at last and without warning he had appeared in the sight of his fellowmen in his true character, but as if an old Italian portrait of a child saint had been defaced by a vicious and idle boy; at Mrs Tull, a strong, full-bosomed though slightly dumpy woman with an expression of grim and seething outrage which the elapsed four weeks had apparently neither increased nor diminished but had merely set, an outrage which curiously and almost at once began to give the impression of being directed not at any Snopes or at any other man in particular but at all men, all males, and of which Tull himself was not at all the victim but the subject, who sat on one side of her husband while the biggest of the four daughters sat on the other as if they (or Mrs Tull at least) were not so much convinced that Tull might leap up and flee, as determined that he would not; and at Eck and the little boy, identical save for size, and Lump the clerk in a gray cap which someone actually recognised as being the one which Flem Snopes had worn when he went to Texas last year, who between spells of rapid blinking would sit staring at the Justice with the lidless intensity of a rat—and into the lens-distorted and irisless old-man's eyes of the Justice there grew an expression not only of amazement and bewilderment but, as in Ratliff's eyes while he stood on the store gallery four weeks ago, something very like terror.

"This—" he said. "I didn't expect—I didn't look to see—. I'm going to pray," he said. "I aint going to pray aloud. But I hope—" He looked at them. "I wish . . . Maybe some of you all anyway had better do the same." He bowed his head. They watched him, quiet and grave, while he sat motionless behind the table, the light morning wind moving faintly in his thin hair and the shadow-stipple of windy leaves gliding and flowing across the starched bulge of bosom and the gleaming bone-buttoned cuffs, as rigid and almost as large as sections of six-inch stovepipe, at his joined hands. He raised his head. "Armstid against Snopes," he said. Mrs Armstid spoke. She did not move, she looked at nothing, her hands clasped in her lap, speaking in that flat, toneless and hopeless voice:

"That Texas man said——"

"Wait," the Justice said. He looked about at the faces, the blurred eyes fleeing behind the thick lenses. "Where is the defendant? I dont see him."

"He wouldn't come," the bailiff said.

"Wouldn't come?" the Justice said. "Didn't you serve the papers on him?"

"He wouldn't take them," the bailiff said. "He said——"

"Then he is in contempt!" the Justice cried.

"What for?" Lump Snopes said. "Aint nobody proved yet they was his horses." The Justice looked at him.

"Are you representing the defendant?" he said. Snopes blinked at him for a moment.

"What's that mean?" he said. "That you aim for me to pay whatever fine you think you can clap onto him?"

"So he refuses to defend himself," the Justice said. "Dont he know that I can find against him for that reason, even if pure justice and decency aint enough?"

"It'll be pure something," Snopes said. "It dont take no mind-reader to see how your mind is——"

"Shut up, Snopes," the bailiff said. "If you aint in this case, you keep out of it." He turned back to the Justice.

"What you want me to do: go over to the Bend and fetch Snopes here anyway? I reckon I can do it."

"No," the Justice said. "Wait." He looked about at the sober faces again with that bafflement, that dread. "Does anybody here know for sho who them horses belonged to? Anybody?" They looked back at him, sober, inattentive—at the neat immaculate old man sitting with his hands locked together on the table before him to still the trembling. "All right, Mrs Armstid," he said. "Tell the Court what happened." She told it, unmoving, in the flat, inflectionless voice, looking at nothing, while they listened quietly, coming to the end and ceasing without even any fall of voice, as though the tale mattered nothing and came to nothing. The Justice was looking down at his hands. When she ceased, he looked up at her. "But you haven't showed yet that Snopes owned the horses. The one you want to sue is that Texas man. And he's gone. If you got a judgment against him, you couldn't collect the money. Dont you see?"

"Mr Snopes brought him here," Mrs Armstid said. "Likely that Texas man wouldn't have knowed where Frenchman's Bend was if Mr Snopes hadn't showed him."

"But it was the Texas man that sold the horses and collected the money for them." The Justice looked about again at the faces. "Is that right? You, Bookwright, is that what happened?"

"Yes," Bookwright said. The Justice looked at Mrs Armstid again, with that pity and grief. As the morning increased the wind had risen, so that from time to time gusts of it ran through the branches overhead, bringing a faint snow of petals, prematurely bloomed as the spring itself had condensed with spendthrift speed after the hard winter, and the heavy and drowsing scent of them, about the motionless heads.

"He give Mr Snopes Henry's money. He said Henry hadn't bought no horse. He said I could get the money from Mr Snopes tomorrow."

"And you have witnesses that saw and heard him?"

"Yes, sir. The other men that was there saw him give Mr Snopes the money and say that I could get it——"

"And you asked Snopes for the money?"

"Yes, sir. He said that Texas man taken it away with him when he left. But I would . . ." She ceased again, perhaps looking down at her hands also. Certainly she was not looking at anyone.

"Yes?" the Justice said. "You would what?"

"I would know them five dollars. I earned them myself, weaving at night after Henry and the chaps was asleep. Some of the ladies in Jefferson would save up string and such and give it to me and I would weave things and sell them. I earned that money a little at a time and I would know it when I saw it because I would take the can outen the chimney and count it now and then while it was making up to enough to buy my chaps some shoes for next winter. I would know it if I was to see it again. If Mr Snopes would just let——"

"Suppose there was somebody seen Flem give the money back to that Texas fellow," Lump Snopes said suddenly.

"Did anybody here see that?" the Justice said.

"Yes," Snopes said, harshly and violently. "Eck here did." He looked at Eck. "Go on. Tell him." The Justice looked at Eck; the four Tull girls turned their heads as one head and looked at him, and Mrs Tull leaned forward to look past her husband, her face cold, furious, and contemptuous, and those standing shifted to look past one another's heads at Eck sitting motionless on the bench.

"Did you see Snopes give Armstid's money back to the Texas man, Eck?" the Justice said. Still Eck did not answer nor move. Lump Snopes made a gross violent sound through the side of his mouth.

"By God, I aint afraid to say it if Eck is. I seen him do it."

"Will you swear that as testimony?" Snopes looked at the Justice. He did not blink now.

"So you wont take my word," he said.

"I want the truth," the Justice said. "If I cant find that, I got to have sworn evidence of what I will have to accept as truth." He lifted the Bible from the two other books.

"All right," the bailiff said. "Step up here." Snopes rose from the bench and approached. They watched him, though now there was no shifting nor craning, no movement at all among the faces, the still eyes. Snopes at the table looked back at them once, his gaze traversing swiftly the crescent-shaped rank; he looked at the Justice again. The bailiff grasped the Bible; though the Justice did not release it yet.

"You are ready to swear you saw Snopes give that Texas man back the money he took from Henry Armstid for that horse?" he said.

"I said I was, didn't I?" Snopes said. The Justice released the Bible.

"Swear him," he said.

"Put your left hand on the Book raise your right hand you solemnly swear and affirm—" the bailiff said rapidly. But Snopes had already done so, his left hand clapped onto the extended Bible and the other hand raised and his head turned away as once more his gaze went rapidly along the circle of expressionless and intent faces, saying in that harsh and snarling voice:

"Yes. I saw Flem Snopes give back to that Texas man whatever money Henry Armstid or anybody else thinks Henry Armstid or anybody else paid Flem for any of them horses. Does that suit you?"

"Yes," the Justice said. Then there was no movement, no sound anywhere among them. The bailiff placed the Bible quietly on the table beside the Justice's locked hands, and there was no movement save the flow and recover of the windy shadows and the drift of the locust petals. Then Mrs Armstid rose; she stood once more (or still) looking at nothing, her hands clasped across her middle.

"I reckon I can go now, cant I?" she said.

"Yes," the Justice said, rousing. "Unless you would like——"

"I better get started," she said. "It's a right far piece." She had not come in the wagon, but on one of the gaunt and underfed mules. One of the men followed her across the grove and untied the mule for her and led it up to a wagon, from one hub of which she mounted. Then they looked at the Justice again. He sat behind the table, his hands still joined before him, though his head was not bowed now. Yet he did not move until the bailiff leaned and spoke to him, when he roused, came suddenly awake without starting, as an old man wakes from an old man's light sleep. He removed his hands from the table and, looking down, he spoke exactly as if he were reading from a paper:

"Tull against Snopes. Assault and——"

"Yes!" Mrs Tull said. "I'm going to say a word before you start." She leaned, looking past Tull at Lump Snopes again. "If you think you are going to lie and perjure Flem and Eck Snopes out of——"

"Now, mamma," Tull said. Now she spoke to Tull, without changing her position or her tone or even any break or pause in her speech:

"Dont you say hush to me! You'll let Eck Snopes or Flem Snopes or that whole Varner tribe snatch you out of the wagon and beat you half to death against a wooden bridge. But when it comes to suing them for your just rights and a punishment, oh no. Because that wouldn't be neighborly. What's neighborly got to do with you lying flat on your back in the middle of planting time while we pick splinters out of your face?" By this time the bailiff was shouting.

"Order! Order! This here's a law court!" Mrs Tull ceased. She sat back, breathing hard, staring at the Justice, who sat and spoke again as if he were reading aloud:

"—assault and battery on the person of Vernon Tull, through the agency and instrument of one horse, unnamed, belonging to Eckrum Snopes. Evidence of physical detriment and suffering, defendant himself. Witnesses, Mrs Tull and daughters——"

"Eck Snopes saw it too," Mrs Tull said, though with less violence now. "He was there. He got there in plenty of time to see it. Let him deny it. Let him look me in the face and deny it if he——"

"If you please, ma'am," the Justice said. He said it so quietly that Mrs Tull hushed and became quite calm, almost a rational and composed being. "The injury to your husband aint disputed. And the agency of the horse aint disputed. The law says that when a man owns a creature which he knows to be dangerous and if that creature is restrained and restricted from the public commons by a pen or enclosure capable of restraining and restricting it, if a man enter that pen or enclosure, whether he knows the creature in it is dangerous or not dangerous, then that man has committed trespass and the owner of that creature is not liable. But if that creature known to him to be dangerous ceases to be restrained by that suitable pen or enclosure, either by accident or design and either with or without the owner's knowledge, then that owner is liable. That's the law. All necessary now is to establish first, the ownership of the horse, and second, that the horse was a dangerous creature within the definition of the law as provided."

"Hah," Mrs Tull said. She said it exactly as Bookwright would have. "Dangerous. Ask Vernon Tull. Ask Henry Armstid if them things was pets."

"If you please, ma'am," the Justice said. He was looking at Eck. "What is the defendant's position? Denial of ownership?"

"What?" Eck said.

"Was that your horse that ran over Mr Tull?"

"Yes," Eck said. "It was mine. How much do I have to p——"

"Hah," Mrs Tull said again. "Denial of ownership. When there were at least forty men—fools too, or they wouldn't have been there. But even a fool's word is good about what he saw and heard. —at least forty men heard that Texas murderer give that horse to Eck Snopes. Not sell it to him, mind; give it to him."

"What?" the Justice said. "Gave it to him?"

"Yes," Eck said. "He gave it to me. I'm sorry Tull happened to be using that bridge too at the same time. How much do I——"

"Wait," the Justice said. "What did you give him? a note? a swap of some kind?"

"No," Eck said. "He just pointed to it in the lot and told me it belonged to me."

"And he didn't give you a bill of sale or a deed or anything in writing?"

"I reckon he never had time," Eck said. "And after Lon

Quick forgot and left that gate open, never nobody had time to do no writing even if we had a thought of it."

"What's all this?" Mrs Tull said. "Eck Snopes has just told you he owned that horse. And if you wont take his word, there were forty men standing at that gate all day long doing nothing, that heard that murdering card-playing whiskey-drinking antichrist—" This time the Justice raised one hand, in its enormous pristine cuff, toward her. He did not look at her.

"Wait," he said. "Then what did he do?" he said to Eck. "Just lead the horse up and put the rope in your hand?"

"No," Eck said. "Him nor nobody else never got no ropes on none of them. He just pointed to the horse in the lot and said it was mine and auctioned off the rest of them and got into the buggy and said good-bye and druv off. And we got our ropes and went into the lot, only Lon Quick forgot to shut the gate. I'm sorry it made Tull's mules snatch him outen the wagon. How much do I owe him?" Then he stopped, because the Justice was no longer looking at him and, as he realised a moment later, no longer listening either. Instead, he was sitting back in the chair, actually leaning back in it for the first time, his head bent slightly and his hands resting on the table before him, the fingers lightly overlapped. They watched him quietly for almost a half-minute before anyone realised that he was looking quietly and steadily at Mrs Tull.

"Well, Mrs Tull," he said, "by your own testimony, Eck never owned that horse."

"What?" Mrs Tull said. It was not loud at all. "What did you say?"

"In the law, ownership cant be conferred or invested by word-of-mouth. It must be established either by recorded or authentic document, or by possession or occupation. By your testimony and his both, he never gave that Texas man anything in exchange for that horse, and by his testimony the Texas man never gave him any paper to prove he owned it, and by his testimony and by what I know myself from these last four weeks, nobody yet has ever laid hand or rope either on any one of them. So that horse never came into Eck's possession at all. That Texas man could have given that same horse to a dozen other men standing around that gate that day, without even needing to tell Eck he had done it; and Eck himself could have transferred all his title and equity in it to Mr Tull right there while Mr Tull was lying unconscious on that bridge just by thinking it to himself, and Mr Tull's title would be just as legal as Eck's."

"So I get nothing," Mrs Tull said. Her voice was still calm, quiet, though probably no one but Tull realised that it was too calm and quiet. "My team is made to run away by a wild spotted mad-dog, my wagon is wrecked; my husband is jerked out of it and knocked unconscious and unable to work for a whole week with less than half of our seed in the ground, and I get nothing."

"Wait," the Justice said. "The law——"

"The law," Mrs Tull said. She stood suddenly up—a short, broad, strong woman, balanced on the balls of her planted feet.

"Now, mamma," Tull said.

"Yes, ma'am," the Justice said. "Your damages are fixed by statute. The law says that when a suit for damages is brought against the owner of an animal which has committed damage or injury, if the owner of the animal either cant or wont assume liability, the injured or damaged party shall find recompense in the body of the animal. And since Eck Snopes never owned that horse at all, and since you just heard a case here this morning that failed to prove that Flem Snopes had any equity in any of them, that horse still belongs to that Texas man. Or did belong. Because now that horse that made your team run away and snatch your husband out of the wagon, belongs to you and Mr Tull."

"Now, mamma" Tull said. He rose quickly. But Mrs Tull was still quiet, only quite rigid and breathing hard, until Tull spoke. Then she turned on him, not screaming: shouting; presently the bailiff was banging the table-top with his hand-polished hickory cane and roaring "Order! Order!" while the neat old man, thrust backward in his chair as though about to dodge and trembling with an old man's palsy, looked on with amazed unbelief.

"The horse!" Mrs Tull shouted. "We see it for five seconds, while it is climbing into the wagon with us and then out again.

Then it's gone, God dont know where and thank the Lord He dont! And the mules gone with it and the wagon wrecked and you laying there on the bridge with your face full of kindling-wood and bleeding like a hog and dead for all we knew. And he gives us the horse! Dont you hush me! Get on to that wagon, fool that would sit there behind a pair of young mules with the reins tied around his wrist! Get on to that wagon, all of you!"

"I can't stand no more!" the old Justice cried. "I wont! This court's adjourned! Adjourned!"

There was another trial then. It began on the following Monday and most of those same faces watched it too, in the county courthouse in Jefferson when the prisoner entered between two officers and looking hardly larger than a child, in a suit of brand-new overalls, thin, almost frail-looking, the sombre violent face thin in repose and pallid from the eight months in jail, and was arraigned and then plead by the counsel appointed him by the Court—a young man graduated only last June from the State University's law school and admitted to the Bar, who did what he could and overdid what he could not, zealous and, for all practical purposes and results, ignored, having exhausted all his challenges before the State had made one and in despite of which seeing himself faced by an authenticated jury in almost record time as if the State, the public, all rational mankind, possessed an inexhaustible pool of interchangeable faces and names all cradling one identical conviction and intention, so that his very challenges could have been discharged for him by the janitor who opened the courtroom, by merely counting off the first members of the panel corresponding to that number. And, if the defendant's counsel had any detachment and objectivity left at all by then, he probably realised soon that it was not his client but himself who was embattled with that jury. Because his client was paying no attention whatever to what was going on. He did not seem to be interested in watching and listening to it as someone else's trial. He sat where they had placed him, manacled to one of the officers, small, in the new iron-hard board-stiff overalls, the back of his head toward the Bar and what was going on there and his upper body shifting constantly until they realised that he was trying to watch the rear of the room, the doors and who entered them. He had to be spoken to twice before he stood up and plead and continued to stand, his back completely turned to the Court now, his face sombre, thin, curiously urgent and quite calm and with something else in it which was not even just hope but was actual faith, looking not at his wife who sat on the bench just behind him but out into the crowded room, among the ranked and intent faces some of which, most of which, he knew, until the officer he was handcuffed to pulled him down again. And he sat that way through the rest of the brief and record day-and-a-quarter of his trial, the small, neatly-combed, vicious and ironlike incorrigible head turning and craning constantly to see backward past the bulk of the two officers, watching the entrance while his attorney did what he could, talked hismelf frantic and at last voiceless before the grave impassivity of the jury which resembled a conclave of grown men self-delegated with the necessity (though for a definitely specified and limited time) of listening to prattle of a licensed child. And still the client listened to none of it, watching constantly the rear of the room while toward the end of the first day the faith went out of his face, leaving only the hope, and at the beginning of the second day the hope was gone too and there was only the urgency, the grim and intractable sombreness, while still he watched the door. The State finished in midmorning of the second day. The jury was out twenty minutes and returned with a ballot of murder in the second degree; the prisoner stood again and was sentenced by the Court to be transported to the State Penal Farm and there remain until he died. But he was not listening to that either; he had not only turned his back to the Court to look out into the crowded room, he was speaking himself even before the Judge had ceased, continuing to speak even while the Judge hammered the desk with his gavel and the two officers and three bailiffs converged upon the prisoner as he struggled, flinging them back and for a short time actually successful, staring out into the room. "Flem Snopes!" he said. "Flem Snopes! Is Flem Snopes in this room? Tell that son of a bitch——"

CHAPTER TWO

1

Ratliff stopped the buckboard at Bookwright's gate. The house was dark, but at once three or four of Bookwright's dogs came yelling out from beneath it or behind it. Armstid swung his legs stiffly out and prepared to get down. "Wait," Ratliff said. "I'll go get him."

"I can walk," Armstid said harshly.

"Sholy," Ratliff said. "Besides, them dogs knows me."

"They'll know me, after the first one runs at me once," Armstid said.

"Sholy," Ratliff said. He was already out of the buckboard. "You wait here and hold the team." Armstid swung his leg back into the buckboard, not invisible even in the moonless August darkness, but on the contrary, because of his faded overalls, quite distinct against the buckboard's dark upholstery. it was only his features beneath his hatbrim which could not be distinguished. Ratliff handed him the reins and turned past the metal mailbox on its post in the starlight, toward the gate beyond it and the mellow uproar of the dogs. When he was through the gate he could see them—a yelling clump of blackness against the slightly paler earth which broke and spread fanwise before him, braced, yelling, holding him bayed—three black-and-tan hounds whose tan the starlight had transposed to black too so that, not quite invisible but almost and without detail, they might have been the three intact carbons of burned newspaper-sheets standing upright from the earth, yelling at him. He shouted at them. They should have recognised him already by smell. When he shouted, he knew that they already had, because for perhaps a second they hushed then as he moved forward they retreated before him, keeping the same distance, baying. Then he saw Bookwright, pale too in overalls against the black house. When Bookwright shouted at the hounds, they did hush.

"Git," he said. "Shut up and git." He approached, becoming black in his turn against the paler earth, to where Ratliff waited. "Where's Henry?" he said.

"In the buggy," Ratliff said. He turned back toward the gate.

"Wait," Bookwright said. Ratliff stopped. The other came up beside him. They looked at one another, each face invisible to the other. "You aint let him persuade you into this, have you?" Bookwright said. "Between having to remember them five dollars every time he looks at his wife maybe, and that broke leg, and that horse he bought from Flem Snopes with it he aint even seen again, he's plumb crazy now. Not that he had far to go. You aint just let him persuade you?"

"I don't think so," Ratliff said. "I know I aint," he said. "There's something there. I've always knowed it. Just like Will Varner knows there is something there. If there wasn't, he wouldn't never bought it. And he wouldn't a kept it, selling the balance of it off and still keeping that old house, paying taxes on it when he could a got something for it, setting there in that flour-barrel chair to watch it and claiming he did it because it rested him to set there where somebody had gone to all that work and expense just to build something to sleep and eat and lay with his wife in. And I knowed it for sho when Flem Snopes took it. When he had Will Varner just where he wanted him, and then he sold out to Will by taking that old house and them ten acres that wouldn't hardly raise goats. And I went with Henry last night. I saw it too. You dont have to come in, if you feel uncertain. I'd rather you wouldn't."

"All right," Bookwright said. He moved on. "That's all I wanted to know." They returned to the buckboard. Henry moved to the middle of the seat and they got in. "Dont let me crowd your leg," Bookwright said.

"There aint anything wrong with my leg," Armstid said in that harsh voice. "I can walk as far as you or any man any day."

"Sholy," Ratliff said quickly, taking the reins. "Henry's leg is all right now. You cant even notice it."

"Let's get on," Bookwright said. "Wont nobody have to walk for a while, if that team can."

"It's shorter through the Bend," Ratliff said. "But we better not go that way."

"Let them see," Armstid said. "If anybody here is afraid, I dont need no help. I can——"

"Sholy," Ratliff said. "If folks sees us, we might have too much help. That's what we want to dodge." Armstid hushed. He said no more from then on, sitting between them in an immobility which was almost like a temperature, thinner, as though it had not been the sickness (after being in bed about a month, he had got up one day and broken the leg again; nobody ever knew how, what he had been doing, trying to do, because he never talked about it) but impotence and fury which had wasted him.

Ratliff asked neither advice nor directions; there was little anybody could have told him about the back roads and lanes of that or any of the other country he travelled. They passed nobody; the dark and sleeping land was empty, the scattered and remote homesteads indicated only by the occasional baying of dogs. The lanes he followed ran pale between the broad spread of fields felt rather than seen, where the corn was beginning to fire and the cotton to bloom, then into tunnels of trees rising and feathered lushly with summer's full leaf against the sky of August heavy and thick with stars. Then they were in the old lane which for years now had been marked by nothing save the prints of Varner's old white horse and, for a brief time, by the wheels of the parasol-topped runabout—the old scar almost healed now, where nearly fifty years ago a courier (perhaps a neighbor's slave flogging a mule taken out of the plow) had galloped with the news of Sumter, where perhaps the barouche had moved, the women swaying and pliant in hooped crinoline beneath parasols, the men in broadcloth riding the good horses at the wheels, talking about it, where the son and perhaps the master himself had ridden into Jefferson with his pistols and his portmanteau and a body-servant on the spare horse behind, talking of regiments and victory; where the Federal patrols had ridden the land peopled by women and Negro slaves about the time of the battle of Jefferson.

There was nothing to show of that now. There was hardly a road; where the sand darkened into the branch and then rose again, there was no trace left of the bridge. Now the scar ran straight as a plumb-line along a shaggy hedgerow of spaced cedars decreed there by the same nameless architect who had planned and built the house for its nameless master, now two and three feet thick, the boughs interlocked and massed now. Ratliff turned in among them. He seemed to know exactly where he was going. But then Bookwright remembered that he had been here last night.

Armstid didn't wait for them. Ratliff tied the team hurriedly and they overtook him—a shadow, still faintly visible because of his overalls faded pale with washing, hurrying stiffly on through the undergrowth. The earth yawned black before them, a long gash: a ravine, a ditch. Bootwright remembered that Armstid had been here for more than one night, nevertheless the limping shadow seemed about to hurl itself into the black abyss. "You better help him," Bookwright said. "He's going to break——"

"Hush!" Ratliff hissed. "The garden is just up the hill yonder."

"—break that leg again," Bookwright said, quieter now. "Then we'll be into it."

"He'll be all right," Ratliff whispered. "It's been this way every night. Just dont push him too close. But dont let him get too far ahead. Once last night while we were laying there I had to hold him." They went on, just behind the figure which moved now in absolute silence and with surprising speed. They were in a ravine massed with honeysuckle and floored with dry sand in which they could hear the terrific laboring of the lame leg. Yet still they could hardly keep up with him. After about two hundred yards Armstid turned to climb up out of the ravine. Ratliff followed him. "Careful now," he whispered back to Bookwright. "We're right at it." But Bookwright was watching Armstid. He wont never make it, he thought. He wont never climb that bank. But the other did it, dragging the stiffened and once-fragile and hence maybe twice-fragile leg at the almost sheer slope, silent and unaided and emanating that trigger-like readiness to repudiate assistance and to deny that he might possibly need it. Then on hands and knees Bookwright was crawling after the others in a path through a mass of man-tall briers and weeds and persimmon shoots, overtaking them where they lay flat at the edge of a vague slope which rose to the shaggy crest on which, among oaks, the shell of the tremendous house stood where it had been decreed too by the imported and nameless architect and its master whose anonymous dust lay with that of his blood and of the progenitors of saxophone players in Harlem honkytonks beneath the weathered and illegible headstones on another knoll four hundred yards away, with its broken roof and topless chimneys and one high rectangle of window through which he could see the stars in the opposite sky. The slope had probably been a rose-garden. None of them knew or cared, just as they, who had seen it, walked past and looked at it perhaps a hundred times, did not know that the fallen pediment in the middle of the slope had once been a sundial. Ratliff reached across Armstid's body and gripped his arm, then, above the sound of their panting breath, Bookwright heard the steady and unhurried sigh of a shovel and the measured thud of spaded earth somewhere on the slope above them. "There!" Ratliff whispered.

"I hear somebody digging," Bookwright whispered. "How do I know it's Flem Snopes?"

"Hasn't Henry been laying here every night since ten days ago, listening to him? Wasn't I right here last night with Henry myself, listening to him? Didn't we lay right here until he qiut and left and then we crawled up there and found every place where he had dug and then filled the hole back up and smoothed the dirt to hide it?"

"All right," Bookwright whispered. "You and Armstid have been watching somebody digging. But how do I know it is Flem Snopes?"

"All right," Armstid said, with a cold restrained violence, almost aloud; both of them could feel him trembling where he lay between them, jerking and shaking through his gaunt and wasted body like a leashed dog. "It ain't Flem Snopes then. Go on back home."

"Hush!" Ratliff hissed. Armstid had turned, looking toward Bookwright. His face was not a foot from Bookwright's, the features more indistinguishable than ever now.

"Go on," he said. "Go on back home."

"Hush, Henry!" Ratliff whispered. "He's going to hear you!" But Armstid had already turned his head, glaring up the dark slope again, shaking and trembling between them, cursing in a dry whisper. "If you knowed it was Flem, would you believe then?" Ratliff whispered across Armstid's body. Bookwright didn't answer. He lay there too, with the others, while Armstid's thin body shook and jerked beisde him, listening to the steady and unhurried whisper of the shovel and to Armstid's dry and furious cursing. Then the sound of the shovel ceased. For a moment nobody moved. Then Armstid said,

"He's done found it!" He surged suddenly and violently between them. Bookwright heard or felt Ratliff grasp him.

"Stop!" Ratliff whispered. "Stop! Help hold him, Odum!" Bookwright grasped Armstid's other arm. Between them they held the furious body until Armstid ceased and lay again between them, rigid, glaring, cursing in that dry whisper. His arms felt no larger than sticks; the strength in them was unbelievable. "He aint found it yet!" Ratliff whispered at him. "He just knows it's there somewhere; maybe he found a paper somewhere in the house telling where it is. But he's got to hunt to find it same as we will. He knows it's somewhere in that garden, but he's got to hunt to find it same as us. Aint we been watching him hunting for it?" Bookwright could hear both the voices now speaking in hissing whispers, the one cursing, the other cajoling and reasoning while the owners of them glared as one up the starlit slope. Now Ratliff was speaking to him. "You dont believe it's Flem," he said. "All right. Just watch." They lay in the weeds; they were all holding their breaths now, Bookwright too. Then he saw the digger—a shadow, a thicker darkness, moving against the slope, mounting it. "Watch," Ratliff whispered. Bookwright could hear him and Armstid where they lay glaring up the slope, breathing in hissing exhalations, in passionate and dying sighs. Then Bookwright saw the white shirt; an instant later the figure came into complete relief against the sky as if it had paused for a moment on the crest of the slope. Then it was gone. "There!" Ratliff whispered. "Wasn't that Flem

Snopes? Do you believe now?" Bookwright drew a long breath and let it out again. He was still holding Armstid's arm. He had forgotten about it. Now he felt it again under his hand like a taut steel cable vibrating.

"It's Flem," he said.

"Certainly it's Flem," Ratliff said. "Now all we got to do is find out tmorrow night where it's at and——"

"Tomorrow night, hell!" Armstid said. He surged forward again, attempting to rise. "Let's get up there now and find it. That's what we got to do. Before he—" They both held him again while Ratliff argued with him, sibilant and expostulant. They held him flat on the ground again at last, cursing.

"We got to find where it is first," Ratliff panted. "We got to find exactly where it is the first time. We aint got time just to hunt. We got to find it the first night because we cant afford to leave no marks for him to find when he comes back. Cant you see that? that we aint going to have but one chance to find it because we dont dare be caught looking?"

"What we going to do?" Bookwright said.

"Ha," Armstid said. "Ha." It was harsh, furious, restrained. There was no mirth in it. "What *we* going to do. I thought you had gone back home."

"Shut up, Henry," Ratliff said. He rose to his knees, though he still held Armstid's arm. "We agreed to take Odum in with us. At least let's wait till we find that money before we start squabbling over it."

"Suppose it aint nothing but Confederate money," Bookwright said.

"All right," Ratliff said. "What do you reckon that old Frenchman did with all the money he had before there was any such thing as Confederate money? Besides, a good deal of it was probably silver spoons and jewelry."

"You all can have the silver spoons and jewelry," Bookwright said. "I'll take my share in money."

"So you believe now, do you?" Ratliff said. Bookwright didn't answer.

"What we going to do now?" he said.

"I'm going up the bottom tomorrow and get Uncle Dick Bolivar," Ratliff said. "I ought to get back here a little after dark. But then we cant do anything here until after midnight, after Flem has done got through hunting it."

"And finding it tomorrow night," Armstid said. "By God, I aint—" They were all standing now. Armstid began to struggle, sudden and furious, to free his arm. But Ratliff held him. He flung both arms around Armstid and held him until he stopped struggling.

"Listen," Ratliff said. "Flem Snopes aint going to find it. If he knowed where to look, do you think he'd a been here digging for it every night for two weeks? Dont you know folks have been looking for that money for thirty years? That every foot of this whole place has been turned over at least ten times? That there aint a piece of land in this whole country that's been worked as much and as often as this here little shirt-tail of garden? Will Varner could have raised cotton or corn either in it so tall he would have to gather it on horseback just by putting the seed in the ground. The reason aint nobody found it yet is it's buried so deep aint nobody had time to dig that far in just one night and then get the hole filled back up where Will Varner wouldn't find it when he got out here at daylight to sit in that flour-barrel chair and watch. No sir. There aint but one thing in this world can keep us from finding it." Armstid had ceased. He and Bookwright both looked toward Ratliff's indistinguishable face. After a while Armstid said harshly:

"And what's that?"

"That's for Flem Snopes to find out somebody else is hunting for it," Ratliff said.

It was about midnight the next night when Ratliff turned his buckboard into the cedars again. Bookwright now rode his horse, because there were already three people in the buckboard, and again Armstid did not wait for Ratliff to tie the team. He was out as soon as the buckboard stopped; he dragged a shovel clashing and clanging out of the dog-kennel box, making no effort whatever to be quiet, and was gone limping terrifically into the darkness before Ratliff and Bookwright were on the ground. "We might as well go back home," Bookwright said.

"No, no," Ratliff said. "He aint never there this late. But

we better catch up with Henry anyway." The third man in the buckboard had not moved yet. Even in the obscurity his long white beard had a faintly luminous quality, as if it had absorbed something of the starlight through which Ratliff had fetched him and were now giving it back to the dark. Ratliff and Bookwright helped him, groping and fumbling, out of the buckboard, and carrying the other shovel and the pick and half-carrying the old man, they hurried down into the ravine and then ran, trying to overtake the sound of Armstid's limping progress. They never overtook him. They climbed up out of the ditch, carrying the old man bodily now, and even before they reached the foot of the garden they could hear the sound of Armstid's rapid shovel up the slope. They released the old man, who sank to the ground between them, breathing in reedy gasps, and as one Ratliff and Bookwright glared up the dark slope toward the hushed furious sound of the shovel. "We got to make him stop until Uncle Dick can find it," Ratliff said. They ran toward the sound, shoulder to shoulder in the stumbling dark, among the rank weeds. "Here, Henry!" Ratliff whispered. "Wait for Uncle Dick." Armstid didn't pause, digging furiously, flinging the dirt and thrusting the shovel again all in one motion. Ratliff grasped at the shovel. Armstid jerked it free and whirled, the shovel raised like an axe, their faces invisible to one another, strained, spent. Ratliff had not had his clothes off in three nights, but Armstid had probably been in his for the whole two weeks.

"Touch it" Armstid whispered. "Touch it!"

"Wait now," Ratliff said. "Give Uncle Dick a chance to find where it's at."

"Get away," Armstid said. "I warn you. Get outen my hole." He resumed his furious digging. Ratliff watched him for a second.

"Come on," he said. He turned, running, Bookwright behind him. The old man was sitting up when they reached him. Ratliff plunged down beside him and began to scrabble among the weeds for the other shovel. It was the pick he found first. He flung it away and plunged down again; he and Bookwright found the shovel at the same time. Then they were standing, struggling for the shovel, snatching and jerking at it, their breathing harsh and repressed, hearing even above their own breathing the rapid sound of Armstid's shovel up the slope. "Leave go!" Ratliff whispered. "Leave go!" The old man, unaided now, was struggling to get up.

"Wait," he said. "Wait." Then Ratliff seemed to realise what he was doing. He released the shovel; he almost hurled it at Bookwright.

"Take it," he said. He drew a long shuddering breath. "God," he whispered. "Just look at what even the money a man aint got yet will do to him." He stooped and jerked the old man to his feet, not with intentional roughness but merely out of his urgency. He had ot hold him up for a moment.

"Wait," the old man said in a reedy, quavering voice. He was known through all that country. He had no kin, no ties, and he antedated everyone; nobody knew how old he was—a tall thin man in a filthy frock coat and no shirt beneath it and a long, perfectly white beard reaching below his waist, who lived in a mud-daubed hut in the river bottom five or six miles from any road. He made and sold nostrums and charms, and it was said of him that he ate not only frogs and snakes but bugs as well—anything that he could catch. There was nothing in his hut but his pallet bed, a few cooking vessels, a tremendous Bible and a faded daguerreotype of a young man in a Confederate uniform which was believed by those who had seen it to be his son. "Wait," he said. "There air anger in the yearth. Ye must make that ere un quit a-bruisin hit."

"That's so," Ratliff said. "It wont work unless the ground is quiet. We got to make him stop." Again when they stood over him, Henry continued to dig; again when Ratliff touched him he whirled, the shovel raised, and stood cursing them in a spent whisper until the old man himself walked up and touched his shoulder.

"Ye kin dig and ye kin dig, young man," the reedy voice said. "For what's rendered to the yearth, the yearth will keep until hit's ready to reveal hit."

"That's right, Henry," Ratliff said. "We got to give Uncle

Dick room to find where it is. Come on, now." Armstid lowered the shovel and came out of his pit (it was already nearly a foot deep). But he would not relinquish the shovel; he still held to it until the old man drove them back to the edge of the garden and produced from the tail-pocket of his frock coat a forked peach branch, from the butt-end of which soemthing dangled on a length of string; Ratliff, who had seen it before at least, knew what it was—an empty cloth tobacco-sack containing a gold-filled human tooth. He held them there for ten minutes, stooping now and then to lay his hand flat on the earth. Then, with the three of them clumped and silent at his heels, he went to the weed-choked corner of the old garden and grasped the two prongs of the branch in his hands, the string and the tobacco-sack hanging plumblike and motionless before him, and stood for a time, muttering to himself.

"How do I—" Bookwright said.

"Hush," Ratliff said. The old man began to walk, the three of them following. They moved like a procession, with something at once outrageously pagan and orthodoxly funereal about them, slowly back and forth across the garden, mounting the slope gradually in overlapping traverses. Suddenly the old man stopped; Armstid, limping just behind him, bumped into him.

"There's somebody agin it," he said. He didn't look back. "It aint you," he said, and they all knew he was talking to Ratliff. "And it aint that cripple. It's that other one. That black one. Let him get offen this ground and quieten hit, or you can take me on back home."

"Go back to the edge," Ratliff said quietly over his shoulder to Bookwright. "It'll be all right then."

"But I—" Bookwright said.

"Get off the garden," Ratliff said. "It's after midnight. It'll be daylight in four hours." Bookwright returned to the foot of the slope. That is, he faded into the darkness, because they did not watch him; they were moving again now, Armstid and Ratliff close at the old man's heels. Again they began to mount the slope in traverses, passing the place where Henry had begun to dig, passing the place where Ratliff had found signs of the other man's excavation on the first night Armstid had brought him here; now Ratliff could feel Armstid beginning to tremble again. The old man stopped. They did not bump into him this time, and Ratliff did not know that Bookwright was behind him again until the old man spoke:

"Tech my elbers," he said. "Not you," he said. "You that didn't believe." When Bookwright touched them, inside the sleeves the arms—arms thin and frail and dead as rotten sticks—were jerking faintly and steadily; when the old man stopped suddenly again and Bookwright blundered into him, he felt the whole thin body straining backward. Armstid was cursing steadily in his dry whisper. "Tech the peach fork," the old man panted. "You that didn't believe." When Bookwright touched it, it was arched into a rigid down-pointing curve, the string taut as wire. Armstid made a choked sound; Bookwright felt his hand on the branch too. The branch sprang free; the old man staggered, the fork lying dead on the ground at his feet until Armstid, digging furiously with his bare hands, flung it away.

They turned as one and plunged back down the slope to where they had left the tools. They could hardly keep up with Armstid. "Dont let him get the pick," Bookwright panted. "He will kill somebody with it." But Armstid was not after the pick. He went straight to where he had left his shovel when the old man produced the forked branch and refused to start until he put the shovel down, and snatched it up and ran back up the slope. He was already digging when Ratliff and Bookwright reached him. They all dug then, frantically, hurling the dirt aside, in each other's way, the tools clashing and ringing together, while the old man stood above them behind the faint gleam of his beard in the starlight and his white brows above the two caverns from which, even if they had paused to look, they could not have told whether his eyes even watched them or not, musing, detached, without interest in their panting frenzy. Suddenly the three of them became frozen in the attitudes of digging for perhaps a second. Then they leaped into the hole together; the six hands at the same instant touched the object—a heavy solid sack of heavy cloth through which they all felt the round milled edges of coins. They struggled for it, jerking it back and forth among them, clutching it, gripping it, panting.

"Stop it!" Ratliff panted. "Stop it! Aint we all three partners alike?" But Armstid clung to it, trying to jerk it away from the others, cursing. "Let go, Odum," Ratliff said. "Let him have it." They turned it loose. Armstid clutched it to himself, stooping, glaring at them as they climbed out of the hole. "Let him keep it," Ratliff said. "Dont you know that aint all?" He turned quickly away. "Come on, Uncle Dick," he said. "Get your—" He ceased. The old man was standing motionless behind them, his head turned as if he were listening toward the ditch from which they had come. "What?" Ratliff whispered. They were all three motionless now, rigid, still stooped a little as when they had stepped away from Armstid. "Do you hear something?" Ratliff whispered. "Is somebody down there?"

"I feel four bloods lust-running," the old man said. "Hit's four sets of blood here lusting for trash." They crouched, rigid. But there was no sound.

"Well, aint it four of us here?" Bookwright whispered.

"Uncle Dick dont care nothing about money," Ratliff whispered. "If somebody's hiding there—" They were running. Armstid was the first to start, still carrying his shovel. Again they could hardly keep up with him as they went plunging down the slope.

"Kill him," Armstid said. "Watch every bush and kill him."

"No," Ratliff said. "Catch him first." When he and Bookwright reached the ditch, they could hear Armstid beating along the edge of it, making no effort whatever to be quiet, slashing at the dark undergrowth with the axe-like shovel-edge with the same fury he had dug with. But they found nothing, nobody.

"Maybe Uncle Dick never heard nothing," Bookwright said.

"Well, whatever it was is gone, anyway," Ratliff said. "Maybe it—" He ceased. He and Bookwright stared at one another; above their held breaths they heard the horse. It was in the old road beyond the cedars; it was as if it had been dropped there from the sky in full gallop. They heard it until it ceased into the sand at the branch. After a moment they heard it again on the hard ground beyond, fainter now. Then it ceased altogether. They stared at one another in the darkness, across their held breaths. Then Ratliff exhaled. "That means we got till daylight," he said. "Come on."

Twice more the old man's peach branch sprang and bent; twice more they found small bulging canvas bags solid and unmistakable even in the dark. "Now," Ratliff said, "we got a hole a piece and till daylight to do it in. Dig, boys."

When the east began to turn gray, they had found nothing else. But digging three holes at once, as they had been doing, none of them had been able to go very deep. And the bulk of the treasure would be deep; as Ratliff had said, if it were not it would have been found ten times over during the last fifty years since there probably were not many square feet of the ten acres which comprised the old mansion-site which had not been dug into between some sunset and dawn by someone without a light, trying to dig fast and dig quiet at the same time. So at last he and Bookwright prevailed on Armstid to see a little of reason, and they desisted and filled up the holes and removed the traces of digging. Then they opened the bags in the gray light. Ratliff's and Bookwright's contained twenty-five silver dollars each. Armstid refused to tell what his contained or to let anyone see it. He crouched over it, his back toward them, cursing them when they tried to look. "All right," Ratliff said. Then a thought struck him. He looked down at Armstid. "Of course aint nobody fool enough to try to spend any of it now."

"Mine's mine," Armstid said. "I found it. I worked for it. I'm going to do any God damn thing I want to with it."

"All right," Ratliff said. "How are you going to explain it?"

"How am I—" Armstid said. Squatting, he looked up at Ratliff. They could see one another's faces now. All three of them were strained, spent with sleeplessness and fatigue.

"Yes," Ratliff said. "How are you going to explain to folks where you got it? Got twenty-five dollars all coined before 1861?" He quit looking at Armstid. He and Bookwright looked at one another quietly in the growing light. "There was somebody in the ditch, watching us," he said. "We got to buy it."

"We got to buy it quick," Bookwright said. "Tomorrow."

"You mean today," Ratliff said. Bookwright looked about him. It was as though he were waking from an anaesthetic, as if he saw the dawn, the earth, for the first time.

"That's right," he said. "It's already tomorrow now."

The old man lay under a tree beside the ditch, asleep, flat on his back, his mouth open, his beard dingy and stained in the increasing dawn; they hadn't even missed him since they really began to dig. They waked him and helped him back to the buckboard. The dog-kennel box in which Ratliff carried the sewing machines had a padlocked door. He took a few ears of corn from the box, then he stowed his and Bookwright's bags of coins beneath the odds and ends of small and still-frozen traded objects at the back of it and locked it again.

"You put yours in here too, Henry," he said. "What we want to do now is to forget we even got them until we find the rest of it and get it out of the ground." But Armstid would not. He climbed stiffly onto the horse behind Bookwright, unaided, repudiating the aid which had not even been offered yet, clutching his bag inside the bib of his patched and faded overalls, and they departed. Ratliff fed his team and watered them at the branch; he too was on the road before the sun rose. Just before nine oclock he paid the old man his dollar fee and put him down where the five-mile path to his hut entered the river bottom, and turned the wiry and indefatigable little horses back toward Frenchman's Bend. There was somebody hid in that ditch, he thought. We got to buy it damn quick.

Later it seemed to him that, until he reached the store, he had not actually realised himself how quick they would have to buy it. Almost as soon as he came in sight of the store, he saw the new face among the familiar ones along the gallery and recognised it—Eustace Grimm, a young tenant-farmer living ten or twelve miles away in the next county with his wife of a year, to whom Ratliff intended to sell a sewing machine as soon as they had finished paying for the baby born two months ago; as he tied his team to one of the gallery posts and mounted the heel-gnawed steps, he thought, Maybe sleeping rests a man, but it takes staying up all night for two or three nights and being worried and scared half to death during them, to sharpen him. Because as soon as he recognised Grimm, something in him had clicked, though it would be three days before he would know what it was. He had not had his clothes off in more than sixty hours; he had had no breakfast today and what eating he had done in the last two days had been more than spotty—all of which showed in his face. But it didn't show in his voice or anywhere else, and nothing else but that showed anywhere at all. "Morning, gentlemen," he said.

"Be durn if you dont look like you aint been to bed in a week, V. K.," Freeman said. "What you up to now? Lon Quick said his boy seen your team and buckboard hid out in the bottom below Armstid's two mornings ago, but I told him I didn't reckon them horses had done nothing to have to hide from. So it must be you."

"I reckon not," Ratliff said. "Or I'd a been caught too, same as the team. I used to think I was too smart to be caught by anybody around here. But I dont know now." He looked at Grimm, his face, except for the sleeplessness and fatigue, as bland and quizzical and impenetrable as ever. "Eustace," he said, "you're strayed."

"It looks like it," Grimm said. "I come to see——"

"He's paid his road-tax," Lump Snopes, the clerk, sitting as usual in the single chair tilted in the doorway, said. "Do you object to him using Yoknapatawpha roads too?"

"Sholy not," Ratliff said. "And if he'd a just paid his poll-tax in the right place, he could drive his wagon through the store and through Will Varner's house too." They guffawed, all except Lump.

"Maybe I will yet," Grimm said. "I come up here to see —" He ceased, looking up at Ratliff. He was perfectly motionless, squatting, a sliver of wood in one hand and his open and arrested knife in the other. Ratliff watched him.

"Couldn't you see him last night either?" he said.

"Couldn't I see who last night?" Grimm said.

"How could he have seen anybody in Frenchmen's Bend last night when he wasn't in Frenchmen's Bend last night?" Lump Snopes said. "Go on to the house, Eustace," he said. "Dinner's about ready. I'll be along in a few minutes."

"I got—" Grimm said.

"You got twelve miles to drive to get home tonight," Snopes said. "Go on, now." Grimm looked at him a moment longer. Then he rose and descended the steps and went on up the road. Ratliff was no longer watching him. He was looking at Snopes.

"Eustace eating with you during his visit?" he said.

"He happens to be eating at Winterbottom's where I happen to be boarding," Snopes said harshly. "Where a few other folks happens to be eating and paying board too."

"Sho now," Ratliff said. "You hadn't ought to druv him away like that. Likely Eustace dont get to town very often to spend a day or two examining the country and setting around store."

"He'll have his feet under his own table tonight," Snopes said. "You can go down there and look at him. Then you can be in his back yard even before he opens his mouth."

"Sho now," Ratliff said, pleasant, bland, inscrutable, with his spent and sleepless face. "When you expecting Flem back?"

"Back from where?" Snopes said, in that harsh voice. "From laying up yonder in that barrel-slat hammock, taking time about with Will Varner, sleeping? Likely never."

"Him and Will and the womenfolks was in Jefferson yesterday," Freeman said. "Will said they was coming home this morning."

"Sho now," Ratliff said. "Sometimes it takes a man even longer than a year to get his new wife out of the idea that money was just made to shop with." He stood above them, leaning against a gallery post, indolent and easy, as if he had not ever even heard of haste. So Flem Snopes has been in Jefferson since yesterday, he thought. And Lump Snopes didn't want it mentioned. And Eustace Grimm—again his mind clicked; still it would be three days before he would know what had clicked, because now he believed he did know, that he saw the pattern complete—and Eustace Grimm has been here since last night, since we heard that galloping horse anyway. Maybe they was both on the horse. Maybe that's why it sounded so loud. He could see that too—Lump Snopes and Grimm on the single horse, fleeing, galloping in the dark back to Frenchmen's Bend where Flem Snopes would still be absent until sometime in the early afternoon. And Lump Snopes didn't want that mentioned either, he thought, and Eustace Grimm had to be sent home to keep folks from talking to him. And Lump Snopes aint just worried and mad: he's scared. They might even have found the hidden buckboard. They probably had, and so knew at least one of those who were digging in the garden; now Snopes would not only have to get hold of his cousin first through his agent, Grimm, he might even then become involved in a bidding contest for the place against someone who (Ratliff added this without vanity) had more to outbid him with; he thought, musing, amazed as always though still impenetrable, how even a Snopes was not safe from another Snopes. Damn quick, he thought. He stood away from the post and turned back toward the steps. "I reckon I'll get along," he said. "See you boys tomorrow."

"Come home with me and take dinner," Freeman said.

"Much obliged," Ratliff said. "I ate breakfast late at Bookwright's. I want to collect a machine note from Ike McCaslin this afternoon and be back here by dark." He got into the buckboard and turned the team back down the road. Presently they had fallen into their road gait, trotting rapidly on their short legs in the traces though their forward motion was not actually fast, on until they had passed Varner's house, beyond which the road turned off to McCaslin's farm and so out of sight from the store. They entered this road galloping, the dust bursting from their shaggy backs in long spurts where the whip slashed them. He had three miles to go. After the first half mile it would be all winding and little-used lane, but he could do it in twenty minutes. And it was only a little after noon, and it had probably been at least nine oclock before Will Varner got his wife away from the Jefferson church-ladies' auxiliary with which she was affiliated. He made it in nineteen minutes, hurtling and bouncing among the ruts ahead of his spinning dust, and slowed the now-lathered team and swung them into the Jefferson highroad a mile from the village, letting them trot for another half mile, slowing, to cool them out gradually. But there was no sign of the surrey yet, so he went on at a walk until he reached a crest from which he could see the road for some distance ahead, and pulled out of the road into the shade of a tree and stopped. Now he had had no dinner either. But he was not quite hungry, and although after he had put the old man out and turned back toward the village this morning he had had an almost irresistible desire to sleep, that was gone too now. So he sat in the buckboard, lax now, blinking painfully against the glare of noon, while the team (he never used check-reins) nudged the lines slack and grazed over the breast-yoke. People would probably pass and see him there; some might even be going toward the village, where they might tell of seeing him. But he would take care of that when it arose. It was as though he said to himself, Now I got a little while at least when I can let down.

Then he saw the surrey. He was already in the road, going at that road-gait which the whole countryside knew, full of rapid little hooves which still did not advance a great deal faster than two big horses could have walked, before anyone in the surrey could have seen him. And he knew that they had already seen and recognised him when, still two hundred yards from it, he pulled up and sat in the buckboard, affable, bland and serene except for his worn face, until Varner stopped the surrey beside him. "Howdy, V. K.," Varner said.

"Morning," Ratliff said. He raised his hat to the two women in the back seat. "Mrs Varner. Mrs Snopes."

"Where you headed?" Varner said. "Town?" Ratliff told no lie; he attempted none, smiling a little, courteous, perhaps even a little deferential.

"I come out to meet you. I want to speak to Flem a minute." He looked at Snopes for the first time. "I'll drive you on home," he said.

"Hah," Varner said. "You had to come two miles to meet

him and then turn around and go two miles back, to talk to him."

"That's right," Ratliff said. He was still looking at Snopes.

"You got better sense than to try to sell Flem Snopes anything," Varner said. "And you sholy aint fool enough by God to buy anything from him, are you?"

"I dont know," Ratliff said in that same pleasant and unchanged and impenetrable voice out of his spent and sleepless face, still looking at Snopes. "I used to think I was smart, but now I dont know. I'll bring you on home," he said. "You wont be late for dinner."

"Go on and get out," Varner said to his son-in-law. "He aint going to tell you till you do." But Snopes was already moving. He spat outward over the wheel and turned and climbed down over it, backward, broad and deliberate in the soiled light-gray trousers, the white shirt, the plaid cap; the surrey went on. Ratliff cramped the wheel and Snopes got into the buckboard beside him and he turned the buckboard and again the team fell into their tireless and familiar road-gait. But this time Ratliff reined them back until they were walking and held them so while Snopes chewed steadily beside him. They didn't look at one another again.

"That Old Frenchman place," Ratliff said. The surrey went on a hundred yards ahead, pacing its own dust, as they themselves were now doing. "What are you going to ask Eustace Grimm for it?" Snopes spat tobacco juice over the moving wheel. He did not chew fast nor did he seem to find it necessary to stop chewing in order to spit or speak either.

"He's at the store, is he?" he said.

"Aint this the day you told him to come?" Ratliff said. "How much are you going to ask him for?" Snopes told him. Ratliff made a short sound, something like Varner's habitual ejaculation. "Do you reckon Eustace Grimm can get his hands on that much money?"

"I don't know," Snopes said. He spat over the moving wheel again. Ratliff might have said, Then you dont want to sell it; Snopes would have answered, I'll sell anything. But they did not. They didn't need to.

"All right," Ratliff said. "What are you going to ask me

for it?" Snopes told him. It was the same amount. This time Ratliff used Varner's ejaculation. "I'm just talking about them ten acres where that old house is. I aint trying to buy all Yoknapatawpha County from you." They crossed the last hill; the surrey began to move faster, drawing away from them. The village was not far now. "We'll let this one count," Ratliff said. "How much do you want for that Old Frenchman place?" His team was trying to trot too, ahead of the buckboard's light weight. Ratliff held them in, the road beginning to curve to pass the schoolhouse and enter the village. The surrey had already vanished beyond the curve.

"What do you want with it?" Snopes said.

"To start a goat-ranch," Ratliff said. "How much?" Snopes spat over the moving wheel. He named the sum for the third time. Ratliff slacked off the reins and the little strong tireless team began to trot, sweeping around the last curve and past the empty schoolhouse, the village now in sight, the surrey in sight too, already beyond the store, going on. "That fellow, that teacher you had three-four years ago. Labove. Did anybody ever hear what become of him?"

A little after six that evening, in the empty and locked store, Ratliff and Bookwright and Armstid bought the Old Frenchman place from Snopes. Ratliff gave a quit-claim deed to his half of the side-street lunch-room in Jefferson. Armstid gave a mortgage on his farm, including the buildings and tools and live-stock and about two miles of three-strand wire fence; Bookwright paid his third in cash. Then Snopes let them out the front door and locked it again and they stood on the empty gallery in the fading August afterglow and watched him depart up the road toward Varner's house—two of them did, that is, because Armstid had already gone ahead and got into the buckboard, where he sat motionless and waiting and emanating that patient and seething fury. "It's ours now," Ratliff said. "And now we better get on out there and watch it before somebody fetches in Uncle Dick Bolivar some night and starts hunting buried money."

They went first to Bookwright's house (he was a bachelor) and got the mattress from his bed and two quilts and his coffee-pot and skillet and another pick and shovel, then they went to Armstid's home. He had but one mattress too, but then he had a wife and five small children; besides, Ratliff, who had seen the mattress, knew that it would not even bear being lifted from the bed. So Armstid got a quilt and they helped him fill an empty feed sack with shucks for a pillow and returned to the buckboard, passing the house in the door of which his wife still stood, with four of the children huddled about her now. But she still said nothing, and when Ratliff looked back from the moving buckboard, the door was empty.

When they turned from the old road and drove up through the shaggy park to the shell of the ruined house, there was still light enough for them to see the wagon and mules standing before it, and at that moment a man came out of the house itself and stopped, looking at them. It was Eustace Grimm, but Ratliff never knew if Armstid recognised him or even bothered to try to, because once more before the buckboard had even stopped Armstid was out of it and snatched the other shovel from beneath Bookwright's and Ratliff's feet and rushed with his limping and painful fury toward Grimm, who moved swiftly too and put the wagon between Armstid and himself, standing there and watching Armstid across the wagon as Armstid slashed across the wagon at him with the shovel. "Catch him!" Ratliff said. "He'll kill him!"

"Or break that damn leg again," Bookwright said. When they overtook him, he was trying to double the wagon, the shovel raised and poised like an axe. But Grimm had already darted around to the other side, where he now saw Ratliff and Bookwright running up, and he sprang away from them too, watching them, poised and alert. Bookwright caught Armstid from behind in both arms and held him.

"Get away quick, if you dont want anything," Ratliff told Grimm.

"No, I dont want anything," Grimm said.

"Then go on while Bookwright's got him." Grimm moved toward the wagon, watching Armstid with something curious and veiled in his look.

"He's going to get in trouble with that sort of foolishness," he said.

"He'll be all right," Ratliff said. "You just get on away from here." Grimm got into the wagon and went on. "You can let him go now," Ratliff said. Armstid flung free of Bookwright and turned toward the garden. "Wait, Henry," Ratliff said. "Let's eat supper first. Let's get our beds into the house." But Armstid hurried on, limping in the fading light toward the garden. "We ought to eat first," Ratliff said. Then he let out a long breath like a sigh; he and Bookwright ran side by side to the rear of the sewing-maching box, which Ratliff unlocked, and they snatched out the other shovels and picks and ran down the slope and into the old garden where Armstid was already digging. Just before they reached him he stood up and began to run toward the road, the shovel raised, whereupon they too saw that Grim had not departed but was sitting in the wagon in the road, watching them across the ruined fence of iron pickets until Armstid had almost reached it. Then he drove on.

They dug all that night, Armstid in one hole, Ratliff and Bookwright working together in another. From time to time they would stop to rest while the summer constellations marched overhead. Ratliff and Bookwright would move about to flex their cramped muscles, then they would squat (They did not smoke; they could not risk showing any light. Armstid had probably never had the extra nickel or dime to buy tobacco with.) and talk quietly while they listened to the steady sound of Armstid's shovel below them. He would be digging when they stopped; he would still be digging, unflagging and tireless, when they started again, though now and then one of them would remember him and pause to see him sitting on the side of his pit, immobile as the lumps of earth he had thrown out of it. Then he would be digging again before he had actually had time to rest; this until dawn began and Ratliff and Bookwright stood over him in the wan light, arguing with him. "We got to quit," Ratliff said. "It's already light enough for folks to see us." Armstid didn't pause.

"Let them," he said. "It's mine now. I can dig all day if I want."

"All right," Ratliff said. "You'll have plenty of help then."

Now Armstid paused, looking up at him out of his pit. "How can we dig all night and then set up all day to keep other folks out of it?" Ratliff said. "Come on now," he said. "We got to eat and then sleep some." They got the mattress and the quilts from the buckboard and carried them into the house, the hall in whose gaping door-frames no doors any longer hung and from whose ceiling depended the skeleton of what had been once a crystal chandelier, with its sweep of stairs whose treads had long since been prized off and carried away to patch barns and chicken-houses and privies, whose spindles and walnut railings and newel-posts had long ago been chopped up and burned as firewood. The room they chose had a fourteen-foot ceiling. There were the remains of a once-gilt filigree of cornice above the gutted windows and the ribbed and serrated grin of lathing from which the plaster had fallen, and the skeleton of another prismed chandelier. They spread the mattress and the quilts upon the dust of plaster, and Ratliff and Bookwright returned to the buckboard and got the food they had brought, and the two sacks of coins. They hid the two sacks in the chimney, foul now with bird-droppings, behind the mantel in which there were still wedged a few shards of the original marble. Armstid didn't produce his bag. They didn't know what he had done with it. They didn't ask.

They built no fire. Ratliff would probably have objected, but nobody suggested it; they ate cold the tasteless food, too tired to taste it; removing only their shoes stained with the dampening earth from the deepening pits, they lay among the quilts and slept fitfully, too tired to sleep completely also, dreaming of gold. Toward noon jagged scraps and flecks of sun came through the broken roof and the two rotted floors overheard and crept eastward across the floor and the tumbled quilts and then the prone bodies and the slack-mouthed upflung faces, whereupon they turned and shifted or covered their heads and faces with their arms, as though, still sleeping, they fled the weightless shadow of that for which, awake, they had betrayed themselves. They were awake at sunset without having rested. They moved stiffly about, not talking, while the coffee-pot boiled on the broken hearth; they ate again, wolfing the cold and tasteless food while the crimson glow from the dying west faded in the high ruined room. Armstid was the first one to finish. He put his cup down and rose, turning first onto his hands and knees as an infant gets up, dragging his stiff twice-broken leg painfully beneath him, and limped toward the door. "We ought to wait till full dark," Ratliff said, to no one; certainly no one answered him. It was as if he spoke to himself and had answered himself. He rose too. Bookwright was already standing. When they reached the garden, Armstid was already in his pit, digging.

They dug through that brief summer night as through the previous one while the familiar stars wheeled overhead, stopping now and then to rest and ease their muscles and listen to the steady sigh and recover of Armstid's shovel below them; they prevailed upon him to stop at dawn and returned to the house and ate—the canned salmon, the sidemeat cold in its own congealed grease, the cold cooked bread—and slept again among the tumbled quilts while noon came and the creeping and probing golden sun at whose touch they turned and shifted as though in impotent nightmare flight from that impalpable and weightless burden. They had finished the bread that morning. When the others waked at the second sunset, Ratliff had the coffee-pot on the fire and was cooking another batch of cornbread in the skillet. Armstid would not wait for it. He ate his portion of meat alone and drank his coffee and got to his feet again as small children do, and went out. Bookwright was standing also. Ratliff, squatting beside the skillet, looked up at him. "Go on then," he said. "You dont need to wait either."

"We're down six foot," Bookwright said. "Four foot wide and near ten foot long. I'll start where we found the third sack."

"All right," Ratliff said. "Go on and start." Because something had clicked in his mind again. It might have been while he was asleep, he didn't know. But he knew that this time it was right. Only I dont want to look at it, hear it, he thought, squatting, holding the skillet steady over the fire, squinting his watering eyes against the smoke which the broken chimney no longer drew out of the house, I dont dare to. Anyway, I dont have to yet. I can dig again tonight. We even got a new place to dig. So he waited until the bread was done. Then he took it out of the skillet and set it near the ashes and sliced some of the bacon into the skillet and cooked it; he had his first hot meal in three days, and he ate it without haste, squatting, sipping his coffee while the last of the sunset's crimson gathered along the ruined ceiling and died from there too, and the room had only the glow of the dying fire.

Bookwright and Armstid were already digging. When he came close enough to see, Armstid unaided was three feet down and his pit was very nearly as long as the one Ratliff and Bookwright had dug together. He went on to where Bookwright had started the new pit and took up his shovel (Bookwright had fetched it for him) and began to dig. They dug on through that night too, beneath the marching and familiar stars, stopping now and then to rest although Armstid did not stop when they did, squatting on the lip of the new excavation while Ratliff talked, murmurous, not about gold, money, but anecdotal, humorous, his invisible face quizzical, bemused, impenetrable. They dug again. Daylight will be time enough to look at it, he thought. Because I done already looked at it, he thought. I looked at it three days ago. Then it began to be dawn. In the wan beginning of that light he put his shovel down and straightened up. Bookwright's pick rose and fell steadily in front of him; twenty feet beyond, he could now see Armstid waist-deep in the ground as if he had been cut in two at the hips, the dead torso, not even knowing it was dead, laboring on in measured stoop and recover like a metronome as Armstid dug himself back into that earth which had produced him to be its born and fated thrall forever until he died. Ratliff climbed out of the pit and stood in the dark fresh loam which they had thrown out of it, his muscles flinching and jerking with fatigue, and stood looking quietly at Bookwright until Bookwright became aware of him and paused, the pick raised for the next stroke, and looked up at him. They looked at each other—the two gaunt, unshaven, weary faces. "Odum," Ratliff said, "who was Eustace Grimm's wife?"

"I dont know," Bookwright said.

"I do," Ratliff said. "She was one of them Calhoun County Dosheys. And that aint right. And his ma was a Fite. And that aint right either." Bookwright quit looking at him. He laid the pick down carefully, almost gently, as if it were a spoon level-full of soup or of that much nitro-glycerin, and climbed out of the pit, wiping his hands on his trousers.

"I thought you knew," he said. "I thought you knew everything about folks in this country."

"I reckon I know now," Ratliff said. "But I reckon you'll still have to tell me."

"Fite was his second wife's name. She wasn't Eustace's ma. Pa told me about it when Ab Snopes first rented that place from the Varners five years ago."

"All right," Ratliff said. "Tell me."

"Eustace's ma was Ab Snopes's youngest sister." They looked at one another, blinking a little. Soon the light would begin to increase fast.

"Sholy now," Ratliff said. "You finished?"

"Yes," Bookwright said. "I'm finished."

"Bet you one of them I beat you," Ratliff said. They mounted the slope and entered the house, the room where they slept. It was still dark in the room, so while Ratliff fumbled the two bags out of the chimney, Bookwright lit the lantern and set it on the floor and they squatted facing each other across the lantern, opening the bags.

"I reckon we ought to knowed wouldn't no cloth sack . . ." Bookwright said. "After fifty years . . ." They emptied the bags onto the floor. Each of them took up a coin, examined it briefly, then set them one upon the other like a crowned king in checkers, close to the lantern. Then one by one they examined the other coins by the light of the dingy lantern. "But how did he know it would be us?" Bookwright said.

"He didn't," Ratliff said. "He didn't care. He just come out here every night and dug for a while. He knowed he couldn't possibly dig over two weeks before somebody saw him." He laid his last coin down and sat back on his heels until Bookwright had finished. "1891," he said.

"1901," Bookwright said. "I even got one that was made last year. You beat me."

"I beat you," Ratliff said. He took up the two coins and they put the money back into the bags. They didn't hide them. They left each bag on its owner's quilt and blew out the lantern. It was lighter now and they could see Armstid quite well where he stooped and rose and stooped in his thigh-deep pit. The sun would rise soon; already there were three buzzards soaring against the high yellow-blue. Armstid did not even look up when they approached; he continued to dig even while they stood beside the pit, looking down at him. "Henry," Ratliff said. Then Ratliff leaned down and touched his shoulder. He whirled, the shovel raised and turned edgewise and glinting a thin line of steel-colored dawn as the edge of an axe would.

"Get out of my hole," he said. "Get outen it."

2

The wagons containing the men, the women and the children approaching the village from that direction, stopped, and the men who had walked up from the store to stand along Varner's fence, watched, while Lump and Eck Snopes and Varner's Negro, Sam, loaded the furniture and the trunks and the boxes into the wagon backed up to the edge of the veranda. It was the same wagon drawn by the same mules which had brought Flem Snopes back from Texas in April, and the three men came and went between it and the house, Eck or the Negro backing clumsily through the door with the burden between them and Lump Snopes scuttling along beside it in a constant patter of his own exhortations and commands, holding to it, to be sure, but carrying no weight, to load that into the wagon and return, pausing at the door and stepping aside as Mrs Varner bustled out with another armful of small crocks and hermetic jars of fruit and vegetables. The watchers along the fence checked the objects off —the dismantled bed, the dresser, the washstand with its flowered matching bowl and ewer and slop-jar and chamber-pot, the trunk which doubtless contained the wife's and the child's clothing, the wooden box which the women at least knew doubtless contained dishes and cutlery and cooking vessels, and lastly a tightly roped mass of brown canvas. "What's that?" Freeman said. "It looks like a tent."

"It is a tent," Tull said. "Eck brought it out from the express office in town last week."

"They aint going to move to Jefferson and live in a tent, are they?" Freeman said.

"I dont know," Tull said. At last the wagon was loaded; Eck and the Negro bumped through the door for the last time, Mrs Varner bustled out with the final hermetic jar; Lump Snopes re-entered the house and emerged with the straw suitcase which they all knew, then Flem Snopes and then his wife came out. She was carrying the baby which was too large to have been born at only seven months but which had certainly not waited until May, and stood there for a moment. Olympus-tall, a head taller than her mother or husband either, in a tailored suit despite the rich heat of summer's full maturing, whose complexion alone showed that she was not yet eighteen since the unseeing and expressionless mask-face had no age, while the women in the wagons looked at her and thought how that was the first tailored suit ever seen in Frenchman's Bend and how she had got some clothes out of Flem Snopes anyway because it would not be Will Varner that bought them now, and the men along the fence looked at her and thought of Hoake McCarron and how any one of them would have bought the suit or anything else for her if she had wanted it.

Mrs Varner took the child from her and they watched her sweep the skirts inward into one hand with the gesture immemorial nd female nd troubling, and climb the wheel to the seat where Snopes already sat with the reins, and lean down and take the child from Mrs Varner. The wagon moved, lurched into motion, the team swinging to cross the yard toward the open gate into the lane, and that was all. If farewell was said, that was it, the halted wagons along the road creaking into motion again though Freeman and Tull and the other four men merely turned, relaxed again, their backs against the picket fence now, their faces identically grave, a little veiled and perhaps even sober, not quite watching the laden wagon as it turned out of the lane and approached and then was passing them—the plaid cap, the steady and deliberate jaw, the minute bow and the white shirt; the other face calm and beautiful and by its expression carven or even corpse-like, looking not at them certainly and maybe not at anything they knew. "So long, Flem," Freeman said. "Save me a steak when you get your hand in at cooking." He didn't answer. He might not have heard even. The wagon went on. Watching it, not moving yet, they saw it turn into the old road which until two weeks ago had been marked only by the hooves of Varner's fat white horse for more than twenty years.

"He'll have to drive three extra miles to get back into the road to town that way," Tull said in an anxious voice.

"Maybe he aims to take them three miles on into town with him and swap them to Grover Cleveland Winbush for the other half of that restaurant," Freeman said.

"Maybe he'll swap them to Ratliff and Bookwright and Henry Armstid for something else," a third man—his name was Winbush also, a brother of the other one—said. "He'll find Ratliff in town too."

"He'll find Henry Armstid without having to go that far," Freeman said.

That road was no longer a fading and almost healed scar. It was rutted now, because there had been rain a week ago, and now the untroubled grass and weeds of almost fifty years bore four distinct paths: the two outer ones where iron wheel-rims had run, the two inner ones where the harnessed teams had walked daily since that first afternoon when the first ones had turned into it—the weathered and creaking wagons, the plow-galled horses and mules, the men and women and children entering another world, traversing another land, moving in another time, another afternoon without time or name.

Where the sand darkened into the shallow water of the branch and then lightened and rose again, the countless overlapping prints of rims and iron shoes were like shouts in a deserted church. Then the wagons would begin to come into sight, drawn up in line at the roadside, the smaller children squatting in the wagons, the women still sitting in the splint chairs in the wagon beds, holding the infants and nursing them when need arose, the men and the larger children standing quietly along the ruined and honeysuckle-choked iron fence, watching Armstid as he spaded the earth steadily down the slope of the old garden. They had been watching him for two weeks. After the first day, after the first ones had seen him and gone home with the news of it, they began to come in by wagon and on horse- and mule-back from as far away as ten and fifteen miles, men, women and children, octogenarian and suckling, four generations in one battered and weathered wagon bed still littered with dried manure or hay and grain chaff, to sit in the wagons and stand along the fence with the decorum of a formal reception, the rapt interest of a crowd watching a magician at a fair. On the first day, when the first one descended and approached the fence, Armstid climbed out of his pit and ran at him, dragging the stiffened leg, the shovel raised, cursing in a harsh, light, gasping whisper, and drove the man away. But soon he quit that; he appeared to be not even aware of them where they stood along the fence, watching him spading himself steadily back and forth across the slope with that spend and unflagging fury. But none of them attempted to enter the garden again, and now it was only the half-grown boys who ever bothered him.

Toward the middle of the afternoon the ones who had come the long distances would begin to depart. But there were always some who would remain, even though it meant unharnessing and feeding and perhaps even milking in the dark. Then, just before sunset, the last wagon would arrive—the two gaunt, rabbit-like mules, the braced and dishing and ungreased wheels—and they would turn along the fence and watch quietly while the woman in the gray and shapeless garment and the faded sunbonnet got down and lifted from beneath the seat a tin pail and approached the fence beyond which the man still had not looked up nor faltered in his metronome-like labor. She would set the pail in the corner of the fence and stand for a time, motionless, the gray garment falling in rigid carven folds to her stained tennis shoes, her hands clasped and rolled into her apron, against her stomach. If she were looking at the man, they could not tell it; if she were looking at anything, they did not know it. Then she would turn and go back to the wagon (she had feeding and milking to do too, as well as the children's supper to get) and mount to the seat and take up the rope reins and turn the wagon and drive away. Then the last of the watchers would depart, leaving Armstid in the middle of his fading slope, spading himself into the waxing twilight with the regularity of a mechanical toy and with something monstrous in his unflagging effort, as if the toy were too light for what it had been set to do, or too tightly wound. In the hot summer mornings, squatting with slow tobacco or snuff-sticks on the gallery of Varner's store, or at quiet crossroads about the land in the long slant of afternoon, they talked about it, wagon to wagon, wagon to rider, rider to rider or from wagon or rider to one waiting beside a mailbox or a gate: "Is he still at it?"

"He's still at it."

"He's going to kill himself. Well, I dont know as it will be any loss."

"Not to his wife, anyway."

"That's a fact. It will save her that trip every day toting food to him. That Flem Snopes."

"That's a fact. Wouldn't no other man have done it."

"Couldn't no other man have done it. Anybody might have fooled Henry Armstid. But couldn't nobody but Flem Snopes have fooled Ratliff."

Now though it was only a little after ten, so not only had the day's quota all arrived, they were still there, including even the ones who, like Snopes, were going all the way in to Jefferson, when he drove up. He did not pull out of the road into line. Instead, he drove on past the halted wagons while the heads of the women holding the nursing children turned to look at him and the heads of the men along the fence turned to watch him pass, the faces grave, veiled too, still looking at him when he stopped the wagon and sat, chewing with that steady and measured thrust and looking over their heads into the garden. Then the heads along the ruined fence turned as though to follow his look, and they watched two half-grown boys emerge from the undergrowth on the far side of the garden and steal across it, approaching Armstid from behind. He had not looked up nor even ceased to dig, yet the boys were not within twenty feet of him when he whirled and dragged himself out of the trench and ran at them, the shovel lifted. He said nothing; he did not even curse now. He just ran at them, dragging his leg, stumbling among the clods he had dug while the boys fled before him, distancing him. Even after they had vanished in the undergrowth from which they had come, Armstid continued to run until he stumbled and fell headlong and lay there for a time, while beyond the fence the people watched him in a silence so complete that they could hear the dry whisper of his panting breath. Then he got up, onto his hands and knees first as small children do, and picked up the shovel and returned to the trench. He did not glance up at the sun, as a man pausing in work does to gauge the time. He came straight back to the trench, hurrying back to it with that painful and laboring slowness, the gaunt unshaven face which was now completely that of a madman. He got back into the trench and began to dig.

Snopes turned his head and spat over the wagon wheel. He jerked the reins slightly. "Come up," he said.

WILLIAM FAULKNER, born New Albany, Mississippi, September 25, 1897—died July 6, 1962. Enlisted Royal Air Force, Canada, 1918. Attended University of Mississippi. Traveled in Europe 1925-1926. Resident of Oxford, Mississippi, where he held various jobs while trying to establish himself as a writer. First published novel, *Soldiers' Pay*, 1926. Writer in Residence at the University of Virginia 1957-1958. Awarded the Nobel Prize for Literature 1950.

VINTAGE HISTORY—WORLD

V-286 **ARIES, PHILIPPE** / Centuries of Childhood
V-563 **BEER, SAMUEL H.** / British Politics in the Collectivist Age
V-620 **BILLINGTON, JAMES H.** / Icon and Axe: An Interpretive History of Russian Culture
V-44 **BRINTON, CRANE** / The Anatomy of Revolution
V-391 **CARR, E. H.** / What Is History?
V-628 **CARTEY, WILFRED AND MARTIN KILSON (eds.)** / Africa Reader: Colonial Africa, Vol. I
V-629 **CARTEY, WILFRED AND MARTIN KILSON (eds.)** / Africa Reader: Independent Africa, Vol. I
V-522 **CHINWEIZU** / The West and the Rest of Us: White Predators, Black Slavers and the African Elite
V-888 **CLARK, JOHN HENRIK (ed.)** / Marcus Garvey and the Vision of Africa
V-507 **CLIVE, JOHN** / Macauley
V-261 **COHEN, STEPHEN F.** / Bukharin and the Bolshevik Revolution: A Political Biography
V-843 **DAUBIER, JEAN** / A History of the Chinese Cultural Revolution
V-227 **DE BEAUVOIR, SIMONE** / The Second Sex
V-726 **DEBRAY, REGIS AND SALVADOR ALLENDE** / The Chilean Revolution
V-746 **DEUTSCHER, ISAAC** / The Prophet Armed
V-747 **DEUTSCHER, ISAAC** / The Prophet Outcast
V-748 **DEUTSCHER, ISAAC** / The Prophet Outcast
V-617 **DEVLIN, BERNADETTE** / The Price of My Soul
V-471 **DUVEAU, GEORGES** / 1848: The Making of A Revolution
V-702 **EMBREE, AINSLIE (ed.)** / The Hindu Tradition
V-2023 **FEST, JOACHIM C.** Hitler
V-225 **FISCHER, LOUIS** / The Essential Gandhi
V-927 **FITZGERALD, FRANCES** / Fire in the Lake: The Vietnamese & The Americans in Vietnam
V-914 **FOUCAULT, MICHEL** / Madness & Civilization: A History of Insanity in the Age of Reason
V-935 **FOUCAULT, MICHEL** / The Order of Things: An Archaeology of the Human Sciences
V-97 **FOUCAULT, MICHEL** / The Birth of the Clinic: An Archaeology of Medical Perception
V-152 **GRAHAM, LOREN R.** / Science & Philosophy in the Soviet Union
V-529 **HALLIDAY, FRED** / Arabia Without Sultans
V-114 **HAUSER, ARNOLD** / The Social History of Art (four volumes—through 117)
V-979 **HERZEN, ALEXANDER** / My Past and Thoughts (Abridged by Dwight Macdonald)
V-465 **HINTON, WILLIAM** / Fanshen
V-328 **HINTON, WILLIAM** / Iron Oxen
V-2005 **HOARE, QUINTIN (ed.) AND KARL MARX** / Early Writings
V-878 **HOLBORN, HAJO (ed.)** / Republic to Reich: The Making of the Nazi Revolution

V-201 **HUGHES, H. STUART** / Consciousness and Society
V-514 **HUNTINGTON, SAMUEL P.** / The Soldier and the State
V-790 **KAPLAN, CAROL AND LAWRENCE** / Revolutions: A Comparative Study
V-708 **KESSLE, GUN AND JAN MYRDAL** / China: The Revolution Continued
V-628 **KILSON, MARTIN AND WILFRED CARTEY (eds.)** / Africa Reader: Colonial Africa, Vol. I
V-629 **KILSON, MARTIN AND WILFRED CARTEY (eds.)** / Africa Reader: Independent Africa, Vol. II
V-728 **KLYUCHEVSKY, V.** / Peter the Great
V-246 **KNOWLES, DAVID** / Evolution of Medieval Thought
V-939 **LEFEBVRE, GEORGES AND JOAN WHITE (trans.)** / The Great Fear of 1789: Rural Panic in Revolutionary France
V-754 **LIEBMAN, MARCEL** / The Russian Revolution
V-533 **LOCKWOOD, LEE** / Castro's Cuba, Cuba's Fidel
V-787 **MALDONADO-DENIS, MANUEL** / Puerto Rico: A Socio-Historic Interpretation
V-406 **MARCUS, STEVEN** / Engels, Manchester & The Working Class
V-480 **MARCUSE, HERBERT** / Soviet Marxism
V-2002 **MARX, KARL AND DAVID FERNBACH (ed.)** / Political Writings, Vol. I: The Revolutions of 1848
V-2003 **MARX, KARL AND DAVID FERNBACH (ed.)** / Political Writings, Vol. II: Surveys from Exile
V-2004 **MARX, KARL AND DAVID FERNBACH (ed.)** / Political Writings, Vol. III: The First International and After
V-2005 **MARX, KARL AND QUINTIN HOARE (ed.)** / Early Writings
V-2001 **MARX, KARL AND MARTIN NICOLOUS (trans.)** / Grundrisse: Foundations of the Critique of Political Economy
V-92 **MATTINGLY, GARRETT** / Catherine of Aragon
V-928 **MEDVEDEV, ROY A.** / Let History Judge: The Origins & Consequences of Stalinism
V-816 **MEDVEDEV, ROY & ZHORES** / A Question of Madness
V-112 **MEDVEDEV, ZHORES** / Ten Years After Ivan Denisovich
V-971 **MILTON, DAVID & NANCY AND FRANZ SCHURMANN** / The China Reader IV: People's China:
V-905 **MITCHELL, JULIET** / Woman's Estate
V-730 **MYRDAL, GUNNAR** / Asian Drama: An Inquiry into the Poverty of Nations
V-793 **MYRDAL, JAN** / Report from a Chinese Village
V-708 **MYRDAL, JAN AND GUN KESSLE** / China: The Revolution Continued
V-2001 **NICOLOUS, MARTIN (trans.) AND KARL MARX** / The Grundrisse: Foundations of the Critique of Political Economy
V-955 **O'BRIEN, CONOR CRUISE** / States of Ireland
V-689 **OBSERVER, AN** / Message From Moscow
V-525 **PARES, SIR BERNARD** / A History of Russia
V-719 **REED, JOHN** / Ten Days That Shook the World
V-677 **RODINSON, MAXIME** / Mohammed
V-954 **ROWBOTHAM, SHEILA** / Women, Resistance & Revolution: A History of Women & Revolution in the Modern World
V-2067 **SAKHAROV, ANDREI** / My Country and The World

V-303 **SANSOM, GEORGE B.** / The Western World & Japan
V-745 **SCHAPIRO, LEONARD** / The Communist Party of the Soviet Union
V-738 **SCHNEIR, MIRIAM (ed.)** / Feminism
V-375 **SCHURMANN, F. AND O. SCHELL (eds.)** / The China Reader, Vol. Imperial China
V-376 **SCHURMANN, F. AND O. SCHELL (eds.)** / The China Reader, Vol. II: Republican China
V-377 **SCHURMANN, F. AND O. SCHELL (eds.)** / The China Reader, Vol. III: Communist China
V-971 **SCHURMANN, F. AND DAVID & NANCY MILTON** / The China Reader, Vol. IV: People's China
V-405 **SERVICE, JOHN S. AND JOSEPH H. ESHERICK (ed.)** / Lost Chance in China: The World War II Despatches of John S. Service
V-847 **SNOW, EDGAR** / Journey to the Beginning
V-930 **SNOW, EDGAR** / The Long Revolution
V-681 **SNOW, EDGAR** / Red China Today: The Other Side of the River
V-220 **SOBOUL, ALBERT** / The French Revolution, 1787-1799: From the Storming of the Bastille to Napoleon
V-411 **SPENCE, JONATHAN** / Emperor of China: Self-Portait of K'ang-hsi
V-962 **STERN, FRITZ** / The Varieties of History: From Voltaire to the Present
V-312 **TANNENBAUM, FRANK** / Ten Keys to Latin America
V-387 **TAYLOR, A. J. P.** / Bismark: The Man and the Statesman
V-322 **THOMPSON, E. P.** / The Making of the English Working Class
V-298 **WATTS, ALAN** / The Way of Zen
V-939 **WHITE, JOAN (trans.) AND GEORGES LEFEBVRE** / The Great Fear of 1789: Rural Panic in Revolutionary France
V-627 **WOMACK, John Jr.** / Zapata and the Mexican Revolution